Praise for N. Lee Wood's
New York Times *Notable Book*

LOOKING FOR THE MAHDI

"Thrilled me in a way I haven't been thrilled since I read William Gibson's *Sprawl* trilogy . . . It shares the near future setting, the compellingly believable political and technological extrapolation, and the murderously fast pace of Gibson's work."

—*The New York Review of Science Fiction*

"An impressive first novel."

—*The New York Times Book Review*

"Wood delivers fast-paced adventure in a hybrid sci-fi/spy thriller that also connects on a personal level."

—*Publishers Weekly*

"Persuasive double-dealing and paranoia . . . a highly encouraging science fiction/thriller debut."

—*Kirkus Reviews*

Ace Books by N. Lee Wood

LOOKING FOR THE MAHDI
FARADAY'S ORPHANS

FARADAY'S ORPHANS

N. LEE WOOD

ACE BOOKS, NEW YORK

FARADAY'S ORPHANS

An Ace Book / published by arrangement with
the author

PRINTING HISTORY
Ace trade paperback edition / June 1997
Ace mass-market edition / December 1998

The Penguin Putnam Inc. World Wide Web site address is
http://www.penguinputnam.com

ISBN: 0-441-00588-8

ACE®
Ace Books are published by
The Berkley Publishing Group, a member of Penguin Putnam Inc.,
375 Hudson Street, New York, New York 10014.
ACE and the "A" design are trademarks
belonging to Charter Communications, Inc.

PRINTED IN THE UNITED STATES OF AMERICA

10 9 8 7 6 5 4 3 2 1

ACKNOWLEDGMENTS

Many people helped to shape this book, and I'm grateful for all of their time, enthusiasm and expertise.

In Oregon, my thanks to Harold Hauser of the Mt. Hood Community College Physics Department. Any of the science in this book that is correct I owe to him; any errors are my own. I wish it were possible to thank the late Arthur C. Anderson, who first provided me with the freedom to write.

In Pennsylvania, thanks to Deb Hickok of the Department of Commerce in Harrisburg, Debby Kammerer of the South Allegheny Tourist Commission and Pug Unger of Pittsburgh. A special thank you to Karen Jensen of the Army Corps of Engineers in Pittsburgh; Linda Day Sauerwein of the Thomas Jefferson University Hospital in Philadelphia; and David M. Axler of Philadelphia.

In Virginia, I'm grateful to George F. Martin, Jr., and ADC Maps, for their donation of very fine detailed street maps.

In California, I'm happy to thank Judy Wollerman-Irwin of the Silverado Flight Services in Santa Barbara for the best helicopter flight of my life. Thanks to the Rotorway Helicopter Company for their help and information. Thanks to Richie Shorr and Cathy O'Sullivan, and to my father, Curt Wood, for helping with the details of aviation and airplane design, and for sharing their pilots' skill and knowledge. Thanks also to Craig Studwell for all his technical information on oil refineries.

In France, *remerciments* to Fabian Prevost, helicopter pilot, and Olivier Dancer of Gretz, glider pilot, both *extraordinaire*.

And thank you very much, Hélène Collon, of Paris, who knows why.

"Walter C. Pitman III and James R. Heirtzler of the Lamont Geological Observatory were able to estimate that over the past 75 million years the earth's [geomagnetic] field has on the average reversed about once every million years. One may note that for the past 20 million years the average interval between reversals has been about 250,000 years, and the largest interval has been 800,000 years and that occasionally the interval was no more than 100,000 years. The next reversal would therefore seem to be due."

—**Billy P. Glass and Bruce C. Heezen,**
Scientific American

"The charts reveal . . . a slow but steady decrease in the intensity of the main dipolar field at a rate such that if it continued, the field would vanish altogether [within the next] 3,000 years."

—**Charles R. Carrigan and David Gubbins,**
Scientific American

ONE

BERK NIELSEN SHOOK OUT THE LAST FEW DROPS OF hot water from the tiny kettle before stuffing it into his pack. The drops hissed and sputtered in the remains of the dying fire as they hit the smoldering embers. He wasn't worried about the smoke; if there were any Rangers around to spot the thin plume as it billowed into the early morning air, he'd be long gone before they reached his camp. The real danger was fire. In the dry heat, one small ember could escalate into a blaze that would sweep out of control across the brittle rolling mountains. Berk kicked over the last of the thin blackened logs, stamping the ashes cold.

He stowed his gear in the small compartment under the helicopter's spare seat, tucking the down sleeping bag around the knapsack to keep its contents from rattling. Then he stood with his hands on his hips, stretching out the stiffness in his muscles from sleeping on the hard ground. He squinted east at the horizon, idly watching the last puff of smoke drift away on the chill air. It wouldn't be long before the sun rose, he gauged. The sky had already turned a pale golden pink.

This was the part of the day he loved the most, cool and silent, before the sun etched out the mountains with hard lines. A fine mist clinging tenuously in the valleys softened these ridges. Hazy purpled shadows allowed the eye to fill in what it wanted to see. The early morning made the Blue Mountains somehow timeless, eternal, as if the Shift had never happened. The air was quickly losing its icy snap, although it was still sweet, and he thought that if he closed his eyes and drew in that cold, clear air through his nose, he could imagine the smell of evergreens and oaks and meadow flowers in the breeze.

He should have stayed with the Juhamit Family at the Alley Tunnel. There was no sense, really, in risking his helicopter, or his life, setting down alone in the wild. But he enjoyed spending at least some of the flight on his own, sleeping Outside under the whole canopy of unwinking stars scattershot across the black sky. The silence, the *openness* from horizon to horizon, these were part of the reason he flew in the first place.

He wasn't in that much danger, anyway. Rangers didn't move much at night, except whenever a band went on a frenzied rampage, and it was still too early in the season. All the same, he checked the small City-issued revolver as he strapped it to his waist. It wasn't safe to linger too long in the open on top of the ridge overlooking the long, narrow valleys stretching north to south.

His City-issued flight map said "Sideling Hill," with the elevation printed along the crest. He spread the worn map carefully against the nose of the helicopter, the folded edges beginning to fray. It still showed the small pre-Shift towns scattered along the long, wide road cutting through the Alleghenies. Towns with odd names like Burnt Cabins, Wells Tannery, Valley-Hi and Needmore dotted the map painstakingly copied from the records. Larger towns nestled in faded yellow blemishes between the mountain ranges drawn in stark outline, green and brown. Even the odd-shaped rings of purple had been reproduced, sections of the country once monitored by radio, instructions for approaching aircraft to contact control towers on silent air channels still diligently printed.

The radios had long vanished and the abandoned towns

were now overrun with scraggly, weather-tortured trees and scrubby undergrowth. Above them, his map also sketched in a wide blue body of water, Raystown Lake, filling the serpentine belly of the dammed valley. Berk had never flown up the corridors of the Alley Oops quite that far north from the old turnpike, but he didn't need to to know what he would find. Nothing. No dam. No lake. Only a brittle-thin river winding its way through the valley.

He folded the map carefully into a square, the area he wanted face up, and tucked one edge into the crack of the passenger seats to hold it where he could glance at it as he flew. The air was heating up and the sky becoming paler, but he was reluctant to let the morning go, to let the reality rule once more. He closed the passenger door and walked around the tiny helicopter, running his hands down the struts of the naked fuselage, checking the welded-on auxiliary tanks carefully. The lettering on the door was old and faded.

FIRST VIOLIN.

His father's joke. The old man had painted on the name after Irene, Berk's mother, complained she was playing second fiddle to a bunch of nuts and bolts. Mom had thought it was funny. Berk's wife, December, didn't see the humor at all, but Berk refused to change the name. It was bad luck, he'd lied to her.

He pressed a small clear cylinder against the stopcock on the main tank. Colorless fluid frothed into the tube. He sniffed it, stared at it intently as he swirled the liquid inside as if it were some rare wine. Grunting noncommittally to himself, he poured it carefully into a spare can bolted to the front of the passenger seat.

The breeze picked up as the sharp edge of sunlight sliced out from behind the mountains. The harsh light turned the blue softness into hard black silhouettes, as if the top of the mountains were on fire. Sunlight glinted against the helicopter's blades as they creaked on their hinges, pulling at the tether that kept the rotors from turning. The twin blades hung down slightly, resting before their flight. Blowing back the hair from Berk's face, the hot breeze was already scorching the trace of moisture from the air.

He flicked at a speck of cracking paint along one strut with his fingernail and checked the rotors for oil leaks. The helicopter was *old*, rebuilt so many times over the years it was doubtful if anything original remained. His father had spent most of his free time with *First Violin* and, later, the *Irene II*, cobbling together whatever it took to keep the copters flying. Venerable, misshapen, ugly, *First Violin* was more than machine. It had been his father's life, *his* life, now.

Keep her flying, Berk . . .

The City controlled the fuel, as it controlled everything within the glass and steel domes, but the helicopter was his. He felt the odd pressure in his chest, one of pain, and of exhilaration, and something else he'd never been able to explain.

It was safe in the City, green and cool and peaceful. Glittering domes arced high above the tallest building, imposing and reassuring. Berk was born and bred a Cityman, and considered himself as loyal and patriotic as any. He loved the lush green parks, the sweet smell of flowers and water, the taste of ripe, fresh fruit, the high clean lines of stones and steel and glass.

But there was nothing, *nothing* that Berk loved so much as leaving the City. To fly high over the huge domes until they were no more than faceted soap bubbles locked into the crook of the Alley and Mong Rivers, tiny blisters clustered in the valley along the twisting green-black waters of the Ohio. The air Outside was hot and bitter dry, the earth a blasted brown, and even the hardiest foliage struggled for survival. But it was the *vastness*, the sheer freedom of sky and ground and nothing else that he loved, sending him laughing wildly, skimming close to the earth just to watch it blur underneath him.

"Just nothin' like it, is there, Berkeley, ol' boy?" he said to himself, patting the grotesque machine beside him with absent affection.

Nothin' in the world, the old man whispered in his memory. Berk had worshipped his father, his love mixed up in the skinny little man and the machines and the freedom all blended together. *But you take care of your equipment.* Again, just for a moment, Berk could almost feel the old man standing behind him. If he turned quickly enough, conjured hard enough, he thought he might even catch a glimpse of his ghost. *City say they own you.* Berk could see the disdain in his old man's dusty, sunburned face. *Maybe so. Own everything else. But they still need good pilots, boy. Don't fuck with a good pilot. Good pilot don't fuck with his equipment.*

He'd only listened with half an ear when he was young, when his father had been immortal. *First Violin* had still been mysterious and new to him out in the dry airfield as harsh winds whipped the dust around them. He'd nodded impatiently at his father's seemingly endless lectures, eager to climb into the cramped cockpit, his fingers tingling to curl possessively around the cyclic grip.

And outside—the old man would cross his thin brown arms, grinning gaptoothed at the boy—*outside the City, you own the rest of the world.*

His mother had understood it, but Berk's wife had none of his mother's gentle, accepting spirit. The rest of the world, in December's opinion, wasn't worth a damn, anyway. Berk stood staring across the layers of mountain ridges, the morning breeze beginning to stiffen into a warm wind, blowing away the fairy mists. He smiled. It wasn't the place his father had meant; it was the *feeling*.

He climbed into the cockpit; the leather seat squeaked familiarly as he settled himself into well-worn hollows. Flicking on the electrical system, he watched the instrument needles swing into position. He went through his mental checklist with the casual ease years of practice had given him and started up the engine. Listening to the sound told him more than watching the instrument display. As he engaged the rotor, the blades began to turn slowly. He glanced up as they arced by, nodding in an unconscious rhythm as they spun. The rotor blades whirled into a blur, the helicopter shaking with the vibration. The chattering noise faded rapidly once the blades had accelerated to speed.

The sun had risen fully now, glaring in the white, empty

sky. Even with his specially filtered sunglasses, Berk could feel the beginning of the headache he'd had since yesterday morning from squinting into the sunlight. It was still early enough in the spring for the sun to arc relatively low across the horizon during the day, blazing into the helicopter's glass bubble. He'd fly only a scant forty miles today, anyway.

He glanced over the instruments again, then tapped the oversized pre-Shift mariner's magnetic compass with its red EXXON logo badly faded by the sunlight. He'd bartered it from Teddy, the bartender at Strawberry's. It was large, bulky, barely fitting into its bolted-on space at the top of his instrument casing, but Teddy had insisted it was The Very Best. It had cost more than Berk had wanted to pay, almost more than he could afford, and December had complained he'd wasted their money. It wasn't all that necessary; the regular gyro flux compass did its job just fine, he knew. But as he rapped his fingernails against the glass in a casually superstitious ritual, the needle jiggled slightly. It was comforting, a talisman, his protective amulet. The needles pointed steadily, reassuringly.

South.

He settled the headset over his ears, the wires stripped long ago, leather earpads patched and repatched. There were no radio transmissions to receive and none to send. Outside the domes' communications systems, radio was almost worthless anyway; frequent sunspots riddled the wavelengths with nearly impenetrable static. It was unlikely that there would be another flier up, especially in this direction, and the headset was only useful to drown out most of the noise from the rotor. The blades idled just below lift speed, a comfortable *whum-whum-whum-whum* in Berk's muffled ears.

He eased the cyclic forward, his left hand resting by his side on the collective control, fingers curled lightly around the throttle. *First Violin* lifted her skids off the ground, tilted her ass up like a runner at the starting line and languidly rose into the air. He had used only a little over twelve gallons of fuel, but he could feel the light difference in the weight, as well as the turbulence from the wind blowing through the mountains.

The ground fell away steadily from under his feet. He turned the helicopter into the wind, tucking as much altitude between him and the ridge as he could before it fell away behind him. The outline of the old highway became visible from this vantage point and he pointed the copter's nose along its path.

The stark mountains slipped by a few hundred feet below him as he climbed slowly into the thin morning air. Pittsburgh to Harrisburg was an even two hundred miles, not that great a distance by airplane or helicopter, but a lot of those miles were over the multiple ridges of sawtoothed peaks making up the Appalachians, or the "Alley Oops" as the fliers sometimes called them. The peaks were deceptively low, nothing much over 3,000 feet, but the hot winds that swept through the valleys could occasionally make the passage hazardous for small craft.

He'd already cleared the worst of it now, the old highway threading its way through the maze of serrated crests heading east. He had wanted to fly a more direct course east-southeast rather than following the old highway, reasoning it would save time and fuel. Cormack rejected the idea and Berk reluctantly agreed. The City Commission wanted revised charts of the ground route from east of Harrisburg, and Berk really couldn't risk missing the Twin Tunnel Outpost. He had fuel enough to reach the Filly ruins, but without refueling at the outpost, he'd never make it back.

He skimmed above the highway at a thousand feet, feeling the rarified air singing in the blades above his head. The ancient forest still stood in vast patches on these mountains, although most of the large trees had died or burned in fires more than two centuries ago. Many had fallen to winds and age, but some were still erect, bleached trunks with naked branches jaggedly amputated. Underneath the dead giants grew the sturdy low trees and hardy grasses that blanketed the Blue Mountains, tough plants that could withstand the fierce summer heat and the dry winter cold.

Berk viewed the huge dead trees with interest, but he had

no sense of loss. For him the world had always been like this; he couldn't miss immense green forests he'd never seen. They were the inhabitants of a world existing before the Shift, extinct monuments still stubbornly standing in endless acres. But he understood the dream the City kept alive and fostered in the people who lived in the fertile protected domes.

One day, soon, they would reseed the earth.

As he flew over the crest of a ridge, he noted a denuded portion of the forest that spread out for several miles, blackened spears of trees burned in a recent fire. He hoped it had been lightning rather than a roaming band of Rangers. Thunderstorms were welcomed, hoped for, lightning driving nitrogen into the soil and ozone into the air. Bright green patches of new spring growth bloomed under the blackened giants in a regular pattern.

Berk hovered above the burn areas, sketching it out in rough outline on his flight map before he flew on. The City Commission would compare his find with the last supplyplane's records, sorting out the natural spring growth from the small garden patches scratched out of the parched soil by primitive Aggies. According to the City theory, the Aggies didn't make a practice of camouflaging their tiny patches, mostly because the gardens were too difficult to assimilate this far from the domes, anyway. What exactly the City intended to *do* with the information, Berk wasn't sure.

The old highway bent slightly north and disappeared in a jumble of rock in the hillside. The old Tusk Tunnel, maintained as a shelter station for decades, along with its sister tunnels to the east. Seven years ago Rangers had boiled out from the north and slaughtered the Tusk's entire St. Clymer Family, twenty-five or so people. Then they set off the Family's own store of explosives to blow the tunnel, along with a good number of themselves, into rubble. The Twin Tunnels farther east had been left completely untouched. Exactly why Rangers had destroyed the Tusk was a mystery, but then the Rangers were a mystery. One best left alone.

The frightened remaining Tunnel Families wanted the City to track down and exterminate the Rangers. But retaliation was, naturally, impossible. The Ranger band had vanished as abruptly as it had appeared. The City was still taking its first tentative steps into exploring and reclaiming the Outside, and the City Commission wouldn't provide the manpower or the money for tracking down a band of Rangers. Instead, the Heber Family's Twin Tunnels and the Juhamit Family's Alley Tunnel seventy miles west, precious links to the tiny newborn domes of Harrisburg, were refortified and heavily armed. The City abandoned any idea of restoring the Tusk Tunnel.

Berk rode the updraft over the ridge of Tuscarora Mountain and watched the road reappear on the other side of the ruined Tunnel. The Tusk fell away behind him as he climbed to clear Kittatinny Ridge, following the road's shattered outline below as it threaded through the valley.

Ten miles farther east, the road widened into a smooth, carefully maintained landing strip leading up to the mouth of the Twin Tunnels. On the three sides of the strip, high barbed-wire fences had been built, completely enclosing it. Near the mouth of the tunnel sat a squat hangar, doors open, the inside empty. No one was on the strip and the tunnels showed no signs of life. That wasn't unusual.

Wysaigh's had been the last scheduled supply plane to land on the runway, more than two months back. Communications past the Juhamits' Alley Tunnel were, at best, infrequent and unreliable, and the Families that defended these outlying tunnels entirely self-sufficient, independent from the Cities.

The Tusk Tunnel disaster, and the City's less than enthusiastic response, had made them wary and distrustful. Other stories that had drifted in with migrant Aggies kept the Families leery of the Cities. While the Families generally welcomed City goods, they rejected even the most tentative proposals they felt might intrude on their autonomy. They remained independent . . . for now.

The domes of Cincinnati were too remote, and the domes at Erie were more of a preserve than a colony. The Harrisburg colonists had repaired the small domes built before the Shift, but kept only tenuous connections to their mother City of Pittsburgh. Like the Tunnel Families, they were fiercely independent and isolated. Pittsburgh, and its City-made goods, remained the sole link to the outside world for the Families that ran the tunnels.

Other than the Rangers and the Aggies, that was.

Berk began his descent towards the runway, making himself visible as slowly as he could. It was unlikely that anyone would actually fire on him. *First Violin*'s belly carried the bright colors of a City carrier. But it never hurt to be cautious.

His right foot eased against the foot pedal, keeping the helicopter's nose pointed towards the face of the Tunnel as the torque pushed against him. He still had seen no sign of anyone. At fifty feet the dust below him on the landing field began to swirl into eddies. He tilted the rotor into the wind, slipping *First Violin* to keep her fuselage aligned, hovering above the runway for a moment, her skids a scant few feet off of the ground. The dust now whipped around him in a brown cloud as he settled her down through the air cushion, skids crunching against the gravel on the old roadway.

He left the helicopter idling, the blades snicking lazily over his head as he hunched under them, darting out and away. Keeping one hand on the handle of the revolver hanging against his hip, he scanned the rock and dry vegetation. The main gates, massive steel doors that secured the inside of the tunnel, were partway open, but seemed abandoned, not a hint of motion in the dark interior. Double rows of spiraling barbed wire arched up across the top face of the tunnel, vanishing around the tumbled rock. Within a few yards of the tunnel entrance he heard the solid thunk of a rifle bolt being pulled back. He stopped, turning slowly towards the sound with his hands help up, away from his gun.

A thin, bronze-skinned girl was hunched beside a boulder on his right, her rifle trained directly at him. Behind her, a younger boy stood up, aiming a similar weapon at Berk's head.

"Afternoon," the girl said, her voice polite, her eyes hostile and unblinking. "Sum'n we c'do for you?"

He kept his hands up, smiling at her. "I'm a City pilot from Pittsburgh. You one of the Heber girls?"

Wisps of hair blew around her suspicious face. "Maybe," she said.

"We're the Hebers," a man's voice behind Berk called out. He turned towards the sound, smiling at a skinny, white-bearded man. Two deeply tanned, skinny boys stood behind the old man, rifles trained on Berk. His cheeks were beginning to ache slightly from his relentless grin.

With a nod the old man motioned one of the boys towards the helicopter. Crab-walking down the hillside, the boy approached cautiously, rifle pointed towards the tiny craft. "Mind the blades, son," Berk called out in a friendly tone. He was more worried about what the boy could do to the helicopter than the chance that he might be hurt. As if he knew it, the boy shot a scornful look in Berk's direction before peering into the cabin.

"I'm Berkeley Nielsen," he said to the old man, his hands still in the air. He pointed with one hand towards his vest pocket. "City pilot. I got ID, if you'd like."

Another thin, somewhat older boy emerged from the rock behind him, equally armed, bullets strapped across his chest. "Show it, please," the old man said.

Carefully, Berk drew out his City pilot card, a small plastic and metal design in a leather folder. The old man jerked his head at the boy with the bullets. In a clatter of loose stones, the boy scrambled down from the hill, glaring at Berk as he took the card. The boy by the copter kept his rifle trained on Berk as the other's eyes flickered towards the photograph and back to the pilot's face. Berk was glad now he'd decided to stop at Sideling Hill for the night rather than fly into this after sundown.

"It's him," the boy announced. A smile creased the old man's face, lines appearing from under his beard. The rifles were lowered at this apparent signal and the Hebers descended from their vantage point.

"Nice welcoming committee you got," Berk said dryly, and lowered his arms. He took back his identification.

The children walked around *First Violin*, studying the helicopter with intense interest. Heber smiled, jerking his head towards the craft. "Never seen no plane like that b'fore, Mr. Nielsen. Could be a trick. Don't take no chances with things y'don't know. Stay alive longer that way." Berk suspected that the old man was more concerned with intimidating Citymen than with security. "You from Pit, eh?"

"Yeah. I need fuel, water, supplies."

"Y'got money?" the old man asked.

"City issue," Berk said, knowing that the paper was completely worthless outside the domes. "If you want it. Or we could maybe trade for something . . . ?"

While the old man stood face to face with Berk, the children circled the pilot as if they were inspecting him for booby traps. They were small people, wiry and weather-beaten from generations of living in the tunnel, dark from the fierce sun. No one knew if the Families had originally come from one of the surviving domed Cities, or if they were off-spring of Aggies. Or perhaps they were the descendants of some ancient band of Rangers-turned-entrepreneurs, before they had become too savage and deformed.

"Got any sweets?" a young boy still crouching on the hill-side asked, his tone unmistakably forlorn.

"Got any alcohol?" Berk returned, eyeing the old man.

Heber laughed, a surprisingly deep and energetic sound from a man as old as he looked. He slung his rifle onto his back as the other children picked their way down the boulder-strewn hillside. "I might have a drop or two," Heber said. "Shut off that flying thing and we'll talk."

The tiny helicopter weighed barely twelve hundred pounds and after Berk had locked on the ground-handling wheels, it was more of a problem keeping the enthusiastic team of children from pushing in the wrong places.

"Watch your feet," Berk called out nervously, "keep your hands where I showed you."

The kids were used to dragging small planes inside the protective hangar, and they were eager to inspect this strange new craft. Berk kept a watchful eye on them as they rolled *First Violin* through the hangar doors. "Don't touch the little blades back there!" he warned as one of the boys reached for the tail rotor with curious fingers. He slipped the tether over the end of one blade and anchored it to *First Violin*'s nose.

The main steel gates that secured the inside of the tunnel were slid back on smooth, well-oiled tracks. Even a child, Berk noticed, could seal off the tunnel against any attack within seconds. He blinked in the sudden twilight as he passed into the interior. A few yards farther on, a second wall of wood enclosed the mouth of the tunnel.

Generations of inhabitants had shaped the waystation into a fantastic melding of primitive survival and luxurious ostentation. Where the outer fortified doors were massive and unadorned, the interior walls looked more like the entrance into some bizarre fairy-tale castle. Ornate engraving covered every inch of wood in the structure, carved and painted in bright colors. Fanciful animals cavorted in impossible flora. High above Berk, multicolored glass glinted in huge windows.

The main door into the house opened; a stringy woman of the old man's age peered out, small children and younger adult women crowding around her. A profusion of carved cats were intertwined along the sides of the door, lacing the top. Each cat had been painted with blue stripes, or blue spots, or simply solid blue. The woman turned aside wordlessly as the two men stepped inside.

The main entrance was huge; in its center was a table massive enough to seat fifty people. The room ended in a hallway that ran the length of the tunnel. Wooden ladders and stone steps led into rooms carved out of the walls. Balconies jutted out from alcoves overhead, young children leaning from the rails to peek and giggle. The walls were whitewashed and clean, making the interior as bright as possible. Lamps set in rows, high along the curved wall of the tunnel, burned even in the daytime, but the interior of the tunnel stayed cool. Berk could feel a hint of circulating air against his skin. Hidden somewhere above, fans rotated, keeping the air from becoming stifling.

As the old woman, evidently Heber's wife, disappeared into one of the rooms off the hall, she glanced at Berk, impassive. "Don't mind Berry," Heber said. He hesitated, then said in an emotionless voice, "We lost one of the girls a while ago." Berk glanced at him, but the old man seemed unconcerned. "Rangers took her." He shrugged. "Happens if you don't keep your guard up."

Berk said nothing, keeping Wysaigh's own disappearance to himself. He dropped the knapsack he'd retrieved from the helicopter onto the massive rough-hewn table. The planks had been worn smooth from years of use, but the sides and legs had been elaborately carved like the rest of the house. Dozens of mismatched but equally ornate plush chairs had been placed around the table, the carvings on these different: smaller, more finely detailed, pre-Shift. A huge crystal chandelier hung from an overhead beam stretching across the arch above them.

Berk could see a corner of the kitchen where the old woman and two of the younger women had gone, and heard the clank of an ancient hand pump drawing water. Heber seated himself comfortably in one of the chairs, looking up at Berk expectantly. "Well," he said, dark eyes eager, "let's see what'cha got, son."

The Families scorned the City's strict authority, and couldn't be forced into supplying fuel to pilots for free. They knew the City needed them much more than they needed the City. But self-sufficient as the Tunnel Families were, they lacked the precise machine-made goods impossible to obtain outside the City. The City began providing the Families with regular supply runs, tempting them with small luxuries among the basics, hoping to lure the Families into a dependency on City goods: lightbulbs, fruit, toilet paper, special medications.

The Tunnel Families grudgingly tolerated the gradual intrusion of long-distance recon pilots. Homemade alcohol could be bartered for these coveted luxuries. The City equipped the pilots with standard supplies, while pilots had to depend on their own instincts and cooperative guesses as to what the Families might find appealing. Long-distance recon pilots hoarded their own stock of candies, cigarettes, batteries, small tools, any trifling item that could mean the difference.

Berk carried a metal case in his knapsack and he placed it on the table, pointedly unlocking it. From it he took several boxes of brightly wrapped candies, dried sugared fruits, a pack of disposable lighters, four packets of pencils, a box of cheap jewelry, a tiny sewing kit with a wealth of steel needles and pins, little glass bottles of perfume, bars of soap, two light bulbs and a stack of paperback books. He laid out his goods in a line on the table wordlessly, as the old man and a growing number of children and adults gathered and watched, silent. When he'd finished, he seated himself opposite the old man and waited.

Heber crossed his arms on the table, leaning over to stare at the stash. After a minute, he pushed the two light bulbs back at Berk with a gnarled finger. "No use," he said. "Solar generator's broke down." He looked up at the pilot. "We get by fine without it."

Berk nodded and repacked the light bulbs carefully. He made a mental note of the broken generator. Parts could be made. The next flier out could strike a better bargain.

Heber continued studying the rest of the goods as Berk glanced around casually. He counted twenty-nine people in the oversized room; younger couples, a few women with babies in their arms and a dozen children, from a toddler to the five adolescents he'd encountered earlier. They all had the same small, dark features of the old man, quite obviously interrelated. They stood quietly, looking bored with the entire procedure. A young boy and the thin teenaged girl who had greeted Berk stood at his side, staring at the table unblinkingly.

"Don't need jewelry," Heber said. He started to push the small box of costume jewelry away. The girl standing by Berk's shoulder started as if she'd been bitten by some small insect, and the old man glanced up at her. She looked back, impassive as the others. Heber lowered his gaze, eyeing the box once more with pursed lips. "Suppose don't hurt to look it over." He pushed the box past Berk towards the girl. "Elissa, y'see if there's anything worth something."

The girl nodded without changing expression and began to sort the jewelry methodically.

"Me too, Dad?" the boy said, unable to keep the longing from his voice.

"Y'don't need tinsel, boy. Think you kids need a couple of them books." Heber picked up the stack of paperbacks, inspecting the bindings, flipping through the pages.

Berk smiled to himself. The Dome River Press was actually one of the City's prides, turning out reprints of books from the treasured collection in the City's private library, in cheap, study editions. The growing number of new novelists had enjoyed some limited success as well, despite strictly rationed paper production, and Berk had packed a mixture of classics and juveniles in with the new, popular books. He had done his research on the Hebers before he'd left and, although he tried to hide it, he was pleased so far with how well he'd judged them.

Heber's wife returned from the kitchen with a steaming pot of tea and two mismatched mugs on a tray. She set one mug, clearly home-fired, in front of her husband, and the other, an ancient pre-Shift mug, before Berk. He looked at the cup with interest. It had to be well over two hundred years old and the ceramic glaze had cracked into a fine spider-webbed maze. The handle showed dark lines where it had been repeatedly glued back on over the years. The design had faded, but Berk could make out the words printed in blue on the side.

"Old truckers never die," it read, "they just get a new Peterbilt." It made no sense to Berk, but anything pre-Shift fascinated him. It took some effort not to bargain for the mug, which had obviously been Heber's intent.

The tea steamed fragrantly, a strong local herbal, and the old lady offered Berk honey to sweeten it. Heber had selected seven paperbacks, pushing the remainder back. "Got these already," he said. Inwardly, Berk winced. He hadn't been as thorough as he thought. "Wouldn't have any electrical manuals, wouldja?" Heber asked hopefully. Berk honestly regretted saying no, and stored that information away as well.

It took more than an hour, three cups of tea and a plate of

brown biscuits before Heber made his final selections. He had chosen the candies, the dried fruit, soap, two packages of pencils, a pack of disposable lighters, seven books. One of the elder Heber women had stared at the tiny sewing kit solemnly until it, too, slowly crept into the pile the old man was making at his elbow. Finally, his teenaged daughter, Elissa, decided on a single thin gold chain, testing it gently between her teeth first. Berk silently repacked the little that remained, but left the packing case open. Just on general principle.

"Now," Heber said, grinning as he leaned back and stretched his arms over his head, "what ken we do fer you?"

TWO

February 15, 2242

THE NIGHT BEFORE WYSAIGH TOOK OFF ON HIS Tunnel-Harrisburg supply flight, he lounged back in the old patchwork couch December had had to reupholster yet again. Berk handed him a beer, condensation streaking the sides of the City-issued Blue Ribbon bottle.

"The only thing in the Filly is a big pile of bricks." Wy crossed his legs, one ankle balanced on his knee. "City wants me out there to resupply the tunnels regular, drop the mail out at the Harrisburg Domes, scout around for any sign of Aggie farms. That's just fine by me. Flyin' over the Filly is an extra chore they decided to throw in for free. Wasn't my idea at all."

Berk sat in the fraying chair across from Wy. "You can't really check out the Filly without setting down inside her."

"But what the hell do I have to worry about setting down in the goddamned city for, Berk? Y'fly over it, y'jot down some scribbles on the map, y'leave it alone. Nobody in his right mind is going to want to *land* in it."

Berk twisted the top off of his beer and took a long drink, grimacing. For some reason, the City standard beer never had quite the same taste batch to batch. This was not one of their better ones.

"And what if you *have* to land, Wy? You'd snap your wings off trying to land inside the Filly."

Wysaigh laughed and spread his arms wide, measuring with his hands. "That's why *The Kid*'s got real long wings, son. I start having trouble, I can glide for miles and miles. Find me a nice flat road still stretchin' out there the other side of the river. You, however, and that overgrown lawnmower of yours, would go down like the proverbial rock."

Cormack had given Wysaigh the recon assignment, explaining to an angry, disappointed Berk that the Council felt Wysaigh's ancient Sundancer IV was less of a risk than his tiny helicopter. Wysaigh's small plane had been rebuilt and modified over the years, as were all of the aircraft still surviving within the Domed Cities, until the original manufacturers would hardly have recognized it. The long wingspan gave Wysaigh's light plane a shallow glide ratio and low fuel consumption, and Wy had modified its fuselage to keep the plane afloat if he ever needed an emergency amphibious landing. He was very proud of *The Kid*, confident of his craft's ability to handle anything that the harsh Outside world could throw at him.

The truth, Berk knew, was that Wy was a trueborn City boy. The City's regimented parochial society that chafed at Berk was comfortable for Wy, the rules clearly established, tolerance of anything outside fixed parameters discouraged. Wy took fewer risks than Berk, never flying more than his assignment, never flying without the Council's clearance. Wy's philosophical convictions were more in line with the Council's political objectives, and the choice assignments frequently went to those more amenable to Council policies, or at least Cormack's definition of same, while the City's few rebellious sons found themselves choked by the Councilman's tight leash. Those who had the freedom didn't use it; those who would use it couldn't get it.

But Wysaigh depended too much on the abilities of his fixed-wing plane, Berk had argued with Cormack. *First Violin* was more maneuverable, and could set down in the midst of a city as easily as the middle of a field, justifying the extra fuel and risk of exploring the Filly ruins. Cormack had smiled his polite reptilian politician's smile, said the Filly wasn't ready for that advanced an exploration just yet, Wysaigh could take all the observation notes the Council needed for evaluation, he was terribly sorry, old pal, maybe next time, and had Berk ushered unceremoniously out of his office.

December settled herself on the arm of Berk's chair, her hand resting casually on her husband's shoulder as the two fliers discussed their differing crash survival strategies. She had listened to this same conversation over the years all too often to be upset by it.

"And that's what you'll be doing as long as you fly fixed-wing, Wy. Flying over nothing but miles and miles of empty hills and nice flat roads, taking pictures as you pass on by. Y'll never really find anything that way."

Wy shrugged. "Never wanted to be the bold and daring hero-type, anyway. I'm a *pilot*, Berk. Not some explorer of unknown frontiers. My job is to find agroland." He drained the bottle of beer, and set it down on the small table by the couch. December picked it up and took it into the kitchen. Berk could hear the water running as she rinsed the bottle out. It would go into the kitchen's storage rack, along with the other empties, and December would return them to the brewery for recycling. A broken bottle was an extra expense the Nielsens didn't need.

"To you it's all some kind of intrepid adventure," Wy said. "For me, it's a steady job. I got a wife and two kids to feed and they don't have too much patience with starry-eyed idealism. I actually *enjoy* the Tunnel-Harrisburg run. Go out once a month, wrangle with a couple stiff-necked cavemen, check out what's going on at the Harrisburg Domes, come home. Simple, easy." He grinned, lowering his voice before December came back into the room, "And it's got its compensations, m'boy, better believe it."

December settled back onto the sofa and gave no indication she'd heard Wy's last comment. Whatever he'd been insinuating, Berk ignored it.

"There's more to being a pilot than carting mail and supplies while eyeballing for wild cabbage patches," Berk said.

"It's exploratory. How else is the City going to reclaim the Outside if nobody wants to explore what's still there?"

Wy waved his hand dismissively. "Reclaiming the Outside is going to take a long, long time, Berk. You've got some kinda idea that now it's possible to walk around Outside without turning into instant crispy critters—we'll all just leap out and undo centuries worth of damage overnight. One small step at a time, buddy."

December had pried open another beer and handed it quietly to Wysaigh. She looked inquiringly at Berk, and he shook his head. Wy drank, burped, and set the bottle on the little coaster on the table.

"There's a difference between small steps and running in place," Berk said. "That's what we've been doing, just maintaining, getting by, for as long as the domes have been around. And maybe that's the problem; we're all so used to just keeping the status quo, we don't have what it takes anymore to get out, see what's left, *use* it."

"That's not quite so, Berk," December put in softly. Inwardly, Berk winced. Not again. Not now. "Sure, technologically," she said, "the domes haven't progressed for a long time, but we *are* doing something. We've got hundreds of strike plates built, and that's doing something. The new Spring Hill Power Domes are almost ready to go on-line, and that will mean less power rationing—that's doing something."

Berk didn't want to argue with her, not in front of Wysaigh, but old habits were hard to shake. " 'Almost ready'? I thought the damn plant's *been* ready for months. What's holding it up, huh, December?" He was baiting her.

December glanced at him with contempt, then said to Wysaigh, "Jacob Chong put me on Markley's team to work up a new graphite rolling design. It looks good. We think it's going to work."

The old photovoltaic plant had been designed to supply the City for three hundred years, keeping the domes habitable through the long years when exposure to the Outside meant almost immediate death. It had done its job remarkably well while the survivors waited to re-emerge. But through the decades electrical power became scarcer as the panels wore out or were broken, and the population inside the domes increased to their maximum capacity. Now that it was finally survivable Outside, at least for useful lengths of time, the old plant was being replaced by a series of new power domes.

Thousands of photovoltaic cells covered each Spring Hill generating plant over 15,000 square feet of active area, strange ridged domes revolving on tracks maximizing the light's energy as they followed the sun across the sky. Under the solar domes, Energy Department personnel lived and worked, protected from both the killing radiation that powered the plant and roving Ranger bands occasionally migrating along the riverfront. Underground cables ran the power into the City. It was a masterpiece of design.

Almost.

"But until then, sweetheart, you need me. Or at least what I'm good at finding," Berk said. "Oil. You can't manufacture that synthetic lubricant crap you're using fast enough to keep up, and it's shit anyway. If it's not *just right*, the tracks will keep on freezing up and the whole fucking works will grind to a halt."

She looked at him, two small points of pink on her cheeks the only indication she felt anything at all. Wysaigh began studying the label on his beer with intense curiosity.

"Then all your brilliant work just sits there," Berk continued. "It won't hold up under something that big, will it? You need what I find. Good, heavy-duty, pre-Shift oil. Lots of it."

Wysaigh looked up from picking the paper label off his bottle, smiling broadly, obviously trying to lighten the suddenly tense mood with a little gentle teasing. "Yeah, we're all real grateful you poked your nose around and discovered The Great Oil Cache in Venango. When was that, anyway—'38? '39?"

Wy's remark just rankled. " '36," Berk answered, attempting to keep the sullen anger out of his voice. He felt as if Wy had joined sides with December against him, his wife and best friend both hostile to him.

"Yeah, that's right—'36," Wy said obviously. "You were still the brash young hero then, eh? Like father, like son. But let's seen, so far the City's reclaimed a hundred seventy thousand acres of good fertile agroland along both sides of the Ohio. How much alcohol do you think a hundred seventy thousand acres can produce?" His eyes crinkled with amusement as he baited his friend. "Petroleum oil's still the best for lubrication, sure it's better than the synthetic stuff the City labs make, and I like all that exotic fruit Erie's starting to ship back as much as you do. But how long did it take to erect the workdomes over Venango? How long did it take Erie, before they even started any recovery work? And look at Harrisburg, already forgetting where they came from, who *paid* for their independent colony."

"We still need oil," Berk said stubbornly, trying to keep his voice from sounding petulant. "Not just lubricants, Wy. Your alcohol just doesn't work for making a whole lot of fancy plastics. Wouldn't it be nice not to have to have a license for camera film?" Berk smiled with an effort. "Old-fashioned oil is still the best, and I'm good at finding it."

Wy snorted. "Licensing film's just like licensing bullets, Berk. Just another way for the Council to keep their hold and make a profit off us at the same time. Anyway, your last oil find ran out pretty quick. I don't think Cormack, or the rest of the Council, cares to wait five more years for another of your miracle oil finds. What we need most is fertile, producing agroland, not oil."

Berk said quietly, "It also takes time to cultivate a hundred and seventy thousand acres of land, Wy. And the people we took it away from haven't exactly been the most cooperative or reliable labor pool."

But Wysaigh apparently either missed or chose to ignore his point. "You're not too likely to find much of a cooperative or reliable labor pool in N'York or DeeCee or Philadelphia, either," he said. "I just happen to think it makes more sense in the long run to reclaim the land, producing our own agro supply. We need the grain for alcohol and bread, hay for paper and animal fodder. And for that we need *land*, a lot of it. Land here on *this* side of the Alleys, to make it productive again. What we *don't* need is worthless, burnt-out ruins packed with crazies."

That was the official City line. Reclaim the land. Reseed the earth. Be fruitful and multiply. And take the profits back to the domes. The rights of a few wizened, deformed Aggies scratching a meager crop from the little fertile land beginning to recover from the Shift were unimportant next to the those of the City's. Any more liberal-minded Citizens who objected were either politely placated or ignored.

December had relaxed, letting the conversation slide past without her, but Berk could feel her tense anger through the cool hand lightly resting on his shoulder.

"Yeah, well . . ." Berk was unwilling to let the subject drop. "I'm still putting in for a run over Filly. There are a lot of areas I checked out on the last recon's notes that look promising. We *need* oil, Wy. That phony sludge the City's making us use in our machines is tearing them up as well. The rivers have shifted, and those docks did a lot of oil business. There were a lot of refineries there. I've done my research. They're still there. There's oil there, Wy, I know it. If anyone can find it, it'll be me." He could feel the pressure of excitement and longing in his chest.

Wysaigh finished his beer and stood, stretching his back. "*If* you can convince Cormack there's really anything worth the trouble to salvage. You'd need a really big find, Berk . . . And I need a good night's sleep." He grinned, happy to be flying in the morning. "'Night, Berk, Sember," Wysaigh said, hand on the door. "When I get back, Fayette and me'll have you up for dinner, okay?"

"Sure," Berk said, trying not to let his envy show. "That'd be okay. Have a good flight, Wy."

For a moment, Wy looked at him, as if he wanted to say something more, his wide face creased in a frown. But he smiled and left, closing the door quietly behind him.

Wysaigh flew off early the next day in the bitter winter chill, and never returned. Cormack canceled any further eastern exploratory runs. Berk honestly did hope that Wy's agricultural knowledge would help him survive. No one would be searching for him.

Not even Berk.

THREE

November 5, 2217

Y OUNG BERKELEY CHEERFULLY STRIPPED A RUSTY IN-
strument panel from the ancient DC-9, pleased his father had finally brought him on the trip to the airfield ten
miles east of the Domed City. The panel itself was worthless, but it could be used to take molds from.

It was late in the season, although it was still hot. The old
man wasn't worried about traveling alone Outside with his
small son. Rangers rarely ventured in that close to a City,
and there hadn't been a report of a band in the area for
months. Berkeley's father had decided it was time for the
boy to learn the business.

Packed into the beetle-shaped pedalcar, jammed between
the old man's legs, the boy had chattered excitedly the entire
journey. The sun was hot even through the dark bubble-glass
of the pedalcar and Berkeley fidgeted, but the old man
would just wipe the sweat off his stubbly face and chuckle.
It wasn't a long trip across the hilly brown terrain, but it
seemed like a vast alien universe to a young boy raised in
the confines of the City's cool domes.

Across the field from the DC-9, the old man was hammering away at another plane, the sound thin and sharp in
the dry air. Berk was busy with all the absorption of a seven-

year-old, screwdriver in hand, when he heard a faint, weird warbling. He ignored it at first, thinking it the call of some animal hunting in the heat, content in his child's iron conviction that his father could keep him safe from anything. The old man stopped his pounding and Berk heard the chilling sound again, closer, louder in the silence. He still didn't understand what it meant and stuck his head out of the dim interior of the derelict plane, scanning the dusty airfield curiously.

"Get down!" his father screamed at him, racing across the field towards Berk, his body hunched over as he ran. Although Berk instantly obeyed, in the confusion he was afraid his father was angry with *him*. He flinched, searching his memory for some offense he'd committed. His father dropped into the dark space next to him, grabbing him by the collar.

"Stay down," his old man said, face close to Berk's. He held a black, snub-nosed pistol. For the first time, Berk saw the fear on his father's face, the leathery skin pale. "Don't come up until I call you, you understand?"

Berk nodded mutely, feeling an unknown dread tug at his bladder. The old man jumped agilely out of the cabin space, his pistol ready in his hand.

Crouched in the darkness, his screwdriver held before him like a weapon, young Berkeley could hear the weird yelping cries, and the *pop-pop* of his father's gun. Metallic drumming, *something* clattering against the plane, echoed through the interior, amplified in the boy's terrified mind.

The drumming stopped abruptly. A scream spiraled up the edge of sound, bubbling away in sudden silence. Dust trickled through the sunlight, a solid shaft of silver gleaming in the hush. Not even the pop of the old man's gun cut the stillness.

A shadow passed the hole. "Dad?" the young boy whispered, blood pounding in his ears. The shadow froze above him and a noise like a disemboweled sparrow chirped. A figure dropped into the space with him. Panicked, Berkeley scrabbled backwards, away from the grinning thing hunched on all fours.

Matted hair and shreds of cloth and fur blurred over the creature's body. Brown-stained teeth filed to points in a lipless grinning mouth snicked open and shut. A gnarled, lumpy arm reached for Berkeley, streaked with dirt, ragged fingernails snagging the boy's shirt, dragging him close. Two lumps of stringy flesh dangled from the creature's chest and Berk vaguely recognized this thing as female. Pressed close to him inside the cabin, it stank, rancid breath hot against his cheeks. Its irisless black eyes glittered close to him, a piglike snout wrinkling with reddened nostrils.

"*Boy*," he thought he heard it say as it stroked his face, hard fingers roughly feeling his crotch, the ribs under his shirt, inspecting the child's muscles in his arms. "*Boyboyboyboy . . .*"

He saw his father's face appear in the hole above him, blood trickling down his forehead, a wide gash ripped across his scalp.

"Hey, you," the old man said, the words oddly calm, almost conversational, as if he were addressing a clerk at the grocer's. He had the pistol pointed down into the hole, and as the thing turned to look up, Berkeley started to scream.

He screamed as the bullet tore away half of the creature's skull. He screamed as its body fell heavily on him, the stench of filth and blood threatening to drown him. He screamed as he kicked, struggling with hysterical strength, while his father jerked the thing's body off of his son. He screamed as blood covered his head and shoulders, scratching himself with sharp bits of bone as his hands rubbed frantically at his face. He screamed as blood and thin-gruel bits of shattered brain dribbled down his hair, dripped down his back, into his mouth, into his eyes, blinding him.

He screamed and screamed and screamed . . .

FOUR

THE SUN BURNED WHITE IN A CLOUDLESS SKY AS
Berk walked across the flat abandoned airfield, watching the rusted hulks shimmer in the low ripples of heat.
Small dust dervishes whipped themselves across the field,
vanishing in the cross-currents. Pulling down the cloth
wrapped around his head from his face, he drank from the
small canteen. The water was warm and metallic, but in this
heat it was life itself and tasted wonderful. He recapped the
flask and let it hang from its chain on his belt.

He walked towards the gutted hulk of a Boeing 787, kicking up small eddies of bone-dry dirt. The plane was scaled
with brown rust, the faded flakes of paint that might have
once clung to its fuselage had long ago been sandblasted
away into oblivion. One wing had cracked away entirely
from the body of the plane, the other sagged with its wingtip
on the ground.

Berk hopped up on it, balancing along the creaking slope,
stepping carefully along the riveted metal where the wing
struts were marked out. In places whole sheets of metal had
vanished, leaving the skeletal framework exposed. The fragile metal skin left clinging to the old plane was paper-thin,
and a man could slice a leg badly if he stepped through it.

The glass in the windows along the fuselage had been broken out and the emergency door hung crookedly against the side. Berk stuck his head into one of the empty windows, smiling to himself.

His father had pushed him through this same window nearly a quarter of a century ago, and the two had pried open the emergency door. The plane most likely had sat untouched since then. The small, thin boy who had once scrambled through the window now pressed his adult head and shoulder against the curved opening. He missed the old man.

He placed his hands against the fuselage for support and crab-walked to the open emergency door. He stepped cautiously inside and stood quietly for a moment to let his eyes adjust to the low light. A few upended seats lay stacked against one wall, the fabric and cushions long rotted away, frames torn from the floor. Cautiously avoiding the gaping holes in the cabin floor, Berk made his way towards the nose of the plane. The small vestibule where stewardesses had once reheated meals and made coffee was still intact, but empty. Behind it was the cockpit, framed by its missing door.

He crouched in the space once occupied by the pilot's seat and wiped grime and dirt caked on the instrument panels with the palm of his hand. There was precious little left of the 787 of any use, little that he and his father had not removed years ago. The wires once coated with brightly colored plastic has rusted away to brittle twists of decay. Empty sockets now stood in the place of glass and chrome displays. Shrugging to himself, Berk stripped away anything remotely of value, gleaning only a few rusty screws left rattling in one corner; an overlooked instrument cup, glass opaque but unshattered, the guts long vanished; a pair of toggle switches that might possibly be salvageable once they were cleaned, if the rust had not welded them together.

Once he had transferred his meager treasure into his knapsack, Berk stared out the glassless windshield, studying the stretch of runway before him. Bristles of hardy grass

grew in the cracks radiating the length of the asphalt paving,
as brown and dry as the dirt blowing across the airfield. The
horizon tilted from his viewpoint as he tried to align himself.
Tipped forward on its nose, the plane leaned towards the
side of the broken wing. He craned his neck, squinting
against the glare of the sun. He tried to imagine the plane
slowly taxiing down an immaculate airstrip, bellying heavily into the sky, engines screaming.

He'd never seen a jet plane in the air, other than in the few
remaining museum photographs and video records still intact. He'd never felt the shudder of engines fighting turbulence, never seen the silent flashes of silvered lightning in
the tops of dark thunderclouds, never heard the whine of
wheels braking against the tarmac. He knew he never
would.

But his father had told him stories, the stories handed down
through generations of pilots. Huge humpbacked planes
gleaming in the sky, massive tons of steel and fuel and human
flesh carried far above the clouds on long, slender wings.
Planes that soared across the continent without stopping, at
heights that made the inhabitants of the world below invisible.
Contorted military fighter jets that turned at speeds so great
the pilot could black out from the pressure. Even during the
years the domes had been clamped shut and the few small
planes waited preserved in their crates, the stories and the
dreams of flight were kept alive.

First Violin weighed less than half a ton, and looked
more like a crippled dragonfly, but she flew. She was too
beautiful, too good, too *useful* to waste as a mail plane.
How long would he have to wait for a decent exploratory
assignment?

Leonard Cormack was a real prick, Berk thought sourly to
himself. How could his father ever have called that petty bureaucrat a friend? His mouth quirked into a frown as his
fragile daydream vanished. He turned away from the cockpit, groping in the gloom towards the emergency exit.
Perched on the edge of the sloping wing, feet dangling like
a child's, he looked towards the low outline of brown hills
in the distance hiding the domes of the City.

Berk cleared his throat, listening to the silence in the abandoned airport. His pedalcar was parked next to the skeletal remains of a hangar, the metal sheeting long stripped away from the lacelike arches. Even though there was little left to salvage at the old airport, the long days between flying had been unbearable. Here, at least, Berk felt at peace. He liked the quiet, the sound of the wing blowing the dust, giving him the illusion that he was utterly alone Outside. It was never quiet in the City.

He wrapped the length of cloth around his face, leaving only his eyes uncovered, and jumped down from the broken wing of the 787. The shadows were lengthening and he aimed the little pedalcar towards the City, looking forward to a cold drink. The wheels creaked as he adjusted his seat, closing the dark-glass door over him.

He turned onto the dry dirt road that had once been a major route into the open city of Pittsburgh, beside the shadowy ribbon of the Mong River. The large wheels of the pedalcar took the bumps and wind-ravaged furrows of the old road well, and the breeze flowing through the vents cooled Berk as his legs pumped at an easy pace.

By the time he pedaled across the bridge, the sun had slipped past the horizon. He pulled the car into the City Transportation lot, just inside the City Gate.

"Cuttin' it thin tonight," the attendant grumbled as he rolled the car into a line. The gate would be sealed after dark, a precaution against the occasional Ranger band insane enough to try and attack the City at night. The attendant locked the gate to the yard behind them both, and headed off in another direction from Berk's.

As Berk passed under the smaller, inner arch at the top of the stone stairs leading down the street, he jumped up with his hand extended over his head, brushing the cold granite arch with his fingers. It was a casual, superstitious pilot's tradition, an expression of boyish exuberance as much as self-confidence.

He jogged down the flight of steps to Smithfield Street, crowded with a workshift change, and he hurried, hoping to get home before December did. He turned left onto First, trotting past brick and steel buildings painted bright colors, not slowing his pace until he had passed Market. At the corner of Stanwix, he looked up at the high-rise, counting the flights until he reached his floor. The second apartment window from the end glowed with yellow light. He grimaced.

"Damn." December had got there before him. He had hoped to have at least one drink before they started their nightly ritual fight. Berk stood, shifting his weight from one foot to the other as he considered. "The hell with it," he muttered finally, and turned away.

He hailed a taxi at Third and told the driver to take him to Strawberry's. He didn't need to bother giving an address. It was a short ride to Strawberry Fields Tavern off Sixth and Strawberry Avenue, and Berk got out, taking his change from the driver. As he pedaled slowly away, the taxi driver scanned the street, alert for any drunks even at this early hour. Berk pushed open the stained-glass door of the tavern.

The place was slightly more upscale than most, although it was relatively small. What it lacked in size, it made up for in style, doing its best to represent what its owner, manager and bartender, Teddy Vandergrift, imagined to be an authentic pre-Shift watering hole. A huge mirror stood behind the chrome and green-glass bar, lined with shelves. The double reflection of the tavern's prized collection of antique bottles, empty except for colored water, made an imposing display. It was rumored that Teddy had a few bottles of original liquors stashed away somewhere. Teddy would smile enigmatically and neither confirm nor deny it.

The tavern was a favorite with the City fliers or those who were simply interested in either flying or the pilots, and Teddy did what he could to encourage their business. Gray-and-white paintings simulating old photographs hung on the walls, depicting men and women in various uniforms standing next to the great planes of a vanished era. Propellers, salvaged or fabricated, hung gleaming from the ceiling, turning slowly but doing little to circulate the air.

Also overhead dangled models of every plane of every pilot who frequented Strawberry's, which, of course, was every flier in the Pit. Teddy's teenaged son made a fairly good profit from scavenging, and Teddy preferred the pre-Shift plastic or metal models that occasionally surfaced. But what he couldn't find, he manufactured himself, amateur model planes replicating the various machines of his regular pilot customers, and painted with their colors. A wood-and-papier-mâché model of *First Violin* hung in one corner, bearing only a vague resemblance to the slender little helicopter. Beside it hung a long-winged amphibious plane, Wy's *The Kid*. Berk appreciated that Teddy hadn't taken down the little model after Wy had disappeared.

Teddy was obsessed with creating exactly his version of what a true pre-Shift tavern was like, studying every pre-Shift book and video in the museum's collection. He had somehow become convinced that true pre-Shift bartenders needed to be of the proper physical size. While there had been no food shortage within the City for generations, people ate a diet consisting mostly of hyponically grown vegetables and potatoes, and grains grown in Outside fields. Tough little goats and sheep who could tolerate the harsh sun on the Outside, as well as survive on the meager vegetation, provided the most common meat and dairy products, but cost much more dearly than farm-bred rabbit and various fowl. Fruit was plentiful, grown in the City's cherished North Side dome groves, and even on Berk's street several trees bore plums or apples once a year. Bananas, pineapples and oranges were rare. Shipped in from Erie, or grown in the experimental agrolabs, they were far too expensive for the Nielsens to buy on a regular basis just for the curious taste.

Part of the Alley River had been enclosed by domes and the water carefully diverted through a series of chambers, forming the City's fisheries. The labs had been working on genetically altered species that would grow both quickly and large, yet survive in the harsh conditions on the Outside, with some success. Most of the fish hatched in the City's fisheries were released when still fingerlings into the wild waters, with the hope they would survive and repopulate the rivers, but those fattened within the locks inside the domes were the main source of fish for the City's population.

Yet on this lean diet, Teddy had diligently pursued his ideal physique, putting on pounds steadily over the years until he weighed nearly twice as much as any man Berk had ever met.

He stood behind the long glass-top counter, a smudged white apron tied around his robust waist, drying glasses with a striped towel.

"Hey, Teddy," Berk said, sliding onto one of the bolted-down barstools. "Lost a little weight, there, eh?"

Teddy grinned indulgently, accustomed to the inevitable jokes. He poured a glass of the standard City-distilled Scotch and set it in front of Berk.

"You 'n' Sember fighting again?" he asked. Teddy had decided, after much research, that the proper pre-Shift barkeep had also been a persistent busybody, always willing to listen to his customer's problems and quick with advice no one wanted or was expected to take.

"Yeah," Berk admitted, taking a sip of his drink. "Still fighting with Cormack to give me something a little more juicy besides mail runs." He scratched his ear ruefully. "He thinks I'm a bad boy, take too many risks and not enough shit from the Council. So, no assignments. I'm getting bored and cranky. Sember's bugging me again to give it up, put in a request for retraining and go into something more steady."

It was a story Teddy had already heard many times before. He wiped the glass counter, glancing up when a pair of customers entered the tavern and sat at one of the three large round tables near the door. Taking drink orders was very simple. Despite the illusion of variety provided by the multitude of Teddy's bottle collection behind the bar, the City only produced Blue Ribbon beer and Allegheny Gold Scotch, neither of which bore much resemblance, Berk suspected, to their original malt ancestry. At a signal from the newcomers, Teddy poured two Blue Ribbons into his reproduction beer mugs and took them to the table before resuming his conversation with Berk.

"I think maybe December's mood might have a little to do with Wy's going down," Teddy offered. "Maybe she's afraid it might happen to you, too."

Berk shrugged. "Maybe. But she knew I was a pilot when we got married. She had the opinion that it was romantic then."

"Well, you need something to cheer y'up, that's what I think," the big bartender said. Now that his duties as self-proclaimed Last of the Great Bartenders had been discharged, he could indulge in showing off his newest toy. Grinning, he reached under the counter and placed a model helicopter, cast in metal, in front of the pilot. Berk recognized it as a pre-Shift Bell Jet Ranger VII. Although it was a different type of aircraft altogether, Teddy had carefully restored the battered model and painted it with Berk's colors. Stenciled on the side was the name *First Violin*.

"My kid found this last week poking around outside the Three Rivers dome," Teddy said with some pride, both in his son and the model. "I figure I'll replace my old model with this one—it's better. I'll rig it so that the rotors move, and hang it up where the propellers can give it a little air, turn the blades, y'know?" He stuck his forefinger in the blades, moving them around in a circle. They wobbled slightly and clicked where not even Teddy's loving touch could even out the dents.

Berk smiled, drinking the last of the second Scotch Teddy had poured for him. "That's real nice," he said, pleased. "I like it, I do." Teddy poured him a third, on the house. The fourth Berk had to pay for. And the fifth.

He didn't bother with a taxi, choosing to weave his way back to Stanwix Street. The lights in the apartment windows were out. The dome arching high over the streets was transparent, stars shining blearily through the hazy condensation on the thick glass. Berk pushed open the street door and climbed on the stairway, listening to the clump-clump of his drunken feet. Pushing the door from the stairwell open, leading onto his floor, he groped along the rows of apartment doors until he blinked at the door reading "716," the top of the "6" broken off to read: "71o."

Home. Jiggity-jig.

He fumbled with the lock, trying vainly to insert the metal key, when he inadvertently turned the knob and found December had left the door unlocked. He stared at the open doorway in dull surprise, and crept as quietly as drunkenly possible into the apartment, hit his shin in the dark against the patchwork sofa, cursed, grabbed his leg and passed out.

FIVE

November 17, 2218

THE CITY NESTLED IN THE CROOK OF THE RIVER'S division, an island of geodesic domes wedged together like half-buried glass mushrooms, their massive triangular panels reflecting golden bright sunlight.

Thin yet hardy trees lined the river's edge, green leaves rapidly beginning to turn gold and red now that the short fall season was ending. In a few weeks the rivers would start to freeze and the bitter, dry winter would drive everything to a near standstill, the population burying themselves inside the City to wait for spring.

Two bridges, one on either side of where the Ohio River split into a Y, were centuries old but meticulously maintained. Curved arches of dark, mirrored glass enclosed the tenuous bridge connection between the residential domes of the main City and the newer agrodomes on the North Side, the glint of sunlight obscuring any pedestrians crossing the river. On the South Side, the bridge had been left exposed, and an occasional pedalcar could be seen leaving or entering the City.

One bore a Council supervisor overseeing the construction of new solar collector domes; in another, engineers headed for the strike plates being built over on Mt. Oliver.

Messengers carried orders or equipment to the Outside irrigation dams along the rivers, armored tandem cars bearing agroworkers to the open Outside agrofields. Homebuilt private cars belonged to the scavenging antique hunters, or even pilots like Berkeley's father in a borrowed, beat-up car from the City fleet, out searching for bits and pieces of old aircraft.

On either side of the surviving bridges stood the broken columns of less fortunate edifices, a few surviving rusting steel stumps of cables curling from their ragged ends jutting out across the water. At the amputated end of one bridge young Berkeley lay on his stomach, fishing pole set beside him, peering down hundreds of feet to the dark water flowing slowly by below. Hidden under the water the remains of the destroyed bridge provided shallows that churned the murky waters, and provided shelter for small fish. His fishing line slanted away from the shallows, marking the drag of the water.

"Berkeley," he heard his father call. The boy sat up suddenly, knowing he'd been caught again, and watched the old man walking down the incline towards the end of the ancient, ruined bridge.

He expected his father to be angry; he'd been warned to stay away from these dangerous wrecks. This time, however, the old man sat down cross-legged at the edge of the bridge, putting his arm around Berkeley's shoulders. He leaned forward, inspecting the fishing line.

"Catch anything?" he asked, no anger in his voice.

Berkeley didn't quite know what to expect. "No, sir," he answered cautiously.

They sat for a while without speaking, listening to the sound of the wind blowing through the fragile leaves of the trees that clung to the shore below. Across the river, a line of goats clambered up the Incline, a vast preserve surrounded by an electrified fence to keep the animals in and Rangers out. Goatherds swaddled in the same protective white robes that covered the backs of their charges swatted the rumps of stragglers wandering too far in search of the last greenery of the season. Rifles strapped across their backs, the herders called after the goats, their laughter and voices carrying through the hot thin air.

The tiny *peep-cheep-chee-chee-peep-peep* of unseen birds carried up to the Nielsens, the last brood of chicks before the winter set in.

"Hear that?" his father asked suddenly, and grinned. "Baby birds," he said happily. "Sparrows, most likely. Hardy little things." And he clapped the boy on the shoulder as if he had personally been responsible for the scarce wildlife. After a moment, he added, "Your mother doesn't like you coming out here."

"I know," Berkeley admitted, staring down at his fishing line intently.

"It's dangerous. These old wrecks aren't solid, and staying out in the sun too long isn't good for you." The old man rubbed Berkeley's short cropped hair. "You didn't even bring a hat," he chided.

"I like it out here." Berkeley said, trying to explain. "It's quiet and I can be by myself."

His father nodded, and curled a gnarled forefinger around the line, jerking it a little as if to entice any hidden fish to bite. Berkeley suddenly suspected that his father had come here when he was a boy, too. He wondered if Grandfather Nielsen had caught and scolded his son, Berkeley's father, for the same transgressions.

"Why did they blow up the big bridges and leave just the two little ones?" the boy asked suddenly, his thoughts changing direction as abruptly as dry leaves in the gusting wind.

His father smiled. "They were too big to defend, Berkeley," he said. "Little bridges can be defended better than big ones. You should be doing your history homework instead of coming out here to play."

But Berkeley *had* studied the Shift, like all young students living in the City, as well as ancient history before the Shift. He could trace the lines of convection currents in the diagram of the earth's mantle, could rattle off about the Time of Zero, when there had been no geomagnetic fields to create Van Allen belts holding the ozone under their blanket.

But it didn't mean anything to him. They were only marks on a chart, large, meaningless blotches of land and water he'd never see.

He'd flown with his father and had probably seen more of the physical world than any of his classmates, except probably for Donica Wysaigh and her older brother, and that world held no oceans, no continents, no islands, no countries. There were only the domes and the vast dry land surrounding them, pale mountains to the east, low humps of land spreading to a flat horizon in the west, and the branching river separating the City from them both, flowing off into an unknown distance.

Berkeley tried to grasp the hugeness. He tried to visualize the great steaks of smoke and light hurtling up into the clouds, a "limited nuclear strike," not against people, but against the earth itself. He understood the words, could stand up with shaking knees in front of his class and recite the memorized texts in his childish voice. The old people tried to balance the Shift with an artificial nuclear winter, fighting the erosion of the ozone and the heat with an umbrella of dust clouds and smoke in the atmosphere.

They had wanted a quick solution, *now*. But in geological reckoning, *now* wasn't in the lifetime of the old people. Maybe it worked, maybe it didn't. Maybe it had carved decades off the Time of Zero, when the atmosphere had been stripped clean, and the earth baked under the relentless radiation of the sun. Maybe not. Berk parroted the words while the concepts were too enormous for him to comprehend.

The planet was too big. The Shift was too big, bigger than God. How could Berk be expected to understand?

So he imagined the soldiers blowing up the large bridges, great clouds of fire and smoke rising into the air, huge shattered pieces of the bridge slowly, majestically, in his mind's eye, crashing to the river below. He looked out across the river, conjuring up crowds on the smooth, empty bank. Ragged, desperate people screaming and cursing in the Great Panic, cut off and locked out of the domed Cities. He tried to understand the Shift by imagining it on a human level. A child's level.

"Do you think they were bad people, the ones who didn't get in?" he asked, hoping they were. He preferred to think of those long-dead hordes as Rangers, evil, frightening, not quite human.

His father shrugged. "I don't think so. They were just people, that's all. They were warned, like Noah had been in the Bible, and they chose not to believe, not to save themselves. Those cities that didn't build domes died. Our City Fathers helped save as many people as they could, but if they had tried to save them all, there wouldn't have been enough food, or clean water, or room to live in. Everyone would have died. It was a hard decision, Berkeley, and very sad."

It was a difficult concept for Berkeley. "Donica says that her father told her it was because they were bad. The old people did bad things to the earth, and they made the Shift happen."

Again, the old man shrugged. "Maybe. I don't know. The Shift is just something that happens, Berkeley. This old earth just sometimes changes without bothering to consult us first. But people always want to believe that they're important, good or bad. That what they do or don't do can change everything. Sometimes, all we can do is grab hold with both hands onto the planet, like fleas on a dog. Just hang on for the ride." He chuckled.

Berkeley grinned at his father, enjoying the joke. He pretended for a moment to be a little black flea on the back of an immense dog, wondering how far apart the hairs would be. Another thought excited him. "Donica says there're people on the moon, too. They got domes just like us, only better 'cause it's millions times worse than here, and they got these real big telescopes so they can see us from up there, and they're waiting for us to come back and get them."

"Wouldn't know, son," his father said. "Maybe they survived, maybe not. Just won't know till we get there." He smiled, running his gnarled hand through the boy's hair.

"We won't be going back there any time soon. They'll just have to wait a while longer."

His father sighed, a sad sound. Berkeley glanced at him quizzically. Was he sad for the people trapped on the moon, waiting for rescue that might not ever come? Was he unhappy because it would take more years than Berkeley could conceive of before people *could* rescue them? At least the moon people had *all* been inside domes, and didn't need City Fathers to choose who would live and who would die.

"Do you think God hated the people who didn't get in?" Berk wondered what the hundreds of millions who died in the Shift could have done to make God hate them.

His father was silent for so long that Berkeley thought he wasn't going to answer. "God loved the people inside the City. He saved them so that human beings wouldn't completely perish from the face of this earth. He saved us so that when the time came, we could restore His land. You are one of God's chosen, Berkeley. That's all you have to remember."

Berkeley knew his father wasn't really a religious man, but Mom went every Sunday to St. Mary Mercy. She was the concert pianist with the City Philharmonic, and said it was just to help out the church with the choir. She respected Dad's cheerful irreverence, while he respected her unspoken need for vague spiritual reassurance. Matters of theology were things Berkeley lost interest in quickly. It was all too complicated for him.

"Do you think there'll be another Shift?" He suddenly thought of the question, feeling a vague sense of alarm at something too big to prevent, something threatening to carry him away, out of control.

"Of course." The old man laughed. "But it won't happen for a very, very long time. We'll be like the dinosaurs, Berkeley. We'll be so old, scientists will be digging us up when we're fossils, and you and me, we'll be put up in a museum for people to come and stare at. How about that, son?" He brushed the boy's head again, affectionately. "You want to be a bunch of bones stuck in a rock hanging up on a museum wall someday?"

Berk laughed, and the fear of the Shift abated. He stared up at his father eagerly as a new idea occurred to him. "D'you think there's still bones over there?" he asked in a hushed voice, hoping there were. "Maybe we can find them now?"

His father chuckled. "That was a very long time ago. Let's leave all the bones for the next Shift, okay? Now we better get on home. Your mother's cooking dinner and you've still got your homework to do."

His father reeled in the fishing line, and they walked back into the City, the old man's strong, wiry arm around the boy's thin shoulders.

SIX

April 6, 2242

IT WAS THE OVERWHELMING NEED TO URINATE AS well as the light that woke him. He lay sprawled on the sofa, with his head over the side and his left arm dangling to the floor. He tried to sit up, pulling one leg from where he had lain on it. His foot hit the floor woodenly, pins driven into blood-starved flesh. He groaned, unable to find his balance with his numbed foot, feeling his head throbbing in his ears.

"Have a good time last night?" December asked.

He squinted up at her. She stood in the white satin nightgown he'd given her for her birthday last year, her arms crossed, one hand holding a glass of dark red juice. Blond hair fell in waves past her shoulders. Disapproval pinched her full lips and hardened her blue eyes, marring the illusion of perfection. He attempted a boyish, chagrined smile, which she didn't return. This was not a good sign.

"I'm in pain," he said, holding his head. "Don't you have any sympathy for a dying man?"

"No," she said flatly, and sipped her juice delicately.

"Went to Strawberry's las' night," he said, trying to straighten his numbed leg, "to see if any of the other fliers got assignments."

It was a very thin excuse and he knew she didn't believe him. "If you'd come home last night at a decent hour, then you could have talked about that with Leonard Cormack himself."

"Shit!" Berk said, trying to stand on his numb foot before collapsing back onto the sofa. "He called? What'd he say?"

December took another long drink of her juice, glaring at him with narrowed eyes, making him wait. "If you'd been here, you'd know. I'm not your damned answering service."

Berk's foot had regained enough sensation for him to stand and take one threatening step towards his wife. "Goddamnit," he cursed under his breath, helplessly fighting the old defensive urge to argue that was springing to virulent life.

She didn't appear intimidated. "Why don't you call him and find out? I have to go to work." She placed a slight emphasis on the word *work*, intimating, he knew all too well, her dissatisfaction with him.

She disappeared into the bedroom to dress as he dragged himself to the kitchen. There was barely any coffee left in the pot, not even half a cup of lukewarm liquid sloshing in the bottom. December had made it for herself, leaving just enough to demonstrate her anger. He shrugged, poured the dregs into her used cup and drained it in one swallow. It did little to relieve the pain around his temples.

The telephone line had only static on the line when he picked up the phone. "Damn, damn, damn," he swore softly. It would probably be quicker to walk down to City Hall than wait for the erratic phone lines to clear. Not that he preferred to meet face-to-face with Cormack any more than he had to.

December emerged from their bedroom, dressed in one of his light plaid shirts and her leather workpants. She carried her protective solar windjacket with the City Power patch on its shoulder. Tossing the jacket over the back of the sofa, she began twisting her long blond hair onto her head, securing it with pins.

"You're going out to the dam," he commented, keeping his voice even. It was obvious she was working on site, and he didn't expect her to answer. "Phone's down again."

"Too bad," she said, sounding not in the least sorry. "Markley and I are working under a deadline." She wrapped a length of white sunscreen cloth around her neck, shrugged on her jacket and headed for the door.

"I don't know when I'll be back tonight," she said venomously, "so don't wait up." She slammed the door closed; the sound was loud and painful. It was unnecessary, if that's what she'd intended. Berk somehow felt uneasy pain every time Markley's name was mentioned.

He sat staring out of the window for an hour after she left, waiting for the phone to ring, waiting for his head to clear. He tested the phone again. Still static. Finally he took a shower, the chilly water not much more than a dribble. December had used up their entire ration of hot water in the recycler, of course. Shivering, he shaved and put on his best shirt and clean pants. It would have to be done in person.

He opened the door to the stairwell and stepped directly into a tiny mound of pale brown dog shit left on the landing by Mrs. Kerowitz's goddamned miniature spaniel.

The day was not starting out well.

Leonard Cormack smiled as he opened his office door, braided tie dangling loosely from his open shirt collar. "Berkeley," he said, his voice warm and jovial. "Come on in. Glad you could come down." Berk rose from the couch in the waiting area and shook the Councilman's extended hand.

Cormack in a congenial mood was never a good omen. Berk sat in a worn chair in his office, waiting for Cormack to return with two cups of grain coffee.

"Milk?"

"No, thanks," Berk said, taking the ceramic cup from him. He sipped carefully as Cormack settled into the large chair behind his cluttered desk, the springs creaking under his weight.

"Council held a vote yesterday. I got you through. Y'want the assignment, it's yours." He took a long drink of the hot liquid and set the cup on a pile of papers, still smiling. Berk didn't smile back.

"Which assignment? Wysaigh's?" he asked, not even trying to hide the bitterness in his voice. Cormack's smile dimmed somewhat, replaced by the more familiar scowl.

"Not exactly. Trade loop, for sure. Regular run, if you want it. But this time we also want you to jump the Alley Oops. All the way. Exploratory," Cormack said shortly.

Berk ran his fingers through this thick, short hair. "Fly-by?" he asked suspiciously, his eyes narrowed.

Cormack shook his head. "Set-down. That *is* what you've been pestering me the last four years for, isn't it?" He scratched idly at the stubby growth of stiff, brown hairs on his cheeks.

Cormack had been smooth-faced and polished when he was just another pilot, a friend of old man Nielsen. Now he always looked in need of a shave. Berk's theory was that Cormack deliberately cultivated that image; a hardworking Councilman wouldn't have time to shave, especially one up for re-election.

"Check the maps, note any changes, any new growth you find. Do the tunnels, take some medical supplies in to Harrisburg, the usual," Cormack was saying. "But we want you to check out the Filly's harbor, look around at any industrial sites. Sniff around. Do what you're best at, Berk."

He'd been waiting for so long for an assignment like this. He'd fought with the Council, begged Cormack, complained bitterly to other independent flyers similarly kept under the Council's thumb. He felt oddly unelated.

"I don't know if *First Violin* can do the distance. She isn't what *Irene II* was," he said slowly, watching Cormack's face. The Councilman grimaced, as if he'd bitten into a particularly sour apple.

"Bullshit," he said. "I know you got extra tanks. Get 'em on her."

"It's almost three hundred miles one way, Leonard." Berk was enjoying goading the Councilman. "She's not going to like climbing over the mountains if she's packing."

Cormack's voice became sharp. "Look, if you've decided y'don't want the job after all, we'll just give it to Finley. I don't personally give a shit whether the great Nielsen flies or not." Cormack looked flushed.

Berk hesitated. It might be enjoyable to make Cormack sweat a little, but not enough to actually lose the assignment. It was odd, though, that Cormack *was* sweating.

Finley was one of Cormack's stable of pilots, a Council employee flying a City-owned plane, not a freelancer like Berk. He had enough experience, and his record, although spotless, showed he was a cautious, reliable flier, never taking any unnecessary risks. Like Wysaigh. And, like Wysaigh, Finley preferred the safe route and a steady job. Finley had the twice-a-week run to the agrofields down the Ohio Riverway, and he'd bitched and moaned often enough over his beer in Strawberry's about having to make all the multiple landings and takeoffs.

Too young, too soft, Berk thought. He'd probably already turned down the job. Probably, Berk realized suddenly, Finley wanted his damned mail run to Erie! Nice straight run up and back would suit Finley just fine. Cormack could have simply bumped him for it, but Berk suspected even Finley would be reluctant to take an assignment with that kind of dirt on it.

But Cormack didn't need to dangle the juicy temptation of an exploratory over the Filly to convince Berk to take Wysaigh's route in place of the Erie run. So why the big smile and warm congratulations all of a sudden?

Of course, Berk. You forget. Cormack isn't that jovial young flier who was your father's drinking buddy anymore. This is a politician, and politicians never give anyone anything out of the goodness of their hearts. So why should you?

"I'm not saying I won't do it," Berk said slowly. Cormack relaxed a little. "You know as well as I do that the maps aren't that good anymore. I'll be putting down in territory nobody knows that much about. There aren't too many friendlies to extend their hospitality much past Harrisburg. All I'm saying is that I ought to be compensated as long as I'm taking on an extra risk."

Leonard smiled, but now the smile was stiff, the eyes narrowed. "Let's not kid ourselves here, Nielsen. We need someone who can take care of himself on the Outside, and you, my boy, are badly in need of a job."

Berk felt his face grow warm, and he sat silent for a moment, lips pressed together in a hard line. "Yeah," he admitted finally. "I need the job, Cormack. I've been waiting four years for your department to give me something more than shit flights just to keep me flying and hoping. So you figure you can jerk my chain, and I'll be so hungry I'll jump at the opportunity. But why the Filly, Cormack? Why now?"

As he asked the question, he knew the answer, could see it in Cormack's eyes. "You're up for another term," Berk said. "You need to come up with something showy enough to get your ass re-elected, don't you? Like maybe another nice big oil field, the kind my father kept telling the Council for *years* was out there. Now that Harrisburg is secure enough to jump from, you can afford to look a little farther than your own safe backyard . . . especially now that you've got the old man's *son* to take the risks for you."

"What the hell's your problem, Nielsen?" Cormack snapped. "You and your old man made your reputations bragging about all your feats of derring-do, all the epic risks you took. Is the old man's son getting cold feet these days?"

Berk surprised himself, refusing to rise to the bait. "Maybe, Cormack," he said coldly, "the old man's son is wising up in his old age. Time to balance out the derring-do with a little looking out for business. Sure, I want this exploratory, you bet.

"But what happens *after* that? I wait another four years? What happens if the Filly turns out dry? What happens if you *don't* get re-elected?" He leaned forward, one hand gripping the coffee mug tightly. "It's real nice of you, Cormack, to offer me this wonderful flight assignment, seeing as how you know I'm not just one of the few who'd want it, I'm probably the only pilot this City's got who could do it. Me, and my fuel-guzzling flying lawnmower."

Cormack glared at him. "So do you take it or not?" he demanded curtly.

"Yeah, I'll take it," Berk said. "But I want a guarantee of

seniority postings when I get back. I'm not going to risk my ass or my helicopter on what I can find in Philadelphia just to give you a little flash for your political career. I'd rather fly around looking for stray Aggies who'd as soon shoot me down as kiss me than to trust you. Maybe I've learned something from Wysaigh as well as from my old man after all."

"Fine," Cormack said, reaching for the telephone. "Thank you so much for coming in, Nielsen. I think we'll give this to someone who understands the value of teamwork and respect towards an office of the Council."

Berk stood up, leaving the half-empty cup of grain coffee on Cormack's desk. "You can always find somebody willing to kiss your fat ass, Cormack," he said, knowing he was destroying his future as a pilot. "You specialize in keeping fliers hungry. And you can sure ground me. But how many pilots or machines have you got can do a city set-down? Who do you have who knows more than I do about recon work? You've already killed Wysaigh, you son of a bitch. How many more pilots are you willing to lose before you're finally stuck with me? That ought to look real good to the voters."

He was already out the door and halfway down the hall when Cormack bellowed his name. He turned, as surprised as the secretaries behind the row of desks flanking the hallway. The Councilman's face was red, furious. "Get back in here, Nielsen."

Berk's pride wanted him to tell Cormack to go to hell, but his sense of survival had him march back into the Councilman's office without protest. He crossed his arms, still standing, as Cormack shut the door.

"I went out on a limb for you, you know," Cormack said, looking grim. "You're not a real popular boy."

Berk said nothing. Cormack shifted his weight onto one foot, his face redder than usual. Frustration, anger, Berk couldn't tell what was passing through the Councilman's mind, but he was enjoying the sight of his discomfort.

"You've got some high opinion of yourself, Nielsen. But it's not generally shared by everyone on the Council. You've mouthed off and disregarded orders ever since you got your

City pilot's certification. It really is too bad your old man isn't still around to kick your butt a little."

Berk said nothing, waiting as the Councilman fumed. At last Cormack said, "Final offer. Seniority posting when you get back"—he thrust a finger in Berk's face—"but *only* if you come up with something worth it. Come back empty-handed, Nielsen, and you can sit until that lawnmower of yours rusts. That's it, take it or leave it."

"I'll take it," Berk said quietly.

The Councilman glared at him. "Fine. You leave in three days."

As Cormack turned away, Berk grinned, a thin, angry smile. "In writing, Councilman," he said.

He couldn't help it.

SEVEN

September 4, 2225

BERKELEY SAT BESIDE HIS FATHER IN FIRST VIOLIN, the helicopter humming contentedly around them as the old man followed the 79 route north. Now that his father was nearly finished rebuilding *Irene II*, the second family helicopter, Berkeley thought of *First Violin* as *his* more and more. But this wasn't a flying lesson. Berkeley, at fifteen, already had more than five years of experience. This, his father had explained, grinning, was a sightseeing lesson.

"All looks pretty much the same, don't it?" the old man said, leaning back comfortably, his eyes hidden behind the protective dark glasses.

And, Berkeley had to admit, it did. Miles and miles of fairly uniform ground, low rolling hills dusty and brown and mostly barren. Far to his right, Berkeley could see the low-lying blue mountain range in the distance, nearly hidden in the curve of the horizon. They had flown over several small towns, all abandoned. Roofs of ancient houses had fallen in, topless boxes like simple mazes standing in rows, wind-blasted into colorlessness.

"Isn't the same, if you know what you're lookin' at." The old man banked the helicopter to the right, flying over a fairly large collection of ruins which the hand-drawn map in

Berkeley's lap told him had once been Meadville. "You see that?" his father said, pushing the cyclic forward gently. They hovered above the remains of a large building, most of it long burned to the ground. The old man's feet played the rudder pedals and *First Violin*'s nose swung around for Berkeley to get a better view.

"Yeah," the boy said cautiously.

"What is it?"

Berkeley studied the ruins for a moment. "A house?" he guessed uncertainly.

"Don't think anybody ever lived there, boy," his father said. "Guess again." The helicopter's nose swung to the left, then steadied facing into the wind.

"Don't know," Berkeley admitted.

"That road we been following used to have thousands of cars on it every day. Not like pedalcars. Like those down back there." The old man pointed to a collection of old pre-Shift cars, all rusted into frail skeletons of their former bulk. Even smashed and wasted away by weather and time, they were easily three or four times as big as a normal pedalcar.

"And what did those cars use for fuel, boy?"

"Gasoline," Berkeley said promptly.

"How far are we from that big road?"

He shrugged. "Not very."

The old man glanced at Berkeley, lowering his head to look at him from over the top of his dark glasses. "So think, boy."

"It's a gasoline refilling post," Berkeley said. It was obvious now.

"Right. A gasoline *station*." His father dropped the helicopter closer to the ruins. "So what's that down there?" He nodded sideways out the window at two barely visible holes in front of the station, no bigger around than Berkeley could make a circle with his hands.

"Um—" He thought hard. "That's where they kept the gasoline?"

"In big underground tanks," the old man affirmed. "Used to be pumps to take it out again and put into the cars."

Berkeley looked at his father speculatively. "There isn't any left anymore, though, is there?" he said.

"Nope."

"You've already looked."

"Yup." His father grinned, and pulled back on the cyclic, heading for the main road. "Some things you can't see from the air, son. You've gotta set down and sniff the ground a little."

He flew past the road, and over a long, flat area. "Now this, you ought to be able to tell me."

"Sure," Berkeley said promptly. "Used to be an airport."

"No planes down there. All covered with weeds. So how do you know?"

"It's shaped like one. See," the boy said, pointing. "Those were runways."

"What kind of airport?"

"Little one for private planes. Runways're too short for the big jets."

The old man nodded, and swung the helicopter back to the north, nose down to cruise straight and level. "There're two more just like it west of here. Isn't much left of them or the reservoir."

They flew a zigzag course all up the old road, his father pointing out various objects. "This all used to be oil country here, boy. Lots of it. Took it out of the ground raw."

"It's all gone now?"

The old man frowned, shook his head. "Nope," he said confidently. "Still some left. Closest stuff, I think, gonna be east of here. Large part of scouting, son, is sticking your big nose in the library. 'Course most of the obvious ones, round in Oil City, Franklin—got those already. Sucked out and capped long ago. So y'gotta look where people mighta forgotten about."

Wars and rising global heat had burned off much of the imported oil. The Great Panic had drained domestic reserves, although Berkeley couldn't imagine where people had hoped to flee, running from city to city until their gas ran out, their planes crashed or they simply died.

"But there was plenty enough oil for millions of people,

then. Lot of it left in the ground." His father smiled, lecturing to himself. He meant the little abandoned wells dotting the wastelands, but Berkeley heard the old man's dream behind the words. The reason his father built *Irene II*. Bigger, with a longer range, he dreamed of heading south, down to the Gulf of Mexico. Bypassing Cincinnati. Finding places with names like Big Hill and Weeks Island, the underground salt domes of the Strategic Petroleum Reserve. "Some things fire and time can't get to at all. Lots more just waiting for eager beavers like you and me."

"Why aren't we going east, then?"

"Because today," his father said, "we're going to Erie."

Berkeley's eyes widened. "Set down?" he asked, excited. "Yup."

Erie had been another small city which had domed itself for the Shift, then been extinguished with the domes mostly intact. No explosions or fire had ruined the small domes, no evidence of any violence. It had perished from much more natural causes.

The engineers who built the domes had underestimated how far and how fast Lake Erie's water level would rise after the Shift. The polar caps melted, water swelling the great Canadian riverways as it poured across the Canadian plains into the Great Lakes faster than either Lake Ontario or the St. Lawrence Seaway could drain it away. The sea level rose several meters, the Atlantic pushing its way up the valley, drowning small towns. The neglected locks from the Lachine to the Thousand Islands sections of the seaway broke under the assault.

The water level rose relentlessly into Erie, pumps failing under the strain. The streets of the City flooded under the domes. The Presque Peninsula nearly vanished, and everything north of Sixth Street was abandoned. The inhabitants crowded to higher ground, hemmed in by the limits of the domes, struggling for survival. Engineers, dying with the rest of the population, couldn't hold back the rising waters. The sewage system finally collapsed, and within a few months, those who had not died of disease abandoned the domed City, fleeing toward Pittsburgh. A bare handful survived the trek, only to be turned away along with the hundreds of thousands of other refugees begging to be let in.

Decades later, the glaciers began to grow again, reclaiming the poles. The waters eventually receded, leaving behind fertile silt. Like Harrisburg, the water-trapping greenhouse had sheltered a small tropical environment of its own, ruined buildings giving way to a jungle of soaring trees and flowering plants. Unlike Harrisburg, however, it had neither solar domes, nor a moving river to put powerdams along to draw electricity from. And, unlike Harrisburg, there wasn't much left that hadn't fallen into ruin or rusted away.

The old man flew over the Erie International Airport, well outside the Erie domes, without bothering to land. There were few planes left on the ground; most had flown away long ago with the desperate citizens fleeing the drowning town. Those that remained were no more now than insect bodies smashed flat against the ruins of the old airport.

Berkeley's attention, however, was on the domes themselves: five, pressed together like fragile soap bubbles, covered an area two miles wide and three miles long. Like those in Pittsburgh, they had been built from light-sensitive, nearly indestructible glass, but even with the panels darkened in the glaring sunlight, the verdant interior filled them with emerald brilliance . . . A half-dome had been erected jutting out over the small bay, arches opening out on the water for the long-vanished boats. There were several gateports leading in, all but one blocked by rubble.

Berkeley's grandfather, not much older than Berkeley was now, had been one of the first fliers to make early, tentative forays into the Outside. Eager pioneers, they had been the first to explore the domed Cities in search of fellow survivors.

Cleveland, Detroit and Chicago, along the Great Lakes, had built domes. So had Toronto and Ottawa, farther up the other side of the Great Lakes. Louisville in the south, and St. Louis and Des Moines in the west. With the exception of those in Cincinnati, all the domes had failed. Jagged fingers of twisted steel beams no longer held their protective glass, broken domes leaving the Cities open and exposed to the Outside.

St. Louis still had the skeleton of her domes intact, the glass shattered in the abandoned streets below. Deep under the crumbling ruins, a labyrinthine maze of tunnels had become catacombs of ancient bones as the doomed survivors slowly died off, waiting for the Zero Time to end, the magnetic fields to return to the earth.

Past the Missouri River very little had been explored as yet; the Great Plains were an immense broiling desert. Even the vast majority of the lowlands was inhospitable, fit only for roving bands of Rangers. After the shock and disappointment at their isolation wore off, the City of Pittsburgh concentrated its efforts on retaking the open land closest to the major rivers, land it could irrigate and farm.

There had been some talk about establishing a colony at Erie. After all, her domes were still intact. It was closer than Harrisburg, a straight route north, not over mountains. And it had a fantastic, tropical environment, rich in plants and fruit.

The City of Cincinnati, however, had also survived under its protective domes. Now that the more hospitable spring and fall months were shortening the lethal summers, the first contacts between the two domed Cities were made, about the same time as Berkeley's grandfather had taken his own son on his first tentative explorations in the dead city of Erie.

Cincinnati was reachable by the Ohio River. Boats covered with protective sunscreening and powered by strong human legs connected the domed sister Cities. Together, the two Cities built a flat-bottomed boat to travel down the Mississippi on a joint expedition toward the unexplored Gulflands. They'd hoped to find another surviving City at Memphis, if not at New Orleans. The courageous men and women setting out had waved and pedaled away to the cheers of their friends.

They never returned.

The tragedy had soured relations between the domed Cities, each side blaming the other for the failure. A new joint venture was shelved after the two Cities couldn't reach agreement on who was to be in charge. Cincinnati became an isolated City, a tiny kingdom hostile to its rival. Pittsburgh turned its eye towards the fragile river ecosystem, throwing its efforts into reclamation agriculture.

Berkeley's grandfather died before his fortieth birthday, skeletal, vomiting blood, riddled with radiation cancer. The price of being a pioneer. His son inherited *First Violin* and his father's dreams.

Erie, lush and beautiful as it was, was reachable only over a large expanse of blasted earth. Or by air. Politics, money, limited manpower, had kept any would-be settlers out of Erie. But with the waning enthusiasm between the only two known surviving domed Cities, recolonizing abandoned domes looked more attractive. It would take a few more years, maybe. But for now, that suited the old man just fine. He preferred leaving Erie just the way it was, unspoiled, untouched, the sweltering domes a nearly virgin playground for pilots like Berkeley's father.

And now Berkeley.

His father set *First Violin* down gently and let the engine and the blades whine to silence. There was no secured perimeter of electrified barbed wire, no safety hangar to put the helicopter in. They would have to leave the machine Outside, unguarded. It wasn't that much of a risk, Berkeley knew. This late in the year, after the ravages of the summer, Rangers were scarce and not too active.

The old man handed the boy one of the machetes he had fashioned in his workshop, the gleaming curved steel salvaged from an old airplane prop. Berkeley strapped the machete to his waist and looped a length of rope around his shoulder before following his father.

There was little difficulty getting into the domes. They simply climbed over the rubble of a gateway, thick roots and vines cracking relentlessly through the stone and concrete. Once inside, however, they were slowed by the thick tangle of old growth. They had to hack their way through the dense vegetation for every step they gained. Berkeley spotted old hatchmarks on the bark of trees and fingered them curiously.

They could have been made by any flier, but the boy wanted to believe that it had been the old man, once young like him, following his own father as they hacked their way into these domes, leaving the scars of their passage behind.

Inside, the temperature was nearly as hot as Outside, but the air was sticky and humid. Within minutes, Berkeley's shirt clung to his chest, his hair plastered wetly against his forehead. Sweat ran in rivulets down his skin, but he felt exuberant as they chopped and climbed their way slowly through the brush.

They stopped to catch their breaths, and listened without speaking to the cacophony of wild alien sound, unseen birds whooping and twittering in the canopy of leaves overhead. A whir of wings startled Berkeley, and he stared open-mouthed at the bright rainbow plumage of a parrot as it screeched its outrage at him, then disappeared into the trees. A blue- and red-striped lizard as long as the boy's arm raised itself on short fat legs to glare at him, its head darting from side to side before it skittered into the underbrush.

He laughed, delighted and amazed by the sight of animals he had only seen in picture books. The old man grinned, throwing an arm around the boy's shoulders. They stood gawking at the bizarre scenery, the warm smell of bright leaves and flowers growing in the rich mold thick in the boy's nostrils. Berkeley had spent many nights sitting longingly at the old man's feet as he spun tales about vines hanging from massive trees and fantastic wild animals roaming free inside the Erie domes.

A black monkey, its face ringed with white fur, shimmied up a tree trunk, an infant monkey clinging under its arms. Berkeley stared at it as he wiped his forehead, feeling light-headed in the unaccustomed humidity. The mother chattered at them, then leaped away into the safety of the overhead canopy. A spray of leaves swirled down as it vanished.

"This is how I imagine the world must have been like once," the old man said, his voice quiet.

Berkeley stared up at his father. "The Outside? All like this?"

"Not all. Some of it. Lots of it." The old man sat down on

a fallen tree trunk, damp and covered with velvet moss and strange fungus. "The Outside can be beautiful in its own way, Berkeley. It's got its own life, plants and animals and even men who've learned to survive. You just have to open your eyes and see what's there. But places like this . . ." He shook his head and looked at the boy. "It almost makes me believe in a merciful God," he said softly. His face was gaunt, lined. The shirt sticking wetly to his chest showed how thin his body had grown. His sunburned skin peeled constantly. His short, stubbly hair had turned white and his eyes were tired.

In that moment, Berkeley realized something he had only vaguely understood before.

His father was dying.

His mother's soft crying behind the bedroom door at night. The too-wide grins and hearty back-slapping of visiting pilot friends. The sores on his father's skin that wouldn't heal. The feverish nights spent on *Irene II*. The sudden crash courses he'd been giving Berkeley in flying and reconnaissance. It had been obvious; the old man was dying. He'd flown too much, been exposed too long, and the merciless sun had finally got him.

"Dad . . ." Berkeley said, feeling his face grow cold.

As if he knew, his father rose, mopping the sweat from his forehead. "Let's go," he said, and smiled. "There's a lot here to see."

They hacked their way along the overgrown trail to a hodgepodge of ruins with walls of rusting, twisted bars. They stumbled out of the brush into a hollow between two shattered buildings. There, the biggest cat Berkeley had ever even imagined lay dozing on a jumble of rocks, sunlight streaking down through the foliage, dappling gold highlights on its striped hide.

His father grabbed him tightly by the arm and they froze as the cat raised its head, green eyes blinking sleepily at them. Berkeley's heart pounded in his throat. The tip of the cat's tail moved gently, unconcerned. Tufted ears flicked at insects buzzing in the humid heat. Then it yawned, a huge red maw of sharp teeth.

"Shit!" Berkeley gasped, jumping back in alarm. The brush behind him rustled. The cat snapped its mouth shut and, in a liquid ripple of muscle, rolled to its feet. His father jerked him down and they crouched in the tall grass, machetes gripped in sweating hands.

The great cat stared at them, tail lashing in agitation. It growled, a low rumble of dangerous sound, then slithered off the rocks and out of sight among the ruins. The muffled crackling among the trees as the cat vanished made Berkeley nervous, yet strangely excited.

"This here was a zoo, boy," his father was whispering, still the teacher. "A place where they kept animals from all over the world. Guess when the people left, somebody still thought enough to let them out, give them a chance to fend for themselves. Might be the last of these creatures on the whole earth, for all we know." The old man had relaxed, but kept his alert eyes on the brush where the cat had gone. "Kind of like Noah's ark."

They skirted the edge of the old abandoned zoo and found a straight path through the center of the domed City, leading towards the lake. Concrete structures had fallen into piles of rubble along the ancient street. Shadows slunk through the caves of empty brick shells crumbling into vine-tangled ruins.

They came out along the lake shore. The water in the bay rippled blue under the dome with crystal-bright light. Five long-necked kudu raised their heads in unison from where they had been drinking along the shore, liquid brown eyes turned in the direction of the boy and the man. Under spiraled horns, the animals' ears swiveled forward curiously, unafraid. Berkeley watched as they turned and picked their unhurried way on long, delicate legs back into the cover of the brush.

Concrete benches still lined the waterfront, crumbling and covered with moss. Berkeley and his father brushed the dirt and leaves off one still relatively intact and sat watching the water. Brightly colored fishing birds skimmed over the surface of the bay, dipping their beaks into the water to snatch up tiny silver fingerlings. Occasionally a larger fish would leap, a flicker of rainbow scales and silken tail leaving radiating circles in the water.

By the time father and son had found their way back out to the helicopter, they were both filthy and tired. Berkeley looked back at the gatepost to glimpse a strange small furred animal sniffing after them, face at the open hole. It blinked and wrinkled its eyes, annoyed by the dry heat, then skittered away from the inhospitable Outside, back to the lush jungle growth.

Berkeley thought that the Outside would look even more drab and barren after Erie, but instead, it was as if his vision had been sharpened, details he might ordinarily have ignored jumping out at him with new life and meaning.

The light had reddened as the day grew old, the tiny shadow of the helicopter rippling as it raced across the land below. The old man was following a different road back while Berkeley's finger traced the route on the tattered map. Berkeley spotted a patch of pale green half-hidden between two low slump-shouldered hills. It was so small they might have missed it entirely had they been flying a few hundred meters to the east.

"Look, Dad!" he said, and pointed.

His father rolled the helicopter slightly, and drew it up over the spot. Below them, a half-dozen men had pulled a primitive camouflage net partway across the garden patch. They scattered as they realized they were too late, the wind from the helicopter blades blowing dust around them. The men seemed to vanish, as if diving into hidden burrows in the ground. A child ran in crazed circles. A woman appeared suddenly, bolting from her hiding place to snatch the child in her arms. They crouched together in the dirt, dark faces turned up at the helicopter, mouths open wide in terror as they cried, unheard over the steady thrum of the blades.

"Rangers!" Berkeley said.

"Aggies." The old man's voice was flat, hard. He stared at the woman and child trapped in the dust below, then pulled *First Violin* away, gliding fast as he pointed the helicopter's nose south.

"We found something!" Berkeley said, excited and happy

to have finally made his first real discovery. But he was puzzled by his father's grim expression. "They'll give you a bonus for an agricultural find, Dad. Aren't you going to report it to the Council?" he asked.

"Report what?"

"That Aggie garden!"

"What Aggie garden?" his father said. He wasn't smiling. "I didn't see any Aggie garden. Neither did you."

"But . . ."

"Listen, son," the old man said fiercely. "That pathetic little patch of dirt probably won't even provide enough food for those poor fuckers down there. Chances are they're taking what they can from it right now, then they'll burn the rest and run, figuring we'll be back to take it away from them tomorrow, anyway."

Then he gave Berkeley a final lesson in "sightseeing" for the day, one the boy remembered more than all the others. "Sometimes, Berkeley," the old man said gently, "what you don't see is more important than what you do."

EIGHT

"HAVE YOU EVER REALLY THOUGHT ABOUT SUICIDE?" December said. In her clear cool eyes, not a hint of depression showed. Not a glint of desperation.

He had made dinner reservations at one of the private outdoor gazebos at the Golden Triangle, the restaurant nestled in the green wedge of land between the Mong and Alley Rivers. The sky through the dome was still a clear blue, deeper with the growing evening. Birds twittered and sang, hopping from one fruit-laden tree branch to another in the open parkway. In the distance, at the tip of the Triangle, a wide fountain sprayed clear water in a glittering fan, reflecting rainbows in wavering arcs. Waiters in crisp white uniforms passed from one tiny round table to another bearing trays of food, savory aromas mingling with the scent of new flowers in the air. It was as unlikely a place to discuss suicide as Berk could imagine.

Momentarily confused, he chose to answer with safe humor. "Actually, no," he said lightly. "Taxes, maybe . . ."

She acted as if she didn't hear him.

"Killing yourself," she mused, as if examining a particularly interesting bug stapled to a biologist's labeled board.

"Putting a gun in your mouth, for example, and pulling the trigger. You can see it, if you really want to."

She speared a tiny portion of fish on the end of her fork, holding it delicately poised next to her mouth as she spoke. "One moment everything that makes you a human being is there, alive and pulsing and intact, and the next, it's just bloody oatmeal stuccoed against a wall like some kind of weird artist's design. And you're not even human anymore, just this slab of meat with bits and pieces of something that *used* to be a person slithering down a wall." She popped the fish into her mouth and smiled as she chewed.

He hoped that would be the end of the subject, but she looked at him, her eyes shining, and said, "If you think about it, it's true you wouldn't actually *be* there to see yourself. You wouldn't be alive to look at your body lying on the floor. But you could *imagine* it, couldn't you?"

He stared at his plate, determinedly cutting and eating the food he had lost appetite for, without answering her. She picked up a piece of bread and tore off a small chunk, buttering it evenly and carefully.

"And because you see it in your mind, it would be as if you were really there, seeing how you could go from being *alive* to *dead* in a second, how the people around you would react. You could imagine yourself lying on the ground with your mouth open, and your eyes open and a great big hole in the back of your head where your brains had been just a second ago, a fraction of a second before you pulled the trigger and stopped being *you* and started being something else."

"Stop it!" Berkeley said sharply, cutting her off, afraid. "Shut the fuck up. What the hell's wrong with you? What are you thinking of, anyway?"

She looked at him, cold blue eyes wide. "I'm not thinking of killing myself," she said, seemingly astonished that he had thought so. "Sometimes I wonder about things like that. Don't you?"

"No." Whatever celebratory mood the meal had started out with had evaporated.

"I would have thought that you would, flying Outside all the time. Anything could happen there."

"It's not like committing suicide." For a moment, Berk saw the blackened smear of a helicopter against the desert sand. "Let's drop the subject, okay?" He stared at the food on his plate, the fear slowly turning to anger as he ate methodically, in silence. He glanced at her, watching as she continued eating, unconcerned.

"Markley says he's promoting me next month," she said, looking up. "The irrigation dam project has gone very well, and my designs seem to be holding together. I'd like to get in on the Lebanon Project, do some of the internal power design. With this promotion, Markley thinks I have a good chance."

The mention of her supervisor's name threw Berk off-balance again; the vague fear returned. She smiled and turned her attention back to her plate. "Anyway, he's written a good recommendation for me to Councilman Chong. Markley says there might even be enough in the budget for a pay raise."

"Good. That's great." He found himself muttering. *Markleysez Markleysez Markleysez* . . . "I'm happy for you, really."

"Then I'd be making enough that we could get a bigger apartment," she said.

He sensed another attack, but couldn't see where it would come from. "What's wrong with our place now?" He had been proud of the housing he'd finally been able to get assigned. A two-bedroom apartment for a childless couple had been difficult to wrangle. But his earnings as a pilot barely covered the apartment's extra expense above the City rent allotment, while December carried the cost of food and clothing and the rest of life's little necessities.

"I wouldn't want you to give up your workshop," December said, the right amount of concern and surprise in her face.

Knowing it was inevitable, he asked grimly, "Why would I have to give up my workshop?" Again, it would be the same old argument. She wanted him to give up flying, get a steady job, maybe even go into the Energy Department with her.

"We'd need another room for the baby," she said, as if it were the most obvious thing in the world. "I've already checked it out, and we're more than qualified for parentage permits."

He sat with his mouth open, dumbfounded. Suspiciously, he asked, "You're not . . ." Without permits, a pregnancy would mean an immediate trip to the public clinic for a mandatory termination, and that would certainly cancel his flight tomorrow. For a crazy instant, he was sure that she had somehow known he would get this assignment yesterday and purposely allowed herself to be illegally impregnated.

"Of course not," she said.

Unlikely as it was for her to be pregnant, he reluctantly dismissed the idea. He sat rigidly.

"Don't you want to have a baby?" she asked softly. A stray wisp of blond hair escaped from her upswept hairdo, and she pushed it away from her eyes with a pale hand, nails immaculately tapered. She was still the most beautiful woman Berk had ever known, and as she smiled tremulously, a hint of an embarrassed blush on her cheeks, eyes shining with tears, he felt his groin stir in response.

He had loved her once, with a passion that was clear and innocent. There was a time when that smile could convince him the earth was flat. Sometimes she reminded him of that.

"What the hell is this all about, Sember?" he said, his voice as soft and gentle as hers. "First you're going on about people blowing their brains out and now you want to have a baby. I don't understand you."

Her eyes shifted back and forth as he stared at her, and he watched the sweet smile fade and her face harden. "No," she said, drawing away from him stiffly, "I don't suppose you do."

He groaned silently. "Okay, Sember. When I get back, we'll apply for parentage and try for a baby, okay?" Anything to make peace, he thought. They could argue about it just as easily in a week as they could tonight.

"Such enthusiasm," she said, her voice sharp. She glared at him, wineglass in her hand. "You'd make a lousy parent, anyway." She drank half of the wine in a long gulp.

"December, please," he pleaded, reaching for her hand across the table. "What do you *want* from me? I'm leaving tomorrow morning. This is the best assignment I've had in years. I just wanted us to go out, celebrate a little, have a nice meal and enjoy ourselves together. Is that so terrible?"

"No, it's just fine for you, isn't it?" she said, jerking her hand out from under his. "Tomorrow you fly off and leave me behind, and I'll do what I do every day—go to work and watch people with less talent and experience promoted over me because *they're* not married to some adolescent flier who's made a career out of pissing off the entire Council. I come back every day to the same apartment and the same stack of bills, and watch you lock yourself into that stupid room and tinker around with your toys. If you're even home and not out scrounging junk in some worthless antique airfield. I can go see Fayette and play with her little girls and come home tomorrow to an empty apartment. My life is just one big thrill after another."

She subsided into a strained silence, her cloth napkin clutched in one hand with white-knuckled force.

"Wysaigh's gone," he pointed out quietly.

"Yes, he's gone," she shot back, "On the same damned flight you're taking tomorrow. But at least he left Fayette with something more than overdue bills and spare helicopter parts."

Their waiter returned and cleared the plates from the table, most of Berk's meal left untouched.

"Care for some dessert tonight, folks?" he asked.

"No, just espresso," Berk said curtly. The waiter nodded as if he didn't notice the simmering tension, and moved discreetly away.

"Is that what you want, Sember?" Berk said. "Would you like me to fly off tomorrow and disappear like Wy? Would that make your life a little easier if I weren't here anymore?"

If he'd hoped to shame her, it didn't work. "What I *want*," she said firmly, "is a real life, Berk. I want a husband who takes some responsibility, for his family and their future. I want a husband who pays more attention to business and his wife instead of his ego and some piece of flying scrap metal.

I'm tired of waiting for you to grow up while you play at being the adventurous hero."

"Someone more like, say, Markley, right?" He was unable to stop the words. "If I'm such a handicap to you, exactly what *did* you do for Markley to get a promotion out of him?"

He instantly regretted it. She stared at him, a mixture of emotions he couldn't read. If he'd expected to shock a confession from her, or a heartfelt denial, what he saw on her face gave him no clue.

"You son of a bitch," she whispered. She threw her napkin down, pushed her chair back and walked away, just as the waiter arrived with two small cups of espresso grain coffee.

"The check, I assume?" the waiter asked, ironic. Berk watched her leave without going after her, her white dress floating around her slim body, back stiff. She didn't look back.

He paid the check and wandered into the Blockhouse, the bar at the edge of the Triangle. He sat in a corner and ordered a Scotch, followed by several more. It was stupid, but he didn't care if he was hungover tomorrow or not. He would fly anyway. By the time he had finished his fifth Scotch, he had worked himself up into a self-righteous rage.

He imagined December and Markley at the irrigation dam. He could see her begging him for a promotion. She'd do anything, he heard her say longingly, *anything*. He could hear the wistful reproach in her voice, a voice that said *he* was the reason she hadn't got where she deserved to be. *He* was responsible for forcing her to degrade herself.

His hand clenched around his drink as he watched Markley smile, a twisted, sadistic grimace. In his drunken imagination, he watched as Markley leaned back against the hard gray stone of the dam, and opened his pants, imperiously ordering December to kneel. She sank, not quite unwillingly, to her knees, her slender hands pressing against Markley's beefy legs. Sweat beading her skin in the hot Outside air, she opened her mouth, and Markley slid his obscene cock in between her full lips. Markley's fat hand grabbed her by her blond hair, pins roughly pulled out, and forced himself deep into her face. Again. And again.

The fantasy played in his head as Berk threw down more money than needed to pay for the drinks, and staggered out. He wanted to kill Markley. He wanted to beat the shit out of December. Still he kept on visualizing December's mouth sliding wetly against Markley's now cartoonishly monster-sized cock, her lips eager, wet and trembling.

He marched along the dark streets, past the arches connecting the Triangle dome to the Center dome, hearing her hungry moans in the slap of his feet against the ground, hearing Markley grunting like a diseased animal. He could see starlight above him as he watched the buttons pop off her workshirt, *his* workshirt, as Markley ripped it apart. It fell open, down her smooth, white shoulders, her naked breasts straining out as she groveled in the arid brown dirt, rubbing them against the rough fabric of Markley's pants. Her greedy mouth sucked him, her lust-filled eyes turned up at her supervisor as he grinned triumphantly down at her.

He climbed the stairway to their apartment, achingly aware of his own throbbing hard-on imprisoned in his pants. Unlocking the door with shaking hands, he slammed it shut, breathing hard, both from the rapid walk and the angry fantasy circling in his head.

December rolled over as he jerked the quilts from the bed, glaring at him, her mouth twisted in disgust. "You're drunk," she said sleepily, one hand raised to shield her eyes, squinting in the light as he stood above her.

"You're right," he said, undoing his pants. She grimaced at his erection, reaching for the quilt.

"Forget it," she groaned, turning away.

Roughly he grabbed her by the shoulder, slamming her back against the bed. His pants dropped to his ankles and he kicked them away as he pinned her down, pulling the hem of her thin nightgown up around her hips. "You want a baby," he sneered. "I thought you wanted a baby, right?" Frustrated by the hem, he grabbed the nightgown by the neckline, tearing it down the front, and ground his chest against her exposed breasts. "The hell with the City permits, let's make a baby right now, Sember!"

Her eyes inches from his face were furious. "Fuck you!" she snarled, struggling against him. She struck him on the shoulder, the blow ineffective coming from an awkward angle.

He grabbed her wrists, bearing down with his whole weight against her. "I'm trying," he laughed, without humor. He felt his hard erection pressing into the soft flesh of her stomach. "Or would you rather be fucking Markley, huh?"

She froze for a fraction of a second, then redoubled her struggles. "You goddamned bastard," she wheezed out as her legs windmilled. She kicked him in the side and he grunted; then they both toppled from the bed, sliding down on the sheets pulled off the bed. He thrust his knee roughly between her legs, prying them apart as she got one hand free. Her fist caught him hard on the side of the head, a painful stinging blow to his ear. She hit him again before he ground his elbow down against her forearm.

"Owww!" she howled in pain and fury.

"Shhh," he said mockingly, "You'll wake the neighbors." He slid his hips down across hers and thrust himself inside her in a long, ungentle stroke. She arched her back, and sank her teeth into his shoulder in a vicious bite. Yanking away, he slapped her hard in the face, and lay with his forearm jammed across her throat, pinning her under the chin. They froze on the floor, staring at each other in trembling rage.

"What's the matter," he said, teeth clenched, "I don't fuck as good as Markley, that it? Or can't I make a better deal for you than he can?"

He jerked as she suddenly spit, blinking as warm wetness hit him below his left eye. He shook her but didn't dare release his grip.

"I don't have to fuck anybody for a promotion," she replied, her voice hoarse. "What did *you* have to do for your prize flight assignment? Say pretty please, bend over his desk and let Cormack plug you in the ass?"

"You're the most manipulative, cold bitch I've ever known

in my life," he snarled. Slowly, almost unbidden, his hips began to move as he slid in and out of her.

"And you're nothing but a selfish, juvenile, washed-up failure," she panted, but she had stopped struggling.

His thrusts became harder, insistent, and he grinned as she lay under him, his hands clamped around her wrists by her head, their fingers tangled in her long hair. The dark color of her torn nightgown outlined her full breasts. He watched as they rose and fell quickly with her labored breathing, wanting to squeeze them in his hands, pinch her small nipples roughly enough to make her cry out. But he knew better than to let go of her hands.

He looked at her face, seeing the red outline where he had struck her, and suddenly, she smiled thinly. She relaxed slightly and raised her knees, opening herself to him. He hesitated for a moment, then drove himself into her again as hard as he could. There was moment of vicious satisfaction as she gasped in pain, her back arching. He slammed into her, wanting to drive his cock deep inside her, through her.

"You wouldn't mind if I crashed Outside, would you?" he said, grunting through his teeth as he buried himself in another long, furious thrust, feeling the hard bones of her hips against his thighs. "You'd like me to die, wouldn't you?"

Her eyes glittered as she stared at him, in fury and hate. No fear showed on her face, no expression of helplessness, even as he had her pinioned under him. Not December.

"Maybe I would," she said, and he rammed himself into her in a savage stroke. She gasped again, and he ground himself against her, feeling the fire rising up through his spine, shivering through his legs. But she kept her narrowed eyes locked with his.

"If you died, then I could fuck anyone I wanted to," she said. The heat flowed through his shoulders, trembling through his arms, and his hands tightened around her wrists, crushing the slender bones. She grimaced with pain, then grinned, a small, feral smile, a hint of triumph in the grim amusement. "I'd fuck a *lot* of men," she said, "and I'd start with Markley." Her voice caressed the man's name sensuously.

The fantasy he'd nursed through several drinks superimposed itself against her face, and as if she could see it in his eyes, she wrapped her legs around his waist, her hips moving against his. Her mouth opened and she ran the tip of her tongue across the edge of her teeth, her breath ragged, taunting him. Her eyes were hard, not a shred of passion in them.

He stretched her arms up above her head and fell heavily down on her. He kissed her roughly, his tongue thrust into her mouth. Her head thrashed, trying to break away from him. She bit his lips, but not like she'd bitten his shoulder, and he groaned, feeling the heat crash over him, down him, through him, emptying out in one long wave of pleasure and agony and hate and desire and helplessness.

He realized, after some time, that his head was pounding with the beginning of a vengeful hangover as he lay across her, her warm breath against his cheek. His anger and his lust faded away in a soft, guilty haze of satisfaction.

"You're heavy," she complained softly, and he rolled off her, sitting beside her as she rubbed her sore wrists. She took off the torn nightgown, inspecting it critically before lumping it into a ball and tossing it onto the dresser. He watched as she remade the bed, efficiently and quickly, and got in, her back to him, not bothering to invite him in also.

Squatting on the floor with his arms around his bare knees, the air seemed suddenly chilly, and he crawled in bed beside her, tentatively putting his hand on her back. "You okay?" he asked.

"Of course not," she said calmly. "You hurt me."

He thought about that. "I'm sorry," he said, although he didn't feel exactly sorry. He fingered the painful marks where her sharp teeth had sliced into his skin, his fingernails picking at the flakes of drying blood.

"You should be," she said, her voice muffled against the pillow. He wasn't sure he'd convinced her. It didn't matter.

"You really wish I would die?" he asked, more curious than angry. He pulled her to him, curving his body around hers, his arm across her waist. He cupped one of her breasts gently. They lay still in the dark.

She didn't answer for a long moment, and he thought she

might have fallen asleep. "Sometimes," she admitted. "You really think I'd fuck Markley just for a promotion?"

He gave the question serious consideration. Now that his drunken fury had subsided, he analyzed the situation from a clearheaded, pragmatic point of view. (No doubt, he thought, that's how December would examine it.) He thought of the years she'd spent in the Energy Department, resenting him for keeping her from promotions she felt she deserved, watching others advance while she struggled vainly for recognition.

He critically assessed his fantasy of December and Markley. Detached now from his emotions, it seemed like some trite and cheap porn vid he'd dredged up from his frustrated adolescence. Without the alcohol and the anger and the lust, he could still imagine December kneeling in the dirt. But in this version, he could see her doing the required job indifferently and expediently, with the least amount of time and bother.

He smiled in spite of himself, imagining Markley leaning against the stone dam, his pants sagging pathetically around his knees, eyes popping from his pudgy red face as he stared at this cool, immaculate woman, amazed at his good fortune as she actually acquiesced to his half-joking, fumbling attempt at seduction.

He could see her distastefully spit out Markley's all-too-eager efforts, getting to her feet and brushing the dust briskly from her pants. He knew exactly the look in her eyes as she'd glare at poor Markley, *a deal is a deal,* and the hapless man would tremble, not about to double-cross this cold, determined beautiful creature.

It had probably never happened, but it wouldn't be beyond her. December would never barter sex for professional favors, if there were any other way. But she wasn't the kind of woman who would be outraged if Markley *had* tried to corner her, no helpless victim indignant at the world's unfairness. She'd use the situation unmercifully, and Markley had better watch his back.

"Sometimes," he said finally.

She didn't protest her innocence, and shortly he heard her

breathing change as she fell asleep. He kissed her gently on the back of her neck, feeling a strange kind of affection and loss. Even if he no longer loved her, he didn't want her to leave, didn't want to lose her, didn't want to live in the cool, green, sweet domes without her.

NINE

April 9, 2242

THE ALCOHOL TESTED ACCEPTABLY CLEAN, A LITTLE muddy by City standards, but remarkably pure for homemade. *First Violin* would have no trouble with it, although Berk decided to change the filter once he got back to the City.

The Hebers manufactured it themselves, along with almost everything else they needed. Many of the makeshift parts of the old man's still, however, bore marks Berk recognized as City-issue. He swirled the alcohol around in his test tube, squinting as he examined the chemical reaction critically.

Heber watched Berk, smiling as he leaned against his still and packed an enormous, ornately carved pipe. "Last pilot out here tested this same batch, Mr. Nielsen," the old man said, lips clamped around the stem of his pipe. Berk glanced at him, wondering for a moment as Heber played with one of the disposable lighters if he was foolish enough to expose the still, and the alcohol fumes, to an open flame. He suspected it was only a show of bravado, aimed at keeping a Cityman off balance.

"It was good enough to fly him out," Heber continued.

That would have been Wysaigh, Berk knew. For a moment, he stared into the pale blue test liquid, not seeing it. "A helicopter isn't the same thing as an airplane, Mr. Heber," he said, keeping his voice even. "She quits on you in the air, it's not so easy to coast in and hope for the best," Berk poured the little tube of alcohol into a waste can before he turned toward Heber. "And I wouldn't know about the last pilot out here. He never made it back."

Heber's smile stiffened, but he maintained his cool gaze. "Wasn't the fuel," he said defensively. "And it weren't us."

"Wasn't saying it was," Berk countered. "Just hard to take the last pilot's word on your fuel."

Berk didn't like using the disappearance of a friend to give him an edge in his bargaining, but he was practical enough to know he had to. They dickered for another hour, but the pleasantness had become strained. He finally agreed to a good bargain; a full tank when he left, his water reserves topped and food enough for two days. When he returned, on his flight back to Pittsburgh, Heber would fill the tank again. Although the handshake was friendly enough, the tension still showed.

It was already late afternoon and Heber offered Berk the hospitality of the waystation for a meal and a bed for the night. He accepted, planning to fly out towards the Harrisburg domes in the morning. One of the Heber boys—around eighteen or nineteen, Berk guessed—filled *First Violin*'s tanks under careful scrutiny. Berk took an oily rag and wiped away the little alcohol that had spilled onto the paint of one auxiliary tank as the boy looked over the copter with ill-concealed curiosity.

Mrs. Heber and the younger children had made supper, a meal of several anonymous birds too tough and gamy to have served any domestic function in their lives, small onions and potatoes in a heavily spiced stew, and some green, leafy vegetable Berk didn't recognize, tasting vaguely like asparagus. Now that the bargaining had been completed, the old pre-Shift mug with its cryptic message had vanished, the table set with a neatly matched display of brown, home-fired crockery.

The meal was eaten in near silence, only the clink of sil-

verware and less than polite slurping of food by the younger
children to break the monotony. Occasionally Berk would
look up from his plate to find the Family watching him with
a strange, expectant look. A few of the older girls blushed
shyly. Uncertain, he would smile back, nod and look down
at his plate again.

Elissa and her older brother brought the two men cups of
strong tea and honey as they finished the last of the meal.

"Come on up and watch the sunset, Mr. Nielsen," Heber
said.

The old man guided Berk down the tunnel, past the war-
ren of interconnected rooms, whitewashed walls and carved
wood. A fortified door led out of the east side of the tunnel
into the open. Between the Twin Tunnels ran a tiny stream,
clear water churning slowly across the valley, replenishing
the pond at the south end. A small shack sat on one bank; the
generator house, Berk guessed. Irregular patches of young
green crops grew along the sides of the creek, irrigated by a
waterwheel set into the stream, slowly dribbling into rows of
neatly tended ditches. The rocky, irregular land between the
Twin Tunnels was enclosed into the Hebers' territory by
high chain fences, one inside the other, topped and lined between with rolls of barbed wire, razor edges glinting red in
the light of the setting sun. As Berk glanced back over his
shoulder, he could see three of the Heber children standing
guard on the high balcony overlooking the crops and the
creek, rifles at the ready.

The second tunnel was used primarily as a warehouse and
the main trading outpost. The far end looked out over the
wide valley floor sloping all the way to Harrisburg. They
crossed the woodcarved bridge spanning the creek, the smell
of the vegetable garden rich in the air. Several neatly whitewashed boxes scattered around the garden hummed with
lethargic bees, a few flashing in the waning light as they returned home for the evening.

Heber led Berk up a stairway to the balcony on the west
side of the second tunnel. Underneath, protected from the
sun and wind, caged rabbits and various birds rustled in the
shadows, rows stacked against the closed face of the tunnel.

One son stood guard and, Berk didn't doubt, another armed sentry guarded the east side. Above them on the mountainous rock face, a ten-year-old boy crouched, rifle balanced between his knees.

"You expecting trouble?" Berk asked.

"Always," Heber answered calmly.

The old man settled himself on a plank bench, his thin legs thrust out in front of him. He packed his huge pipe with a crumbled green herb kept in a skin pouch hanging from his belt. Pale sweet smoke trickled around his face as he lit it. Berk leaned against the railing of the balcony, resting his elbows on the massive, well-worn wood looking out at the mountains.

"Rangers?" he asked. It seemed so tranquil and quiet.

The evening sun had begun its angled slide down through the distant mountain peaks. The breeze was still warm on Berk's face and night insects had started the first chorus of hesitant whispery chirps.

"Sometimes," Heber said. "Depends on whicha them around this time of year." He shrugged. "They migrate, different bands, like wild birds. Sometimes one group'll come in, trade peacefully, then two days later the same group'll try killing everybody they can." He blew a thin trail of smoke into the air. "Crazies. Y'never know."

Berk had read the few existing pilot reports on Rangers, every one ever filed, but he had never heard of Rangers capable of anything but violence against these outposts. "Ranger? Trading?"

Old man Heber chuckled, seemingly amused by Berk's reaction. "Not all of 'em are complete vermin," he said. "A few of the bands come through here got leaders with a couple brain cells left in their skulls. Rest of 'em might be mindless stinkin' mutes, for all I know." He sucked on his pipe for a moment. "Y'can't reason with them. Them y'shoot."

That much Berkeley knew. "How often do they come through here?" His stomach felt sour, and he shivered. He turned his back on the mountains, leaning against the railing, facing the old man.

"Not too regular," Heber said. If he'd noticed Berk's change of mood, he didn't mention it. "Sometimes they'll come in, set up camp for a couple of weeks, then disappear. Sometimes don't see 'em for months on end. No telling when."

"What're they like?" Berk asked. The idea of even semi-intelligent Rangers was a novelty, one he wasn't sure he liked.

Heber snorted. "You new at this, son?" he asked, laughing.

"Not quite," Berk said, irritated. "I got pulled off the Erie run when Wysaigh disappeared. Y'don't bump into many Rangers on a mail run. And those you do see, you see from a thousand feet up."

Actually, he'd been happy as hell when the mail run to Erie had been reassigned. It had been a straight, unbroken hundred-mile flight up, a walk around the miniature jungle slowly being tamed, dinner and a night's sleep after the mail was delivered and the return mail packed away, and another dull hundred-mile flight back, once a week, week after endless week.

The City crews working to reclaim the Erie domes were a hardy, proud bunch, and Berk got along well enough with them. He tried to keep his disappointment and growing resentment to himself as he delivered weekly City orders, plans, family missives. Simple, dull mail runs paid the rent regularly. Or at least kept the peace when he wasn't forced to spend too much of December's paycheck as well.

Then Wysaigh went down, somewhere past Harrisburg, after he'd dropped his supplies, the light single-engine plane and its pilot vanishing without a trace. If Wysaigh had survived a crash, he was somewhere out there, far out in Ranger territory. God help him.

"Well," Heber said, as if he could read the thoughts in Berk's mind. "Rangers ain't too friendly. I wouldn't be taking any hikes for my health in these mountains." He thought a bit as the smoke from his pipe drifted away in the breeze. "We can pretty much handle 'em when they come to trade . . . usually."

"Trade what?" Berk asked, his gaze traveling across the darkening horizon. The night seemed less tranquil than it had minutes before. He sipped his lukewarm tea.

"Lotsa towns used to be around here," Heber said. "Little ones like Amberson, Roxbury, Willow Hill—hell, they weren't much to begin with. Nothin' now but a few houses fallen in cellar holes, stores all gone, cleaned out, burnt down. Y'go south down the valley, there's Chamberburg, Hagerstown, Martinburg, Winchester. T'wards Baltimore, there's Gettysburg, Frederick." The old man casually called off the names as if he were personally familiar with the ancient towns, an impossibility, Berk was sure. "Sometimes, Rangers'll find something interesting in what's left a them. They're too stupid to know what's good, what i'nt. So, they tote in all sorts of junk. Sometimes it's useful. Most times not."

He tapped the pipe against his knee, the ashes falling to the porch floor. "They also bring in meat, skins, anything they can kill. Sometimes Aggie stuff, seeds, vegetables, the like." Heber's eyes seemed pale in the thin light. "Don't know if they trade with Aggies or not. Pro'bly they just kill 'em and take what they want, is what I'd guess."

"I ken show you my sign collection, if y'want," the boy with the rifle said. Berk had almost forgotten his presence and he started at the sound of the boy's voice in the growing dark.

"Only sign you should be interested in, boy," his father growled at him, "is Rangers comin' over the hill to git you."

The boy's face sobered, and he turned back toward the dark hills.

"Sign collection?" Berk asked curiously.

Heber grinned, the now-empty pipe in his clenched teeth. "Yeah. He's got signs from all over. Rangers don't read. Don't even know what they are. Just another piece of junk they got lucky draggin' in, and now they know they can git a pack of good homegrown smoke, or a couple of bullets every time they bring in something new. Gives us some idea how far they travel. Got a barber shop sign clear from Black Ash Swamp way up north just last fall."

Berk's grip around the handle of the mug tightened. "Bullets," he repeated, as if he hadn't heard the old man correctly. "You give the goddamned Rangers bullets?"

Heber paused, his eyes narrowing as he cocked his head to stare at the flier. "Yeah," he said, his voice sarcastic. "Funny thing, they don't seem to be too interested in City-issued currency."

Berk felt himself growing angrier. "Then why trade with the fuckers in the first place? They took one of your girls and you give them *bullets*? Are you out of your mind?" He was shouting now, and he could see the boy with the rifle standing closer, the weapon wavering uncertainly in his direction. He forced his voice into a quiet calm he didn't feel. "What the hell's wrong with you people?"

Heber looked at him steadily, ignoring his worried son, and stood up slowly from the bench. "Mr. Nielsen," he said, his tone resigned, worn, "I can trade with Rangers, or I can kill 'em. Killin' em makes 'em mad, and we live with enough fear as it is. Yeah, they took my granddaughter. They kill the boys when they can, but not my girls. So there's a chance she's still alive. Mebbe later on we can trade to get her back. It's happened before." His voice turned scornful. "Y'think you City folks're going to come out here and exterminate every last Ranger for me? Get my granddaughter back in one piece?"

Berk couldn't answer. He shook his head.

"Didn't think so." Heber scratched his nose, looking off into the night-shrouded mountains. "I prefer tradin' them smoke rather than bullets. A happy, doped Ranger is easier to trade with. But sometimes they don't want smoke. Sometimes they got their own from somewhere else I don't want to know about. Then they want weapons."

Heber paused, his eyes narrowed as he regarded Berk. "Consider this, boy. Better givin' Rangers bullets than knives. Only thing Rangers really know 'bout guns is which end points away. They'nt smart enough to take care of 'em, so they don't work all that good, half the time blowin' up in their own faces. So, before you go telling me my business, live out here for a while, Cityman."

Berk felt the chill of the evening air against his hot face. "I'm sorry," he said. He meant it.

Heber said nothing, then put his hand on Berk's shoulder. "Let's go see if Berry's got you a place for the night." If the old man felt any animosity towards him, Berk couldn't tell.

TEN

THE ROOMS INSIDE THE HEBERS' TUNNEL WERE cool, if not soundproofed. They had put him up in a claustrophobically small chamber carved out of the rock, bare walls rough and chill. There wasn't much more than a tiny bed, a chair and a crude nightstand with a candle and a basin of water. Berry had silently handed him a towel and an empty bucket. He didn't need to ask what it was for.

He put the bucket under the narrow bed, undressed and climbed into the bed, snuffing out the candle. He was tired but unable to fall asleep, listening to the strange sounds in the tunnel. The sheets were clean, homespun rough against his naked skin, and smelled of the thick layer of fragrant straw the Hebers used for mattresses. He turned over, pulling the woolen blanket over his shoulder.

He could hear the murmurings and an occasional faint laugh as the large family retired to their individual rooms for the night. Outside, in the passageway, the Hebers kept a few lamps burning continuously, the yellow line under the door was the only light in Berk's room.

He hadn't realized he'd fallen asleep until a subtle rustling and movement in the bed woke him. It took him a moment to realize this wasn't the City, and the slender naked body next to his wasn't December.

Startled, he sat up, staring in the dark.

"It's me. Elissa," the girl next to him whispered. She put a cool hand on his thigh, her fingers sliding up searching for his groin.

"What are you doing here?" he whispered back, grabbing her wrist and pushing her away.

The girl sat up on the bed, the straw mattress creaking. All he could see of her was a faint outline in the dark. For a moment, she didn't answer, and when she did, her voice was puzzled, hurt.

"You don't like me?" she asked.

Christ. If the old man found Berk in bed with her, he'd shoot him for sure. "I like you just fine, Elissa. But you gotta get out of here."

"Why?" She made another attempt at touching him. He leapt out of the bed, fumbling in the dark with a match to light the candle by his bed. It sputtered to life, illuminating the room with a pale, wavering glare.

Elissa sat on the bed with her feet tucked under her, regarding him quizzically as he hurriedly jammed his legs into his pants. Her thin body had barely passed puberty, her breasts still tiny mounds of budding, pubescent flesh. The small gold chain she'd chosen from the pile of cheap jewelry circled her neck, accentuating her sharp collar bones. "Maybe I'm too young for you?" she suggested reluctantly. "I ken get one of my older sisters, if you want." She smiled tentatively, a hopeful expression. "Maybe you like to do us both at the same time?"

Stunned, Berk stared at her with his mouth open. "Are you *crazy*?" he blurted out.

She frowned, and put one fist on her narrow hip in an expression of exasperation. "Mr. Nielsen," she said, in a voice that said she thought *he* was the crazy one, "what exactly is your problem? 'Cause if it's you like boys instead of girls, my brothers just aren't interested."

Something in her tone made him pause. "Elissa," he said slowly, "does your father know you're here?"

"Of course he knows!" she retorted. "Din't you and him talk all this over? You wouldn't still be here if you din't make a deal."

He sat down in the chair in the corner, not about to get any closer to the girl. "He didn't mention sleeping with his daughters as part of the bargain."

"But it's always part of the bargain," she insisted. "That other pilot who used to come regular, Mr. Wysaigh, he should have told you."

He remembered Wy's oblique mention of "other compensations." "He sort of did," Berk said slowly. "He used to, uh . . . 'do' . . . *you*?"

Her chin lifted defiantly. "What's wrong with me?" she said, defensively. "I got my blood, so I'm old enough."

Now that his heart-pounding fear that old man Heber would come bursting into the room with a shotgun at any moment had subsided, Berk struggled to make sense of the situation without offending the girl. Or, he suspected, her father.

"How old are you?" he said cautiously.

"Fourteen," she said promptly. He lifted an eyebrow, and her eyes wavered. "Almost," she said more quietly.

Almost. Jesus.

"And Mr. Wysaigh slept with you?" Wysaigh's eldest daughter was not much younger than this girl on the bed.

She grimaced, idly picking at the woolen blanket. "No," she admitted reluctantly. "But he promised he'd do me when I got older . . ." She drew the blanket up under her chin, her thin arms wrapped around her knees. Pouting, she looked even younger than thirteen, a point that Berk didn't want to press. "He was real nice, I'm sorry he's dead. I liked Mr. Wysaigh. He'd bring all the girls little presents, candies and things, even the ones he wasn't doin'. He din't play favorites, so nobody's feelin's got hurt. He even used to do two or three together sometimes."

"I can imagine," Berk said dryly.

"I *am* old enough now," Elissa said plaintively. "And it's worse for me than a lot of the others. I'm a second, and most of the other girls got thirds, so they've got more choice than me."

Berk shook his head. "I don't understand."

She stared at him. "Well, you don't expect me to do it with my *brothers*, do you?" she retorted heatedly. "The only boys old enough for me are my own seconds, and Tunnel Families don't do that. It's not clean. I can't make a baby with a third, 'cause *they're* all babies themselves. So Daddy said I could be first to try you. You're not family, so you're safe enough. But he said if you say no, I gotta let the older girls have a chance, too."

Now Berk understood. Old man Heber wasn't offering him a hospitable night's fun with one of his daughters. They needed an infusion of new genes into the family to combat inbreeding. Wysaigh had had the Tunnel-Harrisburg run for over four years. Berk wondered how many tunnel babies were Wysaigh's. He sighed, and moved to sit next to the child on the bed. She sat staring ahead, not looking at him. "Elissa," he said quietly, "this is all a little strange to me. I think you're a very pretty girl, so please don't think I'm saying no because I don't like you."

She blinked and a tear ran down her cheek. He wiped it gently away with his forefinger, then lifted her chin to face him. Her mouth trembled as she tried to force back her disappointed tears. "That's okay, I guess. Maybe you can do me when I'm a little older, like Mr. Wysaigh promised?" she asked hopefully.

He smiled. "Maybe," he said reluctantly.

"I'll get my cousin Chira," she said. "You'll like her. She's real old, and she's got big tits and everything." She moved to get out of bed, and he held her back.

"Elissa, please," he said. "I don't want you to send Chira in. I don't think I can 'do' anyone tonight—I'm sorry." She was looking at him with such an expression of amazement and disappointment that he couldn't help smiling. "I'm married. I have a wife back in the City, and I don't think she'd approve." He was still feeling guilty and depressed about the fight with December, and he didn't need to give her another excuse to make things worse.

"So don't tell her," Elissa said, ruthlessly logical.

He tried another tactic. "And I'm not sure I want the responsibility of having a baby here."

Her eyes narrowed suspiciously. "What responsibility?" she said cautiously. "You do me and I take, then it's a Tunnel baby. You don't *have* any responsibility. And you can't take it out of the Family, either. Don't even you try," she added in warning.

"But I'd be the father, Elissa," he said. This was ridiculous, arguing over a phantom baby he was not about to sire with this thirteen-year-old child. "I would feel obligated to make sure it was taken care of, educated. Got good medical care."

Her eyes were wide with surprise and wariness. "You Citymen got some weird ideas," she said. "Just 'cause you make a baby doesn't make you a father. Tunnel babies have lots of fathers, and they get taken good care of and educated just fine. We're not exactly Rangers, you know."

Berk sighed. "Right," he said, admitting defeat. "I would just prefer to think it over by myself tonight, okay? Maybe your father and I could talk privately in the morning?"

She shrugged. "Okay. I'll tell him." She padded out of the room, still naked, and smiled shyly before she closed the door behind her.

He sat for a while to clear his mind before blowing out the candle and climbing back into bed. Wysaigh had never done more than hint at the "side benefits" of his tunnel supply run, and no other pilot Berk knew who'd flown the route on relief once or twice had ever bragged over a beer about it, either.

Of course, if I were Wy, Berk thought, with a wife and two children, I wouldn't want it to be common knowledge, and I wouldn't want too many other pilots, competitors as well as friends, to know about it either. Certain vices are best kept private. He smiled, imagining Wy lounging naked and grinning, surrounded by numerous willing Heber girls, all eager to "do" the balding, pot-bellied flier.

The thought gave him a half-hearted erection before he

remembered that Wy was quite probably lying dead in the wastelands between here and Filly.

He slept fitfully, unable to get comfortable in the strange bed or in his dreams.

ELEVEN

June 23, 2228

Berk sat in First Violin, the helicopter blades droning above him as he flew west. The Ohio reappeared on his right, a winking ribbon of blue stretching from horizon to horizon. It fell away behind him as he passed over it, heading out into the Ohio flatlands.

He had welded together a spare fuel tank and strapped it snugly under the helicopter's belly between the skids. It made *First Violin* slower and less agile, but gave her more range. It had taken him a while to get used to the helicopter's altered feel, but by now his reflexes had compensated for her sluggish lift. The cyclic in his hand vibrated familiarly again, *First Violin* settling into her new weight.

But that spare tank gave him an additional hundred miles of fuel over his normal range. Just enough extra alcohol that, with a little discreet begging, a little bartering, a little stealing, Berk could fly without putting in for any increase in his City fuel allotment that might have made Cormack sit up and take notice.

Berk was confident no other flier would betray him to the Councilman. Not just because they knew what he wanted the fuel for, but because the new Councilman was making himself despised by the small union of independents. Cormack was determined to crack the whip, prove himself to the Council, climb the ladder up with his feet on other backs.

Only Cormack still thought of himself as a pilot. The Transportation Councilman hadn't flown for over two years, no more than an afternoon's jaunt once in a while to keep his hand in. He wasn't interested in flying, never mind exploring the Outside for anything more than hunting down agrofields. Cormack was a natural-born bureaucrat. Berk's lip curled in disgust.

Less than ten miles from the Ohio, the cluster of temporary purple domes the workers had nicknamed Mingo the Merciless glittered like the faceted eyes of dragonflies in the sun. A barrier of razor wire encircled the entire construction site. Inside the protected zone, a red windsock fluttered on a tall pole at one end of the dirt runway. A hundred yards away, the half-finished strike plates hunched below the ribbed conducting tower. When they were completed, the domes would move on. The wind-cranked engine in the tower would supply enough power in a storm to coax lightning down from angry black clouds, keeping the strike plates baited with a slight positive electrical charge.

The small strike plates littered across the hills were not designed for powering the City. Strike surges of 25,000 volts in a split second was far more than the City needed or could control. The plates were only to lure the lightning out of the sky to strike the ground, the vast amounts of electrical charge dissipated, pouring tons of nitrogen into the surrounding soil while precious ozone rebuilt the air. Little by little, the earth was recovering from the Shift, and the City was doing its part by stimulating her renewing health.

Berk set *First Violin* down outside the main dome, not bothering to shut down the machine. He lifted the satchel of mail, City papers and supplies for the workers out of the passenger seat cubby. A figure darted towards him as he jumped out and ran bent over through the dust whipped up by the blades. It was Steubin, the Second Chief Engineer.

"Good to see you, kid!" Steubin yelled over the rotor noise as Berk handed him the satchel. He handed Berk an identical bag, letters home, City reports to go back. "Shut 'er down, just in time for a cool drink!"

"Thanks anyway," Berk yelled back. "Want to take a look around the area."

Steubin grinned, shrugged. "Suit yourself. Let us know if you spot any fire-breathing Rangers, okay? Enjoy!" Then he was sprinting back towards the shelter of the workdome, eager to sort through the mail and get out of the blinding heat.

In minutes, Berk was back up in the air, slicing west.

He didn't know how many more times he could wheedle the fuel he needed. While no pilot would ever give him away, the work domes were not completely isolated. Sooner or later, some engineer would pedal his way down the old Route 22, and somebody would innocently mention Berk's lack of normal sociability. It would get back to Cormack. He'd run a fuel audit and that would be that.

It wasn't as if Berk held out any hope. He knew better. So did his mother. That had always been the risk in being a pilot; fuel was limited, so was manpower. You go down, you stay down. Nobody will ever come looking for you.

Nobody.

But Berk wasn't *nobody*, and the old man wasn't just another pilot.

Berk had almost blown it with Cormack, naïvely figuring his father's pal, his dear old buddy, would understand.

"Your father was a top-notch flier, Berkeley, the best," Cormack had said in his pleasant politician's voice, sitting behind his desk in an office so new there hadn't been time to even put up pictures on the walls. Books and files bulged from mesh moving crates scattered everywhere. No place to sit. Berk had had to stand in front of Cormack's desk, feeling like a penitent schoolchild before a stern teacher. Somehow, Berk understood that was the way Cormack had intended it. Not even the old man had used the diminutive "Berkeley" since he was a child. "And I'm sure that with time, you'll be as good as he ever was. Nielsens've always been good fliers. But you're still young and inexperienced."

"I've been flying since I was ten years old, Leonard."

Berkeley had yet to make the transition from calling him by his first name to using Cormack's last name like a curse. "I've got more flight time logged and more recon experience than most of the pilots on your regular payroll. I know I can find him."

Cormack had shrugged. "But you don't have the same kind of exploratory experience your father had. The man had a real nose, the kind that comes with years. Besides, those days are gone. What the City needs now is teamwork, people pulling together." Cormack held up his hand, his fingers closing into a fist.

Berk glanced at it, uninterested. Cormack snorted, then leaned back. "You're barely eighteen, Berkeley. This isn't like spotting an Aggie field. And that's not even the point. There's no chance he could have survived this long out there, we both know that. The City must conserve its energy for the living."

"Until we find him, we won't know for certain."

Cormack simply shook his head sadly at Berk's stubbornness. "I'm sorry, son, I just can't bend the rules, not even for you. Your father would have understood."

If nothing else, it was the condescending "son" that made Berk start hating Cormack in earnest.

"I'm not going to get that experience if you keep me on the dam runs, either. At least give me a westside mail drop, Leonard. I can scout as I go, and I'll pay for the fuel myself."

Cormack placed his hands on the desk, steepling his fingers. "I guess I just have to come out and be honest with you, Berkeley," he said. "That machine of yours is fine for quick down-and-dirties, but it eats too much fuel. Money isn't the issue. Now, if you had a fixed-wing, a power glider, maybe . . ." It was an offer left hanging in the air.

"The only thing my family has left right now is my father's helicopter," Berk said calmly. "I can't afford to buy a second plane, even if there was one available. And I won't sell *Violin*."

Cormack shrugged.

The Councilman had built up his own small fleet of ma

chines he'd bought before his election, then sold it to the City. Now he was starting to use the Council funds, and the power of his office, to drive pilots into financial troubles deep enough to force them to sell. Then he would hire them through the Council as salaried pilots to fly their own planes. The choice runs were assigned to his City-owned pilots, the independents left with the scraps.

It had been his idea for the City to own the planes as well, with Cormack, of course, holding the reins. On paper, it saved money, and anything that meant less taxes found easy votes. But in the real world, pilots didn't take the same kind of loving care of a machine they no longer owned, and like most independent fliers, Berk didn't trust his life to the civil service City mechanics who couldn't even keep the public pedalcars in decent shape.

Cormack was determined to gut the heart of the maverick pilot, and he was slowly succeeding. The community was of primary importance, not the individual—that was the party line, yes, sir. Those who had held on to their machines helped each other stay alive and up as best they could, but Berk knew the gypsy pilot was a dying breed.

In more ways than one.

"Tried to talk your father into switching to fixed-wing, but he had a bug about those flying lawnmowers of his. And *he* had the seniority to do pretty much what he wanted to. But you're not the old man, and Taylor's retired." Cormack smiled, a small, triumphant, reptilian grimace. "*I'm* Transportation Councilman now, and it's my job to run this office as efficiently as possible. That means I'll sometimes have to be unpopular with old friends. I'm sorry, Berkeley. The answer is no."

Berk had watched his father wheedle the fuel out of Taylor, and learned from the old man the advantages of keeping his anger in check, how to hide his frustration, how to use favors and guilt, how to lie. Even at eighteen, Berk knew some of the fundamentals of diplomacy and bureaucracy. He reasoned with Cormack, and when that didn't work, he begged. But Cormack wasn't Taylor. So he did what his father would have done . . .

"You're right, of course," he said, putting as much sincerity into his voice as he could. "I understand. I'm sure Dad would too. Thanks anyway, Leonard. No hard feelings, really."

Cormack smiled, satisfied. Berk shook his hand, even let the son of a bitch clap him on the back as he left. There would come a time, Berk knew, when that wouldn't work anymore either. Cormack was a hard-hearted bastard, but he was neither blind nor stupid.

So, being his father's son, Berk simply found a way around the problem. In the end, he'd arranged his own flights himself on the sly. He had talked Malik, the pilot who had been given the westside mail run, into switching assignments. Berk bought the extra fuel chips off Malik out of his own pocket. As long as they could make the reports with each other's names on them, Malik was more than happy to make a bit of profit. Malik would still pull the bigger salary, plus a little for beer on the side. Berk would get the fuel and the time.

In any case, Cormack was no buddy, no dear old pal to Malik, either. There weren't that many pilots, and they tended to be a small, close-knit group. Cormack had bullied his way into the Councilship, selling out the private interests of his former colleagues to gain votes from the other larger and more powerful sections of Transportation. Taylor at least had had some idealism and enthusiasm for exploration, an eye on the future. Cormack's ambitions, it became all too obvious to Berk, all too quickly, were simply for personal power and control under the guise of City unity.

Cormack would eventually find out about the switch, and Malik and he would both catch shit, but that would be later.

Now was now.

For a moment, the ache in his chest brought tears back to Berk's eyes, and he blinked, surprised. He wiped the tears into the sweat on his cheeks, and began weaving across the wide, desolate plains.

Much past the Ohio, the land abruptly gave way to a vast desert, sand shifting between the rolling low hills. As far as the eye could see in any direction, and for more than a thousand miles to the west, was badlands—rocky, parched ground where nothing moved but the wind. The Mississippi still gouged its way through the center of the wasteland, a sliver of life in the wilderness, but Berk knew the land was completely barren all the way to the foothills of the unseen Rocky Mountains far beyond the curve of the horizon.

What his father had been doing this far out in the desert, Berk didn't want to think about too much. If the old man had got it into his head to fly until he dropped, there would be no way Berk would ever find him. But what if he'd just been scouting? What if there's been something in the musty bowels of the library archives that had perked his interest, sent him searching through the inhospitable flatlands? What if he . . . really was still alive?

Irene II was a slightly bigger helicopter than *First Violin*, had more range. There were a million square miles of nothing in the west, and Berk's chances of spotting him were practically nil.

"You don't need to look for him, Berk," Irene had said. "Don't do it for me."

At eighteen, Berk didn't qualify yet for individual City housing. He didn't mind, though, that he still lived with his parents. He sat at his mother's kitchen table, staring at the spot where the old man should have been. He should have been hunched down on his bony elbows, slurping his muddy grain coffee. He should have been furtively scratching at his balding head, angry red patches where the thin hair had fallen out in clumps. He should have been heckling his son in his cracked voice, his laughter wheezing in sick lungs, eyes sad behind the gap-toothed smile.

The walnut-backed chair gazed back at Berk, empty. "I have to look, Mom," he'd said quietly. She nodded. Understood. Neither of them speculated aloud that the old man could not have survived more than a week alone on the Outside. Not in summer.

So when the vague dark mark in the distance caught Berk's eye, he almost passed it by. He didn't want to see it. But he had, and reluctantly banked *First Violin* towards the black smear in the desert sand.

He settled the helicopter on the ground, sand boiling up around him in the rotor downwash. The wind cleared the dust like a curtain pulled back as the blades swiveled to a stop, revealing the ugly scar in the rocky earth. He opened the door, heat hammering down with fierce vindictiveness.

There was no doubt it was *Irene II*. He read the traces in the dirt and saw what had happened in his mind's eye. The helicopter had nosed straight in, blasting into the earth at full speed. The explosion had sent fragments in all directions, a violent flash of ire and exultation in the solitude. The helicopter and the man who flew her had detonated together into a scorching fury, a wild, brief shout of defiance thundering through the silence.

There wasn't enough of the old man's crippled body left to bury. Berk crouched in the sand, fingering shattered pieces of metal, a bit of burned cloth, a shard of bone. His eyes were dry. He had cried for the old man for months, knowing it would be soon. The sun had killed the old man just as surely as the crash had. Now that it was finally over, Berk found himself unable to feel much of anything at all.

He squinted up in the sunlight, wondering. Why hadn't the old man taken *Irene II* far beyond any possible reach of his son's searching eyes? Why had he destroyed the only other helicopter in the City? Why hadn't he at least said goodbye? Was it an accident? Was it impulse? Had he simply gone mad at the end?

Why, Dad, why?

Berk was tempted to gather stones, erect a cross, do something to mark his father's death. Some kind of memorial, a ritual, anything.

Finally, he stood up, and walked back to where *First Violin* waited, the killing sun beautiful on her blades snicking lazily overhead. He left the crash as he'd found it, untouched.

It somehow seemed right that way.

TWELVE

April 10, 2242

THE SOUNDS OF PEOPLE STIRRING IN THE TUNNEL woke him in the early morning and he splashed water from the basin on his face and chest, gasping from the chill.

Dressing quickly, shivering, he opened the door and peered out. A pretty Heber girl with a naked two-year-old child balanced on her hip stopped and smiled.

"Mornin', Mr. Nielsen," she said politely. "Breakfast in an hour, you want?"

"Thank you, yes," he said, staring at the child. It had been crying and now stared back sullenly at him with wet, red eyes, sucking three fingers. He couldn't tell if the child had any of Wysaigh's features or not. It glared at him and clutched at its mother's dress, burying its face in the cloth as it renewed its wailing.

"Don't mind him," she said, shifting the child to her other hip, "He's just cranky 'cause he wants his breakfast, too." Her milk-swollen breasts pressed against the rough cloth of her shift.

He nodded, not knowing how to answer, and followed her down the high arched hall towards the main room. Doors opened and closed as the Hebers went about their morning activities. A pair of young boys scampered, laughing, around a stairway leading to the rooms on the upper level. They stopped when they saw Berk walking beside the woman.

"Morning, Mr. Nielsen. Morning, Chira," they chorused. He glanced at the woman, startled, and she smiled back. She wasn't much older than twenty, which, he thought, might seem "real old" to a thirteen-year-old like Elissa. The boys tittered and darted away as they passed.

Old man Heber was in the main room with Elissa beside him. The large table was half set for breakfast, Hebers of various ages and sexes bustling with tableware and food. Elissa's father carried a wicker basket of supplies in his arms. The girl, now dressed in a boy's shirt and pants, held a rifle in hers. She smiled wanly and looked away.

"Morning, Mr. Nielsen," Heber said. "Let's go pack this away in that spinning thing of yours."

"Morning, Elissa," Berk said quietly.

"Mornin'," she replied. "Gotta go relieve the night watch." She walked away, her thin back stiff.

"I assume you've talked with your daughter, Mr. Heber . . ." Berk began.

The old man held up a hand. "We can talk while we pack your supplies. It's quieter out there."

Out in the hangar area, Berk popped open the helicopter's small storage container under the seat and began tightly packing away the food and water supply. He wasn't sure how to broach the subject, and was relieved when the old man brought it up.

"Told Elissa not to get her hopes up," he said obliquely. "Tough age for the girl. Too old to be a child, not old enough to be an adult."

"If I've offended anyone, I'm very sorry," Berk said.

"No, no," Heber responded with a short laugh. "Actually, Cityman, I should be making apologies to you." Berk looked up at him quizzically. The old man shrugged, grinning under his white beard. "We didn't see quite eye to eye last night, and I just didn't . . . well . . . get around to explaining a few other minor details."

Berk smiled slowly. "Might have made things a little unpleasant for Elissa," he said.

Heber shrugged, still grinning. "Girl's gotta grow up sometime. Rejection is part of life, too, and 'cording to Elissa, you were very considerate, quite the suave and sophisticated City gentleman." Heber stuck out his hand, and after a moment, Berk clasped it firmly. "Even," Heber said.

"Even," Berk agreed. He finished stowing the supplies and snapped the seat back into place, then slipped the handling wheels onto *First Violin*'s skids and pushed the little helicopter's dragonfly boom down gently. Heber helped him guide the craft out into the open area, more a polite gesture than a necessity. Berk faced the helicopter into the light breeze.

"On the same subject, Mr. Nielsen, we'll respect your decisions." Heber said as Berk stowed the handling wheels back in the storage compartment. "But we can always use a little freshening in the Family."

Berk ran his hand along *First Violin*'s framework thoughtfully. "If there's a problem with that, maybe you might consider some kind of exchange of Family members with the City."

Heber shook his head. "I been to the City, Mr. Nielsen. Once. Know you got all sorts of regulations to keep your population even. We don't have exactly the same problem. The Outside and plenty of Rangers keep us 'regulated.' No sense sending boys to the City. My girls, they'd only end up bein' used like whores. City women wouldn't care much for that, and neither would I. City boys don't seem to know much about surviving out here, and we don't need useless mouths to feed. I don't really think too many City women would care that much for tunnel life. Seems to me you people prefer monogamy, mostly, anyway. That kinda philosophy here breeds more discontent than children.

"No, Mr. Nielsen. One willing pilot's good for a bunch of girls. Nice, private arrangement we had with Mr. Wysaigh, worked just fine. Now he's dead, you taking his route, thought you might be interested."

Although Wy was probably the father of any number of tunnel children, Heber didn't seem too distraught over his disappearance. That bothered Berk.

"I'd have to think about it," he said, not sure what else he could say.

Heber shrugged. "Like I said, up to you, no offense taken."

Watching the old man walk back towards the tunnel doors, Berk smiled ruefully.

"Different world out here, Berkeley, boy," he said to himself. "Different rules."

Above him, perched along the tumbled boulders with her rifle cradled casually in her thin arms, Elissa glanced at him, then back at the expanse of rolling brown hills. Beside her, an adolescent Heber boy spoke to her, inaudible in the distance. Berk didn't need to hear the words to see the eloquence in Elissa's defensive shrug.

He headed back for breakfast, eager to eat and fly before it got too late and hot. He didn't think he'd be taking Heber up on his "hospitality." Another Heber woman opened the door for him, smiling shyly at him through thick lashes.

Well, at least not just yet.

The early morning sun was still low on the horizon, but heating up the air quickly by the time Berk had hurried through his breakfast. He ran his preflight check on *First Violin* as the Hebers gathered in the shade of the tunnel to watch and wave goodbye. He had already settled into his seat and adjusted his sunglasses over his eyes and the stripped headset against his ears. A quick check of the instrument panels showed no problems as the blades hummed overhead contentedly, the engine warming up.

Elissa had been relieved by an older brother or cousin, and had climbed down from her perch overlooking the tunnel. She stood a little away from her family, watching him with sullen eyes, her brothers jostling her good-naturedly, teasing.

Berk hesitated, then impulsively opened the helicopter door and jumped out. He darted over to her, kissed her firmly on the lips and ran back, crouching under the thrumming rotor blades. She blushed bright red and glared at him with a mixed expression of anger, embarrassment and, he hoped, happiness, as her cousins and brothers cheered raucously. He grinned at the girl, readjusted his sunglasses and gently lifted *First Violin* into the air, a cloud of dust obscuring the family below.

He accelerated slowly, using the updraft against the mountain ridge to carry him up and over. He preferred flying in the early morning; *First Violin* operated better if he avoided the worst of the harsh midafternoon heat and the thin air. It would be only a short flight into Harrisburg, where he would drop off mail and medical supplies, but it was as far as he would go today.

The large cities on the eastern side of the Alleys, N'York, DeeCee, the Filly, had been too large, too sprawling for domes. Without the domes, they died like dinosaurs in the Shift, leaving behind huge crumbling ruins like abandoned gravestones of an ancient world.

Berk planned to fly into Philadelphia early the next morning, spend the day searching through the outskirts before he found somewhere relatively safe for the night. The following morning, he would head straight back, stopping only briefly at the Twin Tunnel to top off his fuel tank. The return flight would be less than four hours over what had taken him three days to cross.

The center of Philadelphia, exposed to the Outside and infested with crazies, was not a place he cared to visit for any length of time. He was supposed to search the outland areas, find what he wanted and get out. But, Berk thought, what was the point of flying all that way if he didn't at least take a little look around?

After Harrisburg, there would be no further friendly outposts, no emergency repair or refueling stops. Civilization, as far as the domed Cities were concerned, ended at the Susquehanna River.

Harrisburg had erected two major domes on each side of the Susquehanna River, connected by a minor dome on the tiny island bearing twin covered bridges. The bridges on either side of the island had been blown. But for all the careful plans, Harrisburg, like Erie, hadn't been able to prevent disaster. The first pilots exploring the Outside had been ecstatic when they had seen the crystal glitter of the Harrisburg domes in the distance, and equally discouraged to find the City completely lifeless.

Ancient explosions had ripped out huge panels, and a great fire had consumed the major portion of buildings inside the western Lemoyne dome. Inside the eastern Harrisburg dome, buildings crumbled. Still partially protected from the harsh Outside environment, a tiny savannah-like jungle had crept over the remains; wild animals scurried in their shade. There had been no human being, other than perhaps the stray Ranger, inside these domes in well over a century.

Not long before the Tusk Tunnel catastrophe, the City sent a major recovery team out to Harrisburg. Not a temporary dome erection, the quick salvage-and-abandon job the City had done numerous times before, nor another Erie reclamation; this was to be a more ambitious, satellite City. Harrisburg was over the Alley Oops, isolated, and the City intended to colonize and repopulate the Harrisburg domes to make it a new domed City.

At the time, Berk had been as enthusiastic as any, sure that it meant more exploration opportunities for pilots and that Cormack would have to loosen the chokehold he'd kept on Berk since his father's death.

The colonists had sweated and grunted through the mountain ranges in armored tandem trucks. Wary and armed to the teeth, fifty men and women bulled their way by land, over the broken backbone of the Pike, across the Alley Oops, dragging their monstrous load of equipment and supplies mile after agonizingly slow mile. Berk had flown scout, circling above to watch for Rangers. The colonists finally reached Harrisburg and the scouts flew home.

Wy had been assigned the mail and supply run to the tunnels and Harrisburg, while Berk flew the mail run to Erie. And waited.

It was almost a straight shot into Harrisburg, the road directly crossing the wide curving valley between dwindling mountain ranges. Carlisle had nearly vanished, perennial summer fires sweeping through roofless houses along the barely visible streets. Berk flew over the few small ruins, all that remained of Mechanicsburg and Camp Hill, and caught sight of the tiny domes of Harrisburg glittering in the sunlight along the broad, shallow Susquehanna riverbank.

He circled above Harrisburg domes, dropping altitude as the river shimmered below, and turned to approach the east dome facing into the wind. Like the Hebers, the colonists had cleared and renovated a section of the old roadway as a landing strip for airplanes, razor wire set in rows on either side and at the far end, and a rude hangar built next to the dome entrance. As he descended towards the enclosed strip, dust boiled up from the rotorwash. He hovered, feeling the cushion of air under him, and settled gently, loose gravel grinding under the skids.

Two men and a woman stood at the gatepost of the dome waiting as the rotors whined down. As Berk climbed out of the helicopter and unloaded the small package of mail and supplies, they strolled out to greet him.

"Good to see you!" the woman said, extending her hand. She was older than the two men, iron-gray hair pulled back from a wrinkled, tanned face. Berk shook her hand, feeling the strength in her grip.

"You don't want to see ID?" he asked.

She shook her head, grinning. "If you're a Ranger, we're all in trouble." She squinted up towards the sun. "Let's get this thing inside the shed and we'll get out of this heat."

It wasn't Pittsburgh, but it was certainly cooler inside the eastern dome. The colonists had cleared away major sections of the old City, recycling building material as they renovated small neat houses around squares of orchards and gardens.

The woman was Durene Thombly, the "mayor" of Harrisburg. The original fifty colonists had expanded to a little under a hundred inhabitants. A group of children played a game of kickball in a wide, green field, high sweet laughter in the distance. "You're new," Durene observed dryly. "What happened to Wysaigh?"

"Nobody knows," Berk said simply.

Durene pursed her lips and nodded. "Too bad. Good man." They strolled down a wide avenue lined with trees towards an imposing group of long buildings in the center of the dome. "Want the grand tour before lunch or after?" Wysaigh wasn't mentioned again.

The City Hall had been preserved, more or less. The outside shells were still standing, and the colonists had restored quite a bit of the interior. The buildings could have housed the entire colony, and did at first, until individual farms were carved out.

"The old rail yards were about the only place we had to store material when we started demolition work," Durene said. "Mostly what we've salvaged is bricks." She smiled, her teeth very square and white. "Lots and *lots* of bricks. We need the land."

The dome still contained long blocks of ruins, and the colonists' primary activity was the gradual hacking and chopping and carting away of rubble to clear the land for planting. What was unsalvageable was either dumped off what remained of the north bridge, slowly being transformed into a pier jutting out into the river where the colonists hoped to erect a small boat dock, or simply carted a few hundred yards outside the domes and unloaded in a ragged semicircle.

It neither looked nor felt like a "City" to Berk, but there was something appealing about the *emptiness* of it all. He stared in disbelief at a small herd of fat, spotted cattle grazing in the small open fields around the City Hall.

"They're not a luxury," Durene said, following his gaze. "We don't eat them. We got farm equipment, but we can't produce alcohol fast enough to fuel 'em. So, we use the animals as engines." She indicated the herd with her firm chin. "We started with five cows and a bull calf we hauled with us from Pittsburgh. We process bull sperm to control the sex, and we've increased the herd up to nearly a hundred animals." She laughed, green eyes crinkling. "Give us a few years more, and we might just be exporting beef to the Pit."

In the shade of the state capitol building, a young woman shooed away a dozen geese from a group of diners. Twenty or so people dressed in rough-spun farm overalls sat at a dozen café tables draped in white linen and set with glistening porcelain. The geese flapped blindingly bright white wings, their orange beaks open as they honked their annoyance.

They joined a group of other colonists for lunch, but took a table by themselves. Around them, a few people nodded at the mayor deferentially, the clatter and tinkle of silverware and glasses mixed with conversation. Durene pointed with her fork towards the capitol behind her. "Designed after St. Peter's Basilica," she said proudly. "The dome's a little cracked, and we've got it braced on the inside until we've got enough time and manpower to repair it right, but, by God, it's still there. After lunch, I'll show you the staircase. All marble. Supposed to be just like the old Opera House in Paris."

Since Berk would likely never see Italy or France, he took her word for it. He was more amazed and fascinated by the abundance of crisp lettuce, fat tomatoes and fresh cheeses than by Durene's civic lecture, and helped himself to a generous portion out large communal bowl of salad as it was wheeled by their table on a trolleycart.

"Lotta the stained glass is gone, really a shame, but we've got all of the bronze doors repaired. Think some of the murals can be restored. Used to be a museum here full of old manuscripts, papers, books. They're pretty much rotted away," Durene went on. "But this was the heart and soul of the old City, and we'll do what we can to preserve it. Chicken?"

"Get much problem with Ranger attacks?" Berk asked as he took a couple of crisp pieces of fried chicken from another wheeled trolley. He hesitated, not wanting to appear greedy. The young woman pushing the cart smiled.

"Not too bad," Durene said, taking a half dozen pieces of fried chicken for herself from the cart. A teenaged boy waited with steaming vegetables. The woman with the chicken went on to another table. "This is the start of the season for them, though, so we'll be a little more watchful. Not that we really have too much to worry about. We've only lost one citizen in an attack, and he got caught in one of our own boobytraps."

Berk glanced up at her in mid-chew. "Uh . . . booby-traps?" he asked around a mouthful of onions and broccoli.

Durene chortled. "It may not be pretty, but that ring of junk we've got outside the east dome isn't as harmless as it looks," she said. "We don't have that many people to spare, so unless some Ranger is extraordinarily tough or extraordinarily lucky, he isn't gonna get too far before something either falls on him, blows him up, cuts him in half, poisons him, shoots him full of nails, or drops him down a real deep hole." Durene laughed in earnest. "We've become fairly imaginative in our strategic defense network. Most of the Rangers seem to have figured it out, and they leave us pretty much alone. Only one way in or out, by air."

"That also isolates you," Berk said slowly. "Cuts you off from the Outside." And from the City, he noticed.

Durene shrugged, unconcerned. "We've got decades of work to do right here. When we're were done with this side, we got even more to do across the bridge on the west dome. When we're done with *that*, we'll worry about the rest of the Outside." She looked at him, green eyes iron.

Durene showed him around the rest of the City after lunch. It didn't take long. The bridge connecting the two domes on either side of the river to the domed island in the middle was very much like the bridge between the City center and the argodomes of Pittsburgh. Berk leaned against the handrails and looked through the smoked glass at the island in the distance. Irrigated fields along the riverfront below thrived, and blue-overalled colonists strolled through the rows, vigilant and protective. It was a nice colony, Berk decided. Plenty of room, more or less friendly people, good food.

"There're no taverns here. No entertainment halls, no sports arenas, no theaters," Durene said, as if she could hear his thoughts. She pointed at the dome glass overhead. "During the high summer months most of the solar power goes for the heat regulators, and it still gets damn hot. This old glass can't screen it all out by itself, and we just shut down the whole colony. We get indoors, and that's when we make repairs, renovate interiors of buildings, do the canning and preserving, spin and make new clothes for ourselves. It's hard work, and we don't have time for 'relaxation.' There's enough resources here to support the stable population we have now. We don't need any more immigrants. We're a completely self-reliant City, Mr. Nielsen. We plan to stay that way."

Berk nodded. She stared at him for a moment before she smiled thinly. "Don't get the wrong idea. We like the occasional visitor." She emphasized the word "visitor" slightly. "And while most of us might have been born in Pittsburgh, our families are here. This is our home. We are as much a real City as you are, or Cincinnati is. We expect the same respect for our independence as any domed City would."

This little speech, he thought, was not so much for his benefit as it probably was a veiled message to carry back to the City Council. The rumors that Harrisburg was about to declare a break with its mother City were probably true, then. He grinned, one eyebrow raised, and she laughed.

"If you've got anything else you'd like to send back to Pittsburgh, let's have it," he said.

"Just mail," she replied.

They found an extra bedroom for him with one of the families in a rehabilitated old house, not as Spartan as the tunnels had been. They were friendly, if somewhat aloof. This time, however, he had no offers of nocturnal company.

The family was up, dressed and gone by the time he woke, the domes still dark in the hours before sunrise. They had left a small package of food on the rough-hewn kitchen table for his journey, as well as a cold breakfast.

Durene Thombly met him at the gateport with another package of food to take along with the return mail sack. She shook his hand firmly, and walked back into the dome, leaving Berk to take off before the sun shattered the early morning cool.

THIRTEEN

April 11, 2242

BERK HAD A LITTLE OVER A HUNDRED MILES IN FRONT of him from the Harrisburg domes to the outskirts of Philadelphia, but the Alley Oops were no more now than a low line of hazy blue mountains. The old road twisted away from Harrisburg, ambling through gentle rolling hills. He passed over the occasional remains of small towns; once, a herd of tiny deerlike animals with huge ears bolted from beneath the cover of trees clinging to the edge of a thread-thin creek. Panicked, they bounded away in clots, a dozen dappled hides rippling through the high brown grass.

The dry savannahs quickly faded into a desert grown up in the barren wastes between Philadelphia and Harrisburg. Wind and fires had erased large areas, leaving only traces of past habitation. Whole towns lay buried in shifting dunes, their angular corpses under the desolate sand-shrouds barely visible from the air. A few clumps of brush speckled the arid badlands, tapping into hidden oases of underground water. The sky was cloudless, a deep, rich turquoise through the protective dark glass of the helicopter. The horizon shimmered in the heat. Berk popped the air vents on *First Violin*'s bubble, letting the wind cool the inside of the cabin.

In the distance, towards the old city of Reading, he no-

ticed a thin line of drifting white smoke. Dropping a few
hundred feet, he circled, his hand curled around the cyclic
suddenly sweating. As a hot breeze pushed *First Violin*'s
belly over the rise of a low dune, he spotted the band.

Two dozen Rangers, maybe more. They didn't scatter and
hide like Aggies, concealing themselves in underground
burrows. Here was no frail garden camouflaged and tenderly
cultivated. The Rangers had heard the thrum of the helicopter blades, and danced as if to its music, leaping up and
down, stamping the dusty ground, waving spears. Hideous
painted faces stared at Berk, open mouths grinning in animal
ferocity. Black and white and red streaks covered their half-
naked bodies in weird patterns. A few pointed rifles at him
and he banked *First Violin* away sharply, putting as much
distance between himself and the Ranger band as quickly as
possible. Whether or not the Rangers had the bullets or skill
to bring down *First Violin*, he didn't want to take the chance.
His hand shook as he adjusted the trim, cruising on towards
the Filly.

By late afternoon, Berk reached the first signs of the old
city of Philadelphia. The desert abruptly fell away behind
him. Short, gnarled trees were scattered thinly across the
gentle hills. In the late spring, thunderclouds would rumble
through the sky, violent lightning storms torching the tall
dry grass. Huge raging fires would sweep across the desiccated landscape, leaving a vast black scar. The brief torrent
of rain would bring an equally brief flush of green to the barren ground below. Creeks and rivers would flood, turning
from blue to muddy brown, eroding into sharp-edged
troughs. The rainy season would be over all too quickly, and
the new green plants would sizzle in the summer, turning
again to brown weeds and other scrubby growth covering
the hills. The land would wait through the dry, bitter cold
winter for the next thunderstorm to begin the cycle again.

It was too early in the year for the rain, but Berk could see
an occasional patch of green here and there along the banks
of small streams. He circled a few of the larger ones, examining them for signs of Aggies. These small, irregular areas
of green could as easily be natural growth as evidence that

humans other than Rangers were scratching out an existence on the Outside. Even within his own lifetime, Berk had seen the increase in life recovering from the Shift, rainstorms lasting longer, the edges of the deserts slowly shrinking, the long, scorching summers and dry glacially cold winters not quite as devastating season to season.

Below Norristown, the road converged in loops and curls on others like itself, old overpasses fallen. The ruins below grew denser. Rows of buildings and houses, looking as if they'd been bombed into their skeletal shapes, radiated towards the Delaware River. Neat white rows of marble slabs marked an old cemetery, the empty cairn of a small church in its center. Faint, wandering scars of roads straightened into the clean geometric lines of an abandoned town tucked in the curve of the river. The ancient highway followed along its banks, and as Berk flew over the fringes of Philadelphia, he could still see signs of a once-large population, an immense, abandoned field of broken stone and red brick.

He followed the Schuylkill River through the heart of Philadelphia. The regular square lines of the ruined city split away as the river wandered through what Berk's handdrawn map—*Large part of scouting, son, is sticking your big nose in the library,* the old man whispered in his memory—told him were the industrial park areas, a large expansive delta of empty flatlands. Once a huge center, past explosions had obliterated immense areas. Holding tanks which once held millions of gallons of oil and other chemicals stood as empty, open towers or in ragged shards. Most of the deserted office complexes and factories had burned long ago, reduced to long rows of jumbled, twisted piles of rubble. A few were still disconcertingly whole, untouched and waiting. He circled one, the paint chipped and faded on its tower. He could barely make out a checkered pattern and a single word—PURINA—on its side.

He followed the traces of old roadways, scanning the few intact structures webbed with thin pipes, massive tubes and shafts, tumbled smokestacks that once billowed foul steam, matching them to the map he'd copied from the library archives until he'd found what he wanted: a mazelike refinery, its aggregate of towers and flyways, pipes and bulky tanks much like any other factory rotting away in the wind-blown silence of the industrial parkland. He set *First Violin* down gently onto a small cracked asphalt-paved lot near the factory and shut her down.

The first plant he searched was empty, its three tall domed-top tanks drained. Inside, decayed machinery littered the floor, the cavernous space gutted and dangerous in the gloom. Berk scrambled down off the creaking ladderways, scratched and sneezing in the dust he'd stirred up. The second was a repeat of the first. By now it was after noon, the Outside sun baking the metal under his hands and feet as he labored up and down the disintegrating stairs welded to the storage tanks. The insides of the abandoned refineries were nearly as blistering hot. The third was so badly wrecked he didn't bother to probe too deeply into its interior. He could *feel* its emptiness. The old tanks had crumpled, ancient explosions blowing their skins apart.

Berk fought down the prickle of not-quite-fear, needing to find something to prove to Cormack it would be worth sending him out again. He couldn't go back empty-handed. The worry sat in his chest, sour, itching.

The sweat ran into his eyes, dripping onto the crumpled map as he hunched over it in *First Violin*, sitting quietly on the ground. One left. He'd done his research, already knowing which of the few big plants had been searched long ago and come up dry. He also knew which factories produced fertilizer and cattle feed, and which had been oil refineries. If there was an abandoned cache here, it would be in one of these small places, easily overlooked by the pilots in search of bigger fish. Places not as simple to set a fixed-wing plane down in, get out and explore. Sniff the ground a little.

But if they were all dry, that was it. He wouldn't need to look any farther in the delta. He could probably not even bother going back, he thought grimly. He took the helicopter up, heading for the last plant on his map as the shadows lengthened. It was the smallest of the assortment, not much more than an auxiliary refinery and storage facility of a minor company. Tall, slender distillation columns still stood next to the squat, cracking towers. He landed in a rocky clearing and hoped.

Empty coke drums littered the ground, broken pipes scattered. Bits and pieces of anonymous parts sprinkled among the wreckage crunched under his boots. All five of the main crude tanks seemed to be in sad shape, more than two hundred years of extreme weather having taken their toll. At least they had never caught fire. Three of the five squat, hulking tanks were completely empty, fractures along the sides exposing their contents to slow evaporation and leakage. What remained inside was no more than a cracked, blackened stain.

The fourth and fifth tanks sat side by side in the shade of the desolate refinery, protected from most of the grinding, direct sunlight. Sand and gravel had drifted into the space between the refinery walls and the tanks, forming a dune halfway up their sides. He climbed the dune to the ladder still fastened to the side of one tank. His belt weighted him down with tools as he clung to the corroded metal stairway. His ears were rushing with fear as the steps creaked underfoot. Prying at the edges of the rusted access hatch at the tank's domed top, he hammered with a chisel and crowbar at the rust fusing the hatch shut. Slowly, the recalcitrant hatch gave. He cursed as he scraped his knuckles yanking it open.

And smelled it.

His heart pounding, he shined his small flashlight down into the pitch-black gloom, seeing the glitter of success below. The tank had held up through the decades. Berk laughed, the sound reverberating through the stand of silent pipes and flyways of the empty refinery. He let himself dance a quick, if cautious, celebratory jig on the hazardous stairway before lowering the collecting can into the sludge for a sample. Sticking his little finger into the black liquid, he tasted it and grinned. Sweet, whole crude.

The volatile butane and lighter hydrocarbon gases had long since evaporated away, seeping through the microscopic gaps in the tank, the slow Outside heat performing approximately the same distillation job the ancient factory once did. Probably a percentage of the gasoline had evaporated as well. What was left in the tank was a thick ink-black sludge of unrefined crude oil. Hundreds and hundreds of barrels of it.

Enough to keep the single small refinery Pittsburgh still operated running for months. Enough to supply lubricating oil for all the pedalcars and the airplanes in the City. Enough to grease any gears and wheels and chains in the dozens of irrigating dams along the Mong and Alley Rivers. Enough for every photovoltaic dome track in the known world. Enough for every machine in every City factory for decades. Enough left over for the City chemists to play with for a long, long time.

Enough to get Cormack re-elected and really despise Berk.

All that was needed now was a way to get it all from *here* to *there*. But that wasn't Berk's job, was it? He grinned.

First Violin's engine was still warm by the time he'd tenderly packed away the sealed can under the seat. He devoured the lunch Durene Thombly had given him, not even tasting it, as he leaned against the smooth metal hide of the helicopter and listened to the shrill call of marsh birds, faint in the wind. Ten minutes later, he was back in the air. Time to find shelter.

The Schuylkill twisted through the parkland, draining into the wide Delaware. Pockets of marsh ponds glittered in the sunlight. Buried at the end of this bleak land was the deserted International Airport. The long, triangular runways had been nearly reclaimed by the river, cattails and razor grass growing along their sides. Shorter weeds grew through the webs of cracks in the tarmac. The terminals glared with empty faces out over the wasteland. A small flock of birds rose in a cloud from the tall cover as Berk slowly set *First Violin* down on an abandoned runway, the first craft to land at the airport in over two hundred years.

It was obvious that there was nothing left here to salvage. Most of the great jets had flown off long ago for their final destinations. A few planes still littered the airfield, crushed and deformed, like beached steel whales rusting into immense oblivion. Berk didn't even bother to get out; he simply sat in the helicopter, the rotors humming above him. He felt a strange ache, the vastness of the ancient airport overwhelming him.

Taking off his sunglasses, he wiped at his eyes and told himself he was just tired, it was the heat making them watery. When he pulled *First Violin* back into the air, he didn't look behind him.

On the other side of the Schuylkill River, the long boat docks were decayed, empty. Piers had fallen into the water, jutting out in black outline along the river, ragged teeth of naked pilings. The marshes had encroached into the streets of the old Naval Reservation, the bridge across the mouth of the basin long broken up.

Berk flew north, following the bend of the Delaware, the water below a deep blue. The edge of the city crowded up against the open strip of land bordering the waterfront. Several large ships still moored to the sides of the quay had sunk, some with bows or sterns out of the river, others no more than shadows of wavering black under the water. Some of the wharfs had been not much more than warehouses built on square jetties, still standing with roofs caved in. The floating docks and the piers had sagged into the water, a few with small boats sunken alongside them.

Identical stone towers on either side of the river and colossal steel grids supported part of the old bridge between them, although the center span had broken in two. Snapped cables trailed in the water below, the naked girders like fragile lace. Berk hovered above it, awed by its sheer size. Time and weather had severed the bridge, not man-made explosions, but even collapsed, the lines of the suspension bridge were still graceful.

He circled around a barren island in the middle of the river, and looped over the bridge, turning away from the water as he headed for the center of the city. A thick, compacted stand of skyscrapers marked the old city's downtown section, surrounded by a sea of low red brick houses, the smaller, older tenements of a vanished era radiating as far as his eye could see. A few of the monolithic towers had collapsed, smashing like giant dominoes against their neighbors as they fell into twisted rubble. Most of the towering highrises seemed intact, although much of the glass was gone. Some had been gutted, square shells that he could look down into as he flew overhead, their floors nothing more than latticework holding the façade upright with ancient dignity. It felt odd to see these tall buildings naked under the sky, still defiant even in death.

He skirted the edge of the square spires, searching for landmarks he'd seen only in ancient photos or as marks on maps. He found Independence Hall at the edge of an empty stretch of ground, the old red brick edifice still presiding over what had once been a park. The cupola had been knocked from its bell tower, the hands on the clock vanished. Giant buildings hovered over its back. Another, no more than layers of glass and steel beams, had narrowly missed the old Hall when it had shattered to the ground an unknown number of years before.

He was tempted to set down and explore the Hall. Windows gazed blindly out, empty black squares where anything could be hiding behind their shadows. The Hall was too close to the surrounding wreckage of houses, warrens of unknown danger. He spotted signs of new, haphazard building among the rows of decaying houses, fresh scorch marks of recent fires. In the deadly heat of the sun, it was no surprise that he'd seen no one, no movement, no sign of life. But Berk knew that didn't mean the city was sterile.

He sighed and turned to follow Market Street back towards the Schuylkill River, weaving his way around the immense columns of boxlike buildings. The safest place for the night would be on the top of one of these buildings, high above the wild streets, he decided. But, while there was still enough daylight, he wandered through the old city, a skyborne tourist, amazed by its open, naked immensity, both fascinated and vaguely saddened by the lost power below him.

At the very center, where the two rivers pinched in the land like a woman's slender waist, stood a white stone church, dwarfed by the empty cenotaphs surrounding it. Berk hovered, smiling, enchanted by the medieval filigreed steeples, sculpted minarets, peaked spires. The old church faced another ancient white building, larger, competing with its own fairylike layers of columns and ornate façade, blue slate tiles still clinging to its dormered roofs. A massive pillared clock tower tapered to a stone-laced point, a bronze eagle patinaed with verdigris perched over the cornice above the clock, wings spread ready to fly. One bronze figure still remained on its pedestal, spear in hand, his tarnished dog faithfully by his side. Gaping holes in the roof below explained where the vigilant statue's companions had gone.

Searching through the forest of abandoned towers for a place to land, Berk examined those with their roofs still intact. Finally, he chose one with a flat expanse to land on, picking it as much for its apparent sturdiness as its view overlooking the old city.

He hovered, the dust under him blowing in a brown cloud from the rooftop, and settled down gingerly. *First Violin* whined as her blades slowly spun down and shuddered to a halt. On the roof, a fairly brisk wind blew; he didn't get too close to the edge to peer down. A squat, smaller structure in the center held nothing more than huge fan ducts. The few entrances out onto the roof were blocked by rubble.

The air cooled rapidly as the sun set far to the west, the blue mountains hidden behind the curve of the horizon. Berk pulled his sleeping bag out from the storage bin under his seat and unwrapped his supplies.

Enough junk and splintered old wood littered the rooftop to provide a small fire. The sky faded from purple to black, stars bright and steady in the thin night sky. The rise and fall of the wind gusting through the streets didn't quite cover up other sounds, different now in the night. Slowly, Berk could make out flickering lights below, fires hovering in the distance inside buildings invisible in the darkness. Once he heard faint laughter, a high thin coughing wail like that of a wild animal in the bush. It sent shivers through him; the hidden life of the city was both frightening and exciting.

He curled up in the sleeping bag between *First Violin* and the embers crackling as they glowed themselves to death, his hand on the gun by his side, and fell asleep.

He didn't sleep long.

His eyes shot open as he was snapped out of his dreams by the barest scrape of noise. He caught a glimpse of them as they poured out like rats from a hole in the wall of the ventilation building. They were tiny, amazingly small, slithering from under piles of debris and crushed machinery, slipping like snakes through impossibly narrow spaces. He had wrenched himself halfway out of his sleeping bag, his gun already raised when they swept over him. A metal pipe struck him in the arm. The gun flew out of his numbed hand, vanishing into the darkness. Another pipe thudded into his stomach, and he crumpled. Within seconds, they had him pinned down.

He struggled desperately under their weight, astonished by the utter lack of sound. Steel bars and iron pipes beat at him, swinging up and down into his body in a frenzied rhythm.

He saw a flash of a vicious grin, tiny; spaced nubs of teeth, heard the whistle of breath as one of them grunted, and turned his head just in time to watch the pipe slam into his forehead.

White light exploded in his eyes.

Then he saw nothing.

When Berk woke, he was lying face down on the graveled roof, his legs still twisted in his torn sleeping bag. He struggled to his knees, his head pounding. A stab of agony made him clutch at his right arm, and he realized dully that it was broken. His sleeping bag had cushioned some of the blows, but his face was badly beaten, blood oozing from his scalp. One eye had swollen nearly shut. Dazed, he looked around. The sky was an amber hue, the air still cool in the early morning. Tiny bare footprints were scattered through the gray ashes of his fire.

First Violin was gone.

They were children. Little children. For a sluggish, confused moment, he thought they had flown off with her. His brain refused to work. Then, with a sudden, sinking feeling in his gut, he dragged himself to the side of the building and leaned over the waist-high wall around the edge. Wind blew his hair back from his eyes.

Twenty stories below, *First Violin* lay shattered on the littered pavement, a forlorn child's toy broken and tossed carelessly aside.

He stared down at the wreckage below, blinking in disbelief. Slowly, he turned away, let himself slide down to sit with his back against the rooftop wall, his legs splayed in front of him. He clutched his broken arm to his chest, breathing in shallow gasps through his mouth. He stared, no longer seeing, slack-jawed.

He didn't know how long he sat on the roof. That he'd passed out a few times he knew because he'd jerked to painful awareness, red and black scintillating flecks stirring behind his eyes. The sun beat down on him mercilessly. He struggled to think.

You're a dead man.

He pushed the thought away in sudden panic, the rush of adrenalin clearing his head slightly. He had to get out of the sun. He blinked, focusing on the pile of rubble against the walls of the ventilation building.

No good. He couldn't build any kind of shelter with one arm broken, and he was sure the creatures would be back as soon as night fell. He had to get the hell off this roof, out of the building. Find someplace safe, or at least defensible, to hole up until he could figure out what to do next.

The children had taken his knapsack, the kettle, the gun, everything except the sleeping bag. White down feathers floated in the hot dry air like a parody of snowflakes as he tore strips of cloth from out of the bag. He found a short piece of splintered board and tied his broken arm to it as best he could, one-handed, with the cloth strips.

Then he sat on the shaded part of the roof, panting, trying with an effort to keep himself conscious. It took him several hours to slowly clear the trash and rubble away from an entrance into the ventilation building. The metal door hung on one rusted hinge, and it took all his remaining strength to push it open wide enough to admit his adult-sized body.

He chose a large, twisted chunk of pipe, hefting it in his good hand, and squeezed into the doorway as quietly as he could.

The ventilation building had no roof, huge extinct fans frozen in the open air. A stairway led down into the lightless bowels of the skyscraper. His heart beat wildly, pulsing waves of fear and pain in his head as he crept down into the darkness.

It was cooler inside, and once his eyes had adjusted to the dimness, he started the long climb down.

He kept his pipe half-raised, clutching it tightly, his good arm shaking badly as he made his way along littered hallways, doors torn from shattered walls, floors sometimes crumbled into jagged holes. The building seemed deserted, empty, but when he stopped to rest, crouching in the shadows, he could hear muted scuffling and murmurs in the walls.

He found a stairwell leading down several stories before it ended in midair, concrete steps chopped off, stumps of iron rods unraveling. He climbed back up to the level above, stopping to catch his breath by an open hole punched out the side of the building. The wind moaned through the streets below him, whispering in hot gusts through the opening. He brushed the moisture from his forehead and stared at his hand. Blood, not sweat, trickled down his face. Wiping his hand against his pants, he groped with desperate strength along the hallways towards the heart of the building.

A yawning gap in the floor opened above the next level down, an iron girder exposed in the middle of the hole. He lowered his legs over the sides, holding onto the girder with his good hand, and let himself dangle briefly before dropping to the floor below. He landed badly, crumpling with a moan as he fell. The sound seemed to ripple through the air, calling out to the hidden creatures.

He froze. The murmurs in the walls had stopped, the building was silent, listening. Hurrying towards the stairwell, he almost cried in relief to find it had resumed its square spiral down. He nearly ran down the stairway, jumping where steps had fallen away. The wall had collapsed in one part, taking several steps with it, exposed to the outside. His eyes hurt in the sudden brilliant sunlight as he leapt the breach down towards the broken steps, scrabbling for a handhold as he fell. The pipe clattered down in front of him.

The board he had tied his broken arm to smacked against the wall, and he nearly fainted as agony slivered through him. He lay on his stomach, his lungs burning as he struggled for breath. The dust he had stirred up in his fall swirled in lazy clouds, sparkling white in the sun.

In numbed disbelief, he watched a small blackened hand reach from around the corner of the stairwell to curl around the lost pipe, tiny pale fingernails chewed ragged. He stared down in terror as a small naked boy followed the hand, and squatted on the steps. The child grinned with square baby milk teeth bright in his dark face. Miniature doll-like genitals dangled below its pot belly, little navel protruding. Stick-thin arms crossed equally thin legs. Black eyes stared at Berk from a delicate, angelic face. Berk lay shaking, exhausted, panting shallowly.

Two more small children stepped out into the sunlit stairwell, a boy and a girl, their dark skin streaked with gray ash. Another child slithered out of a hidden passage cut in the walls. The first child laughed, a chittering, insect sound. Berk rolled onto his side, looking back over his shoulder, up the stairwell. A dozen more had materialized above him, crouching down in the dust, watching him with bright feral eyes.

Babies. They were only children, none older than five or six. They crept toward him, jagged bricks, rocks, some with thick metal pipes, clutched in their hands.

Berk hadn't the strength left to fight them off as they jumped on him. The children beat him, pummeling him with bricks, pipes arcing down on him glittering in the sun. He curled into a ball, his arms over his head. A pipe thudded against his ribs, a baby's fist gripping a brick slammed against his ear. He wept helplessly, his face pushed against his drawn-up knees. Something struck the side of his face, and he heard the crack of teeth snapped off in his jaw. Black sparkles of pain drew him down.

They beat him long after he lost consciousness. He didn't notice when they stopped, dragged his inert body down the last remaining flights of stairs and dumped him by an open doorway.

FOURTEEN

April 12, 2242

PAIN.

Red sharp awareness that streaked up his spine to explode in his skull. He heard someone whimpering, was startled to realize it was his own voice. His shoulder ached and his head throbbed.

He was lying on his side, his torso wedged half-propped into a corner filled with rubble, his legs twisted under him. He moved groggily and felt the broken edges of bones in his arm grind agonizingly together. He gasped, tasting blood in his mouth.

Something jabbed him in the chest.

His eyes snapped open and he stared at someone crouching in front of him just out of reach. He scrabbled backwards, cringing from the expected blow. The figure didn't move.

His eyes focused in the gloom, barely making out the shadowed features of a girl silhouetted in the shattered doorway of the building. Crudely sewn skins of scabrous fur draped over her shoulders in a ragged cloak and covered her legs in rough pants. Beside her, a sack of the same material lay in the rubble. She brushed back a handful of matted

black hair tangled around her face, and peered at him critically with dark eyes in deep-set hollows.

She held a long metal bar, a flattened notched hook on
one end and a round knob on the other. It dangled between
her crouched knees, glinting lethally in the dim light. She
leaned forward, her nose wrinkling a bit as she sniffed at
him audibly.

"Y' dead?" she asked.

He didn't know what to answer. Eyes narrowed, she
brought up the iron bar, poking him in the chest again with
the flattened hook. Defensively, he raised his good arm over
his face, flinching against the wall. She cocked her head,
staring at him.

"Y' dead?" she repeated.

"No," he said, his voice cracked and raw. "Please . . . I
won't hurt you."

She smiled thinly, more an expression of grim amusement
than reassurance. She turned towards the reddish sunlight
streaking through the doorway, sniffing the air like an animal, alert, wary. After a moment, she turned back toward
him.

"Her you?" she said.

Her accent was thick, strange. He wasn't sure whether she
had asked "how" or "who." Or maybe it was "hurt you?"

"My name is Berk. I'm from . . . a city far away, over the
mountains. I'm hurt. My arm is broken," he said, covering
both questions.

She squinted at him as if he were speaking some garbled
foreign language she couldn't understand. A scrabbling
sound from somewhere above, like rats deep within the
walls, made her glance sharply around, peering into the
shadows. It stopped.

"Nothin' good here," she said, speaking quietly to herself.
She looked at him, the interest dying in her face. She
grasped the bag in one hand and hefted the bar in the other
as she began to back away, leaving him.

The scrabbling noise was closer. His heart pounded in his
chest, making his head spin with dark sparkles at the edge of
his vision. He knew he probably had a concussion as well as

a broken arm, and was perilously close to passing out again.

"Wait," he called out frantically to the girl. "Don't leave me here. Help me, please . . ."

She stopped at the edge of the rubble spilling out of the hole in the building, looking back at him with surprise in her eyes. "Why?" she asked, as if the idea was novel to her.

He managed to crawl to his knees, trying to ignore the sharp pain in his arm. "Please," he gasped, unable to think, suddenly terrified as he realized that the girl intended to leave him behind for the weird children to finish off.

She frowned, sniffed the air again. "Nothin' good here," she repeated, and vanished down the other edge of the rubble, leading to the outside. Berk sank to his belly, all his injuries burning now like fire. The noise in the walls was louder. He could hear the chittering of the children coming closer.

"Oh God, oh God," he wept, dragging himself towards the hole where the girl had gone. The swirling blackness flooded into his consciousness, dragging him down. He stopped, his one good hand digging into the gravel and dirt as he fought to stay alert. When he looked up, the girl was back, crouched in front of him again. She spoke, a rapid blur of words he couldn't quite make out. Her free hand made a choppy gesture.

"What? What?" he pleaded, desperate.

"I help you, you help me, yes?" she demanded, speaking slowly.

Anything. "Yes," he agreed, his voice no more than a whisper.

She hesitated, then slipped down the pile of rubbish, loose rocks clattering. Grabbing him under his arms, she dragged him up towards the hole. Behind him, the chittering became louder. Something slithered in the blackness.

She released him and jumped over his body, hissing at the dark in a staccato burst of words he didn't understand. The chittering stopped, an ominous silence. She whirled, shouting and smashing the iron bar against a naked column supporting what was left of the roof. He shrank away as it shuddered, sending a shower of dust and loose debris tumbling down on them.

Then she grabbed him again, hauling him roughly towards the exit, grinning fiendishly. He moaned in pain and fear, unable to stop the sound. They stumbled out into the blinding light, the abrupt heat pouring down like molten lead. He gasped, and his knees buckled. She thrust him upright against a wall, holding him by his shirt. She started at him with slitted eyes as he managed to find his feet, standing shakily. Then she nodded.

Hefting her pack onto her back, she dragged him by his shirt collar down the littered street, her iron bar held at the ready. They kept close to the wall, moving quickly. She stopped suddenly, turning to push him into a sagging doorway, its maw sealed with fallen bricks and half-rotted timber.

"Shut up," she whispered, squeezing up against him in the narrow space. He clutched his broken arm against his chest, blood again beginning to ooze from the wound, his fingers slippery. He clenched his teeth in an effort to keep silent. She leaned cautiously out towards the street, sniffing. How she could smell anything over her own stench he couldn't imagine.

She yanked him down brutally by his shirt to squat beside her in the doorway with their backs against the rubbish pile. At the far end of the street shadows rippled along the wall. The girl arched her neck and warbled softly, a weird wordless sound that raised the hairs on the back of Berk's neck, a cry out of his childhood nightmares. He whimpered involuntarily.

Immediately, she jerked him close to her, close enough for her hair to brush his face, her sour breath against his skin. "Y' dead?" she whispered. He shook his head slightly, unable to speak. He could see sweat beading her dark forehead, streaks through the fine powdered layer of pale dust on her skin. Her narrowed bloodshot eyes glared at him unblinkingly. "Then y' shut up y'mouth, or y' all time dead f'sure." She shoved him back against the rubble, hard fingers locked around his collar.

The shadows along the wall had frozen and after a long moment a deeper warble echoed along the empty street. The girl beside him relaxed slightly. "Squeeze," she whispered.

He didn't know whether that was a command or a comment, so said nothing and remained still, waiting. She released her hold and ignored him as he slid farther down to kneel on the ground, rummaging in her sack for a moment before bringing out a small wrapped package. She rose swiftly, tossed the bundle out into the street and was squatting again before it hit the ground.

It lay in the middle of the street while they remained crouched in the doorway. His legs were beginning to tremble. His broken arm wobbled at the break, fresh blood running over the dark dried blood in shockingly bright red rivulets. She sniffed the air, idly scratching at her crotch under the hide cloak.

A few minutes later, he saw one of the shadows detach from the far wall. A small boy, half-naked and covered with colorful streaks of paint, darted into the road to snatch up the package, then retreated. The girl grinned fleetingly, her teeth flashing white in her dark face. Then the shadows disappeared. She nodded to herself and stood, her hand again clenched on his shirt.

He stayed on his knees, his head filled with the ominous scintillating red and black flakes, cold sweat making him tremble. "Wait, please . . ." he begged, his bloody hand gripping the girl's wrist. "Just a second . . ." He vomited suddenly, bent over, shivering.

"Y' done?" she demanded impassively. He nodded mutely.

She tugged him back up on his feet and dragged him relentlessly down the street at a crouching run. They turned the corner, opposite where the shadows had been, and then another. A numbness began creeping over him. Half-aware, he fought to keep on his feet, keep staggering after the girl, keep moving. She picked her way nimbly around huge tumbled ruins spilling into the streets, a winding, treacherous route, staying in the shadows and against the walls.

She darted down a narrow alley between two tall brick

buildings. He glanced up at a carved stone lion scowling in the corner of a marble entrance and stumbled over the head of its mate lying broken on the pavement below. He stared at it dumbly as if it meant something, something he'd forgotten, maybe. She wrenched him roughly inside.

Out of the glare of the sun, the air within the building was cooler. She stopped, allowing him to sink to the floor, trying to catch his breath while his eyes adjusted to the gloom. The interior of the building was relatively intact, although it had long been stripped bare.

"Mine," she said. "Safe here."

He nodded, feeling strangely detached, cocooned in shock. She squatted in front of him, watching him. "My arm is broken," he said again, lethargically, his voice sounding dull and distant in his ears. The black-edged sparkles on the edge of his vision returned, tempting him to lie down on the floor, let it wash over him.

She reached over and took his chin between her thumb and forefinger. "Open," she said. Leaning close, she sniffed his breath, then wiped the sweat from his forehead with rough fingertips. She sucked the moisture from her fingers, grimacing.

He was beyond caring now. The pain and fatigue and shock rushed in; his knees buckled. He slid down, wanting nothing more than to lie on the cool stone floor.

"No," she said, "not here," and tugged him to his feet, sharp stabs of needle pain shooting up his arm. He sobbed at the sudden agony, tears running wetly on his face, his head pounding.

Somehow, she pushed and pulled him down a stairway into a lightless tunnel, then hauled him at a swift walk through the pitch black. Light burst in his eyes as he saw crooked steps, flashes of wide, glittering spaces, colors blurring together until he was unable to take another step. He didn't care whether he lived or died anymore, he just wanted to stop, lie down. A distant murmur of warm darkness rushed in like a heart beating, a swirling haze crashing down on him as he sank, pain and light fading away . . .

He woke slowly, disoriented and weak, the smell of mold

thick in his nose. He was lying on an old, musty pile of rough cloth sewn together into a homemade mattress. A tattered blanket lay across his naked body, some holes crudely patched, some not. He moved slightly, hearing the creak of leather woven to the iron bed frame on which the mattress rested.

Across the dim room, he saw the girl glance up at him, expressionless. He lay still, gazing at her until she turned away, back towards a low, rickety table, its legs sawn to stumps, covered with an odd assortment of things he didn't recognize.

His arm ached with a steady dull throb and he looked down at it. It rested on a smooth flat board that lay across his chest, expertly bandaged, another thin strip of cloth holding it snugly against his body. It smelled bad. His exposed fingertips were puffy and bruised, curled around the board's edge. He tried to wriggle them, sending a fresh tingle of pain through him. With his uninjured hand, he touched his head experimentally, feeling thick bandaging around his forehead. One eye had swollen completely shut, the skin around it tender. His mouth was dry, lips cracked. His jaw ached and he touched his tongue to the spot where two back teeth were missing.

But he was alive.

He examined the room. It was large, a thousand square feet, he estimated, and, except for a miscellaneous collection of rubbish littering the floor, mostly empty. On the far side, a row of tall windows covered with heavy drapes let in strips of light and warm air around their edges. A pile of splintered ancient lumber, broken wooden chairs and thin twisted grayish branches of dead wood were stacked carelessly in the corner near a blackened, battered garbage can propped up on a platform of loose bricks. Smoke had created a fuzzed soot trail up along the peeling wall to a ragged hole broken through the ceiling above.

The girl sat crouched on her thin haunches in front of the table, her back to him as she mixed strange-smelling powders and mysterious bottles of liquids. Behind the table, a long metal cabinet had been nailed to the wall, glass missing from its doors. It was jammed with an assortment of jars filled with murky liquids of varying colors, anonymous metal canisters with illegible labels peeling away, trays of small metal tools and enigmatic packages. Occasionally, she would open an unmarked jar, sniff experimentally, or touch a finger of the contents to her tongue.

She looked back at him when he coughed gently. "Excuse me," he said quietly. "I'm very thirsty."

She stared at him blankly for a long moment, then resumed wrapping small amounts of her mixtures in pouches. He waited for a moment longer.

"Is there any water?" he asked. His voice was hoarse, his throat dry.

She jerked her head in the direction of the garbage can. "There," she said without looking up.

He nodded, bemused. "Okay, thanks a lot," he mumbled. Carefully, he sat up, letting his feet down over the side of the bed. He spotted his pants and shirt lying in a careless heap on the floor. Leaning over cautiously, he felt dizzy. It took him several slow and painful minutes to pull his pants up over his naked, dirt-streaked legs. He didn't bother with the shirt. He sat still for a long moment, panting with the effort.

Pushing himself up on weak legs, he managed to teeter towards the garbage can and found the water bucket. There was no cup. He dipped his good hand into the murky water, wondering briefly whether it was safe. It didn't matter much, he decided. He'd probably die sooner without it. It was warm and tasted brackish and metallic, but he drank, sucking the water out of his cupped palm greedily.

He stood with his hand on the garbage can to steady himself, looking at the grease-coated grill balanced on its top and the collection of small animal bones behind it. He realized with almost stupid surprise that he had reached the end of his strength. His legs wobbled and he sank to the floor, another wave of darkness rushing up to take him.

When he opened his eyes, the girl had somehow got him back into the moldy bed. His teeth chattered uncontrollably.

He was drenched in sweat, feverish, yet his head seemed remarkably clear and light.

She was unwrapping the bandages from the splint. His broken arm, exposed on the rough board, lay like a dead thing, swollen and purpled. The hole in his skin oozed where the jagged ends of bone had ripped through, yellowing pus laced with blood. The cloth bandages smelled like his arm, pungent, wet with a strong stink of disease and rot. Livid streaks radiated up from the break. Gangrene, he was sure of it.

"Oh God," he mumbled, shocked and scared.

The girl touched a finger to the suppurating raw wound, rubbed it between her fingers and sniffed at the smell. Then she touched her fingers to her tongue. Before he could react, she had leaned over him and licked the sweat from his hot forehead. She looked thoughtful, frowning.

"Don' move," she said, and went to the low table. He watched as she mixed miscellaneous powders and ground dried plants into a bowl, pouring a few drops from one of the glass bottles to make a greenish paste. She returned and smeared the dark green poultice into the infected wound. Scooping up the last of the paste with her fingers, she thrust it at Berk's face.

"Eat this," she said.

Unresistingly, he let her scrape the thick pulp into his open mouth. It tasted bitter and resinous and he swallowed it quickly with a slight shudder.

What the hell, he thought. Maybe it would mercifully kill him quicker than the gangrene.

She rewrapped his arm against the splint, taking care that the exposed wound was completely covered with the green paste. The fresh cloth looked no cleaner than the previous one, but at least it was dry. As he watched, his ears began to buzz, his body suddenly feeling heavy and detached.

"Oh," he said, surprised. "I feel strange." Or at least he thought he said it, but the words came out garbled, and she didn't react.

The girl wound the cloth around his arm, over and over in endless sequence, a monotonous spiraling motion going on and on until he realized she wasn't there at all. He had some-how drifted off to a disturbing twilight sleep, with no border between dreams and awareness. The girl dissolved into am-biguous shapes, moving uneasily in his consciousness, cir-cling just out of focus, irrational and vaguely frightening.

THANK YOU FOR
USING THE BOSTON
PUBLIC LIBRARY

Boston Public Library

BPL

FIFTEEN

April 15, 2242

W HEN HE WOKE AGAIN, THE SEARING FEVER HAD
broken and his migraine ached with a steady dull
throb. He sensed that hours had drifted by without his notice. The light was dim, gray and cool, the feel of early
morning to it. He peered through the gloom to see the girl
asleep, huddled in a pile of rags and furs, her hand curved
firmly around the heavy metal bar by her side.

Nervously, he examined his injured arm, moving the fingers slightly. It hurt less, and although it was hard to tell in
this light, his fingers appeared less swollen. His bruised eye
had cracked open, lashes caked with dried pus, but his vision seemed okay.

In the silence, he couldn't sleep. He stared up at the ceiling, and let his mind wander. He thought about *First Violin*,
his last image of her as she lay on the street below, shattered
and abandoned. His throat tightened, chest aching. It was
more than being marooned and half-dead. He had lost his
machine, his friend, his father's legacy.

Tears burned down his cheeks as he finally let himself
weep with grief instead of pain. He allowed an immense
rush of self-pity to wrack through him, then lay exhausted

and dry-eyed until the morning's yellow sunlight crept around the edges of the heavy curtains, warming the room.

The girl stirred and sat up. She had discarded the cloak, wearing only the ragged leggings, her torso bare. She stared at him warily, no lingering sleepiness in her eyes. Scratching herself idly, unselfconsciously, she suddenly smiled, a self-satisfied expression without warmth.

"Y' better." she said. It was a statement, not a question.

She examined his arm, unwrapping it slowly and flicking away the dried paste on his wound. His arm was still bruised, but the swelling had gone down. The wound had scabbed over, no longer infected, now puckered and dry.

She reapplied more of the green poultice and rewrapped his arm against the board. This time instead of feeding him the remainder, she wiped the paste from her hand onto her grimy pants. She pulled his feet unceremoniously over the end of the bed, forcing him to sit upright, and tied a sling around his arm and neck, bracing the splint against his chest.

He had no idea how long he had been unconscious. He fingered his chin, judging by the stubble that he'd been out quite a bit longer than he first thought. He was also hungry, which seemed a good sign.

She stepped back from the bed, squinting at him with her head cocked slightly to one side. "Y'ugly," she said finally.

Surprised, he blinked. Half-dead, filthy, starving, injured, sunburned and blistered, he didn't imagine he presented a pretty sight. All the same, he was startled.

"What?"

"Why y'so ugly?" she demanded. She spoke slowly, as if to a child. "Y'skin like a fish belly too long dead inna water."

Her own skin was a deep chestnut brown; she was darker than anyone he'd ever known, as dark as the children in the skyscraper. Her soot-black hair hung in matted ropes falling well below her shoulders. She was bone thin, her elbows and knees knobby and rough. Tiny breasts scarcely more than black nipples protruding from her bare chest did nothing to hide starvation-thin ribs. Dark, deep-socketed bloodshot eyes watched him curiously, tired lines radiating underneath. She couldn't have been more than twelve or thirteen, but there was nothing childlike about her, no softness in the harsh planes of her face.

"I don't know," he said, bemused. "Just born this way."

"You kinda sick like Ferryman maybe, but y'got no blood eyes," she said speculatively, studying him. "Skin like that, maybe sun'll kill you shorttime quick."

He carefully touched his broken arm and grinned. "I'll worry about it," he promised sardonically.

She grunted and turned away, moving back to the table at the far end of the room.

Feeling less light-headed, he stood and hazarded the walk over to the windows. The heavy curtains of musty fabric, some rough handwoven material, kept out most of the light and heat. The window frames had vanished long ago, as well as the glass they had once held, rectangular openings nearly six feet tall. He lifted the hem of the curtain to look out at a brick-faced building opposite. The light slanted low, early morning shadows obscuring the narrow littered street three stories below.

He let the heavy curtain drop back over the window and turned to study the girl at the other end of the large room. She sat cross-legged before the long table, ignoring him as she worked. He picked his way unsteadily over to a short metal stool against the wall beside her and gingerly levered himself down onto it. Smiling, he tried to catch her eye.

"You got a name?" he asked.

She looked up at him slowly, her dark eyes hostile.

"Sadonya," she said finally.

Her hands moved restlessly among the jars and vials and pouches of strange powders, crushed vegetable matter, murky liquids. She lit a candle with a battered cigarette lighter and held a dented spoon of dark powder over the guttering flame. It smoked and melted into a tarry liquid which she dribbled over an anonymous ground herb in a small bowl. The candle cast a flickering yellow light on her grim features, glinted on an assortment of metal instrument he didn't recognize.

"Sadonya," he repeated. "Nice name."

She said nothing.

He touched his bandaged arm again. "Thank you," he said.

Her eyes narrowed to suspicious slits. "What me?" she asked flatly.

"I'm grateful for your help," he attempted to explain, a little confused. "I just wanted to thank you."

She said nothing for a long moment. "Y' don't thank me. Y' don't nothin' me. Y' touch me, I frag y' alltime dead," she said warningly. "I help you, you help me. Deal. Tha's all."

He nodded slowly, noting the ever-present iron bar propped up against the table next to her. "Okay," he agreed. Whatever.

She stared at him for several moments, only her hands moving among the clutter on the table. He met her eyes steadily. Abruptly, she leaned towards him, snuffling at him. He pulled back in surprise. She grunted and returned her attention to the table.

She poured the cooled contents of the bowl into a small leather pouch, tying the top securely and placing it in a pile with other, similar bags.

He sat quietly, watching her. "What are you doing?" he asked at last, curious.

She didn't look up. "Cooking."

He was hungry, but it didn't look very appetizing. "You eat this?" he asked skeptically.

"Some." she said. She peered up at him. "Y' ask a lotta stupid howcums."

"Sorry," he said. Conversation didn't appear to be one of her stronger talents. He watched her work in silence, leaning back against the rough wall.

She took out a small pipe and crumbled a few pinches of dried green leaves into it, lit it and smoked, pipe in her mouth as she worked. A blue haze of sweet smoke drifted in the currents of the room, smelling very much the same as what old man Heber had smoked. After an hour, she had filled a dozen or so pouches with various mixtures and stacked them neatly to one side. She blew out the candle and stood. When she had tucked the pouches into hidden pockets in her cloak, she pulled it on over her shoulders.

"Y' stay here," she said, eyeing him. "Safe s'longs you in my place. I gotta go make some bizniz. Don' touch my things."

"All right, whatever you say," he agreed. "But I'm hungry. May I please have something to eat?"

Any attempt at politeness was lost on her. "Everybody all-time hungry," she said scornfully. "Y' wait. I bring back some takeout. Okay?"

"Okay," Berk agreed without quite understanding.

She stopped at the door, glaring at him distrustfully. "Y' don't go nowhere, an' don' touch nothing," she repeated warningly, "Touch my things I frag y'dumdum ass y'do." Then she was gone.

After an hour or so, the room had become stifling hot, dust motes floating in the dry air. He was hungry, but still feeling weak. Groping his way back to the rickety bed, he lay down, dozing while the afternoon crept past.

He waited.

The afternoon folded into night, and some time after midnight, he woke, shivering in the cool. The room was in total darkness, small sounds in the street below making him feel vulnerable and nervous. Now that his fever-drugged sleep had gone, the ache and hunger of his slowly healing body didn't allow him much rest. Wrapping the mildewed blanket around him, he slept fitfully, still waiting.

She didn't return until late the next afternoon.

The change in the sounds below him in the building, although faint, were enough to snap him to instant awareness.

He scrambled off the bed and grabbed the nearest weapon he could find, a broken-off chair leg in the firewood stack. When he saw Sadonya walk into the room, he exhaled a sigh of relief, the burst of adrenalin shivering through tortured muscles. She spotted him crouched behind the woodpile with his makeshift club in hand, and laughed, an unpleasant snort of mirth.

"Y'a *lot* better," she said, grinning.

"You've been gone a while," he explained, trying to keep his annoyance from showing.

She shrugged, a large stuffed sack over her shoulder. "Don' matter," she said, and smirked. "Y'bin scared?"

He stood, dropping the chair leg back into the pile with a clatter. "I've had some reason to be," he said dryly.

She shook her head, obviously amused. "Nobody come here. This's my place." She dropped the sack to the floor. "Y' still hungry?"

"Yeah," he said. He sat back down on the bed, the leather straps holding the grimy mattress creaking. His head still ached with murderous intensity, but his skin itched under the bandage wrapped around his skull. He scratched at his greasy hair.

She had pulled out several things from the sack, some wrapped, others disturbingly not. "Y'know how t'make a fire?"

The room was sweltering hot. "You want a fire? Now?" he asked in disbelief.

She impaled four small, skinned animals, their heads and tails missing, on two thin steel skewers. He noticed their tiny feet uneasily, digits curled, almost human-looking.

"I gotta few sides," she said, "but I don't trust maindish les' it's nuked damnfine crispy."

Silently he agreed, and began one-handedly building a fire in the battered garbage can. He positioned the pieces of broken furniture and gnarled firewood over a mound of dried grass stalks and twigs, working with his left hand making him awkward. When he had it ready, she lit a handful of crumpled paper (pages from what looked to be pre-Shift books, he was appalled to see) with her ancient cigarette lighter and dropped the burning wad into the garbage can. The fire soon licked at the grill balanced on the can's rim. She placed the decapitated skinned corpses over the fire to roast.

She pulled a few vegetables out of the sack, a half-dozen withered potatoes, a handful of stunted carrots and some onions, as well as a few miscellaneous plants Berk didn't recognize. She set a couple of the potatoes on the top of the grill, and hung most of the other things in a bag on a hook near her table. The smell of roasting meat overcame Berk's resistance, his mouth watering.

After the meat and the skin of the potatoes had been charred black, she picked up one of the skewers of meat with the end of her cloak to protect her hand, impaled a potato with the tip and retreated into a corner with her meal, watching him with amusement in her eyes.

Berk hesitated, looking around for something to pick up the hot metal skewer with. He spotted his shirt draped over the foot of the bed, and wrapped it around his hand. He speared the remaining potato, and moved away from the fire. The room had turned broiling, and he blinked away the sweat running down into his eyes.

Sitting on the bed, he broke off a leg of the animal, resisting the sudden nausea tightening in his stomach, and made himself eat. He chewed slowly and swallowed, forcing down both the stringy, juiceless meat and his revulsion. Methodically, he worked his way through both animals, then ate the dry brown potato. The food, repulsive as it was, took the edge off his hunger.

Sadonya watched him from her corner, smiling faintly. "Y' really outatown man?" she asked, wiping a smear of grease from her lips across her cheek with the back of her hand.

He nodded.

"Where from?"

"West of here. A City," he said. He gestured vaguely with his skewer. "It's called Pittsburgh."

She tossed a gnawed-clean bone behind the garbage can, and tore another limb from the second carcass. "Not like here?" she asked, her mouth full of meat. She didn't seem to comprehend the concept.

"No," he said. "Not much." He didn't feel much like talking. "Sadonya, why don't you tell me about here?"

She shrugged. "Here is here. This my place. Y'safe here, s'long you stay inside."

"You live here alone? By yourself?"

She nodded, chewing as she watched him. "Nobody live

with me I don' want," she said. "Nobody fuck w'a cook. Not Mouse. Not Squeeze. Nobody." There was an unmistakable note of pride in her voice.

"I'm . . . real dumdum, Sadonya," he said. "Howcum?"

She chuckled, as if his attempt to mimic her speech was funny. "Okay," she said, in a tone a patient teacher would use to a particularly dull student. "Not too many cooks. Me, I'm inna middle of Squeeze and Mouse, but me and my place neutral terror tory. Everybody needa cook, both want, both get, both lee me alone. Go make their ravs elseplace. Frag each other alltime dead, I don't care. Lee me alone, I'll be cook for allside. Neutral. Y'understand?"

Berk thought so, nodding.

He tried a different tactic. "Where exactly is 'here'?"

"My place," she said. This time he stared at her until she finally laughed, a stillborn, humorless sound. "This place total sum mine," she said, carefully explaining. "Some name it oldtime Tom'n Jeff, but that don' matter. Mosta unions jess call it cook's place, everybody know it's mine. Nobody fuck w'me, 'cause all the unions need cookin'. I don't like runamill misters, and I'm too smart sidin' with one whip-cock over 'nother, so I don't choose nobody. Live here alone. Cook for everybody. Fine by me."

A lot of her words made no sense to Berk, but the gist of it was clear. "Cook," he asked. "Is that like a doctor? A healer?"

She shrugged. "Cook's a cook. Make what y'want." She nodded towards his arm, her hands still full of roasted meat. "Make a mender paste like what I gi' you, suck out all the poisons. Make a lotta other kinda funbanes. Munchies, smokes, what y'want, I make it. Mosta time funbanes, but sometimes bluecross, like after some unionpacks go rav. I don' retail no sneaky frags, but I could if I wanted. No sense in't for me."

She smiled at his puzzled expression. "I sell a frag to Squeeze, then maybe Mouse don't go down, and he maybe kill me alltime dead, just to make sure don' happen twice-time," she explained. "Or maybe he *do* go down, and his Nextup think maybe I frag him, too, so he decide he get even. Mark me dead. Maybe it start one big mother rav, fuck everybody up. One side down, disturbs the natural balance, make me too many enemies."

She worked at her teeth with a ragged, dirty fingernail, then turned her head, and spat out a piece of gristle. She stuck her grimy finger back into her mouth.

"Let everybody else be enemies," she said around her finger. "If I make frag, it's for ownuse, nobody else. Mosttime I just make mender bluecross and funbanes, mind my own bizniz, let everybody else mind theirs."

Berk considered that an intelligent attitude, somewhat impressed with her innate common sense. For a young savage, not much more than a misplaced Ranger, she had the rudimentary instincts of a natural politician. He smiled to himself. She might even have been able to teach Cormack a few things. "And you trade these for food?"

"Food. Yeah. Other stuff." She threw the last bone into the pile behind the garbage can, then sat with her forearms resting on her knees. "But lotta stuff gotta do myself. Make me alltime tired," she said, watching him. "Nobody say y'dead, nobody mark you their prop'ty, fine with me. Y'lucky."

She wasn't smiling any longer, and her expression made him feel suddenly chilled.

"I'm lucky?" he asked cautiously.

"Y'ugly, outatown man, but you still voting age. Some baby buck frag you, I'd guess that'd be good enough to pass entrance exam to a union. Me, I don' care nodamn fuckin' unions. I don' belong to nobody, and I want it stayin' that way. I don' need submittin' trial evidence to no jury o'my peers."

The corner of her mouth, shiny with grease, quirked up in a strange smile. "Y'lucky I find you. Maybe I'm lucky, too. We make a deal, privatelike deal, right?" Her voice was harsh.

"Right," he agreed. "You help me, I'll help you. That was the deal." Within reason, he added to himself.

"Damnstraight," she said dryly. "Sides, not like y' going anywhere inna hurry, i' you?"

No. He guessed he wasn't.

SIXTEEN

May 2, 2242

T HE WOUND ON HIS ARM HAD HEALED OVER FAIRLY well, although he could see it would be puckered, a permanent grim souvenir. It had been only a few weeks, but the broken bones seemed to be knitting, and his migraine headaches had lessened until they were at least bearable. At least he was no longer throwing up.

That was the good news.

While he was still shaky on his legs, he had to ask for Sadonya's help for even the most basic amenities. The girl had brought a dented bucket for him to sit on, holding him by one arm as he lowered himself, pants around his ankles, onto the makeshift toilet. She didn't notice his loss of dignity any more than she seemed aware of her own nakedness. She left the used bucket by his bed, where it stank, until he complained sufficiently enough for her to remove it from the room when not needed.

But shortly after he was able to stand, he'd gone to one of the tall windows, drawing back the rotting curtains with the elbow of his bandaged arm while fumblingly unzipping his pants with his left hand.

"What y'doing?" Sadonya had demanded from where she sat, constantly "cooking" on her low table.

"Taking a piss," he said wryly, peeing over the windowsill down into the street. She stood, and walked over to stand beside him and watch, frowning as he finished. "Do you mind?" he said, a bit exasperated.

"Yeah," she said. "Damnsure. Y'don't piss in the street."

"Well, then," he said with exaggerated patience, "where would you prefer me to piss?"

She glared at him and jerked her head towards the door of the room, walking out without waiting to see if he was following. He shook himself and zipped his pants quickly, trotting on still-weak legs to catch up with her.

It was the first time he'd been outside the large room. He stood in the doorway, leaning with one hand against the frame. A long corridor stretched in either direction, bending away at right angles at the ends.

Sadonya reappeared around the corner on his left. "Come on," she said crossly, and vanished. He hurried as quickly as he could, feeling light-headed. Turning the corner, he saw her standing waiting for him impatiently, halfway down an enclosed hallway, a glass-in overpass suspended dozens of feet over the street below. He got a glimpse through the filthy streaked glass of the surrounding low red buildings as he walked after her. The ramp twisted into another long hallway.

He passed another corridor punctuated with empty doorways on either side. Sadonya waited for him at the end of the hallway, which opened out onto a wide balcony ringing the edge of an enormous double atrium below. Sunshine poured in from a skylight nine stories high, long rows of peaked glass splashing a white radiance across the blank faces of the windowed walls. A single skywalk bisected the atrium, three stories above a sunken courtyard.

"Jesus," he breathed, staring around.

It was hot inside the cavernous atrium, but not unbearable. A hint of moisture in the air caressed Berk's unshaven cheeks. Below, dirt had been dragged inside to fill the courtyard, fashioned from paving stones broken from streets, rough low retaining walls and paths connecting garden plots. Young plants grew in rows of green stubble.

Sadonya jerked her head towards the skywalk stretching above the garden. He followed her.

A long, low trough sat in the middle of the bridge, a simple distillery. Panes of glass stretched over part of it. It reeked, a vile, acrid odor. Sadonya pointed to one end. "Y'piss there," she said. The urine, he could see, flowed down the trough, where the glass acted as a vaporizer. Condensation of the evaporating water dripped down the sides of the glass into small gutters running into a large capped metal drum. Yellow crystals of dried piss clung to the edges of the trough's belly.

Sadonya picked up a hose attached to the bottom of the collecting barrel, turning a stopcock. A trickle of water dribbled from a little sieve on one end. The end of the hose was tied to a long pole. She held the trickling water as far out over the edge of the walkway as the pole would reach, drizzling water down onto the plants below.

"When y'gotta shit, that 'nother place," she said, jerking her thumb toward another metal barrel at the edge of the garden below. Crude steps led to the top of the drum over which a white porcelain toilet was perched on a shaky platform. At the bottom of the stairs, he spotted the dented bucket. He had no doubts as to what Sadonya used to fertilize her garden. Her sanitation was primitive, but ruthlessly logical.

" 'Kay?" she demanded.

He nodded. Satisfied, she turned the stopcock shut and draped the hose over the railing. "S'long you stay inside, y'can splore anywhere y'want." She regarded him for a moment. "Y'go outside, y'dead," she added flatly. He wasn't sure whether it was a warning or a threat.

But once he had a bit more strength, he did explore.

At first he went no farther than to walk gingerly up and down the stairways to the open toilet below. He lingered at the garden for longer periods of time. He discovered her tools, a shovel, a collection of disintegrating brooms, a nearly toothless rake, a couple of homemade hoes, stacked in a tiny room on a level under the atrium courtyard. The dirt under his bare feet felt warm, good against his skin.

Little more than two weeks after she had rescued him, his

broken arm still bound in its sling, he started hacking, one-handed, at the weeds among the vegetable shoots. He could work only short minutes at a time, stopping to catch his breath, dizzy and weak. But he was bored, and maybe a bit of exercise would aid in his recuperation.

Once when he'd had to stop, leaning against the hoe out of breath, he'd looked up and caught Sadonya staring down, watching him with dark, unblinking eyes. He smiled, giving her a cheery little wave. She didn't react, finally turning away.

The little exertion in the garden exhausted Berk. That evening, when Sadonya returned from her "bizniz," he sat on the bed, leaning against the wall to rest, muscles trembling in fatigue. She pulled a large bloated fish from her leather bag, its bulbous eyes and gaping mouth frozen in an expression of surprise, as well as a small sack of tiny brown spotted beans. Wordlessly, she handed Berk a handful of beans from the sack for planting in the garden, and put the rest into a scorched black child-sized bedpan, covering them with water from the bucket. She added a few sprigs of plants from her worktable. After an hour over the garbage can fire, Sadonya continually adding bits of chairs to keep the room sweltering, the beans had boiled into edibility. She put the fish beside the bedpan to grill.

His mouth watered as it roasted over the garbage can fire, sizzling smoke, his energy returning with his impatient hunger. Sadonya pushed the roasted fish with a stick onto a greasy board.

"Y'getting strong 'gin quicktime," she said. She set the board on the floor between them and they sat cross-legged, breaking off steaming chunks with their hands.

He nodded, not about to contradict her with his mouth full of fish. His fingers were edged with black half-moons under his torn nails, and he smelled as badly as she did. He crammed as much of the fish as he could in his mouth, eating greedily, ignoring the dirt.

Water was for plants, cooking and drinking, *only*. He was allowed to drink as much as he wanted, but she'd once withheld two days' food from him as a punishment for attempting to wash himself. He learned to live with the stink and to eat as much as he could when he could. She never seemed to mind if he ate most of the food, anyway.

"Tha's real good," she said, peering at him critically. He paused, suspiciously. "Y' strong alltime soon, help me damnfine. I maybe make a good bizniz w'you, afterall."

He continued eating, watching her without comment. After a moment she grunted and looked away, unconcerned. They finished the remainder of the fish in silence.

She cursed loudly in the night, startling him awake. Jumping to her feet, she stomped the floor around her, bare feet slapping in the dark. "Fuckin' bugs! *Hate* fuckin' bugs. Mutherfuckin' *bugs*." There were other curses, a quick deluge of words he didn't understand. He stared wide-eyed in the dim light, watching her dancing silhouette.

She screamed, an inarticulate shriek of insane rage, and grabbed her ever-present iron bar. Berk recoiled as she pounded the walls and floor with it, flinching as she smashed the bar against the side of the garbage can stove, the impact driving it over onto its side. It rolled jerkily to a stop under the windows.

She stood immobile in the gloom, only her hoarse breathing audible. "Gettin' tired sleepin' onna floor, outatown man," she said, quietly now, her voice calm. "Gettin' chewed by mutherfuckin' bugs." He jumped as she abruptly threw the iron bar across the room. It cracked loudly against the door, nowhere near him. His heart thudded against his ribs. "Y'strong 'nough alltime now. 'Morrow, y'find me 'nother bed," she said.

He realized, guilt mixed with wary dread, she'd given up her bed while he recovered. "Sorry, Sadonya," he said to the darkness, anxious to appease her.

Her silhouette retrieved the fallen iron bar, and she rustled back into her pile in the corner. "Don't care nodamn y'fuckin 'sorry.' Y'get me 'nother bed," she said, her voice muffled in the corner. "Fuckin' *bugs*. Frag alla fuckin' bugs inna *world*," she muttered to herself. Minutes later she was snoring lightly.

He had trouble falling back asleep.

The next morning she left on her bizniz, the night's fury forgotten. Berk began his search for another bed. He had almost instant success as he had realized not long after he started to explore the old building that Sadonya's "place" had once been a large hospital. There were hundreds of rooms lining the long corridors, floor after floor filled with beds.

A lot of beds still held occupants.

Yellowing skeletons lay supine on rotted mattresses, scraps of cloth covering thin sticks of bone, brittle cracked leather stretched over exposed skulls, empty sockets staring, teeth gleaming. Hundreds of them. Some in jumbled piles on the floor where beds had collapsed under them. Some scattered in disassociated pieces, perhaps dragged there by scavenging animals long dead themselves.

In one large room someone had arranged the bones into neat piles, skulls balanced one atop the other into a three-sided pyramid, blank eyes and empty grins facing outward. Long bones were laid out with layers of knobbed ends alternating patterns in stacked rows, gradating from femurs and tibias to tiny phalanges all organized in meticulous cubes. Ribs curved in and out, stacked in columns like hollow baskets. A thick blanket of gray dust covered the macabre ossuary, shrouding it in decades of neglect.

He found an unoccupied bed still in relatively good shape on the fifth floor. It took most of three hours to disassemble it, using odd instruments he found in other rooms. He carried pieces of it, a bit at a time, down the rickety stairwell, and put it together again. The ancient hospital beds were bulky and complicated, hinged in sections frozen into rusted folds. He'd had to break it apart, removing the useless machinery attached to it, then reassembled the pieces into a rough approximation of a simple bed frame.

The fragile rusted springs that had once supported the mattress cracked and splintered worthlessly in his hands. He pulled back the decaying mattress on his own bed, seeing how strips of leather had been woven to their edges. He found old boards to use instead, making a solid support for Sadonya's mound of musty cloth and fur. The bed ready, he picked up the pile, shaking it out vigorously. A fat cockroach as long as his middle finger dropped out onto the floor and skittered in a crazed dance before it fled under the rubbish heaped in the corner.

"Uughh," he muttered in disgust, and dropped the pile onto her new bed. He sat on his own bed on the far side of the room, looking around dispiritedly. The filth, the intense heat, the squalid grimness of the room, the stench, finally overpowered him. In near panic, he pushed away the thought that he would spend the rest of his life here.

Don't think about the future. Just now. That's all that matters. Only here and now. Worry about later, later . . .

After a while, he found enough energy to bring back one of the brooms from the garden storage room and begin sweeping the grimy floor with one hand, the broom tucked under his sweating armpit. He rolled the garbage can stove back and stood it upright again, then restacked the splintered wood and chair wreckage neatly beside it, stomping on the exposed cockroaches as they raced for new cover. He hesitated by Sadonya's low table, eyeing the fresh gouges in the wall and floor, then pushed the broomstick under it to pry out the rancid accumulation of trash jammed underneath.

He had to stop and rest frequently, his head spinning as it began to pound with another vicious migraine. But by late afternoon, he had scooped up the most of the litter, years worth of rotted vegetables, crumbling paper, discarded animal bones and vague things he didn't want to speculate too much about, and thrown it all out the window. He swept the floor again. Dirt still stubbornly crusted the bare tiles, but finally he was satisfied.

He lay down on his bed, curling onto his side and tried to rest as his head throbbed agonizingly. His vision began to double again, pain pulsating against his eye sockets with every heartbeat. His stomach rumbled in hunger, and his broken arm hurt steadily. The empty tooth sockets in his mouth ached. He wrapped his arms around his knees, barely able to lift his head to look at Sadonya when she returned.

She stood in the doorway, a pair of large dead rats tied by their necks slung across her shoulder, blood crusted on their matted black fur. Silently, she looked at the cleaned room, her eyes narrowing as they darted back and forth. She stared at him, expressionless, eyes cold.

"Have a nice day at the office, dear?" he said, attempting a smile to go with his joke. Her eyes flickered before she turned towards her worktable, minutely checking her supplies. "I didn't touch your things, Sadonya, honest," he said tiredly, closing his eyes and letting his head fall back onto the bed. If she was going to be angry, it was too late now.

He listened to the rustle as she moved around the room wordlessly, drifting through the steady beat of pain in his head toward sleep.

He dozed, and wakened to the smell of cooking meat. Outside, the air was cooling in the purpling twilight. She had skewered the dead rats, roasting them over a fire she'd made herself, the firelight dusting the gloom with yellow shivers dancing along the walls.

He sat up groggily, focusing his eyes on two severed rat heads where they lay, sharp teeth grinning in stupid expressions under their crushed skulls, dropped carelessly on the floor along with the pile of shiny gutted entrails. The matted fur had been tacked skinside out to a wide slab of wood that had once been the top of a desk. It leaned up against the wall as Sadonya, her thin back to him, scraped the hides bare of clinging wet gristle.

"Home sweet home," he muttered to himself.

SEVENTEEN

May 12, 2242

THE PLANTS IN THE GARDEN WERE GROWING quickly, thick green shoots sprouting bright leaves. They liked human shit, apparently, and Berk thrust his shovel into the crude opening at the bottom of the toilet barrel, ignoring the stench of rotting excrement. He carried another shovelful of the crumbling fertilizer to the garden and worked it into the dirt. Holding the shovel awkwardly in his left hand, he used his bandaged arm only to balance the handle. He stopped, panting, and wiped his forehead with his good arm.

The plot of beans he'd sown a week before already had bare tips of shoots poking through the shit-enriched soil, pale green nubs against deep brown. The section he worked today he planned to plant with potatoes, a large, compact square of them. He'd carefully cut the eyes out of the potatoes Sadonya had brought back on yet another of her bizniz trips. Potatoes could be dried and made into a flour, he'd explained to her with as much enthusiasm as he could muster; you could make bread out of it. Or maybe some kind of pasta. All sorts of things you can do with potatoes . . . She listened to him impassively, silent.

His broken arm still ached steadily, but had started healing, the bones underneath the puckered scar knitting together. When he probed the fracture under the dirty cloth securing his arm to the board, he could feel a solid lump where the bones had fused. His eye had returned to normal, although he still had trouble with double vision when he was fatigued. He hadn't seen a mirror in a month, but his fingers could feel the wide, jagged scar on his forehead. The gap in the back of his mouth where two teeth were missing made eating slightly difficult, but he learned to chew on the left side. The mass of bruises on his chest and limbs had faded from livid purple to a greenish cast against his peeling sunburnt skin.

Sadonya had sewn up a dozen lacerations on his body, using gleaming forceps and metal clamps as expertly as any doctor he'd known in the City. She pulled out the stitches a week later, and seemed satisfied with how well he was healing.

He scratched the month's worth of unshaven beard, the sweat itching as it trickled down his face. Then, catching his breath, he started in again, slice, turn, slice, turn, chop, chop, chop with the shovel blade, then step back and slice, turn, slice, turn . . .

If he'd held any expectations that Sadonya would be grateful that he had taken over the work of the garden, or that his housecleaning might have been appreciated, he didn't have them long. He'd given up hope that Sadonya might learn to be a little cleaner herself. At least there hadn't been any repeat of her destructive temper.

But the more he did, the more she expected. Freed from the garden, she spent most of her time outside on her bizniz. In what little remained of her working hours, she sat hunched over her table "cooking" her drugs and potions. She had repeatedly made it clear that if he ventured outside the confines of her hospital, he would be killed. Damnsure quicktime fragged. And, for that matter, stay away from the windows. For the moment, she was upstairs, busy cooking while he was quite content to stay where he was, out of her way.

Sadonya's place was situated between two of the "unions,"

rival factions that divided up the city. Squeeze owned Olde Hill, controlling access to a tiny fleet of fishing boats, stashed inside one of the old piers along the Delaware, by patrolling the no-man's strip along the old Highway 95 up to the bridge. A primitive entrepreneur, Squeeze had set up a safe-zone for a permanent market, of sorts, in an enclosed parking garage near Tomb Square. On certain days his union traded fish, and sometimes clean river water, in exchange for anything he considered of value.

Like weapons. Or Sadonya's "cooking."

Mouse, on the other hand, dealt almost exclusively in terror and violence. Bordered on all sides by rival factions, his union had nothing of any real value to trade other than intimidation, prospering by payoffs and bribery, or killing members of rival unions when they could, taking what they wanted. He held the center of the city, and, although his sphere of influence was the underground subway system, he based himself in an old department store two blocks away from Tom'n Jeff's.

There were other factions farther away; someone calling himself Primaverdi controlled a region to the north, bordered by "Chinkton," and someone else Sadonya called the Moleman claimed sovereignty over a large portion of ruins in the southwest. Those borders didn't affect Tom'n Jeff's, and they, apparently, had their own cooks. Unions coexisted in uneasy balance, the occasional flare-up of violence stimulating Sadonya's trade.

What was left over were burned-out hulks infested with "baby bucks," abandoned children left to survive on their own until they were old enough to pass examinations for admittance into a union. Examinations, apparently, were simple: kill a member of a rival union. Join the club.

Then there were the loners, like Sadonya, who managed to survive within their own tiny kingdoms, useful enough to deal what they could and pay a tribute to the unions to be left unmolested . . . most of the time.

"So you're the only cook for both sides? Both Squeeze and Mouse?" Berk had asked, drawing out the story from her as the beans and fish dinner filled his always hungry belly with a pleasant warmth. Their diet was simple, beans and fish, or beans and rats. Or sometimes just beans. Or nothing. Funny, he'd realized, how quickly hunger could overcome repugnance. He preferred fish to rats, and rats to nothing.

They sat in the hot room, the dying embers in the garbage can flickering on the ceiling with an orange glow. Sadonya had put the water bucket on the grill, her sole concession to his plea for better sanitation. While any lingering bacteria in the greenish water didn't seem to affect her, his bouts of dysentery had let up considerably. He'd found a few battered metal cups and plates from the hospital wreckage, and sat with his empty plate balanced on his lap, the severed fishhead staring back at him with its blind eyes grilled pale. He picked at what little flesh was left in the skull.

"Yeah. Jess me." Sadonya shoved her little finger in one nostril, unselfconscious, as she talked. He found something else to look at for the moment. "Timeback was meen Mama was two. Mama did Mouse, an' Squeeze say me okay, even I too young. Squeeze not so bad, we get long okay. Mama gonna give me to Squeeze's union soontime venchilly, she stay here but she still be Mouse's cook. I be with Squeeze when Mama she get alltime dead." She withdrew her finger to examine her efforts critically before flicking the results off into the darkness.

"How long ago?"

Sadonya shrugged, her forehead wrinkling as she thought. "Longtime. Two years and soma. Squeeze, first he say he *got* a cook, me's who, he don' borderline cooks tween him and fuckin' Mouse. Mouse"—she made a vague gesture with one hand—"he got his reasons, too. I think maybe be fuckin' badtime rav end up no cook f'nobody, don' shate that idea."

Flies buzzed in the heat, searching out the shadowy places to escape the killing sun. The boards of tattered drying skins propped against one wall crawled with the iridescent greenbottled flies, strange little flickering jewels in the grimy dusk.

Berk leaned against one wall, his legs dangling over the

edge of the creaking bed, drowsy, listening. Sadonya had removed her cloak and leggings, her dirt-streaked body sweating as she sat naked, cross-legged on the seat of the only chair, which Berk had repaired from the pile of firewood.

"Tha's when I say Mama's place now my place. I don' go Squeeze's union, make this Dee Em Zee alltime, little bitty piece for me, I be my ownsum whipcock. Squeeze don't like that much, but he smart. He know was th'only way. Let me go. So far, s'kay."

Berk imagined this barely pubescent child, orphaned and alone, caught in a power struggle, balancing between two factions, maintaining a delicate, fragile peace. For a moment, he pitied the scrawny dark girl. "Two years alone," he said, musing aloud. "It must have been very lonely here for you."

She knew exactly what he was saying, and smiled, a bare quirk along the edges of her mouth. "Y'not damnsure look like my mama, and I bigga nuff now don' need a *sourgut*, special some old fishbelly ugly outatown man. I take care myself damnfine," she said, cold amusement in her voice. "Maybe I merger sometime whipcock make me a real good buy-out offer, you be obsleet. That kinda make it *you* walking onna razoredge, now, dunnit?"

That it did, he knew. Sardonya had no room for sentiment, she made it very clear. Until his body was completely healed and he formed some kind of plan, his only hope for survival was in his continued usefulness to her.

So, here he was, hacking weeds and shoveling shit, sweating like some poor City-opted Aggie, trying to grow a little more variety into their diet. Later in the day, when the garden atrium got too hot, he could slink through the lightless tunnels and cooler passageways buried under the hospital with an eye out for anything he could use to his own advantage.

He had an idea about water, maybe tapping into some well or holding cistern he had yet to discover. He was deep in thought, shovel still churning the shit into the dirt, designing a pump in his head to draw water into the old building, a hundred times more than Sadonya could get from her scattered hodgepodge of stills. A furtive motion jolted him out of his daydreams.

Three men, boys actually, had silently entered the building, and climbed the short stairway to the sunken courtyard. They stood a few yards away, watching him with expressionless eyes. The tallest of the three, thin corded muscles rippling under shining dark skin, held up one hand. With an audible *snick*, a thin bright blade materialized in a magician's trick from his fist, slivering the sunlight.

He walked towards Berk as the other two drew to one side, waiting. Berk stepped back, hefting the shovel up and around to hold it out defensively. He was breathing fast, breath whistling through his clenched teeth. The tall boy's mouth opened in an ominous smile, the knife held out in front of his body weaving slowly like a serpent's head waiting to strike. He stepped up on to the edge of the garden, spilling dirt over the low stone retaining wall.

"Mine," Sadonya's voice said clearly from above.

The boy stopped. Berk didn't take his eyes off the sinewy boy with the knife. The boy, however, relaxed, squinting up at the sound of the girl's voice. Looking over his shoulder, he glanced at the smallest of the three, a barrel-chested boy with a jagged scar running down from his scalp, across his nose and cheek. He nodded and the boy with the knife looked back again at Berk, shrugging slightly. The gleaming blade disappeared again into his fist.

The smallest one spoke, a rasping sound pulled up from deep in his chest. "You," he said to Berk. He jerked his head towards the stairway leading to the upper levels.

Berk held the shovel out in front of them, motioning them back from the stairway. The tall one with the knife threw an angry, questioning glance at the boy who had spoken. The raspy-voiced boy chuckled, amused, then shook his head and pushed his friends back gently. Making an elaborate gesture, he motioned Berk ahead of him.

Walking sideways, the shovel pointed down, Berk climbed the stairs until he stood near Sadonya, unsure of what to do as the three followed him at a prudent distance.

He still held the shovel in front of him protectively, blocking them from the girl.

Annoyed, Sadonya brushed him aside with a derisive snort to meet the trio face on. In a rapid-fire patter Berk couldn't quite follow, she held a quick conversation with the short, scar-faced boy. It wasn't that they spoke in another language so much as the speed of the jargon, their hands weaving in elaborate punctuation. He caught a word or two—"outatown," "totalsum" and "fuckin' outta my face." Sadonya made a quick, twisting chop with one hand.

The scarred boy looked up at Berk suddenly, black eyes crinkling in amusement as he laughed outright. The knife wielder kept his bland expression, while the third boy grinned humorlessly with pointed rat teeth.

The scarred boy's laugh dissolved in a deep wracking cough and he bent over, hands clenched on his knees as he struggled for breath. A thin yellow line of mucus and drool slid from the corner of his mouth.

Sadonya turned and pushed Berk, with a small shove, like a guardian nurse with a stupid child, stiff fingers jabbing his back propelling him down the corridor in front of her towards her room.

Once in the room, the scarred boy sat immediately on Berk's narrow bed, the knife wielder hovering by his side. The third boy sprawled across Sadonya's bed proprietarially, and smirked at Berk.

Sadonya shot Berk a quick look, motioning him with her chin towards a corner by the garbage can stove. He squatted on the floor, his shovel balanced across his legs, and watched.

The boy on Sadonya's bed, arms and legs draped over the frame, held out his hand to her imperiously. She handed a small pouch to him with an impatient look of disgust. He jerked it from her.

"Fuck you, bitch," the boy said clearly, a mean smile pulled over his sharp, filed teeth. He upended the contents of the pouch into his mouth, chewed and swallowed, then tossed the sack to the floor and lounged back insolently. Sadonya's eyes barely flickered as she bent down to retrieve the empty pouch. The boy laughed, then grabbed at his leather-covered crotch obscenely.

"You bes' hope, Third," Sadonya said, slowly enough for Berk to understand, "I keep Squeeze a live round alltime. He go, you go."

"I frag you down first, l'il bitch," Third said, waggling his crotch at her. "An' ha'some fun firsttime, maybe." He snapped his teeth together with an audible clack, and laughed.

The small scarred boy on Berk's bed—Squeeze, it appeared—smiled ambiguously. "Third got his uses, Sadonya," he said mildly. "Bes' thing all be friends." He glanced at Berk.

Sadonya grunted, and turned her back pointedly on Third to step over to Squeeze. He held up his hand, wrist up, and she wrapped her fingers around it, searching for his pulse. It seemed to be a familiar ritual. Wordlessly, she bent towards him and he opened his mouth, sticking out his tongue. She sniffed his breath, then licked his tongue with her own.

"Nextup," Squeeze said quietly to the boy standing beside him and held out his hand. The blade reappeared in the tall boy's hand, but this time he jabbed the point into one of Squeeze's outstretched fingers, a fat drop of blood oozing ruby bright from its tip.

Sardonya sucked it from his finger, then crossed the room to squat by her worktable, her mouth working as she rolled the taste around in her mouth. Squeeze no longer noticed Berk; instead he watched the girl's face intently in a thinly disguised mixture of fear and wariness and hope.

She nodded finally and started mixing together different powders from her conglomeration of pouches into a shallow wooden bowl, turning the mixture into a thick paste with a trickle of syrupy black liquid. She stirred it briskly for a minute, then walked back to Squeeze and handed the bowl to him. He ate it without a word, a slight grimace of distaste on his face, the only sound in the room the scrape of the metal spoon against the bowl.

The boy on Sadonya's bed moaned loudly, and Berk's head snapped around to look at him. Third seemed far from being in pain. With his eyelids half shut, he stared unseeing at the ceiling, a wide, foolish grin on his face. His palm rubbed the rising bulge of his crotch under the ragged leather pants, sweat shining on his arms and chest. He started to drool.

Sadonya looked sidelong at him with slitted eyes, mouth twisted in hate and disgust. Squeeze shook his head ruefully, gesturing the knife-wielder towards the boy. Reluctantly, the tall one strode over to Third and slung the drugged boy's arm around one shoulder. Third giggled as Nextup dragged him out of the room.

"He *do* have uses, Sadonya," Squeeze said apologetically, "but I think when I go, maybe best thing Nextup do frag him out." He glanced at the girl. "That bein' soon?" he asked, indifferently.

"N'can tell, Squeeze," she said.

"You can."

She shrugged. "How soon's soon? Y'goin' down, tha's alltime sure. I can make you slide maybe easy, but you slide, Squeeze, no lie. I don' lie good, not t'you." She retrieved the small pipe from the cabinet, and stuffed the bowl with dried leaves.

The boy nodded, and coughed quietly. He turned his head to stare at Berk. "He marked?" Berk said nothing, listening with what he hoped was an unreadable expression.

Sadonya looked away. "Mine," she said simply, a little uneasily, it seemed to Berk.

"Huh," Squeeze answered, his eyes amused.

She concentrated on lighting the pipe, inhaled deeply, then handed the pipe to Squeeze. He took it, dragged in a lungful of the pale sweet smoke and leaned an elbow on the bed frame, his scarred angular cheek resting on his fist. "She say you outatown man." The boy spoke slowly, his voice, although hoarse, surprisingly cordial. He was smart, this thin sick boy, Berk decided.

"Yeah," Berk said, wary.

"Huh," the boy said again, then, "Where from?"

"Pittsburgh."

"Where that?"

"West. About three hundred miles."

Squeeze said nothing for a moment, then glanced at Sadonya, his lips pursed. She shrugged.

"Thatta long way?" Squeeze asked reluctantly, obviously unwilling to expose his own ignorance.

"Yeah. A real long way," Berk answered, smiling.

After a moment, the boy smiled back. "How you get here, so long way, huh?"

"I flew. In a big machine with blades on top," Berk made a whirling motion with one upraised finger.

Squeeze's eyes widened slightly. "Yeah," he said. "I seen it, backtime some. Look like a big metal bug flyin' around." He studied Berk with new respect showing in his eyes. He took another draw on the pipe, holding the smoke in his lungs as he regarded Berk speculatively for a moment, then held the pipe out to him. Berk took it from the boy's hand, cautiously inhaled a lungful of sweet smoke, and then returned it, the gesture accepted. Squeeze kept his shrewd eyes on Berk.

"Somebody frag it, I hear." he said.

"Baby bucks," Sadonya added. "Almost frag him, alltime. I do a salvage job. Deal."

"Huh," the boy said. He looked at Sadonya, then back at Berk, his mind working behind the dark eyes. "Think maybe y'be careful," he said, his eyes on Berk but speaking to Sadonya. "I hear Mouse sniff that fragged bug. Y'outatown man get him perked, maybe."

Sadonya slowly shook her head. Squeeze shrugged. "Good offer, Sad. Mouse a problem, alltime for you. Me slidin' gonna make him jump. Me take him down first, better play, I think."

"No ravs my place," Sadonya said simply. "Notime."

"Sometime," the boy warned her, one eyebrow cocked. Berk understood as Squeeze glanced back at him knowingly. "Sun never do stay down." His mild eyes were sad.

Nextup came back, alone, nodding silently at Squeeze. Coughing gently, the boy stood and left without another word. Sadonya sat huddled by her worktable, crouched with her elbows on her knees, chin in her hands, deep in thought.

Berk watched her as the minutes stretched out. The smoke had given him a pleasant buzz, a strange, comfortable sensation.

Finally, her bloodshot eyes flickered to glare at him. "Howcum you stilltime here?" she yelled suddenly, her voice shrill. He started. "Fuck out!" It was the first time Berk had seen her scared.

He didn't like it.

EIGHTEEN

May 15, 2242

S ADONYA LEFT BEFORE THE SUN WENT DOWN, AND
didn't come back that night. She didn't return for nearly
three days. The first day, Berk ate the few remaining potatoes and worked in the garden. It wasn't unusual for
Sadonya to disappear for a day and return with something to
eat later. But by the second day, he was angry and worried.

He couldn't fool himself into believing that he really cared
about Sadonya, not with any warm feelings of affection. But
he did care what happened to her. He was acutely aware that
he needed her much more than she needed him. He was, she'd
spelled out in words of one syllable, *non-union*. Venture outside the confines of her place, and without the protection of
an escort, he wouldn't make it five blocks before some ambitious halfgrown baby buck hoping to join a union would eagerly frag him.

He searched the hospital, hoping to find something to put
into his starving body. Between the occasional bouts of
dysentery and the meager diet, he had lost a frightening
amount of weight. His pants hung loosely on the bony ridges
of his hips, and the joints of his arms and legs were growing
larger than his muscles. Berk had never been fat, but he

knew he was approaching skeletal. He finally pulled up a few of his precious garden plants, eating the shoots.

He couldn't afford to do that twice, and on the third day, he had stopped being angry and was simply frightened. He stayed inert, dozing when he could and moving as little as possible to save his strength. He drank the remainder of the fetid recycled piss water.

She jarred him out of a half-sleep, dropping a large sack heavily onto her worktable. He sat up abruptly.

"Where the hell have you been?" he demanded, his anger returning to mingle now with his relief.

Unapologetically, she stared at him. "Out," she said, surprised. "My bizniz."

"It's my bizniz, too, Sadonya," he snapped, unable to stop himself. "You just trot off and leave me here with no food and no water. What the hell did you expect me to do? I thought we had a deal, I help you, you help me, right?"

She crouched down slowly next to her table, thin arms stretched out over the top of her knees. Her face clouded in annoyance, her eyes barely slits in the dark hollow sockets. "Don't like this," she warned. "You think maybe you make a bad deal, go find nother place. Get out. Fuck you." She turned her back to him, and started emptying her sack onto the table, dozens of her little leather bags and tied bundles of shriveled, dried plants.

He stared at her back, open-mouthed, for a moment, then punched himself mentally. *Stupid, Berkeley, very stupid.* This skinny brown girl was not a child, and the ruthless laws of survival that operated here were not his. He stood on watery-kneed legs, and crossed the room to squat down beside her.

"I'm sorry, Sadonya," he said, putting as much sincerity into his voice as he could. "I didn't mean to yell at you. I was . . . worried about you. I thought maybe something bad happened to you, that's all."

She turned her head slowly to look at him, a sardonic smile curling her lips. He hadn't fooled her for a second. "Don't care nodamn your sorries," she said. "And I can take care my ownsum. You hungry, outatown man?"

He gave it up. "Yeah, I'm hungry."

She nodded, stuck her head into the bag and pulled out two large dead rats, their flattened crushed skulls oozing with oily black blood. She held them out to him. "Then why don' you nuke us up some damnfine maindish, 'kay?" She was grinning broadly as she handed him a double-bladed knife. "Make y'ownsum *useful*, outatown man."

He shuddered as he took the rats, and found a board to clean them on. The knife grated through the sinews and bones of their necks as he cut the heads off. Black itching specks covered his hands, fleas jumping off the dead animals onto his skin as he slid the knife through the hide of their bellies, slippery putrid-smelling entrails spilling onto the board. He gagged, and cut off the tails and feet. Stripping away the skins and tossing them in the corner where Sadonya would later tack them to boards to dry, he impaled the naked pink bodies on the metal skewers, then laid them to one side while he started a fire on the garbage can. He placed the carcasses on the grill as Sadonya mixed herbs into cold cooked beans. She set the bedpan of beans beside the rats to reheat.

He took the cutting board to the window and pushed the bloody entrails off with the knife, out into the street below. When he turned, Sadonya was shaking her head. "I keep telling you alltime, stay way from the windows," she said. "Nexttime, you put that shit where shit go usual. Plants like guts, too."

"Sorry," he muttered. She smirked, a mean look in her eyes. "I know, you don't care nodamn my sorries." He brushed away the clinging fleas hopping up his arms, tiny welts already rising, red and itching along his skin. No doubt he'd come down with some loathsome and probably fatal disease.

God, he hated this place.

They ate in silence, the single rat and a scraping of beans from the pan filling his shrunken stomach. He felt drowsy and leaned against the wall, scratching idly at the sweat itching under his armpits. He closed his eyes, the firelight filtering through his eyelids with a warm red glow. With hunger and fatigue diminished he felt almost good.

After a while, he realized he'd been hearing a humming noise for some time. His skin felt prickly, thick, and his brain sluggishly detached. His crotch ached with an uncomfortable erection rising in unerotic confusion under his ragged pants. He opened his eyes, and looked at Sadonya.

She wasn't there. Neither was the room. Exactly.

Mrs. Kerowitz flowed up out of the bedpan still lying on the dirty floor by his feet, tiny brown specks of beans hopping around her. She pointed a finger at Berk's erection.

"Don' touch my dog," she warned, her voice altered and whizzing by his ear like the passage of an airplane far overhead.

Shocked, he goggled at her, his mouth dropped open. "You hate my dog, alltime, didn't you, Mr. Nielsen, you never did like poor little Happy, never did you any harm, such a good puppy, isn't you, sweetie," Mrs. Kerowitz shook her finger at him, cradling a mass of amputated miniature golden spaniel hair in her arms. He blinked, focusing on the dog as it turned its head towards him.

It grinned obscenely, one popped eye at the end of a slick thread of sinew bobbing loosely from its socket in its crushed rat skull, sharp little teeth dripping thick slick black petroleum oil, leaking down drop drop drop spattering on the floor by his feet. "Frag you alltime dead," the dog said, laughing in a wheezing voice choking like spittle, wet pulpy lungs squeezing out ha ha ha.

"What the fuck!" Berkeley said, but the words didn't come out right. They vomited from his mouth like cockroaches, chittering as they spilled into the air, flying with tiny silver helicopter wings on bodies brown as beans simmered in a bedpan. A burned-bean brown color coated the bedpan where Sadonya stood with her dark naked skin peeling away to yellowing brittle dry leg bones, little toe bones wriggling like maggots in the burned-bean pan. She laughed ha ha ha wet pulpy laughter spilling out a haze of blue smoke, snakes writhing through the air, heads filled with sharp-filed black rat teeth twisting searching, poison oozing from their nostrils in pale drops of white rancid semen splattering sizzling to the floor.

And December said, "Markley do it better, damnsure," and Markley was leaning back against the wall of marching cockroaches chitter skitter skittering up the stones of the dam. He opened his leather ratskin pants and a grayblue-veined smoky serpent writhed out over his fat thighs, bloody slivered cum slipping out of its dead eyes, and December's mouth slid over it wetly with little sharp rat teeth scratching long red lacerations. Markley glared at Berk with furious snarling hate, then vanished in a huff puff of noise moaning behind Berk's eardrums, rumbling deep in his wet pulpy chest.

December arched towards Berk, her head whipping on an impossibly long thin neck as she sank her sharp teeth viciously into his broken arm. Teeth burrowed down the puckered scar, searching for the fractured yellow bones writhing under his skin. He knew she had infected him, the tiny red welts of brown burned beans snapping hop hop hop.

"Face it, Berkeley," she said, her voice dripping scorn and black drops of snake cum that shivered out of his puckered scar down his pale bruised skin, "I told you you were nothing but a selfish, juvenile washed-up failure." Her voice changed, deeping into a rich, rolling politician's voice, scolding him like a child. "You blew it, son, you screwed up and now you're stuck and the old man isn't around anymore to ball your braindead ass out quicktime, is ho?"

"Shut up, just shut the fuck up," Berk howled, a wind of sound that sliced through the echoes in his mind wheezing in the hollow sockets of his eyes. He wrapped hot arms of dread around his chest, squeezing down on his racing heart. His fear rushed through his head, filling his skull with the murmur of his pounding heart, his cock swelling painfully in a blurred throb that pulsed evilly between his own naked thighs, lying fat and wet between dried leather skin stretched over long sticks of yellow dry bones.

And Sadonya said, "You look badtime sick, outatown man, maybe you die on me, huh?" She curled her fingers around his wrist, his heart clamoring to escape through the vein and artery worms eating their way through his peeling bruised wet pulpy flesh. Little brown fingers with half-moons of shit and filth and blood grinning at their ends like the black mouths of leeches. Little black grinning mouths sinking sharp leech teeth into the life pulsing in his wrist.

He yelled, jerked away, shaking off the little brown leeches in desperation, weeping in terror. They dropped and wriggled and jiggled and writhed over the floor. Fat little grubs endlessly flowed around in swirls and whirls and twirls over the floor and up the walls and onto his bed of stacked yellow dried bones, where he couldn't escape, where he was tied down, staked out spread-eagle with his back bowed over the mounds of yellowing, brittle bones, the skin on his naked chest crisping curling under the brutal hot sun in the desert sands, helpless as the fat little maggots rasped their blind tongues over his naked purpled skin ha ha ha with their sucking pursed mouths biting, black razor rat teeth making swelling red welts that puckered along his peeling skin, peeling away in shreds down to the yellow bones of his arms and legs stacked end to end in a neat pile, a bed of bones, tables and chairs of bones. He tried to slap at the little brown maggots, and his skin sloughed off as his hands jerked in panic, get off of me get off of me get off of me, crying like a child, waiting for the old man to shoot the fuckers between the eyes and make everything okay again.

Sadonya turned around to gaze at him with empty sockets in her brittle skin face peeling away like rotting shreds of leather down to a burned black skull and opened her mouth and the old man said sadly, "I'm sorry, Berkeley, son," the jaw moving as he spoke so that the crumbling edges of his charred skull chipped off with each clacking whacking movement. "I'd love to help you, damnsure quicktime I would, but right at the moment I'm a little dead."

The skull fractured, disintegrating into tiny hopping black spots that covered the walls, moving in scintillating formations, shiny wet pastel geometric rainbows as they marched marched marched across the peeling paint peeling like his skin away from yellowing bones, bright yellow, golden yellow, yellow as fetid pus turning to greenish purple bruises, pale as young green plants under the yellow sunlight roaring down from the skylights, torching the black shitdirt crawling with roaches and worms and maggots under his writhing back as the shovel dug slice turn slice turn chop chop chopped around him.

His head jerked up, neck arcing back, the tendons in his arms and legs straining guitarwire taut against the snakes that twisted and slithered around his wrists, crucifying his rigid naked body into the hot black desert dust with their rat sharp teeth, his cock feverishly jutting towards the shrill sky.

Irene II thundered above him, a wild echoing laughter ripping across the boiling clouds as the old man nosed her down into the hot cumwhite shitblack pusyellow bloodred sand, straight down at Berk until he could see the old man's face, sad eyes grinning, his burning skull under his skin making his face glow as he laughed with wet coughing spasms ha ha ha and slammed the helicopter into the center of the desert sun while the blades screamed with manic joy and the old man screamed like a man coming and Berk screamed in terror wanting so badly to wake up and knowing this wasn't a dream he would be here forever damnsure totalsum alltime.

NINETEEN

May 16, 2242

H IS MOUTH WAS DRY.
That was the first thing he was sure of. He listened
to the shallow sound of his own breathing, hearing it whistle rhymically out between his teeth. He knew he'd been listening to it *hush hush hush* and not understanding what it
meant.

Then he suddenly knew what it meant. He was alive, and
he knew he was awake and he knew where he was and he was
afraid to open his eyes. His muscles ached, trembling. He
tried to curl up, turn over, slip back into the cushion of sleep,
but the snakes still curled around him, tethering him to the
desert sand. But the snakes were limp and the desert felt more
like his mattress, lumpy and suffocatingly rank, a musky hot
smell in his nose.

He swallowed, forcing his salivary glands to concede a
few drops of moisture. He licked his lips and forced his eyes
open.

A cockroach wandered up the wall by his bed, a single,
timid insect, waving its antennae furtively. A real cockroach.
A real wall. He felt oddly disoriented, as if everything were
a shade too bright, too solid.

He lay naked on the bed, his ankles and wrists tied tightly

with leather straps to the frame, even his bandaged arm stretched out and fastened by his head. His hands and feet had swollen, purpled with congested blood. His penis lay flaccid over one gaunt thigh, glued to his skin with dried semen. He stared at it, mildly perplexed.

He swiveled his head, searching for Sadonya. She squatted on the chair, her chin propped on arms folded across her knees, watching him with bloodshot eyes. Pale smoke from her pipe drifted in a thin nimbus around her head.

"What . . . what happened?" he asked stupidly. But of course, as soon as he asked, he remembered.

Sadonya shrugged. "Don' know," she said simply. "Mosttime funbanes jess *fun*. Y'gotta lotta bad things inside your head, outatown man. Say lotsa weird shit, flapping around like y'crazyman. Tie you down so don' hur' your ownsum."

She'd doped him with one of her vile concoctions. He gaped at her, sitting there staring at him without the slightest bit of shame.

"You put it in the food," he accused her. Anger started boiling up from his spine, shivering through his aching shoulders. He felt his heartbeat pulsing painfully behind one eye.

"Yeah. I like funbanes sometimes," she said. "I think I be like what you alltime sayin', *'preciative.'* " She glared at him, as if he somehow was at fault. "I *share* it with you." She gestured towards his crotch with her pipe. "Endtime, seem you like it anyway."

"You put it in the food, and you didn't tell me," Berk said, his words coming out thick and slow. His head felt as if it were about to explode.

She shrugged, apathetic.

He lost it.

Completely.

"You put it in the food and you didn't tell me!" he screamed at her. "You stupid fucking bitch!" He felt the cords in his neck distend as he yelled, his wrists and legs wrenching against the leather restraints. His broken arm throbbed. "You put it in the goddamned food without me knowing and *poisoned* me with your fucking horrible shit, you moronic little cunt, I'll kill you, I'll kill you!"

He thrashed against his bonds, arching his back, straining to break free. *"I'll kill you!"* His shouts unraveled incoherently into a final howl of fury and frustration, and he fell back onto the bed, his muscles trembling as he panted, staring at her.

She hadn't moved.

She watched him unblinkingly, her shadowed eyes lifeless. Smoke curled up around her face, muscles unmoving.

Suddenly, he was very, very frightened.

"I'm sorry, Sadonya, honest to God, I didn't mean it," he pleaded. "Come on, it's just the last of the funbane, that's all, really . . ." He tried a smile to prove it.

Standing slowly, she put her pipe down on the table and picked up her metal bar.

"Oh, God, no, listen, I'm sorry, Sadonya, please don't, I didn't mean it, I'm *sorry* . . ."

She came to stand over him, looking down impassively. "Don' care nodamn your sorries," she said, her voice flat. "Fraggin' you don't do me ownsum favors. I break your leg, or nother arm, you don' work so good, eat a lotta my food's all. I jess down you slowsome, make you think a little."

She leaned over, her words slow and careful, her breath whispering against his face. "You listen good t'me now, outatown man. Nex' time, I kill *you*."

She lifted the bar and quickly, expertly, broke two ribs.

TWENTY

June 5, 2242

SADONYA HAD LET HIM LIE THERE, PLEADING WITH her for several hours, before she finally released him. It hurt to breathe, hurt to talk, hurt while he wept uncontrollably with the pain. He'd fumbled with his shirt, tears smearing down his face, trying to wrap his chest with it one-handed, until she'd grudgingly helped bind it tightly over his broken ribs.

They hadn't much to say to each other the next few days, but when he did speak, he was very careful, very polite. He'd finally given up. Numb, crushed, he worked the garden as best he could because he couldn't think of anything else to do.

She owned him. She had made that unspoken point quite clear. Body and soul. Totalsum. He knew it, in a wooden haze of acceptance. He did what she told him to without a word of complaint or question, working until he couldn't. Then he sat quietly, staring at nothing, trying to keep from thinking at all.

When he did think, it was the frantic scurrying of a trapped animal under his skull, a flutter of wild fear. *Gotta get out of here, gotta get out* . . . before he could will himself to push the panic down, clamp it tightly shut, accept the endless *now*.

He still cringed when she walked up unexpectedly behind him, still trembled whenever she picked up her iron bar, hating himself for it. She left him for days at a time on his own, and he waited patiently, saying nothing at all when she returned. When she handed him food, he forced the rank meat past his terror and down his throat, never sure whether she'd added any little surprises to it or not.

If she ever got any pleasure out of keeping him prisoner, she didn't show it. He simply existed in her life, as if it were natural, always had been. After a while, it felt natural to him as well. There was a strange sort of comfort in his surrender, a twisted dependability to the future rolling out blankly in front of him, reassuringly bleak and unchanging.

He felt almost irritated when Mouse changed all that. Squeeze's rival union leader had indeed been perked by rumors of the outatown man. Berk had been up on the skywalk, had just finished drizzling the meager supply of recycled piss over the double atrium garden and was rolling the hose up when four boys pushed through the broken panel in the revolving door and strolled into the lower level. They hadn't spotted him yet, and for a moment, Berk simply studied them with dulled interest.

The four jostled each other good-naturedly, laughing quietly and talking in low voices, their words rolling together in a fast tattoo while hands flickered in a silent language of their own. Arrogant, swaggering, they were whip-thin, corded muscles covered in the same rude leather that Squeeze and his companions had worn. Their dark faces were streaked with bright-colored patterns and the leather was decorated with a profusion of beads and glittering chunks of metal ornaments. When they reached the stairway, it dimly occurred to Berk that he should do something.

"Sadonya," he called out loudly, his ribs shooting pain through his chest in reproach. The four at the foot of the stairs froze, odd-colored faces turned up towards him. Berk kept his voice noncommittal, "We've got company."

She'd heard him, even from as far as the room they shared

down the corridor. By the time the four had climbed the stairway, she'd appeared on the balcony, squinting at them suspiciously. Berk stayed by the distillery on the bridge, leaning against the railing for support as he watched.

"What you want?" she demanded.

"Mouse send you Aye Pee Bee, nowtime. *Him*, too," the most garishly decorated of the four said, jerking a thumb at Berk.

Sadonya said nothing, sullen. She shot a quick, calculating look at Berk. "I get my things." The four moved as if to follow her down the corridor, but she cut them off with a quick chopping movement of her hand. "This still my place, not Mouse. You fuckin' not invited," she said sharply. "You wait here."

The leader of the four snorted derisively. "Little bitch think she got mean chop," he said, grinning to expose stained sharp-filed teeth of his own. The others laughed, but the group stayed where they were, eyeing Berk malevolently until Sadonya returned with her bag.

Two of the boys pushed past the opening in the revolving doors. The plate glass had been replaced with thick sheet-steel and the doors no longer revolved completely but turned far enough to create a shallow, angled opening, creaking in protest as it moved. The last pair followed Sadonya and Berk out the doors.

It was still early enough in the morning that the towering buildings overhead cast their cool shadows through the streets. The group trotted quickly down the wide sidewalks, staying in the shadows as if by instinct, following the shapes of sharp-edged dark. For the first time in days, Berk's head seemed clear, his lethargic spirit catching a spark.

Down in the streets, the city seemed an immense maze, closed in and ominous. Berk caught glimpses of signs as they hurried past. REGAL CAMERAS said one in faded raised letters, the paint stripped away from cracked plastic. PARK HERE! thrust an arrow down over a wide gaping hole. The side of a tall red brick building still had traces of faded paint reading YOU SAVE MORE AT BUDGET, in dingy red and blue.

The boys turned a corner, sprinting across the sliver of

sunlight. Their glass beads and metal embellishments sparkled briefly before they vanished into the twilight interior of a large building.

Berk blinked, blind in the sudden darkness, seeing nothing more than vague movement as he was jostled through a portico cluttered with dark shapes, then through an archway into an immense room. He could *feel* the emptiness before his eyes had adjusted to the candlelit gloom.

The floor was paved with marble, clean, smooth white squares inlaid with jade-green counterpoints, long strips of jade tracing the length of an expansive enclosed courtyard ten times bigger than the atrium of Sadonya's place. Massive square pillars with gilded capitals stretched up five stories to a vaulted golden ceiling. Far above, behind the pillars, dim silhouettes flitted through candlelight, leaned over balconies, whispers and muted laughter echoing through the cool air. A huge bronze eagle stood in the center of the vast room, folded wings jutting forward menacingly, a silent snarl in its open beak.

Something creaked rhythmically, unseen, overhead, oiled machinery rasping in the dark. Beside him, Sadonya stopped. Even in the dim light, he could see her scowl. The four boys flowed around them, leaving them standing isolated by the bronze eagle.

A sudden sound struck Berk with physical force, pressing down, around, squeezing from all sides. He crouched over as an inhuman bellow rippled through his skin, vibrating in the pit of his stomach. It took him a stunned moment before he realized it was music.

Or at least music of a kind. It might have been Mozart or Beethoven in a former life, but the notes stumbled over themselves like exuberant children playing tag, preoccupied with volume rather than any semblance of harmony.

He turned to stare behind him at gleaming columns of pipes. They towered above him, burnished gold in the candlelight. The organ music welled to a heavy crescendo, pulsing through the chamber. When it abruptly stopped, Berk's ears were ringing.

"That be Mouse," Sadonya said, her voice scornful.

As if to answer her, a high-pitched giggle cut across the room, ice-thin and boyish. A weird, grinning face appeared for a second over the edge of the organ's banister, then vanished, reappearing a few moments later in the huge court. He strode towards them, wrapped in a voluminous red cloak, then stopped, pausing theatrically. A dozen other boys dressed in the same outfits as the four who had come for Sadonya and Berk flanked out behind him in an almost formal arrangement.

He spread his arms, huge wings of frayed red velvet suspended from his shoulders to the ends of handheld rods, the cloak sweeping out five feet on either side of him. Where his four messengers had merely adorned themselves with stray bits of odd baubles, Mouse dripped in rococo excess. The cloak streamed behind him, encrusted with jewels and beads and sequined trappings sewn in swirls and circles and crude geometric patterns. Hundreds of chains hung from his neck, covering his chest in a solid sheet of glittering precious metal. He turned, the velvet wings sweeping the floor as he circled once and stopped. Above his grinning mouth, a mask covered his nose and eyes, huge peacock feathers fanning out in a lacy rainbow crown above his head.

"Welcome!" Mouse roared, pronouncing the word as if it were two, sounding as pretentious as he looked. Berk reminded himself that this ridiculous-looking boy was as deadly as any Ranger, and fought down his impulse to laugh.

Sadonya crossed her skinny arms, cocking her head to one side as she frowned.

"No hello for Mouse?" the boy said, his voice normal now. He pouted, a broad, comic gesture. As he lowered his arms, two of his attendants stepped up behind him. A quick shrug and the tattered red velvet cloak dropped from his shoulders into their waiting hands. They folded it reverently as Mouse walked towards Berk and Sadonya.

"I don' hold your union card, Mouse," she said.

Mouse reached up with long, delicate-looking fingers, taking the mask in his hand. When he pulled it away, he was looking at Berk. His face was bare. He hadn't painted it with garish colored patterns like his companions wore. He was older than Bcrk had expected, twenty-five or six; lines around his mouth under sharp cheekbones. Mouse handed the mask to his two attendants without even glancing at them. He stared for a long, silent moment at Berk before his eyes shifted towards Sadonya. His mocking smile had faded away.

"Your mama did," he said, his expression not matched by his mild tone.

"Only shortime. She lef'. *You* cudn' hold her. My mama special," Sadonya said contemptuously. She hawked and spat on the marble floor between them. "Like me. I don' think you all that special, Mouse. I gotta give you shit-nothin'."

Mouse barely glanced at the wet phlegm on the immaculate floor. His two attendants exchanged brief, worried looks that Sadonya didn't appear to notice.

"I don' vite you muchtime here," Mouse said, his voice calm, controlled. Berk didn't relax. "Maybe we cuss this out over drinks, like jemmin, kay?" His hands moved in a quick intricate flutter. His companions glided up noiselessly on either side and Mouse steered his unwilling guests towards a small doorless elevator set in a wall.

Mouse stepped into the lift, and turned, smiling and gesturing to Berk and Sadonya to join him. With a lurch, the elevator jerked upwards unevenly, its open face exposed to scabrous blank walls and lightless levels as they were hauled up above the court. The clanking sound of old machinery didn't cover the faint laboring grunts echoing in the shaft as somewhere below them, Berk imagined, sweating human muscles powered the cable. At the third floor the elevator shuddered to a nervous halt.

A wide gilded terrace overlooked the marble court, the gigantic organ silent on the opposite wall. The terrace had been crammed full with looted art. Paintings impaled on thick nails driven through their ornate frames completely covered the walls, Old Masters jammed side by side with soot-darkened Impressionists, Pollack and Klee flaking genteelly next to Renoir and Brueghel. Rodin bronzes and broken Greek marble sculptures were littered around so thickly, the group had to squeeze past them.

A single ornate wrought-iron table sat at the edge of the terrace. Around it, dozens of teenaged children lounged on worn Persian carpets thrown down in multiple layers. Mouse alternately stepped over or kicked at them to clear a path to the table, Sadonya and Berk trailing behind him.

The stuffing in the musty chairs had rotted to dry dust that puffed through the ripped fabric as they sat down. The table had been set with matching Wedgwood porcelain, a profusion of spoons, knives, and forks of varying sizes placed decoratively around them obviously with no clear purpose in mind. In the middle of the table a dozen cut crystal goblets surrounded an antique gold candelabrum, murky foul-smelling candles dripping yellow stalactites from its holders.

Mouse snapped his fingers, staring at Berk challengingly. A girl appeared with a green bottle of wine in one hand and an elaborate corkscrew in the other. Like the others, she wore homesewn skins of anonymous animals decorated with miscellaneous trinkets. Her furred leather vest, Berk noted somewhat uncomfortably, laced tightly under her large bare breasts, pushing them up into wide nippled mounds.

She flashed a quick smile at Mouse that slid to regard Berk curiously, the smile not quite fading. She bent over, bottle clamped between her knees, and drove the corkscrew in, heavy breasts hanging as the lean muscles in her arms rippled. She pulled—pop—and set the opened bottle on the table, letting one breast brush Mouse's shoulder as she turned to leave.

Mouse noticed Berk staring and his eyes crinkled in amusement. He grabbed the girl by her waist, pulling her down onto his lap and twisting her face around for a wet, unfriendly kiss. She gasped as he released her mouth, and sat passively as Mouse tucked his chin into the crook of her neck. Stroking her possessively, Mouse and the girl gazed steadily at Berk, his eyes mirthful, hers sullen, hostile. She didn't react as the boy fondled her body, barely wavering under his brutal, callous fingers digging into her flesh. Berk blinked, unsure of the implication in their eyes.

"Mine," Mouse said languidly.

The girl's lip curled up in a proud sneer as Berk felt his face grow hot.

Sadonya appeared not to notice.

Mouse glanced at her and scowled. Losing interest, he pushed the girl from his lap, shoving her away roughly.

"I hear Squeeze drop you by," Mouse remarked casually as he poured a bit of the wine into a goblet. He stared for a moment at the label pasted on the bottle, the paper faded into a completely blank square. Holding his glass up to the candlelight, he swirled the red liquid gently before he sniffed and sipped a mouthful, swishing it through his teeth like a medicinal mouthwash. He swallowed it and smacked his lips loudly. "Alltime good shit," he pronounced gravely, and poured three full glasses. He set one in front of Sadonya. "I hear true?"

Sadonya picked up her glass and took a deep gulp of the wine before she spoke. "My bizniz," she said. "What you care?"

Mouse ignored her question, staring at Berk quizzically. He leaned over the table to set down Berk's glass of wine. "I doubletime quick hear *everything*," he said, watching Berk. "Like you mark some outatown mister. You slidin' low, Sadonya, y'gotta mark some ugly old non-union scab with a Dis Ease." Mouse shifted in his chair, staring at Sadonya now, an angry muscle working along his jaw.

Sadonya smiled brittlely, leaning back in her chair, the red wine in her hand winking. "Like mosttime, Mouse, you don' hear good. Must be all that shit in your ears. I don' mark him, an' he'nt sick, he ugly natural like that."

Berk didn't speak. Understanding neither the vernacular, nor the politics involved, he preferred to watch and listen, keeping his mouth safely shut. All the same, he was edgy, tense. He shifted in the musty chair and nervously sipped his wine.

It was warm vinegar.

He forced it down with a hard swallow, set the glass back

gingerly on the table. Glancing around the terrace, he noted that the people sprawled over the carpets were mostly girls, a few thin effeminate-looking younger boys mingled among them. It seemed life in the ruins was short as well as nasty and brutal. The older boys, some barely old enough to be called men, stood stiffly around the room, cradling an assortment of weapons in their arms. One, he realized with a small shock of recognition, held Berk's own pistol in one hand, resting it in the crook of his crossed arms. He stood behind Mouse, glaring at Berk defiantly.

No one spoke except the group at the table, only the flicker of silent finger motions any evidence of conversation between Mouse's retainers.

"I gonna mark you, Sadonya, you be mine," Mouse was saying, his voice still casual. "I hear Squeeze, he gotta bad problem. Maybe I 'side I don' borderline cooks with him no more. Then I mark you f'sure." He leaned across the table to play at a matted curl of Sadonya's hair. She twisted her head away from him. "You still got looks, but you gettin' old quicktime, little bitch. Soon, maybe you need me, yeah?"

"Fuck you, Mouse," Sadonya said, sipping at her spoiled wine. She didn't appear to know it should be any different. Neither, it seemed, did Mouse. "You never gonna mark me. I push little nastics up my hole, you stick yourself there, something tiny bite you, make you swell up like a rotted dead toad, make your eyes bleed, kill you slowtime mean. Y'gonna beg Nextup frag you jess to make it stop." She smiled evilly at Mouse.

The muscular boy with Berk's gun stiffened, shifting uneasily behind the union leader. Mouse's casual smile didn't quite match Sadonya's. "That a lotta shit, Sad," he said. "Kill you, too, you know it." He didn't completely mask the uneasiness in his voice.

She shook her head slowly. "Huh-uh." Her voice carried in the room, a general warning broadcast at large. "I *mune*, Mouse. My mama *mune*. That why I'm cook and y'not. You not mune. You not shit." She sneered openly at him. His eyes flickered from her face to the impassive expressions of the coterie around him. Berk had no doubt that at the slightest hint of derision someone would die.

The moment stretched out silently. "We cuss this out 'nother time, Sadonya," Mouse said quietly, a brittle, dangerous edge in his voice. "Got other more importants worrying me nowtime."

Mouse turned his attention on Berk, his dark eyes set into deep hollows. Berk kept his own eyes steady, forcing down the fear.

Mouse snapped his fingers again, and this time a boy hurried to the table, setting down a small wrapped bundle. Mouse slowly uncovered it and Berk's heart lurched.

"What's this?" Mouse demanded.

Berk reached out to touch it gently, his hand trembling. It lay on the table like a guillotined head, a much loved face frozen into ugly death. "It's a rotor assembly," he said, not caring if Mouse understood or not. The swashplate was twisted, blade pitch linkages crippled, bolts popped off, ripped violently from the shaft.

Featherlight wings had once sung around this broken metal, had once suspended Berk high in the air, carried him safely over the brown deserts, taken him through wisps of clouds and stark blue sky. The metal was cool to his touch, a thin film of oil feeling vaguely like silk. He wanted to cry.

Mouse looked self-satisfied. "Tha's right," he agreed, nodding smugly. Berk looked up at him, his eyes burning. He had the sudden urge to grab this pretentious overgrown peacock by the throat and choke him, choke him until the silly grin went away, choke him to death. He swallowed, his ribs aching suddenly. If Mouse could read his expression, he gave no indication.

"I hear you fly this thing, outatown man," Mouse said. "I hear right." He leaned towards Berk, in a phony conspiratorial gesture. "Y'not marked, y'be a freeman, then maybe I make you a merger offer."

Sadonya started slightly, anger pinching her mouth. Berk slid his hands back from the bones of *First Violin*, letting them fall inertly into his lap. He leaned back and looked at Mouse, saying nothing. His eyes stung, dry.

"I got it all," Mouse said, waving his hand nonchalantly at the rotor head. "Maybe you fissit." He paused, watching Berk narrowly. "Maybe you fly oncetime more, yeah?"

"He mine," Sadonya said sharply, her hands balling into fists.

Mouse chuckled, an oddly pleasant sound not reflected in the spiteful twist of his lips. "Sadonya," he said condescendingly, "he not marked, then he not *yours*. He jess some grownbig baby buck, s'all. Y'notta union leader, he don' hold your card."

Sadonya glared at Berk, her lower lip trembling in fury. "We make a deal," she reminded him irritably. Her eyes were troubled, apprehensive.

Berk stared back at her, not answering.

"Maybe he be in arrested makin' a better deal?" Mouse suggested. "You fly this again?"

For a moment, hope flared in Berk, even though he knew better. *First Violin* was dead. Even if Mouse had scraped every last bit of her smashed corpse from the pavement, he couldn't rebuild her. *All the king's horses* . . . The helicopter would never fly again.

But . . . why throw away any leverage he might gain?

"Maybe," Berk said cautiously.

It was what Mouse wanted to hear. He grinned hugely, and quickly outlined his absurd idea. Berk would repair the copter. He would take up homemade bombs to drop on rival territories, allowing Mouse to expand his union from riverfront to riverfront. In return, Berk would be a card-holding member of Mouse's union, a high official in the company. Mouse would even give him a piece of conquered territory for his own property to rule as a union leader himself, to do whatever he wanted, subject, of course, to Mouse's authority.

"You be almost like Nextup, but I make you besttime offer," Mouse added expansively. "I let you mark's all you want, 'foretime you even ownsum union leader." Agitated hand movements fluttered through the room. The girls eyed each other, astonished; a few of the older boys looked sullen. Mouse glanced at Sadonya. " 'Cept her," he added. "Nobody ever gonna mark her but me. Deal?"

Sadonya had slouched down in her chair, obviously sure Mouse had made Berk an offer he wouldn't turn down. She scowled bitterly. Berk had no reason to feel any particular affection or loyalty toward her. The choice being set on the table was between remaining her virtual slave and a chance at relative freedom.

Except, of course, that it was impossible to repair the helicopter. But she didn't know that any more than Mouse did, now did she?

"Maybe I think about it," Berk said slowly. "I made a good deal with Sadonya, kinda like where I am. I'd feel bad having to break it. If I break my word to her, how much can you trust me? I should really talk it over with her first, come to another arrangement."

She darted a puzzled, suspicious glance at him as Mouse's face twitched before he hid his anger behind a laugh.

"I like that," Mouse said approvingly. "I can respect that."

Berk doubted Mouse respected anything. He held up his broken arm, and indicated his bound chest, smiling ruefully at Mouse. "Anyway, I can't do anything until I've healed." Time, he needed time. He also need something else. "But maybe in the meanwhile you can first make me a kind of good faith gesture . . ."

Mouse cocked his head slightly. Something about the movement disturbed Berk. "Good faith gesture?" Mouse asked, his mercurial humor restored.

"A small gift to show you mean what you offer," Berk said, shrugging offhandedly. He was trembling.

Mouse's eyes glittered in the candlelight, suspicion and merriment in his face. "What kinda 'gift'?"

"Nothing important, just something that shows me you really do have all the pieces of my machine. Then I know your offer's good, and I go home and think about it. Make my decision. A metal can about this big"—Berk measured with his hands—"full of thick black oil."

Mouse snorted. "That all?" he said scornfully. "That easy." He spoke rapidly to the boy holding Berk's pistol. Berk considered for a moment asking for the gun, and decided against it. His mind sorted rapidly through his problems, and he spotted Sadonya regarding him through side-long hostile eyes.

One obvious problem, he realized. She might decide to frag him alltime dead before he got a chance to make up his excuses. He'd have to take the gamble.

A moment later, the boy had returned. He set the battered can before Berk, miraculously still sealed. "You make y'deci-sion quicktime, outatown man, get it worked out with *her*," Mouse warned him amiably. "Special limited offer, good one-time only."

Berk nodded, and cupped his hands around the small can. A quick twist and the precious oil shimmered in the candle-glow.

He grinned, happy.

TWENTY-ONE

June 5, 2242

S ADONYA SULKED AFTER THEY HAD BEEN ESCORTED
back to Tom'n Jeff's. Berk had quickly run through several different stories, weighing them carefully. The last thing he could do was tell her the truth, not trusting her to keep from selling him out to Mouse. He wasn't about to admit to her that he had absolutely no more power over his own life than he'd had before the meeting.

Mouse's boys left them at the door. Sadonya started up the stairway.

"Let me explain, Sadonya," he said, going after her.

She cut him off angrily. "Don' want you fuckin' splains," She twisted around on the stairway to glower at him, hurt and fury in her voice. "You wanna jump, go jump, don't have to make no *arrangement* w'me. I don' give nodamn." There were actually tears in her eyes.

He sputtered, astonished. She had used him, drugged him, tortured him with starvation and driven him to exhaustion, punished him by breaking his ribs, reduced him to a crippled, helpless captive and now *she* was reproaching *him*? Did she really expect *loyalty*?

Of course she did. She pulled you half-dead out of the garbage dump and saved your worthless life. Why wouldn't she feel entitled to do anything she wanted with you after that? *Finders keepers, losers weepers.* She owned you with that simple ruthless logic. And now that her property was slipping from her grasp, she was reacting with all the outrage of a child at the unfair theft of a toy.

She turned away, climbing quickly. Charging up the remaining steps, ignoring the sharp pain bursting across his ribs, Berk caught her at the top of the stairs. He grabbed her by one arm, forcing her around to face him. "Listen to me, Sadonya!"

The dark eyes flickered at him, like the nictitating membrane of a desert lizard.

"Let's you and me cuss this all out private," he said, forcing his voice level. *Be calm, be calm.* "Maybe it's time we make a new deal. Maybe a different deal than what Mouse thinks, yeah?"

She stayed rigid, her body vibrating slightly under Berk's hand. "What kinda new deal?" she said slowly.

Berk had to sit down suddenly, pain making it hard to breathe. His knees wobbled, and he sank down at the top of the stairs. "Come on, Sadonya," he said, wheezing slightly, smiling and patting the step beside him. "Here's fine."

She sat down, hunched as far away from him as the steps would allow. Drawing her knees up towards her chest, she wrapped her arms around her legs and waited.

"I don't trust your friend Mouse," he said. "I think maybe he makes a whole lot of nice promises because he doesn't intend to keep any of them. I repair my helicopter, he frags me and takes it for himself." Her eyes narrowed slightly. She hadn't believed he was capable of working that through, had she? "So maybe I'm not that eager to rush right on over to good old Mouse, after all, hm?"

He could see her thinking. "Kay," she said. "So what?"

"So I think maybe you also gotta bad problem with Mouse. If I were you, I'd frag *me*, make sure Mouse doesn't get his private flying machine, doesn't drop his bombs, make some kind of a big rav and mess things up here for you." She didn't react, her eyes staring at him unblinkingly. He smiled nervously. "I think maybe I got big problems with you or Mouse either way, huh?"

"Yeah," she admitted grudgingly. "You really walkin' onna razoredge now, outatown man, no lie."

"No lie," he agreed. "I also think," he added hastily, "if you frag me, that would make Mouse very unhappy. He'd come after you, no matter what kind of nasties you've booby-trapped yourself with. You gotta big problem, too, no matter which way I choose."

She was nodding pensively. "No lie," she said. She was regarding him with new respect. The dangerous flat look had gone. "You gotta eye dee?"

He grinned. *Gotcha.* "You and me, Sadonya. We're in it together. We make a new deal, and it's a lot like the old. You help me, I help you. This time, though, we help each other like—" He hesitated, wanting to say "friends." But, even if he could bring himself to consider her a friend, he wasn't sure she even truly understood the concept. "—like partners. No more pushing me around like you're the whipcock and I'm some stupid baby buck. Equals, fifty-fifty. You understand? Then, maybe, we'll both stay alive." He sat and stared at her, holding his breath.

She sat quietly, her eyes thoughtful, for a long, tense moment. *Come on, Sadonya, it's not that hard* . . . She gave him a reluctant sideling glance, licked her lips, tongue pale pink. "Maybe we jump fenceways, go over to Squeeze?" she suggested feebly.

Just don't want to give up the upper hand, do you, bitch? Let it go, girl . . . "You tell me. Help me now. Equal to equal, be honest with me."

She considered, then sighed. "No. Squeeze, he slidin'. He die soontime," she admitted. "His Nextup, he good, but he not Squeeze. Maybe he make a rav with Mouse, lotta people fragged. Mouse side, he bigger than Squeeze side. He prolly stomp quicktime shit outta Squeeze's Nextup. Maybe Nextup, he know it, too. He gotta good thing, freezone market, wanna keep that one piece, damnsure. He rollover you an' me to Mouse, so Mouse don' make a rav after all. You an' me"—she made a gesture with her hand he recognized—

"we fucked both ways." Her hand said *real bad*.

"What if you and me, we frag Mouse first?" he suggested.

She didn't have to think that one over for very long. "That fuckin' stupid," she said, but there was no scorn in her voice. He breathed an inward sigh of relief. She'd accepted it, finally, equals, partners. "Mouse, he want me for ownsum reasons. His Nextup no fool. He don't care markin' me or not, being private cook's good nough. Mouse gone, he come down stomp me out the other side of the earth, quicktime. He take me, take you, we both wish we totalsum dead alltime."

They sat quietly on the steps, looking at the waning light in the garden, floating dust twinkling.

"So, you think any more eye dees?" she demanded. No fear in her voice. Had she ever been a child? Had she ever seen the world through innocent eyes? Had she ever clung to her mother's legs and whimpered in confusion and fear, needing someone to take care of her, hold her, comfort her? Love her? Somehow, he doubted it.

"No," Berk admitted. "Not yet." He paused. "Why does Mouse want you?"

"My bizniz," she said promptly, firmly.

"It's my bizniz now, too, Sadonya," he insisted gently, and curled one hand firmly around her bony wrist. Her skin was cool, fine-textured against his palm.

And he waited.

Finally, "Mouse, he think he bees some stud, got damn-fine gentick material up his dick." She spoke in the fading twilight, eyes turned away. "He mark every hole he got, even boys, keep everybody to ownsum, don' share notime nobody. He alltime makin' a lotta baby bucks, but no cooks. He hate that, damnbad. Kill a lotta his ownsum bucks he so mad. So he think maybe he can make another cook on me. Alltime pressin' me. He jealous cause my mama got the taste an' he didn't. He hate my mama and their mama alltime for that."

"Your mama was his sister?" Berk wasn't sure he was hearing correctly.

"Yeah. She got it from her mama, and she alltime tellin'

me all our mamas got the taste. Never been daddies notime be a cook. I keep tellin' him, slits get the taste, no misters." Her voice was bitter.

"Then he's your uncle," Berk said, repelled. "He's your family."

She snorted. "Yeah, he *family*, damnsure. He also my daddy. He Nextup for Kovar pastback longtime. Kovar mark everybody, keep alla slits for ownsum, my mama too. Alla union boss do, that usual gameplan. Misters, they only get wholesale slits passed out for Chris Miss bonuses. Keep 'em mean. Get too bad, they sometime gotta get satisfaction offa sugarboys or funbanes, or maybe they do something earn out a dividend and then they getta freebee."

Berk shivered, remembering Third's eyes rolling back in his head, and his own experience with Sadonya's funbane.

"That usual good way of keepin' meanmisters finetuned for ravs. Kovar, he no different most other union boss, but he don't like Mouse. He don't give Mouse any notime, even when Mouse get to be his Nextup. Kovar treat my mama special, real nice, want my mama ownsum, never share her ever."

She was still for a moment, then took a deep breath, almost a sob, which echoed in the still of the atrium. "I think Mouse frag him quiet, then he beat up my mama. He beat her real bad, almost frag her alltime, then he mark her public, over and over, everybody standin' round watchin'. He make me on my mama right there, her lyin' on the ground bleeding. He brag bout that alltime. My mama hate him. He keep on braggin' even after I born, struttin' around tellin' everybody he gonna make lotta cooks on me too.

"Tha's when we 'scape to this place. My mama tell him she kill me fore she kills ownsum he don't leave us alone. Woulda, too. Then Mouse don't have no cooks."

"Jesus," Berk breathed. Sadonya didn't seem to notice.

"Mouse, he so fuckin' proud of ownsum, say alltime how his gentick dick best. Tha's only reason why his Nextup don' frag *him*, think maybe it true Mouse got cook genticks."

Speechless, he stared at her profile, half hidden in a cave of matted hair. She spoke quietly, her words calm, clipped.

"Mouse, he selfish mean. He keep it all for himself, give nobody any fun, ever. Alla slits gotta pertend alltime he so damnfine, he only one get up w'a dick, or he beat 'em dead. He frag his own Nextup if he even look at a slit funny. But I don't hold his union card, an' he can' stand eye dee maybe I mark with othersum. Gotta be his, he wanna make a lotta baby cooks, then he kill off everybody's else's cooks, he be King Shit over all the unions, quicktime.

" 'Cept he know better. He know I get the taste from my mama, don't get but shit gentick outta his ugly dick. He know I can anytime make baby cooks anyone I want, and he hate that damnsure bad." Her voice cracked, anger finally showing. "I hate him alltime. I fuckin' *die* before he mark me." She swore, a thick patter of words he couldn't follow, cut off with a snap of her wrist, a silent signal of disgust.

Now he understood why Mouse's gestures seemed so familiar.

She turned her head, hate burning in her eyes. "Now you know, outatown man," she spat out. "This help you thinka eye dees, huh? No? Kay, you so smart suddentime, what *we* do, partners?"

"We wait," he said, making his voice sound more assured than he felt. "We stall for time, and we watch and we wait."

"Huh," she snorted, sarcastic. "No lie. You a real alltime genius."

She stood up and left him sitting alone in the blue-washed twilight. His thoughts spun around in circles, like a helicopter searching for elusive camouflaged Aggie gardens, whining irritably in the dusk.

TWENTY-TWO

June 18, 2242

THE BEANS AND POTATOES WERE DOING WELL, although the corn stood only knee-high, stunted withered stalks grudgingly producing one or two tiny corncobs. There were other plants, plants he didn't recognize but which Sadonya kept a careful eye on. It had become almost a pleasure, keeping the garden rows cleared of weeds, the warm brown dirt under his feet friendly, comfortable.

The ache around his chest slowly eased. His arm had almost completely healed, but Sadonya insisted he keep the splint tied on, at least in public. It still made him clumsy, but it didn't hurt much. He was as reluctant as she was to admit he was nearly whole again.

Especially once Mouse started sending his boys over to sit in the lower lobby to watch him. Then the routine changed, everything altered, transforming the delicate and fragile balance into a deadly struggle of wills.

Sadonya caught three of them squatting on the stair landing, silently staring as Berk shoveled more of the decomposed air-dried shit into a new patch, churning it over to ready it for another crop of small brown beans. He'd been steadfastly ignoring his mute audience.

"What you doin' there?" Sadonya shrieked, and he

stopped while she screamed at the trio, resting his free arm on the shovel. He looked up at her and realized, surprised, she was yelling at *him*. "I tell you alltime, you too sick be workin' like that! You get y'ownsum ass back where it go, for you drop flydead."

He let the shovel drop and shuffled toward the stairway. He sagged halfway up, clutching the banister in faked distress. "I'm sorry, Sadonya," he said for the benefit of Mouse's not so discerning spies. "I'm trying to get my health back as soon as possible so I can go work for Mouse. I guess I just pushed myself too far, huh?"

She favored Mouse's sentinels with an angry glare as she caught him under the arm. Supporting him up the remaining steps and down the corridor out of sight, she whispered angrily in his ear, "Jess you be damnsure not push *me* too far, asshole, I make sure it be the truth."

So he stayed in the dark stuffy room, or observed her from the shadowed concealment in the mouth of the corridor while she hacked at the garden, stopping occasionally to yell at the ever-present watchers, carrion birds hovering over a near-dead carcass.

"This *my* place, get out, you fuckin' not 'vited here!" She threw clods of dirt and shit at them. They would dodge the vehement hail of filth, grin with sharp, filed teeth in their painted faces, and resettle like flies brushed from the surface of drying rat hides.

The summer was growing, the nights no longer chilled the shadows, heat ripening the stench of rotting garbage outside the windows. Even from three stories up, it stank. Their shared room was still the coolest one in the place, heat rising on the higher floors (where the stink wasn't as bad) until it was unbearable.

They moved the garbage can stove to another room, however, struggling in the dark at night to disguise Berk's returning strength, and he convinced Sadonya her leatherworks would be better off out of sight and smell elsewhere.

It was getting hotter, sapping at their energy relentlessly. They sat in the dim room, a single candle guttering in the suffocating, still air. He raised his hands, making shadow dogs with his fingers, a flying bird, a crowing rooster, a galloping horse, in the fluttering light on the wall. Sadonya eyes widened curiously, and he grinned. She watched him, then tried it herself, a child's game to temporarily push away the heat and boredom. Eventually, their hands fell away, tired.

"You getting better," Sadonya said, breaking the silence. "We not foolin' Mouse too longtime more."

"Uh-huh," he agreed. He sat naked on the bed, back to the wall, the sweat prickling under his armpits. He felt the questioning touch of insect legs exploring his shoulder, and brushed the cockroach away casually. Interesting, he thought dully, how used to things you can get.

It was too hot for sleep, too hot for talk.

After five minutes or so, she said hopefully, "Maybe I break y'other arm, then you go fall down the stairs? Itta be acid dent, Mouse have to wait little moretime."

It was too hot to laugh. "Thanks for the offer, Sadonya," he said wryly. "But I'll pass."

She stared at the candle, then blew it out to conserve the remainder. "I damnsure getting tired, outatown man," she said in the dark. "I back doin' allthing nowtime, while you sitting here thinkin' up your eye dees." He heard the menacing reproach in her voice. "It's cuttin' in my bizniz. I not sure 'bout this partners shit."

"Teach me how to make your funbanes," he suggested. "I don't like this sitting around on my ass anymore than you do."

Flies buzzed quietly outside, unconcerned with the heat as they crawled through the trash in the street below, eating and mating and laying their eggs in the fetid offal.

"You can't make my things," she said. It was a statement of fact, neither a challenge nor a boast. "I tell you that. Nosuch mister be a cook."

"Why not?"

"I got my mama's taste. You don'."

"Well, maybe you teach me how to make just a few, something simple even a dumb outatown mister can cook."

She snorted. Her laugh. "You don' hear good. You so

dumb. Here, I show you . . ." She rustled in the lightless room, a mere outline of movement. Then she crossed the room, padding on bare feet, and sat down next to him on his bed. "What this?" she said, and poked something into his mouth.

He sat up abruptly, spitting frantically. "This going to give me another one of your fun times?" he asked suspiciously. "You promised no more . . ."

"Uh-uh. Not doin' nothing. You jess taste it, tell me what this." She shifted, the leather creaking under the mattress, holding up a dried sprig of leaves. It brushed his lips. Hesitantly, he mouthed them, then wiped them off his tongue with the back of his hand. "So?" she demanded.

"I don't know," he said.

"What it *taste* like? Sweet? Maybe musty smell on y'tongue like old rat fur? Maybe bitter like how y'shit smell when it get sick runny?"

"It just tastes like dried up old leaves to me," he admitted.

"That," she said with some satisfaction, "is 'cause I got the taste, an' you don'. I show one more . . ." She pressed pinches of crumbled leaves in each of his hands. "That las' one go with one these, make a bluecross. Make it when y'get too hot inside, y'cool off. You taste, tell me which."

Dubiously, he touched his tongue to each, carefully wiping it away when he'd finished. They tasted the same. He said so.

"You don' see it inside y'head?" she asked, obviously knowing he didn't. "Y'don' see how *this* onc"—she closed her fingers over his left hand—"go with firsttime? See how they take y'tongue juice and when they gonna be hot 'nough, they get close, like they markin' each other, how they trade around w'corners, join together an' making rings dancing round and round? Little pieces flyin' off, gon' back and so?"

He realized suddenly what she was saying.

Sadonya was a natural chemist. A taste, a smell, she could read the chemicals intuitively. A lick of sweat off the forehead, and she could taste the poisons excreted through the pores. A whiff of anonymous liquid in any one of the hundreds of bottles she kept stocked near her table, and she could see the chemical structures in her mind's eye. A jab of a knife, a drop of blood, and she knew every secret detail carried in your system. She knew how to mix this with that, knew exactly how much, knew what it would make, knew what it could do. She couldn't tell you the names, couldn't diagram formulae in neat, white chalk rows in squeaking charts against a blackboard.

She simply . . . *knew*.

As if she could feel his realization, she smiled, tiny highlights on her small teeth all that showed of her face. "Tha's why I'm a cook. An' y'not."

"Huh," he said. "Damnfine." Impressive.

"Yeah," she said, pleased. She sat next to him, until he started feeling wary. "Y'think you so smart. Y' think I'm dumb. But you don' get any new eye dees what we do, huh?"

"No," he said. "Not about Mouse. Not yet." For a moment, he had an impulse to tell her about the helicopter, admit he'd stalled, not because he suspected Mouse of any double dealings, but because he'd lied. There was no way to rebuild the helicopter. Oh, he might put something together, some phony piece of cobbled junk that looked good but would never fly, keep tinkering and bullshitting, and buying time until Mouse figured out he'd been had.

But he couldn't tell her that, let her in on the secret. As soon as he jumped, Mouse would try to take her. She'd kill Mouse, or kill them both if she didn't know, or sell him out quicktime if she did.

Of course, if she knew he was simply trying to buy enough time until the worst of the summer heat had gone past so that he could slip away and escape, abandon her to her own goddamned problems, she'd frag him quicktime herself. He clamped down on his sudden surge of amiable goodwill, kept his mouth shut.

She moved back across the room, and he breathed a silent sigh of relief.

"Still don' solve no problems," she said petulantly. Except that her petulance was anything but minor.

"I'll figure it out," he promised.

"Huh."

He was beginning to doubt too.

"Fuckin' hot," she muttered half an hour later.

"Can't solve that one right at the moment, either, Sadonya," he said.

TWENTY-THREE

June 21, 2242

S HE LOCKED THE DOOR WHENEVER SHE LEFT, WHICH
kept Mouse's boys from prying too closely, but it also ef-
fectively locked Berk in, more a prisoner now than before.
Without the cross-current in the room, the heat seemed even
worse, stifling.

He hadn't figured out how he was going to delay his decision much longer, but he couldn't tolerate the enforced
boredom anymore. And he couldn't stand the heat, either.
Building a water pump in the basement was impossible with
Mouse's vigilantes keeping guard. But he sent Sadonya out
scrounging the various floors in the building for the scraps
he had seen and mentally catalogued, describing, nagging,
cajoling, anything to get her to retrieve the supplies he
needed.

She'd watched him dubiously as he tinkered with the miscellaneous bits and pieces, hammering and cursing the old
metal scrap and the makeshift tools. But by the time she'd
returned from another shopping day at Squeeze's small free
zone market, he had cobbled together two working fans.
He'd even sacrificed a little of his precious raw black oil to
grease the gears. Waiting impatiently with his ear to the

door, he listened to the silence of the old abandoned hospital, wanting, for some reason, to surprise her.

When he heard her yelling at Mouse's ever-present watchdogs, spitting angry insults at them, he sprinted to the bed and hooked his feet into pedals on a crank, pumping a self-generated breeze. The key rasped in the ancient lock, she walked into the room and stopped in disbelief. Lank greasy strands of hair blew back from his face.

"Ahhhh," he breathed, grinning like a fool, "feels so *good!*" He stretched his arms over his head with fingers laced together in an exaggerated pose. The fan blades, scavenged from forgotten ventilator shafts, whirred almost flawlessly, clacking with a slight noise that reminded him, for a brief painful moment, of Teddy's model helicopter hanging in Strawberry's.

She set her bag down on the worktable, and circled his fan incredulously, sniffing at it. She put her hand out to feel the breeze it generated, jerking it back distrustfully. He couldn't help laughing, and pointed to a similar machine on her side of the room.

She perched reticently on the edge of her own bed, arms braced, and thrust her bare feet into the leather stirrups. Studying his movements, she began to pedal slowly, the fan blades moving jerkily until she'd got the rhythm, turning faster until a breeze lifted the clumps of matted hair off her face. She blinked, the air blowing in her eyes, pumping faster. The twin blades sang together.

She grinned at him wordlessly, stained teeth shining in her dark face. It was the first time, he realized, that he'd ever seen her smile without malice, the first time he'd seen actual joy, real pleasure in her eyes. She pulled off her cape, letting the air stream over her bare flat chest.

She pumped as hard as she could, bouncing on the bed as her thin legs spun the blades around the crankshaft, grinning and squinting in the stiff wind she'd generated. He matched her as if it were a race, the fans blurring, gears *sh-clank sh-clank sh-clank*ing happily. It lasted only a minute before their starved, malnourished muscles tired. They slowed, panting, and silently pedaled, letting the slight breeze push back the killing heat for an hour.

"Y'know, you not so dumb after all, outatown man," she said finally, reluctantly.

"Y'know," he said amiably, "my name's Berk, not 'outa-town man.' Berrrrk," he enunciated slowly. "It's really a very simple, easy name. You think you can remember that? Bet you could if you tried hard enough."

"So okay, *Berk*," she said, grimacing at his sarcasm. "You get any more bright eye dees while you sittin' around mak-ing this shit, *Berk*? Like how we gonna outlive Mouse?"

"One thing at a time," he said.

"Huh." She laughed, and leaned back against the wall, closing her eyes and letting the cool air flow past her.

They pedaled until their muscles gave out, tired, perhaps even hotter after all the exertion, but the momentary respite from the heat had lightened both of their moods.

"Maybe I gotta bonus in my pay check, too, *Berk*," she said. She began pulling out the inevitable pouches and sprigs of dried leaves, bunches of herbs tied with string from her bag. At the bottom lay four unhealthy-looking dead rats, their skulls crushed, a slightly bloated fish, half a dozen potatoes, the usual bag of brown beans he'd come to loathe, and a couple of withered onions beginning to sprout.

And three small tomatoes.

Immediately, he was on his knees at one side of her table, open-mouthed and staring incredulously at the three round, bright red, plump tomatoes. "Where did you get these?" he asked, his mouth watering.

"Squeeze, he not doin' so good," Sadonya said, her face enigmatic. The answer didn't seem correlated to the ques-tion. He looked up at her, puzzled. She shrugged. "I damn-fine cook, but I not God. He slidin' and slidin' fast. I give him somethin' make the pain not so bad. He happy, he give me these." She paused for a moment, "Squeeze, he okay. Damnshame. Should be fuckin' Mouse, stead."

Berk nodded, unable to keep from staring at the tomatoes. "We'll be careful and save the seeds," he said. "Maybe we can grow our own."

She snorted, but didn't say what he knew they were both thinking. They wouldn't live long enough to see the results. Admitting it aloud would have been too much like an admission of defeat.

He cooked the fish and two potatoes over the garbage can in the other room, while she played with her fan, listening to it faintly clacking away. When dinner had been nuked damnfine crispy, they ate in silence, sucking on their tomato halves for dessert, nibbling on them slowly to make them last as the night deepened the sky.

Then, food in their bellies, the fans moving night-dark air, Berk formulated another part of his plan. He considered it, not liking it too well, and realized there wasn't much other choice.

Three steps outside Tom'n Jeff's and he was as good as dead. If there was any chance at all of escaping Mouse, he would have to get as far away from Philadelphia and the union territories as he could. And there was only one person who could take him that far.

"Sadonya," he said conversationally, "your mama ever tell you bedtime stories?"

She squinted at him, brushing away a few of the more aggressive flies from her face. "What that?" A couple of the buzzing insects circled, annoyed, and landed again, jockeying for position on her body.

Berk took a deep breath. "They start like this: 'Once upon a time . . . '"

TWENTY-FOUR

January 6, 2231

H E'D KNOWN HER ALL HIS LIFE, OF COURSE. IN A
City of less than a hundred thousand inhabitants, it
was hard to be strangers with anyone. And December Pindar
was not a woman who blended well in a crowd. He'd seen
her, admired her and immediately written himself off as not
standing a chance with a girl so ethereally beautiful.

Berk Nielsen was not a homely man, merely average.
Short and lean like his father, brown eyes, brown hair, good
tan, he was the standard physical example of an unremark-
able Cityman. Far too commonplace for someone like
December.

Most of the people who had first survived the Shift hud-
dling under the domes had been Caucasian, the more afflu-
ent and powerful guaranteeing themselves a reservation
inside their landlocked arks. The sun, however, once the Van
Allen belts had vanished and the ozone layer stripped away,
favored darker-skinned individuals, a layer of subcutaneous
melanin sometimes being the sole fragile edge standing between surviving and dying of hard solar radiation, regardless
of how thick the protective dome glass was.

There were limits.

Rangers and the tunnel-burrowing Aggies who survived

in the open wastelands and the savages who lived in the shadowed bowels of open ruins were exclusively dark-skinned. For the most part, the Citizens of Pittsburgh had been homogenized into a standard racial group, mostly Caucasoid, but intermarriage and the surviving generations becoming shorter, thinner, dark-haired, dark-eyed, and tanning easily.

A few of the tiny ethnic enclaves had remained tenuously intact. A single square block incorporated the City's miniature Chinatown, Japanese, Chinese, Korean, Vietnamese, a dozen different Asiatic races intermingling, trying to preserve languages, cultures, identities of countries that hadn't been seen in more than two hundred years. Jews still went to the synagogue while Christians attended their churches. Any other dissimilarities were minuscule and, as long as you were a Citizen, ignored. The differences still remaining between what was considered "black" and "white" had become so vague as to be more a matter of arbitrary degree, the preservation of culture and languages dependent on individual interest rather than because of any racially pure heritage. The domed City of Pittsburgh was simply too small for anything else, or anything less.

Which made December Pindar part of an exotic minority. It wasn't just that she was tall and blond, with blue eyes like deep river water, she was beautiful. More beautiful than Berk would have hoped himself likely to be able to attract.

So, when Kilian had strolled into Strawberry's with December's arm safely tucked through his, Berk, as well as most of the other male pilots in the tavern, had turned to look, admired December for the thousandth time, and had to admit that the handsome, square-jawed, tanned flier and the tall blond girl made an attractive couple. Berk surreptitiously eyed the reactions of the women pilots, smirking slightly. Then he'd gone back to his beer.

Which made *him* nervous, if flattered, when December had walked over to his tiedown on the protective community hangar where the pilots kept their machines.

"This actually flies?" she'd asked, not bothering with any usual social conventions such as a preliminary Hello, what's your name. She was looking at the helicopter, squinting critically.

He'd stood, flustered, anxiously eyeing Kilian busy at the other end of the hangar while racking his suddenly empty brain for a witty response. "Uh, yeah, it flies," was the best he could come up with. He had never been much of a ladies' man, but he wasn't usually this inept.

"It looks funny," she said.

"Flies funny, too," he blurted out. "Maybe you'd like to check it out up close and personal sometime." Mentally, he kicked himself, which he imagined hurt a lot less than what Kilian might decide to do later.

That, lame as it was, made her look at him. A hint of a smile pressed dimples on each pale smooth cheek, full lips curved. She stood self-confidently, a full inch taller than he, hands in the pockets of her Energy Department-issued vest. Her long legs supported a well-proportioned torso undisguised by baggy pants and a work shirt. "Sure," she said simply. "How about now?"

"But . . . aren't you Kilian's girl?" Berk asked, suddenly alarmed.

Her smile widened, showing even white teeth. "I'm hardly a 'girl,' " she said, "and I've never liked the idea of people belonging to each other, not even in the romantic sense. I'm a human being, not anyone's property."

"Yeah, well,"—he nodded reluctantly—"I'm not sure that Kilian feels the same way."

She shrugged. "If you feel like you should ask his permission, that's up to you." Although there was nothing insulting or sarcastic in her tone, Berk felt chagrined.

"Of course not," he said immediately. "You want to check out the difference between your average, ordinary, run-of-the-mill fixed-wing and a real flying machine, then let me introduce you to *First Violin*." He patted the helicopter affectionately.

Kilian had finished tarping his *Laser Chaser*, and walked over in time to hear Berk's last statement. "Sember," he said, chuckling, "you don't want to go up in that thing."

"Why not?" she asked before Berk could retort.

"One,"—Kilian held up a finger—"you'd be flying with Berserker Berk, and two, there's a very old saying that a helicopter is a treacherous piece of shit whose sole purpose for existence is to get half a chance to slam you straight into the ground and chop you into little itty bitty pieces."

"Of course," Berk said, feigning perplexity. "That's what makes it so fun to fly, and why I have to be ten times better a pilot than you."

Kilian laughed. "Okay, have fun, ladies!"

He walked off, seemingly unconcerned that December was about to go off with another man. Even more disconcerting, he didn't consider Berk to be much of a threat.

"You really called Berserker Berk?" December asked him ingenuously.

"Uh, no," Berk said, uncomfortable. "I think he made that up."

He slipped the handling wheel into *First Violin*'s skids and pressed the boom down to roll her out of the hangar into the cold winter light. It was one of those sharp, clear winter days Berk loved, the frozen crystal-blue sky stretching away cloudlessly overhead. It had rained a few nights before, the shallow ice-puddles traced with lacy patterns. Dead stubbles of frosted grass crunched underfoot.

Her hands still in her pockets, December followed him Outside, without any offer or attempt to help, no giggling insistence on getting in the way. She stood watching him calmly as he carefully checked over *First Violin* before opening the passenger door. She stepped up confidently into the seat, and he fumbled self-consciously with her safety harness before she stopped him with a smile. "It's like a fixed-wing's, isn't it?"

"Yeah, exactly," he muttered as she snapped it around herself. "Right." He closed the door and walked around the helicopter's boom instead of the nose for the private opportunity to squeeze his eyes closed in a grimace of self-disgust. No other woman had ever made him feel as nervous and insecure as she did.

But once the helicopter thrummed to life, the vibrations caressing through his body like a lover's touch, he let his reflexes take over, a feeling of almost merging with the machine. He only had to think of what he wanted and the helicopter responded instantly and willingly. He knew what December felt, looking down at the ground sliding under her feet. The illusion, sitting surrounded by the glass bubble, was like a magic-carpet ride, a dream of flying like Peter Pan, free and weightless in the air. Two chairs and a tiny instrument panel was all that stood between their bodies and the infinity of the Outside.

She wasn't like the other women Berk had taken up before. She wasn't like any woman he'd ever known. *First Violin* dipped and spun, looped and buzzed its way through the dry canyons at breakneck speed. Usually, the women he took up were either pilots themselves, with an affected air of slightly superior amusement at the strange little helicopter, or they were ordinary City girls who tended to scream, either in pretended or real fright.

But December was neither a pilot nor a screamer. She simply hung onto the sides of the passenger seat with clenched hands, more for stability than fright, her body snugly strapped to her seat. She said nothing, smiling faintly, clear blue eyes wide as he twisted the helicopter tortuously through the sky.

Eventually he straightened *First Violin* and cruised down the Ohio River Valley, the Alley Oops a low line of hazy purple hills far in the distance. The river, swollen after the winter rains, was muddy brown. A brief explosion of green grass and flowers would sweep through the hills along the river in a few weeks, a burst of short-lived color that would shrivel and disappear by the beginning of April.

He rode the currents up until they could see the edge of the white Great Desert to the west. Rolling sand dunes shimmered between flat hills, stretching a thousand miles to the feet of the far-off Rockies, cutting the continent in half. Were there domed cities surviving in the West? Was there still life along the Pacific Coastal lands? It was as if the other half of the continent belonged on another planet, lost, unknown. They hovered above the hills slipping down to that vast, barren ocean of sand, gazing wordlessly until he turned the helicopter back towards the City.

He couldn't afford to burn up too much of his fuel allowance on personal flights, but he decided on one more small thrill before he had to take her back to the hangar. He headed straight for the dome cluster at top speed. Set in the distance, surrounded by the emptiness of the Outside, they looked fragile, tiny. But closing in, the faceted domes suddenly grew huge outside the wind bubble.

He veered around the summit of the main dome, *First Violin* a shaky multiple reflection sweeping across the mirrored panes, each triangular panel thirty foot a side. The helicopter looked like a tiny insect next to the giant center dome rising nearly a thousand feet above the rivers. It was a breathtaking instant, the dome looming close enough that Berk could have almost reached out and touched it. Then it rolled away like the monstrous belly of a metallic whale beside them as they whipped past. Instead of a yelp of surprise or fear, or the bored ho-hum a jaded woman pilot might have forced, December craned her neck to look back. That pleased him, somehow.

He flew her down the winding Mong River and hovered above the Duquesne Project. Still under construction, the outline of the monster structure spread out along the curve of the river, sketching promises in the soil.

"I work here," December said, looking down at the project's foundation.

"I know," he said. "which one's yours?"

She smiled sidelong at him, gently mocking. "None of them are *mine*," she said. She pointed down towards one of the arms radiating from the backbone of the structure. "I'm on the crew for subtropical rain forest design, second to the end."

The Duquesne Project was the first truly ambitious project the City had attempted since the domes had been opened, the inhabitants taking their first steps Outside. Jacob Chong, the Councilman for the Energy Department had teamed up with a designer from the Environmental group of Isidra Stachan's Science Department. Combining forces, the Council had developed plans for a massive solar photovoltaic collecting system that could generate enormous amounts of power, enough for a truly independent, self-contained recycling agricultural dome.

"It'll be huge," December explained as she stared down, her eyes glowing. "Interconnected domes two miles long and half a mile wide, with five extended annexes a half mile each. Each arm will have its own PV plant, twice the size of anything we have now, and it'll be bigger than the main dome you just tried to scare the shit out of me by kamikazing."

He coughed, reddened. The helicopter gave a tiny lurch, as if responding intuitively to her pilot's embarrassment. "It'll be the world's biggest PV-powered greenhouse, then," he joked to cover his chagrin.

She chuckled. "The world's *only* PV-powered greenhouse!"

"But why does it have to be so big?" Berk knew the basics. He just didn't know what else to say. If she noticed his nervousness, she was polite enough not to react to it.

"You need that kind of space to re-create all the climatic zones we want. We'll be able to simulate *anything*. High, cold mountain tops. Deep, humid jungles. Prairies."

"Antarctica?" he teased her.

She grimaced dismissively. "All right, *almost* anything. But who cares about a miniature Antarctica?"

"Penguins?"

"Very funny."

He pulled *First Violin* around, adjusting her nose into the wind to hover above the structures. Below, small human figures ambled, some carrying building materials, some climbing the steep curving lattices of the new domes. Tiny workers in huge machines dug a canal through either end of the main building, a diversion for the future water supply. A few of them looked up at the helicopter above, minute hands shading unseen eyes.

"Eventually, the water will be completely self-contained, almost zero percent humidity loss," December was saying. Berk didn't care about the technicalities of the Duquesne Project.

He did, however, enjoy watching her talk. The sound of her voice, the way her hands moved as she spoke fascinated him. That she loved her work, believed in what she was doing, made her eyes shine in a way that made it hard for him to concentrate on her words.

"Then we'll only need the canal for what little we lose to evaporation. Once they're sealed, the interconnecting domes will be big enough to generate spontaneous climatic cycles of their own, independent of the main dome. And when the PV plant goes on line, there'll be enough power to completely control the temperature."

"But what's the point?" he asked, just to keep her talking.

"The point is, we can develop genetically altered seeds tailored for each environment. Grow all the pre-Shift plants we've still got in the Archives' deep storage, mutate the DNA so that they're more resistant to hard radiation, temperature flux, whatever."

He liked that idea. He groped with one of his own. "Then design long-range planes and drop the seeds from the air," he mused. "You could do it. Not with a helicopter, unfortunately, but maybe some kind of glider, use a lightweight engine for takeoff, and maybe a gear chain and flywheels you'd pedal for the generator, let air speed take over once it's airborne. That'd cut down on the weight of battery cells . . ."

"I'd think solar cells would be more practical," she said, eyeing him with interest.

"Yeah, but they don't absorb enough energy for lift."

"What about with Artie supercoils?" she suggested.

For a moment, he blinked, unsure if she were joking with him. Her smile was teasing, but she seemed genuinely interested in the idea. "Room temperature on the Outside is a bit warmer than the inside of a lab," he said.

She smirked. "I'm an Energy engineer," she reminded him, "and a pretty good one, I'd like to think. How hard do you imagine it would be to use a fraction of the PV input to wrap a temp stabilizer around an Artie coil?"

"Not that hard, I guess," he admitted. Her optimism was wonderfully infectious. "You still can't use more than what comes in, though," he said. "There wouldn't be enough photon energy to get the plane off the ground, but maybe . . . put solar panels along glider wings"—he found himself sketching the idea in the air with one hand. She kept looking at him speculatively, and he liked that too—"miniaturize the Arties and put them in series and you'd get better efficiency. You'd have to use fuel and an engine for takeoffs and landings, but switch in flight to solar power, and use thermals when you could, save on how much fuel weight you'd need for multiple landings, and you could have a truly independent long-range aircraft."

"High-flying modern-day Johnny Appleseed." She smiled. "Is that it?"

He grinned foolishly, warmed by her interest, her enthusiasm mingled with his feelings of sexuality. He banked away from the Project, heading back towards the City.

Later, while he still basked in the glow of her attention, he would remember and sketch those ideas, slowly growing them into an obsession. He'd always been good at designing things, and he knew engines, but not that much about fixed-wing. Badgering his best friend, Wy, into taking him up in *The Kid*, he learned to fly fixed-wing, crawled over every inch of *The Kid*'s frame, soaked it into his skin. The urge to impress December, win her approval, gave him restless energy.

Wy had thought him crazy, but eventually he got caught up in Berk's inspiration. They hunkered over multiple beers at Strawberry's, scribbling diagrams on scraps of paper, arguing passionately. Berk's designs were modified and revamped, until he finally, painstakingly transferred to finished detailed plans for a long-range recon glider plane to expensive draft paper, each tiny item precise even down to the recommended screw size. Blueprints still danced in his head when he submitted his plans to Cormack, the last of his idealism not yet extinguished.

In the long months while he waited for Cormack's decision, Berk's concerns were caught up elsewhere, chief among them December Pindar. Cormack eventually shot the plans down as being too farfetched, too expensive, too ambitious. The Council looked them over, sure, maybe in the future they'd be useful. Not now. Besides, Cormack sniggered, what the hell did a helicopter pilot *really* know about fixed-wing, anyway? Forget it, son.

So, Berk would shrug, busy with other matters, and let it go. His wild dreams would fade away, eventually gathering dust in the back of his mind.

But in the first few days of conception, bright and new, they juggled in his libido with the faint perfume of the blond girl beside him, machinery and flesh mixed disturbingly together.

The hills undulated beneath them, the river slicing away around their bend. "Now I'll show you the real difference between a fixed-wing and a helicopter," he said. Her quiet smile intrigued him.

He landed in a tiny patch of clear ground near the top of Mount Washington and shut down the helicopter. The blades snicked slowly to a halt.

"Try getting a fixed-wing plane to land in a spot like this," he said as he jumped out. He trotted around to the passenger side to open her door.

She stepped out and stood with him at the edge of the plateau, looking down the Mong Incline at the massive domes glittering silver below. The land at the top of the plateau sloped down towards the riverbank, cut into terraces and ledges where houses and streets once covered the hillside. A small stand of leafless trees stood in a protected hollow, a flock of speckled starlings flitting from branch to bare branch. In the sudden quiet, the wind whispered through the trees, ice crystals in the air stinging cold cheeks.

December shivered, her face blushed red with the cold. After a moment's hesitation, Berk put his arm around her shoulders, drawing her in close to him to share their body warmth. She turned to look at him, and suddenly kissed him.

Surprised, he kissed her back.

Three months later, he married her.

TWENTY-FIVE

THE HEAT HAD BECOME SO SEVERE THAT EVEN THE flies were dying.

During the height of the day, the surviving insects ceased their activity, hiding in any shadows they could find to escape the relentless summer sun. They swarmed in from outside, the searing heat leaching any trace of humidity from the air. They crawled on Berk's and Sadonya's skin, insistently creeping towards eyes and the corners of their mouths, attracted by the moisture.

The two of them lay immobile, the air motionless, stifling. Breathing it felt like hot ash being dragged inside Berk's lungs. His nose, completely desiccated, began bleeding. He tried panting, his mouth open. Eventually, his tongue felt like fur and his lips cracked. Dehydrated, he didn't even seem to sweat much anymore, his skin gray and flaking. His head ached continually and his eyes felt as if they had somehow grown too large for their sockets.

Sadonya had abandoned the bed altogether, sleeping on the cooler, bare floor despite whatever bugs might crawl there in the night. She no longer kept the door shut against Mouse's prying, the cross-breeze too precious. She and Berk spent most of the time dozing, waiting for the relentless heat to break.

Nothing moved during the day when the sun baked the life out of the dust of the city. The free zone market had closed shop, the evenings too hot for commerce. Even the rats had burrowed deep into the bowels of the ruins, dormant. Sadonya brought out meat she'd preserved, slowly baked into thin strips of rat jerky. It was undeniably too hot for nuking any fresh maindish.

The ripening plants in the atrium began to wilt. The distilleries couldn't produce enough moisture, and the skylight greenhouse was radiating too much heat through the glass. Berk had found a cache of ancient bed linens and bath towels, still folded neatly in their storage cupboard, although they tended to crumble if they weren't handled with excruciating care. He took them up on the roof, after the sun had set, the sky still an electric sizzling blue, and spread them as best he could over the glass roof to filter the light.

He had taken the splint off his arm; the bones had knit and the puckered scar was fading from angry red to sullen pink. He still wore it whenever Mouse's watchdogs were skulking through the corridors of Tom'n Jeff's, but now they had taken to coming only at night, vanishing before the sky had turned from pale copper to scorching white blue. Even Mouse didn't seem to be in such a hurry at the moment.

Which, Berk hoped, would last until after the worst of the summer. Because he already knew there was no solution to his and Sadonya's predicament . . . because he'd already figured out his only option. What do you do when you're stranded, and the place you're in is slowly killing you? When there're three hundred miles of brutal desert and mountain between you and home? When no one is going to come to your rescue? Well . . .

. . . you walk.

First, of course, he needed to get out of the city, and for that he needed Sadonya, at least as far as the other side of the Schuylkill River. He doubted she'd be willing to escort him across hostile union territories, especially if they were being hunted.

Late at night, when the temperature had dropped slightly, after they had used up whatever meager energy they had left slowly pedaling the fans to take the edge off the shimmering daytime heat, he told her stories in the dark. Stripped naked, leaning against the wall with his limbs splayed out, he made up bedtime stories for little girls, even psychotic little girls like Sadonya, just to pass the hellish days.

Once upon a time, he'd tell her, there was a fabulous domed City where green meadows peppered with little white and yellow daisies grew under trees practically dripping with juicy sweet fruit, where it was cool, even in the middle of summer, and warm in the worst of the winter. There were no bugs creeping up the walls, and no flies sucking the moisture from your eyes. There were no union bosses there making ravs against rival groups, nobody had to frag anyone, and every woman could choose who she wanted to mark. Water was plentiful, fountains and pools on every street corner, pumped directly into people's homes clean and fresh to drink, no one had to endure foul water distilled from piss and boiled to kill the breeding microbes infecting them with constant dysentery. Nobody ate rats, because there were lots of different kinds of meat, chicken and duck, lamb and goat, hundred species of fish. Everybody ate good food, as much as they wanted, whenever they wanted. The people were always healthy, and everyone loved each other. They all lived happily ever after.

He even started believing it himself.

They had both managed to drop off to a fitful sleep, the tepid night breeze drifting through the decaying curtains. At first, Berk didn't know what woke him. His eyes opened, seeing nothing in the lightless room. He turned his head at the sound of a faint scraping, groggily puzzled.

A second later, something smashed down against his side, a steel bar slamming into his sleep-stunned body. Another blow clipped him on the side of the head; black stars exploded in his eyes.

He half rolled, half fell to out of the bed, hearing the grunt of the shadow as it smashed the bar into the mattress.

Sadonya? The ancient bed frame shuddered, cracked. Legs collapsing, the bed fell on Berk's terrified body. *Why?*

No, it couldn't be, because he could hear Sadonya screaming furiously as another shadow launched itself against the skulking figure standing over him, upraised metal glinting dimly. He knew it must be Mouse, coming to frag them both.

Must have figured out he'd been lying.

Damn.

In the nearly total darkness he scrambled away as the two shadows grappled, twisting and clawing, whirling past Berk and into Sadonya's table, somewhere very far across the room. He crawled into a corner, and felt warm blood trickling down his side. Searing pain in his chest made it hard to breathe. He blinked. How did the blood get in his eyes? He curled up as the two shadows reeled past him, slamming against the wall, bouncing away again like billiard balls. For a moment, Berk thought he was going to throw up, his face flushed cold, ears prickling in sudden heat. His head buzzed, spinning. Sound was painful and he had trouble focusing his eyes.

Broken glass tinkled gaily, strange music to accompany the silhouetted dancers spinning crazily, heavy breathing no more than a fine line between lust and terror. They pirouetted against a curtain, ripping it from the window, dim light trickling in as they whirled away into the darkness of the room.

"You motherfuck," he heard Sadonya say, her words as sharp as crystal wind chimes, slow and clear, oddly out of place. A high-pitched giggle answered her. He'd heard it before, but he couldn't remember, couldn't remember.

"Funtime!" a thickened, strangulated voice said in the dark. "Jess a little funtime, l'il bitch."

He heard Sadonya cry out in pain, a scream of fury that ended in a rasping, sliding noise, a sudden wet gurgle and the sound of a body thumping to the floor.

Then it was quiet.

His heart hammered against his eyes, straining to see in the dark.

"*Berk*," he heard her say, and almost wept in relief.

"Yeah," he said. "I'm okay . . . I think."

Click-click-click.

The sudden glare of the alcohol lighter hurt his eyes, the shaking flame all he could see for a moment. Sadonya lit the candle and set it on the floor. The low table, along with most of her equipment, had been smashed, herbs and broken bottles and small ratskin pouches scattered around the floor lying in glimmering pools of spilled liquids.

A body lay on the floor, limbs contorted. A puddle of dark red blood seeped out from underneath it.

It wasn't Mouse. Too bad.

It was Third.

Then the body moved, rolling to one side as it whimpered. The eyes opened, and Berk stared into the face of a scared child. The boy gazed back, stunned, tears dribbling down cheeks of a too young face.

"He's still alive," Berk said, alarmed. He started crawling towards the boy, unsure of what exactly he intended to do once he got there. He had to help, there had to be *something* he could do.

In two strides, Sadonya reached Third. She kicked the boy onto his back, squinting down at him in the flickering candlelight. She looked around the room, searching; her head snapped to one side, the other, then down again at Third. Her eyes were impassive, dead. Berk recognized that look.

Third moaned. Before Berk could reach him, Sadonya had grabbed the boy under the arms, dragging him along the floor, leaving a trail of slick blood glistening like the slime of a garden snail. Third's legs flopped uselessly. His face twisted from frightened vulnerability into animal fury. Berk realized at the same moment as the boy what Sadonya intended.

"*Sadonya!*"

Third clawed, whipping his arms behind him, battling futilely with Sadonya as she grunted and jerked the boy's injured body toward the window. Berk scrambled towards them, scuttling on hands and knees frantically.

"*For God's sake, he's still alive!*"

She had Third half over the low sill, the boy's hands gripping the ledge desperately. She hesitated, then calmly, deliberately spat into Third's face before she kneed him hard in the crotch, driving his body up over the edge. Crippled legs slid over the side, the boy's own weight wrenching his hands from the sill.

There was a long second, when time stood still, frozen silent. Berk crouched on all fours with his mouth open in soundless horror.

Then the body crashed into the street below, a sickening wet thud crunching against piles of debris. Sadonya peered down, a hazy outline against the window, then turned towards Berk, her face a weirdly shadowed blank in the candlelight.

"No more, he not," she said, thin satisfaction in her voice. Then she slid down to sit on the floor, breathing hard. "Ah, shit," she added calmly. "We fucked damnsure now."

Berk rose from hands and knees to sit cross-legged on the dirty floor. "Then why'd you kill him?" he asked. Numbness was setting in on one side of his face. Touching it gingerly, he felt drying blood along his swollen cheek, a rip in the top of his ear throbbing.

Sadonya stared at him. "You don' understand a thing, do you, outatown man?" she said scornfully. "*Think*. How Third get by Mouse's misters, get up in here, huh? He sneak tiptoe by them? How come nobody come running quicktime all this noise?"

"I don't know," he said dully.

She grimaced. "Because they *dead*, is why." She shook her head at him, exasperated. "An' if they dead, it 'cause Third, he don' care about stigating a rav. How come? Make sense to you?"

"No," he said, exploring the torn edges of his ear.

"You stupid damnsure. Maybe he hit y'skull too hard. Third come here by ownsum, it 'cause nobody wanna be with him. It 'cause he marked alltime dead. You get it now?"

Yeah. His stomach sank. He got it. "Squeeze is dead," he said.

"First smart thing you say," she said. "Time we go."

She got to her feet, and began stuffing things into her bag, picking her way carefully in bare feet through the broken glass shattered over the floor. She found Third's double-edged knife, wiped the blade with her cloak, the boy's blood a smear of black.

"What are you talking about? 'Time we go'?"

"Don' play no fun with me," she said, not bothering to look up at him as she hurriedly sorted through the littered floor. "You chat chat alltime 'bout this great place you from. I think eye dees same as you, I know we fucked we stay here. I know you need me get you out, I know you been pulling on my head."

She squatted in the wreckage for a moment, and glared at him, her eyes burning. "You think alltime I stupid. You act like I some kinda headsick baby buck, you bigshot outatown brain. I pastime thinkin' too. I think you lie to Mouse, you lie to me, you fuckin' lie bout fissit your flying thing."

He didn't trust himself to speak.

"I think maybe nowtime we make nother new deal. Same like the old. I help you, you help me." She mocked him, her voice hard. "I take you Outside, you take me back this fancy City." She slipped her ratskin leggings on, hefted her bag to her shoulder and grabbed her cloak. "We go," she said firmly. "Now."

"Sadonya," he said, "you don't understand." Her face clouded in anger. "You're not stupid," he added quickly. "I'm not saying that. You just don't understand how *far* it is!"

"You wanna stay here, get fragged quicktime stead?"

"No," he agreed. "But we can't charge out the door just like that. It'll take days and days, a lot of days to walk to the City. We need food, water. It's across a goddamned *desert*, Sadonya!" He gestured frantically at his naked body. "It's the middle of the summer! We'll be nuked damnfine crispy shorttime without some protection from the sun. *You* get it now?"

"Yeah," she said reluctantly.

"How much time do we have before Mouse comes?" he said, thinking fast.

She shrugged. "Don' know. 'Fore sun is up."

He struggled into his pants, fingers clumsy with dread. His shirt was gone, torn to rags to bind his broken ribs. "Shit," he cursed quietly. "I'm going to fry with only this."

She looked thoughtful. "You wait," she said, and slid quietly out of the room.

His feet had swollen too large for his boots, but he slipped on his socks. He had stripped the moldy blanket from the bed trying to figure out how he could use it, when she returned. She handed him a mass of ratskins sewn into a sack, and a cloak similar to hers. "They my mama's," she said simply. "Kinda old, but they still kay. You too big for her leggins, though, I leave it."

"Thanks," he said, touched. He ripped the blanket in half, handing her a piece. "You'll need this to wrap your head in."

He tied the laces of his boots together and hung them around his neck. Lifting up the broken bed, he retrieved his precious can of oil. "*Now* we go."

She stopped in the doorway, and looked back. "Wait." Lifting the bar, she smashed his pedal fan, pieces flying off. He winced. She turned and demolished her own in a few blows. "Don' leave nothin' useful for Mouse."

He had to agree. "You go get as much water out of the stills as you can carry. I'll be down in the garden."

She'd been right about Mouse's boys. Third had killed two of them before they could even react, bellies ripped open. Their faces still held wide-eyed expressions of astonishment. The last of the trio had almost made it to the revolving door before Third had crushed his skull. Berk ignored the corpses as he systematically stripped the garden, pulling up half-grown potatoes, ripping green bean pods by the handful and stuffing them into the sack.

Sadonya hurried down the stairway, cans of water thunking together in her own sack. She also began jerking whole plants from her mysterious herbal plot, pushing them, roots and all, into her already bulging bag.

"You can't carry all that," Berk hissed, afraid of unseen assailants lurking in the shadows. "Leave it. It's just junk!"

She pointed to the can of oil resting on the stone curb. "You takin' that shit?"

He let it go. His sack was nearly full. He stuffed the can of oil in and slung the bag across his shoulder. "Let's go." Violently, she shook her head, and began pulling up every remaining plant in reach, throwing them across the atrium. "What are you doing?"

"*Nothin'* for Mouse," she panted, crab-walking down the aisles, arms windmilling destruction. "We never comin' back here, Berk. We leave fuckin' Mouse *nothin'*."

He didn't attempt to argue with her; instead he helped her demolish his lovingly tended, painstakingly grown garden. He was surprised to find he was crying.

Sadonya darted up to the overhead skywalk, draining the last of the water from the still. With a laboring grunt, she pushed it over the edge. It tumbled down, impacting into the garden with a muffled explosion of broken glass and metal.

"Now we go," she said in the sudden quiet.

She led him through the lightless tunnels buried under Tom'n Jeff's, squeezing past hidden spaces leading down corridors he hadn't seen before.

They came up out of the tunnels into the ruins of a building that had fallen long ago, weeds crisped in the summer sun, wilted in the cracks of piled brick. Twisted columns of steel beams speared into the ground. It would be hours before the sun rose, but there was enough ambient light that he could make out blue shadows, looming larger and more ominous in the silent dark.

Sadonya pressed her hand against his mouth, a clear signal he didn't need repeated.

They scrambled as quietly as they could down the mounds of rubble to the street below. She hugged the sides, staying in the shadows of a maze of little streets, small red-bricked houses standing in empty dormer-windowed rows. Behind them rose the blind façade of the tall buildings, bleak against the dark sky.

His legs were becoming cramped from running bent, scuffling along to keep his noise to a minimum. At first, he'd looked around as they ran, trying to keep his bearings. They ran past a turreted building, a tiny out-of-place castle, rows of identical square houses facing narrow alleys, squat buildings draped with the torn lace of fire escapes.

She stopped, pressing up against a doorway, breathing shallowly. There was enough light to see her fingers flashing a quick signal at him. When he shook his head, she grimaced, then snapped her hand in disgust. He knew without needing to understand the hand language that it meant *Nevermind*.

She led him along the small streets, winding farther away from the center, turning corners hunched over and trotting so quickly he lost his sense of direction. North? South? What difference did it make to him? Even if he'd dared to speak in the silence, he couldn't have made use of the information. He simply had to trust her, follow her wherever she was headed.

The towering highrises were mostly behind them, off to his right, and his sense of direction kicked in again. They had taken an elliptical path, heading now northwest, toward the Schuylkill. They veered again, straight north, running in earnest. Sadonya's bare feet slapped faintly against the street, Berk's lungs burning as he ran behind her. Four marble eagles, wings swept back from their breasts, tips brushing against a low pillar of stone, guarded the corners of a bridge. Lions' faces peered snarling from the stone. The center span of the bridge had fallen into the water, cutting off access to the far bank of the river.

Sadonya turned back towards the center of the city, racing down a street leading to the blocks of glass towers, a needle-tipped skyscraper outlined in blue against a slowly lightening sky. She was headed straight back into Mouse's territory. Berk heard a muffled sound in the distance, astonished when he realized it was a dog barking. A large dog. Two large dogs.

He ran to catch up with her, grabbing one arm and turning her so that she could see his questioning face. She shook her head.

Hurry, hurry.

They ran one block and Sadonya popped down into a hole

in the ground, like a rabbit into hiding. On his own he would have missed the old subway entrance covered with bricks, wasted lumber, shattered remnants of a dead city. Concrete steps vanished into coal-black depths. He stumbled down into the lightless station, jumping when her hand closed around his wrist. She pressed him against a wall, and they froze, listening.

Angry disembodied voices echoed through the tunnels, the patter of feet amplified in the dark. Holding tightly to his wrist, she groped along the wall, stopped, and bent close to him. "Feel up here with your hand. Something?" she whispered in his ear.

His fingers spasmed up the length of the wall, groping blindly until he felt a jagged opening a foot above his head, a slight bitter wind against his fingertips.

"Lift me up, then you come," Sadonya directed.

He boosted her up into the hole, then pulled himself in after her. He scooted along on hands and knees until her feet in his face stopped him.

"Shh."

He lay down in the cramped passageway, the smell of rancid urine thick in his nose. Rat droppings ground under his arms and hips. Something squeaked in front of them, a quick scrabble of tiny claws. A light outside in the tunnel flickered, voices louder. On a platform on the opposite side, a boy with a torch sprinted by, his painted face distorted in its wavering yellow light. The soft jingle of trinkets sewn onto his clothes vanished into the darkness along with his light.

She kicked him and he hunched behind her, crawling along the tight space after her, dragging his sack beside him. The passageway branched, and she turned right, the small sound of her breathing all that guided him.

It seemed to go on for miles, the occasional sound of muffled voices through the pipes spurring him to baby-crawl faster, his knees and palms scraped raw. Somewhere, he lost his boots. In several places, he had to squeeze through crushed openings, his shoulders and chest nearly too wide to fit. Once he had to remove part of the load from his sack to thrust it through, slither after it, sweating, and repack the bag on the other side. Fear and claustrophobia closed in around him until he thought he would scream, not caring if he was caught and killed.

He nearly fell through the uneven hole punched through the passageway. It opened into a deeper, wider conduit, smooth round walls cool in the blackness.

A rumbling sound grew louder; then they were close enough to hear words, a man singing in a rough, low voice. A light appeared around the bend. Sadonya thrust her feet and legs through, and jumped out, splashing. The singing stopped. A dog barked, close by.

Berk pushed himself to the edge of the opening, staring out. Sadonya stood calf-deep in water, her fingers flickering silently as she conversed with an old man in a narrow, flat-bottomed boat. The man glanced up at Berk, and Berk saw he wasn't that old, more his own age.

His skin was chalk-white. Stringy wisps of ivory hair floated past his shoulders. Toothless and skinny, his long, thin limbs wasted, he wore nothing but a dirty length of cloth wrapped around his hips, secured to his waist by a rope belt, and a blue leather cap. The man's eyes glittered red in the dim light, staring steadily at Berk under the shiny bill of the cap, a silver badge fastened to its peaked crown. Two Dobermans sat expectantly at the prow of the boat, long tongues hanging over sharp white teeth as they panted, watching him.

Berk lowered himself down cautiously, dropping the last few feet into the black water. The bottom was slippery with soft mud, fuzzy algae growth fertilized by decomposing rat, dog, and, quite likely, albino human shit. It squished between his toes. A lantern hung several feet above the water, suspended from a post on the curved prow of the boat. Golden lights sparkled in the black water.

Sadonya looked around. "This Ferryman. He call own-sum Charon. He don't talk same as me."

"Bullshit," Charon said. "Same as you."

His fingers moved, and Sadonya grinned. "Yeah," she snorted. "Kay, same as me."

"Ply twosum across the wilds of damnfine Styx?" Charon

demanded, staring at Berk unblinkingly with blood-red irises. "Be thou fuckin' lost souls, or mere wandering turds along the night, all pay up ante first, or no go, let Cerberus champ you skinny ass quicktime." The albino laughed, a warbling mad sound that the two dogs picked up, howling like wolves, muzzles in the air as they voiced their opinions.

The water was ice-cold, amazing Berk at how quickly he chilled after months of broiling heat. He stood, shivering and miserable, watching Charon warily.

"Damnsure," Sadonya said. "What you want?"

"What you got?"

"Maindish?" she suggested.

"Awww, shit." The albino pulled a disappointed face. "Lotsa maindish dwell deep within the bowels of the river Styx," he said. "Cerberus champ me quicktime four-legged fucks, get me fish offa pole. Toads ofttimes alight the night seasons. Sometimes Cerberus, they get me a juicy fat baby buck, mmm-mmm finger-lickin' good. We eat jess fine. Don't need maindish." He tsked. "Spose you stay here, wasting amongst the gloomy doom for a hundred years of purgative." The man spoke with an affected lilt to his garbled words, obviously proud of the nonsense he spouted.

"Make you a bane?"

Charon sat down on the plank in the center of his little boat and stroked the chisel head of one Doberman. Whining neurotically, the other baby-killing dog pawed his master's thigh insistently, begging to be scratched. "What kinda bane?"

Sadonya shrugged. "What you want?"

"Something that sing along the blood until the sands of all time are extruded across the shores of far-flung stars in the churlish heavens. Make me feel good forever, damnfine."

"That *im*possible, Ferryman," she said flatly.

He shrugged. "I got Eel come make me banes when I want."

"Eel not me. Eel got no taste. I best cook ever be, Ferryman, damnsure you hear from all the unions."

Berk longed desperately to get out of the slimy water and into the Ferryman's boat. He imagined he could feel tiny unseen mouths sucking at his flesh under the glimmering black surface of the water.

"Eel not beatin' feet outatown, neither, Mouse breathin' fire he so mad. He frag your sorrowful ass, then Eel be best cook ever be, fuckin' quicktime, eyah?" the albino said cheerfully.

"What do you want, then?" Berk snapped. "If we've got it, we'll give it to you." Sadonya turned to stare at him angrily. "We haven't got time enough to dicker around on a price."

The albino looked sad. "Don' get lotta company," he said. "I perfer bitta civil spice to negotiations." He brightened. "But I also perseptic nuff to know when a man's inna hurry. I'll settle for the complete works of Homer. Y'got that?" He pursed his lips, and added, "In Greek, prefabrically."

Berk's mouth dropped, and he stared at the insane albino uncomprehendingly. Sadonya elbowed him roughly, purposely, as she turned and rummaged through her bag.

"Jess so happen," she said, and smiled at Berk.

She pulled a battered pre-Shift book out of the sack, its pages warped and brittle. The gold print had long worn away from the cover, but the letters were still pressed into the leather-covered boards. *Physician's Desk Reference, Volume III, Seventy-third Edition*, it read.

She handed it to the Ferryman, who promptly flipped through the pages. He frowned. "This not in Greek," he complained.

"No," she said. "This much better. It older even than Greek."

The Ferryman glanced up, his red-irised eyes widening. "Not . . . Minny Ocean?"

"Damnfine," she agreed.

He smiled, a toothless black hole in his pasty white skin. "That be fine," he said. He dumped the book unceremoniously into the bottom of his boat, and pushed the dogs away to make room. They sniffed the pages that were slowly curling as the book soaked up the water sloshing in the bilge. "I shall ply the way transvestite the watery path of murky hells, damnquick, for Mouse he be comin' down the barrel Mach Five."

Sadonya slung her bag into the boat, and clambered over the side, her feet and ankles covered with ink-black ooze. Berk scrambled in after her, the boat rocking gently.

The Ferryman kicked the shallow boat away from the side of the wall, poling it through the low tunnel lit only by his lantern swinging from the prow. Wet curtains of fungal growth hanging from the vaulted ceiling brushed Berk's face. Condensation dripped like rain. The Ferryman began singing, a hoarse voice enthusiastically bellowing unintelligible lyrics, the dank tunnel walls echoing weirdly. The two dogs howled. Grinning as if she were on an afternoon's pleasure outing, Sadonya crouched in the bow of the boat, arms wrapped around her knees.

"Used to be three, y'know," the Ferryman said to Berk, suddenly breaking off his tune.

"Three what?"

"Three dogs. Cerberus sposed to got three heads, but one dog, he get real sick, stomach swell up, he whimpering all-time like a champed up baby buck. He died. Make me sad, cry all day long." The Ferryman looked distraught, standing motionless as the boat drifted aimlessly. His pale red eyes stared off in the lightless distance, pole dangling limply in his hands.

Berk didn't know quite how to respond. "I'm sorry," he said.

The Ferryman suddenly grinned. "It 'kay," he said. "We nuke him up, he taste damngood. Eat him all day long, we near splode."

Berk stared at him uncomprehendingly.

Sadonya laughed from the prow, and lay down, resting against her sack. "You funny, Ferryman," she said appreciatively.

"Everyone's a comedian in Hades," he said, and bowed, the boat rocking precipitously. He reached into the hidden folds of his loincloth, his hand working as if he were masturbating, then extracted something in his clenched fist. He offered it to Sadonya. "Magic," he said.

Mystified, she held out one hand. He placed a tiny albino frog in her palm, its neck fluttering for a moment behind bulging red eyes before it leapt into the air. She squealed as it splashed into the water, golden circles glittering on the ripples. The two dogs whined, writhing around Charon's legs, sniffing at Berk with hot dog-smell breath. The Ferryman began poling again, howling his monotone song.

I've died, Berk decided. I've died and this is hell. He would be stuck here, caught in an underground tunnel with a homicidal girl and an insane albino with killer dogs, forever.

But a moment later, the Ferryman pulled up against the subway platform, water lapping over the edges. "Please watch you damnstep as you exit the train," he exhorted, his words echoing in the tunnel, his gaze fastened on the ceiling. "No pushing, shoving, or horseplay permitted in the cars, frag you ass you do. Present you fuckin' ticket at the boarding gate, thank you for riding Septa, have a nice day!"

TWENTY-SIX

July 6-7, 2242

THEY WORKED THEIR WAY UP OUT OF THE TRAIN tunnel, climbing smashed steps when they could, crawling through lightless ducts, walking nearly upright through a maze of empty conduits Berk suspected were part of an ancient sewage system. Several times they stopped, listening, and heard only the faint rustle or squeaking of hidden rats. Berk's eyes made out little in the deep gloom as he stumbled over loose bricks and debris littering the curved floor of the channel. The sudden light hurt his eyes as they emerged blinking into a vast, abandoned station. Except for the Ferryman, the trains that had once terminated here were cut off from the city center by the river.

Huge pillars held up only open sky, the roof of the station collapsed. A massive bronze angel had toppled from a pillar to the floor, lying on its back in the wreckage with broken wings. The angel still tenderly cradled a sleeping man in its stiff arms. Sadonya didn't even glance at the statue as she scurried out the door, into the early morning sunlight. Somewhere in the underground tunnels, she had lost her iron bar. Berk smiled thinly. Good.

"Think Ferryman'll tell Mouse where we've gone?" he

asked, crouched in the early morning shadow of the station, resting to catch his breath.

She shook her head. "Not yet, but venchully. He not asked, he don' say. Mouse most like think we hiding inside. It too crazy be running in the open. Crisp to death. Take him time figure it out." She glanced at him, her eyes hard. "But he will, quicktime sure. 'Kay, outatown man," she said, "I done my share. Now you do yours."

He wanted nothing more than to put as much distance between them and the Filly before they had to find shelter out of the sun and wait for evening. He had lost the map in *First Violin*, but it was simple enough to follow the old road bordering the river.

While part of him rejoiced at finally breaking away, a sense of purpose restored, he was frightened. Fry to death was right; this was insane. He was never going to make it back on foot, and he'd dragged this girl along with him into certain death. They walked briskly, expending far more energy than either of them could afford. He forced himself to slow down, convinced that not even Mouse would chase them this far outside his union territories. He hoped.

But at the moment, he was too busy to worry about it. They were still following the river when they stopped in the ruins of a small suburban community overgrown with weeds and inhabited by wild birds. The roof of one house was still intact, more or less, and they sheltered there, out of the blinding heat, sleeping fitfully. Berk started awake at every sound, heart pounding. When he glanced at Sadonya, she was peacefully snoring, almost smiling in her dreams.

The sudden whir of tiny beating wings snapped his eyes open. Insects hummed in the air, stirring on the breeze as the evening grew. "Let's go," he said as he shook Sadonya awake.

He made her drink as much as she could from the water she'd brought along, drinking himself until his stomach ached. Then he waded into the river to refill the water cans. It felt good, glorious to be in clean water, and he dunked his head, soaking the torn blanket he'd wrapped his head in, as well as his pants and cloak. He shook the water from his eyes, grinning.

"You should too, Sadonya," he said. "This road turns away from the river soon, and you'll need to stay as cool as you can."

Gingerly, she stepped in the water. When it came up to her hips, he tried dunking her playfully. She squealed in real fright, clawing at him as she scrambled back to the safety of the shore. It was, he realized, the first time she'd ever been in that much open water. She had never known a bath or a shower in her life. Glaring at him, water dripping from her sodden, matted hair, he felt pity and remorse. He didn't bother with apologizing, but his momentary happiness vanished completely.

They marched down the road in the waning light without speaking. By nightfall, the river turned to cut its way through the remnants of a small town, while the road veered away into the desert. They stopped a last time to replenish their water.

"How come we don' jess keep followin' the river?" Sadonya complained. They drank as much as they could again, splashing water on themselves. The moonlight cast a wan, grudging light, just enough to see by.

"Because it doesn't go where we want to go," Berk said.

She packed the water cans away in her bags as he filled them.

"How come we can't stay here, then?" she said after a long moment. He turned to stare at her. "We got water, we gotta place outta the sun, damnsure lotta maindish scurrying round, no way Mouse come to frag us way out here." She shrugged. "I like it."

"Then you stay here if you want to," he said hotly. "Maybe Rangers won't get you. Maybe the sun won't kill you. But I'd rather die than stay here, Sadonya. I'd rather die."

He shouldered his bag, and marched down the road without looking back. For a moment, he hoped she *would* stay behind. It would be easier and quicker without her, and he was damnsure she could take care of her ownsum. He didn't bother to slow down when he heard the quick patter of feet as she ran to catch up with him, her water-cans clinking.

Actually, he thought, hating himself for it, what she said made good sense. It was foolish to try crossing the desert in the middle of the summer. They should have set up a camp along the riverbank, settled down to wait out the worst of the hot weather.

But, he argued with himself, if they made twenty miles a day, actually a night, sheltering where they could out of the sun during the day to sleep, they could make the Twin Tunnels in a week, and wait out the summer there. Maybe a pilot would make a run. If not, they could walk the rest of the way in the cool of the late autumn, and be home in another week. All they had to do was survive the first week.

No problem.

The road cut through a cemetery, the shell of a church hunkered on the hill in the moonlight like a bad omen. They turned away from the river, following the road past another small, ruined town, through a snarl of interconnecting roads, picking their way over the remains of fallen overpasses, and out into the desert.

After another mile, Sadonya began complaining. "I gettin' bumps on my feet, they hurtin'," she whined. "I tired now, less stop and rest."

"We got a long, long way, Sadonya," he said. "Best to keep going while we're still strong."

She glared, and dumped her sack on the road, sitting down abruptly. "I restin'," she said defiantly.

"Fine," he said. "Catch up with me later, then, I don't care." This time there were no hurrying footsteps behind him. He glanced back over his shoulder, seeing her only as a shapeless dark lump on the roadbed in the pale light. He started down over the rise of a hill, Sadonya disappearing behind him.

A canopy of stars overhead winked, millions of them sprinkled through the clear night sky. He watched a meteorite curve gracefully towards the horizon—a blink and it was gone. Night insects chirruped. After a while, his resolution wavered. He stopped, sitting in the road to wait for her. Five minutes later, she trudged over the low hill.

She stomped past him. "You a real fuck, outatown man," she said angrily as she passed him.

He shook his head, got to his feet and followed her.

He had wanted to walk throughout the night, as quickly as they could, but by midnight he was exhausted. They sheltered in an old golf clubhouse, the once green courseway buried under the desert dust. Rusted golf clubs still neatly lined the racks, old lounge furniture wasted away to genteel corpses. Tiny lizards scrabbled through cracks in the walls, lidless eyes in their triangular heads examining the two invaders before their scaly bodies whipped around and vanished. Part of the internal structure of the building had collapsed, but the roof was still intact. It was cool inside the old building and by morning, Berk decided to spend the day resting, out of the sun.

They slept restlessly, the sun slowly heating the day. A musty earth smell permeated the old building, an odor Berk didn't recognize but rather liked. He lay on the floor curled up with his bag under his head, drowsily watching as Sadonya poked, half curious and half angry, at the blisters on her feet. She made herself a salve from the supplies she'd brought along, not bothering to offer Berk any for the blisters he'd developed as well, his socks quickly unravelling. He was damnsure not going to ask her for any of it, though, screw her. He turned over on his other side, back to her.

Conserving their food, they chewed on small bits of dry rat jerky, and sipped at their water carefully. At sunset, he was roused by a sudden noise reverberating in the roof, the throbbing beat of hundreds of wings. He jumped to his feet, nervously crouched over as he searched for the source, then watched in open-mouthed wonder as thousands of tiny black bats swept down from the high ceiling, out of an open window overhead, dainty black wings flitting in the pale red twilight. He laughed at himself.

He felt rested, stronger. Sadonya's blisters had shriveled, almost completely healed. For a brief moment, Berk regretted his stubborn pride, but still he couldn't bring himself to ask her for the favor.

The desert had both destroyed and preserved the land along the old auto route. The road itself had been buried in drifting sand in places, depressions in the hills the only shadow of its existence. The tops of ancient tombstones in half-buried rows neatly lined cemeteries along the roadside, pallid white ghosts in the shadowy night. A lonely post office waited at the top of a hill, a dried-out, preserved husk of a vanished past.

The clumps of houses along the road petered out after a few short miles. They trudged along the open, naked road for mile after mile without speaking, the bare slap of feet and dull clank of water cans the only sound. Berk was pleased at first with the speed they were able to go, despite Sadonya's constant complaints. But the night was too brief, and as the sun began to pink across the horizon behind them, he realized they had a problem.

They had to find shelter out of the sun, soon.

Small roads split off from the main highway, leading temptingly towards unknown, invisible towns, right over the hill, just out of sight *there*, or maybe *there*. Without his map, Berk couldn't tell exactly where they were, or how far away, and it was an effort not to be seduced by the lure of secondary roads turning away from the old Route 76.

But when the sun finally muscled its way over the horizon, heat blasting against their backs, Berk's worry gave way to dull panic. He nearly cried in relief as the road passed through an old toll barrier.

It wasn't much. The roofs of the toll booths were gone, glass shattered out of the windows, leaving not much more than chest-high, topless boxes. Berk huddled against one wall of a rubble-floored booth, Sadonya preferring her own. They had to shift positions as the sun climbed, staying in the shadows, dozing until a laser-hot streak of sunlight creeping into the shade burned them awake.

Berk felt lethargic in the dizzyingly fierce heat, his head pounding feverishly. His mouth was dry, lips cracked, but even half-mad with thirst, he willed himself to conserve their sparse water supply. He woke as his legs started burning, the midafternoon sun beating straight down, eradicating any useful shade. He unwound the torn blanket from his head, and draped it from one low wall to form a makeshift tent. With Sadonya's half, he thought, they could huddle underneath until the worst of the killing heat was over. Then he noticed his pack was open.

His water cans were missing.

He walked around the side of the nearest booth to find Sadonya finishing a can of water. Another empty can lay next to her.

"You're drinking all the water!" He gasped, stunned and horrified.

She wiped her mouth with the back of her hand, staring at him without the slightest remorse. "I thirsty," she said reasonably. "Y'*sposed* drink water when y'thirsty."

"You bitch," he breathed. "You stupid little bitch."

He reached down and jerked her bag away from her, turning it upside down and shaking out the contents roughly.

"Hey!" she yelled. "What you doin'?"

Bundles of dried plants, tiny shriveled potatoes, ratleather pouches spilled out onto the cracked asphalt roadway, along with five more empty water cans. There were only three left. She scrabbled on her hands and knees in the sand, grabbing at her supplies. White powder spilled out from a burst pouch, looking oddly clean against the heat-cracked roadtop.

For a moment, he couldn't think, couldn't react, his muscles pulling in every direction, vibrating in fury. Then he kicked the kneeling girl, sending her sprawling.

She landed on her back, arms splayed, knees drawn up. She blinked in the sudden sun, more bewildered than hurt. He saw her eyes squinting in the light, a moment before he jumped on her.

A part of his mind was surprised, shocked, as he started beating her, operating rationally somewhere behind him. It was the raging animal part that saw the flicker of steel, caught her wrist as she brought the knife up. He felt the blade graze his cheek, narrowly missing his eye, before he punched her in the face. He slammed her knife arm down against the ground, once, twice. The knife spun glittering away. This was insane, he knew it. Neither of them had the energy to spare. He punched down, all his strength surging out his fists as he pummeled her chest, her face, her arms, legs, back.

Stop this! Stop! Stop!

She had curled into a ball, shielding her face and stomach from his fists, grunting under the blows. The fury switched off like a light burned out, his arms suddenly aching, leaden. He fell back, sitting down woodenly on the roadway, not caring that the sun was searing his exposed flesh. She huddled, weeping.

He watched her as she cried, stupefied. Then he got to his feet painfully and picked up the knife where it had fallen. He tucked it into the waistband of his pants, poking the blade through the cloth in a makeshift sheath. Collecting the scattered contents of her bag, he dropped them one by one into the sack. She watched him pack the three remaining water cans into his own sack, wordlessly.

She had moved out of the sun, sitting in the shade, her tears drying on her cheeks. Her eyes followed him, pure hatred in her face. He didn't care. When he finished picking up her things, he tossed the sack into her lap.

"I gonna kill you, outatown man," she said softly. "Damn-sure."

He almost laughed. "You'd be doing me a favor, Sadonya," he said, his voice toneless. "You've just killed us both already."

Her eyes narrowed, uncomprehending.

"We don't have enough water now to make it across the desert."

"We still got water. This some big fuckin' desert we can't walk cross damnquick," she said sarcastically. She didn't believe him.

"Yes," he agreed. He rubbed his eyes with a thumb and forefinger, tired, very tired. "It's some big fuckin' desert. We have another two or three days in front of us, if we walk fast, and the sun is going to leach out every drop of water in our bodies.

There's not enough water left for two people to make it." He looked at her.

Slowly, fear replaced the anger in her eyes as she began to believe him. He reached down to pick up an empty can and handed it to her.

"When you piss, you piss in this. When you get thirsty, you drink it. When I give you water out of the cans, you drink until I say, and no more." He heard his voice, leaden and dead. He put his hand on the hilt of her knife in his pants. "If you give me any more trouble, I'll kill you and keep all the water myself. Do you understand?"

She nodded, mute.

"Fine," he said. He felt nothing. It didn't matter now, anyway. They wouldn't last another day.

He took her half of the torn blanket, and they huddled together in its shade, sweating, until the sun set. As soon as the last red glare sank behind the horizon, he disassembled their camp with a few shakes of the cloth, and started walking. Sadonya hefted her sack and walked beside him.

"We gonna try anyway?" Sadonya asked, her voice small.

He didn't look at her. "Yes."

"Why?"

"Because I say so."

She didn't answer, and they walked through the night in silence. They stopped to rest and she watched as he drank half a can of water, handing the remainder to her. She sipped it slowly, making it last, and stuffed the empty can in her own sack.

But by morning, the water was gone and they were both drinking their piss. They staggered into the shelter of a farmhouse shell, three walls still standing. Collapsing out of the sun into the shade, Berk sat with his back to one wall, arm resting on his knees, watching the heat shimmer in waves across the desert. Sadonya slept beside him, her chest rising and falling in shallow breaths. The sun, hovering in the west, turned the sky a solid bloodred.

His burned skin blistered an angry crimson, his eyes ached in the dry heat. He nudged Sadonya occasionally, but the girl barely moved, her dark skin hot and parched. As the sun moved overhead, he half-carried, half-dragged her around the crumbling wall to the shade. She muttered incoherently, eyes closed.

The sand baked against his skin. Huge sunburn blisters along his legs broke, and he tried to suck the moisture into his mouth, knowing he was going crazy and not caring any longer.

From the north, a bobbing movement in the quavering mirages floating over the desert sand attracted his dull attention. One heat-striated bob split into three split into five. Fluttering dun-colored figures shuffled out of the heat waves toward them, solidifying into human forms sheathed in robes of sand. Berk made no effort to hide. His mind still worked, and he wondered with a vague, detached curiosity as they approached whether they were real or hallucinations.

Rangers or mirages, he decided, it really didn't matter. He and the girl were still dead.

TWENTY-SEVEN

July 10-12, 2242

T HEY GAVE HIM WATER, WHICH JOLTED HIM OUT OF his stupor. One of the figures squatted in front of him, holding a canteen to his mouth. Berk drank greedily, his shaking hands clamped around the warm metal, slurping the water down as quick as he could before they changed their minds and took it back. Reluctantly, he let it go as they pried it out of his hands.

He stared at the figures, panting, his swollen tongue licking at the water drops on his lips. If this was a hallucination, it was a damnfine one, he decided. One of the illusions spoke, unfamiliar words, as it held the water back to his mouth. *Slowly, slowly . . .* they seemed to say. Berk nodded, keeping his eyes locked on the phantom as he drank.

The eyes that stared back were dark and concerned through the light brown cloth wrapped around its head, and Berk knew this was not a mirage. More words were spoken, soft, murmuring, totally incomprehensible. A wet cloth touched his face, shockingly cold against his feverish skin.

The water began to revive him, and he looked around for Sadonya. Another of the dun-robed figures bent over her, touching the soaked edge of its robe to her face and neck. The girl stirred, moaning, but she was still unconscious.

The figure next to Berk stood and loosened part of the cloth wrapped around his head, exposing his face. Leathery, wrinkled black skin, darker even than Sadonya's, made an odd contrast to the man's pale curling beard. He smiled at Berk, and reflexively, Berk returned the gesture.

The bearded man put fingers and thumb to his lips, a loud whistle cutting through the hot air. Almost instantaneously, the desert seemed to come alive around him.

The faint bleat of goats *meh-heh-hehed*, and two dozen spindly legged animals trotted through the tremorous shimmers of heat, followed by two more of the robed figures. The goats' slit-irised brown eyes regarded Berk curiously, huge ears flickering. For some reason, dried bushes had been tied to their backs.

The bearded man spoke to Berk again, his tone friendly, questioning, but the words unintelligible.

Berk shrugged. "I'm sorry," he said, his voice hoarse and cracked from thirst. The bearded man smiled with stained teeth, apologetic, and helped Berk to his feet. He was shorter than even Sadonya, and gazed up at Berk with wonder in his eyes.

Another man cradled Sadonya in his arms, wrapping his robe around her against the sun, and the group turned away from the old road, heading south. The short, bearded man tucked his shoulder under Berk's arm, helping him as he limped with bare feet across the still hot sand. The goats called to each other with muted baas, quiet laughter was exchanged between a couple of the herdsmen. It was all surrealistically peaceful to Berk.

He wasn't astonished when he spotted the low, mounded tents pitched in the desert. He was too dazed to feel surprise. The bearded man led him into one of the tents as Sadonya was taken off to another. Berk sank gratefully to its woven-reed-carpeted floor. A tiny charcoal fire, actually no more than a few glowing coals, heated a brass kettle suspended from a tripod hook.

Another robed figure offered him more water, helping him to sit up, and wiped his face and shoulders with a wet cloth while he drank. The bearded man left and returned with a second man, his face uncovered. Like the first, his skin was a leathery black, but he was a much younger man.

A short beard grew white along the sides, a dark, curly stripe running down from his chin, making his lean face look even longer. The whites of his eyes were tinted brown, nearly as dark as the iris; like an animal's, Berk thought. He smiled slightly, exposing black gums and brown-stained teeth. His nose was long and thin, with wide nostrils.

He was not a Ranger. Berk had seen plenty of Aggies up close, at least those the City kept in camps to work the co-op farms under supervision. Although they were just as dark, these people didn't behave much like the sad, wizened creatures Berk expected.

For one thing, they could speak.

The younger man sat down cross-legged on the floor of the tent in front of Berk, hooded dark eyes regarding him curiously. "Eengglees?" he said slowly, his pronunciation careful. One front tooth was missing, the gap creating a slight lisp.

"Yes," Berk acknowledged and smiled.

"Cit-tee man?" the man asked, smiling back.

Berk hesitated, then said, "Yes, Pittsburgh."

The man shook his head and smiled apologetically. "Talk me very bad," he said. "Slow, slow."

The one who had wiped Berk's face and given him water poured tiny cups of a hot drink, handing one to Berk. He realized, as he took it, the hands that held it were delicate. He glanced up into the shy smile of a young woman.

"Thank you," he said.

She nodded, then spoke quickly to the younger man before she left the tent. He made motions for Berk to drink.

It was not much more than sweetened hot water with the faint, bitter taste of a nameless herb, but, surprisingly, it cooled Berk as he drank. His ears tingled. He started to feel almost whole, giddy and lightheaded.

Berk pointed to the cup. "Good, very good," he said to the stripe-bearded man. He paused, then held out his hand. "My name is Berk," he said slowly, clearly.

The man nodded, smiling. "My name is Amminadab," he

said, and put his palms together. After a moment, Berk set down his cup and did the same.

It was a slow, halting conversation, but between hand motions and the little English Amminadab knew, Berk understood. These *were* Aggies, of a sort. They were a small tribe of wandering people calling themselves the Brethren.

Berk had learned a smattering of obligatory Italian in his early school days, in the City's attempt to preserve all the languages it could. The Brethren, at least to Berk's untrained ears, sounded vaguely Germanic. His City education so far hadn't proved all that useful.

Amminadab unwound the cloth from his head, and put it to one side. Around his neck, he wore a crude necklace, a carved-bone cross with tiny arrows at each tip, against his loose tunic. He noticed Berk looking at it, and smiled, touching it with a gnarled finger. "*Zishen af Gottum*," he said. "God's touch."

They made him comfortable, and he slept that evening in the small tent, a dozen other men smiling politely and dozing on the floor along with him.

In the early morning, the tent stirred to life. A woman gave him an undyed robe identical to theirs, laughing quietly behind her hands while he struggled with wrapping the headcloth in the same fashion. Amminadab led him across the camp to where most of the tribe gathered in the shade of a ruined wall, smiling up at Berk around his missing tooth unselfconsciously. The tribe sat in neat rows, cross-legged in the dusty sand, waiting expectantly.

Berk spotted Sadonya, her black hair bare against her own tunic. She glanced at him impassively, one eye bruised and swollen shut. He felt remotely ashamed and looked away.

A hunchbacked old man stood up, holding a carefully wrapped object reverently in his arms. He held it out to the gathered people, and they responded by holding their hands together as if praying. Slowly the group bowed, once, holding their heads low to the ground. Berk glanced around, then copied their movement.

After a long silence, the Brethren straightened. And that, apparently, was that. The wrapped object went back into a

tiny square box, and the group dispersed, breaking camp.
Tents were dismantled in minutes, and before the sun had
risen to warm the air, the tribe moved on, heading south.

Berk walked with Amminadab, chatting as best he could.
His self-appointed interpreter had learned his smattering of
English from another Aggie who had died when Amminadab
had been still a child. Where that one had learned it was a
mystery. "Cityman" seemed to have no particular meaning to
Amminadab. The Brethren, Berk decided, were too far away
from the City for their tiny gardens to have been of any
interest to the Council.

The Brethren had not had the unfortunate contact other
Aggies had experienced. They had not had their painfully cultivated gardens stolen, and themselves co-opted, pressed into
working their own land for the greater benefit of the domed
City.

Yet.

But Amminadab seemed pleased to have the chance to
improve his slight skill and Berk was happy to simply be
alive.

There had always been Brethren in the desert, according
to Amminadab. Even before the *Ferangd'rung*, before
Christ had returned. With shining-eyed enthusiasm, he rat-
tled on in a mélange of his vernacular generously spiced
with English and animated hand motions.

These Aggies, from what Berk could piece together, were
the descendants of the Amish and Mennonites once in the
area, although whether spiritually or physically wasn't
clear. This expanse of desert, pitilessly hot, nearly barren,
the Brethren called Paradise, much to Berk's barely con-
cealed amusement.

The Shift, Amminadab explained in his energetic if somewhat scanty English, had been the direct result of the Second
Coming of Christ, wasn't that obvious? Their ancestors, although they had lived modestly, doing their best to follow
God's law, had failed. They had not lived simply enough as
God had truly intended, so He had decided in His infinite
wisdom the only way to teach His children was by re-
creating ancient Israel in Pennsylvania. God was merciful,

great was His compassion. He was giving them another chance to get it right this time.

The Brethren had adopted what they believed was God's true role for them, following their biblical interpretation of ancient Holy Land customs. Seminomadic, the Brothers lived in tents made of skins, and dressed in rough cloth. Herding tough, wiry goats, they foraged for wild food and in the mild seasons grew what they could in tiny plots of land camouflaged to blend into the surrounding brown hills. Not, it seemed, from City pilots, but from the *Tuivels*, the Rice Wolves.

Rangers.

At the end of spring, they harvested their crops and abandoned their little gardens. Heading for Eden on the River Jordan, they rejoined other tribes along the river, where they would wait out the hot summer months, trading stories and exchanging members, breeding their goats until it was time to migrate again, returning to their individual territories to plant their winter crops. Then it was a race to preserve enough food and avoid or minimize the losses from assaults by the Rice Wolves to make it through the barren winter.

From a rough calculation of the sun's angle, added to an estimate of where the Brethren had found them, Berk calculated that Eden would be farther southwest, past the old city of Lancaster, the River Jordan sounding suspiciously like the Susquehanna.

The sun climbed rapidly into the pale sky, and a voiceless signal ran like a tremor through the tribe. Within a few minutes, the round little tents had sprung up, and the tribe vanished inside, goats and all. It was easy to see, Berk realized, why he hadn't detected them from the air. A small group like this would be easy enough to miss, and the little tents blended almost seamlessly into the desert sand.

Amminadab beckoned him into a tent, where four other men lounged in depressions they'd made in the sand, woven dried grass carpets spread over the floor. A woman had again set a small brass kettle on a tripod hook over barely glowing embers. They carried the live coals with them, it seemed. She smiled, pressing her hands together, and left. Berk peeked out the tent flap, watching as she ducked into an identical mound tent not ten yards away.

Berk pointed to where the woman had gone. "Why," he asked awkwardly, "she goes there, we stay here?"

Amminadab squinted at him questioningly.

"Men," Berk said, vaguely indicating his crotch. "Women." He pantomimed breasts. The other men grinned, amused. Berk made a motion with his hands to indicate separate tents.

"Yes, yes," Amminadab agreed happily. "True."

"Why?"

"*Ghezetzbuk*," Amminadab said. "God this say."

"You—" Berk pointed to the gap-toothed man smiling at him. "No wife? No women . . ." He laced his fingers together.

"Yes, yes," Amminadab said enthusiastically. "Maybe, no."

"Okay," Berk said, giving it up.

Amminadab seemed pleased with himself. "Okay," he agreed. He turned towards the other men talking quietly in the small tent. Each man took his turn in pouring the tiny cups of scalding hot tea. Amminadab unrolled a long sausage and a stack of flat bread from his little pack. He cut small chunks of the meat and handed them out to each man with a piece of bread. Smiling, he gave a generous piece to their guest. Berk ate it almost greedily, grateful for something other than rat. It was heavily spiced and Berk thought it was the most delicious thing he had ever eaten.

They finished the hot drink and dozed in the tents, waiting out the worst of the day. Berk's body throbbed, nerve endings in his burnt skin hypersensitive. Even the weight of the cloth against his shoulder was painful. He watched the men as they slept peacefully, until his drowsy eyes closed, his chin dropping to his chest.

He was startled out of his slumber, the camp coming to life as if at an automatic, silent signal. The men rolled up the thin grass carpets, transforming them into backpacks. One stirred the coals in the cast-iron pot, tossing a few scraps of wood in with them, and clamped a lid over the top. Tiny perforations in the top puffed a thin trickle of smoke as he set it over his shoulder, swinging at the end of its tripod. He carried nothing else.

They scuttled out of the tents, and within a few minutes, the camp had vanished like before, leaving behind not a single trace in the sand that they had ever been there. The little flock of goats, their brush umbrellas on their backs, skipped over rocks and sand, bleating quietly as small boys waved switches to guide them.

Amminadab chattered on, laughing, unconcerned, when Berk shook his head rucfully, undaunted when the Cityman failed to understand. The gap-toothed man was persistent, and Berk found himself admiring these strange little people. They had adapted, somehow surviving the centuries in the Outside.

The only Aggies he had ever encountered had been drab, simple-minded mutes, as stoic and passive as cattle. The Brethren were Aggies, but they were not uncivilized, backward aboriginals scratching out an existence in the hostile desert, nor were they the solar-radiated genetic defects City propaganda had continually professed all Outsiders to be. They had rescued him and Sadonya when they could as easily have left them to die, feeding and sheltering them in their homes ungrudgingly, without the slightest indication of resentment or expectations. Berk was troubled by the idea that there could be such wide differences among these people and the kind of Aggies he was familiar with ... or were there similarities he'd never bothered to notice before?

They had walked perhaps five miles, the sun glowering redly in the west, when the lead figure halted. Instantly, the Brethren seemed to shudder down into the sand. The goats sank to their knees, their necks bent to hide their faces in the brush, freezing into stillness. Even from close up, knowing the animals were there, it was difficult to see more than a dry clump of dead brush, like any number that grew in spotted patches across the desert.

Amminadab pulled Berk down beside him, his eyes suddenly worried, solemn. "Rice Wolves," he breathed. The Brethren lay huddled on the ground, flicking sand over their

robes to blend in nearly invisibly with the ground. The entire camp vanished in seconds, like a mirage, neatly camouflaged.

From under his headcloth, Berk peered through a tiny slit,
watchful, scared. He saw and heard nothing. Then, far off to
his right, he saw a thin strand of smoke in the air. He thought
he heard the warbling cry of Rangers, but it was too faint for
him to be sure.

The camp stayed immobile and silent for hours, no one
moving, not a child crying or a goat bleating. Once, his leg
starting to fall asleep, Berk shifted position. Amminadab
touched him lightly, shaking his head nearly imperceptibly,
revealing frightened eyes before he pulled his headcloth
back over his face.

A sharp whistle cut through the air, the sound of desert
hawks shrilling. The Brethren rematerialized like wraiths
out of the sand. Berk's joints ached as he lumbered to his
feet, Amminadab seeming no worse for wear. The little man
chuckled, amused, and slapped the sand from Berk's robes.

They walked until it was too dark for the men guiding the
small band to see, setting up camp again within minutes.
Sand tossed up along the edge of the tents blended them into
the desert floor. The man with the coal pot set up the tripod
in the center of the little tent, blowing on the ashen coals to
stir them back to life.

Amminadab pulled the robe from Berk's back gently,
sucking air through the gap in his teeth as he grimaced. He
shook his head as he soaked strips of cloth in water, and laid
them across the Cityman's sun-parched back. Berk sighed
with overwhelming relief, the cool water drawing off the
agony.

This time the women brought food, a small pot of pungent
goat-meat in a thick, heavily spiced sauce. The men ate with
their hands, chunks of bread serving as plates. Amminadab
handed Berk a round of soft white cheese, spiced and sweetened, small pelletlike seeds in the middle. It was good, much
better, in Berk's opinion, than the bitter fermented drink
made from goat's blood that Amminadab insisted he share
with them. His tent mates chortled knowingly as Berk tried

not to grimace and pronounced it very nice. It did, however, get him rather drunk, and that *was* very nice.

The life was simple, direct. Each evening was a repeat of the previous one; men talked quietly and drank, the women flitted like shadows from tent to tent before they drifted into sleep. The sky paled before the sun rose, one day the same as the next. After the brief early morning devotion, the camp continued southwest. By midafternoon a few days later, the sparkling waters of the River Jordan were in view.

TWENTY-EIGHT

July 28, 2242

FOUR TRIBES OF BRETHREN MET ALONG THE SHORES of the River Jordan, a total of less than fifty people. It was not the usual joyous occasion it might have been, Amminadab explained falteringly. One tribe had been reduced to three men, the rest killed or taken off by Rice Wolves. The tribes would have to hold a meeting to decide what to do.

Berk stayed with the Brethren for another week, resting, healing, helping when he could, learning. He saw little of Sadonya, which didn't bother him in the least. He secretly hoped that the girl would choose to stay behind with the Brethren when he left. He could cover much more ground without her, he reasoned, unwilling to admit he simply didn't like her.

In the meantime, he bathed with the men in the clear water of the shallow river, washing the grime from his body and hair. He hadn't had the chance to cut his hair since before he'd left Pittsburgh and it hung ragged past his shoulders. He decided to keep the beard, scraggly as it was; it was hot, but at least protected his face from the sun. He did allow Amminadab to treat his hair for lice, sitting still in the tent as the little man raked through his scalp and beard meticulously with a fine toothed bone comb, pinching the white nits between his fingernails.

Amminadab had not been the only one fascinated with Berk's peculiar straight hair. The women in the camp, their own dense, curly hair plaited in tiny rows, took turns with trying to braid his into intricate patterns, combing and tugging until his scalp ached. They giggled when his hair slipped out of the plaits by morning, then argued spiritedly whose turn it was next.

He took his turn watching the goat herd and learned how to milk them in the evening hours. He mastered the technique of tending the little coal stove, how to make the weak herbal teas, how to preserve the live coals in the cast-iron pots. He learned the social order of who poured after whom, who moved aside to make room to sit down. The men with whom he shared the single mound tent taught him how to erect and disassemble it within a minute, cheering him on as he raced clumsily, applauding when he finally got it right. Amminadab taught him how to drop to the ground and flick sand over his robes, the best position in which to remain motionless for hours without straining his body. The women chattered at him as they showed him how to spot edible plants he would have never seen with his untutored eyes.

In the evenings, he practiced slinging the sand under the tent to lounge comfortably on the reed carpets. He let Amminadab put tiny seeds in the corner of his eye that stained his sclera darker. Chewing on sticks of gnarled dry root dyed his teeth and gums a walnut-brown, and his tent mates examined the results, murmuring their approval. His burnt skin sloughed off in large patches, the pink underneath turning deep brown as it healed.

He picked up a few words of Dushprek in exchange for helping Amminadab improve his meager English. The little man worked earnestly at it in his wholehearted determination to learn, stopping occasionally to explain to their tent mates this word or that enthusiastically. They, in return, responded delightedly whenever Berk was able to stutter through his sparse handful of Dushprek.

He studiously went through the motions of the morning

ceremony, bemused by their casual, almost indifferent religious observance, until he realized they made no distinction
between their faith and their everyday lives. Although men
and women lived separately, there was no particular sexual
hierarchy that Berk could perceive, other than attention to
the needs of others first. Women came and went as they
pleased, choosing their partners, it seemed to Berk, almost
randomly. Children and women were precious, and treated
as such. Individual families had no particular demarcation;
everyone was part of the larger family, every child belonged
to every adult. It was not so much deliberate adherence to an
egalitarian order as it was a simple intuitive consideration
for mutual survival.

They were just nice people.

Berk and Amminadab sat on the gentle slope overlooking
the riverbank, watching the women bathing nude with their
children before the morning became too hot. Sadonya was
perched on a wet boulder, her feet dangling in the river. Berk
knew she'd seen him, but she avoided him and pointedly sat
with her back to him. Fine, he really didn't care.

Amminadab studied the crude map Berk had drawn in the
dirt, his eyelids occasionally blinking away tiny moisture-
seeking gnats. With a thin stick, Berk traced the line of the
river, including the reservoir behind them. Then he pointed
the stick at the water.

"Okay? Understand?"

"Yah." Amminadab nodded earnestly. "Jordan." He
pointed to the water, then at the line in the dirt.

Berk drew a series of curves, then pointed towards the
low line of dull, serrated mountains in the west, tinged blue
beyond the river. "Alleys," he said.

"Bergen." Amminadab smiled, pointed and nodding.
"Yah."

Berk carefully drew in a line, bisecting the river above
where he had drawn the reservoir. "Road."

Amminadab looked puzzled.

Berk mimicked the state he had been in when the
Brethren had found them, pointing to himself and Sadonya,
who was still deliberately ignoring him. His fingers walked

down the little drawing he'd made in the sand.

"Ah!" Amminadab said, suddenly enlightened. "Boz weg."

"Boz weg," Berk agreed, trying to translate. "Old road." He drew into his diagram the outline of the old towns of Reading and York and Lancaster, then sketched in the domes of Harrisburg at the place where the river and the old auto route intersected. "City." He tapped his stick on the circle he'd scratched in the dirt.

"Very bad," Amminadab said, solemn. "No go, city. Boz city, *bad* city."

It took more scratching in the dirt and exchanges between the pilot and the little man before Berk understood. The Brethren would not go anywhere near Harrisburg, having quickly learned how unhealthy it was to get too close to the booby-trapped barrier. They feared even the ruins of the old abandoned towns, and, except when forced to cross them, avoided major roads whenever they could.

The Brethren were not as nomadic as the Rangers, needing to stay in one place long enough to plant their crops in haphazard, natural-looking plots, to keep them from the notice of the ever-greedy Rice Wolves. The Rangers, Amminadab explained laboriously, would take an entire crop when they found it. If the Brethren tribes resisted, they were simply killed. Sometimes some were killed anyway, like the families of the few despondent survivors Berk had seen huddled with their few remaining possessions.

"Fight back!" Berk said.

Amminadab stared at him blankly.

Berk mimicked two people struggling. Amminadab looked shocked. "No, no! *Neemer!*" Agitated, the little gaptoothed man began a rapid-fire jumble of Dushprek, English and gyrating hands. Brethren did not kill. Ever. Not even Rangers. It was forbidden by the Ghezetzbuk, the book of God's laws.

"But Rice Wolves kill you," Berk pointed out.

Amminadab shrugged fatalistically. "No kill," he said with finality. He acted out an escalating conflict, more and more dead. First them, then us, then more of them. More of us. Where does it stop? Here. It stops with us.

But, Amminadab explained, the Rice Wolves had learned, at least somewhat. They rarely massacred the Brethren wholesale and usually left enough grain to plant for the next season. Dead Brethren grew no crops to freely pillage. The Wolves always left a few Brethren alive, mostly children, but took all the women they could find. A parasite that kills its host will eventually die itself. Even Rice Wolves were intelligent enough to understand that much.

Brethren, on the other hand, grew several hidden gardens each season, expecting at least one or two to be raided. It was a hard life—Amminadab grinned cheerfully—but after all, this was Paradise.

Berk shook his head, bewildered.

In its own way, he recognized, it *was* a bit like a bizarre Eden. A gentle, benign people had, amazingly enough, managed to evolve in the harshest environment imaginable. They prospered in the wilderness, only to be hunted by savage Rangers. If they chanced too close to a domed City, they were exploited by the more advanced survivors of the Shift. Yet they survived, persevering in their compassionate beliefs.

A small boy waving a stick over his head ran back and forth in front of a group of goats, edging them down towards the river to drink. The child never struck the animals, Berk observed. He hadn't seen an adult hit a child. And while the women lived separately from the men, they mingled freely, laughing and touching, unselfconsciously happy.

Even the three surviving men of the Rice Wolves' attack were beginning to smile again, if somewhat sadly. All the women were remarkably attentive to the survivors, chatting congenially with them at the river. Two of the men helped to wash clothes, side by side with the women as they scrubbed the cloth against a flat rock. The third, as naked as the bathing women, dandled a child in the river. He held the squealing child up by one arm as he splashed water over its little potbelly while the mother watched. The rest of the menfolk took an interest in the exchange, but none of them seemed jealous.

These men had lost all their women and children, Amminadab had told Berk, but at the meeting it had been decided they should remain a separate clan. When the summer gathering dispersed again, the women of the other tribes would confer among themselves to decide which of them would go with the three widowers to form a new tribe.

Cormack, Berk decided, and the entire Council, could go screw themselves. He would never tell them about the Brethren. Stay away from Citymen like me, he wanted to warn Amminadab. We're maybe worse than the Rangers.

It depressed him.

If Amminadab noticed the change in Berk's mood, he was gracious enough to ignore it. They watched the women splashing in the river, laughing quietly as they played with their children. Their naked bodies gleamed wetly, dark skin even blacker in the water, as black and glistening as Berk's precious oil. Amminadab grinned and winked at Berk, making the same motions with his hands that Berk had used to indicate breasts. "Zhooeeta, yah?"

"Yah, damnfine sweet," Berk agreed, and laughed.

TWENTY-NINE

July 31, 2242

AMMINADAB KNEW BERK WAS LEAVING. HOW HE knew, Berk wasn't sure, but the little man handed him a brass water canteen and a small rolled package of bread, spiced meat and cheese, smiling broadly. Berk stowed the parcel with his battered water cans, the last of his supply of Sadonya's rat jerky, and his oil sample in the sturdy cloth sling he'd exchanged his decaying rat-fur bag for.

"Good luck, my friend," Berk said, and shook the little man's hand. Amminadab nodded, and turned to join the others in their daily devotions as Berk slipped away before the last star had faded into morning.

Apparently, Sadonya knew, too. Berk had hoped to put enough distance between himself and the small gathering by the river before she discovered he was missing. He'd convinced himself it would be for the best if he left her behind. She'd be far better off staying with the Brethren. When he turned the bend in the river and found her sitting under a thin stand of trees, waiting for him, his stomach sank.

She rose as he walked past her without speaking, slinging her bag over her shoulder and falling in step behind him. He threaded his way along the riverbank, his buoyant mood gone.

They stopped midday, sitting in the shade of an old dam, the river spilling over its moss-covered remains. He hiked up his plain robe around his knees and let his aching feet soak in the water. Sadonya squatted down beside him.

"You a real fuck, outatown man," she said belligerently, finally breaking the silence.

"Guess so," Berk agreed, unwilling to argue with her.

She didn't want to let it drop. "Y'gonna quicktime 'bandon me there, huh?"

"Tried to. Tried real hard."

"We make a deal, y'forget that? You jess a lyin' face alla time, break a deal quicktime. I never break my deals, did I?"

He leaned into the river, splashing water against his face, letting it trickle through his hair and beard. Already his braids were unraveling, sticking to his sweating face. "No, you don't, Sadonya, and I didn't forget. I pretty much figured by now you hated me as much as I hate you, and you'd be happier staying behind with them. I guessed wrong."

"Damnstraight." She was quiet for a long time after that. "Fuckin' alltime lyin'," she muttered at last.

He leaned back against the wall of the dam, and closed his eyes. The sound of rushing water, insects buzzing in the heat, relaxed him. The afternoon humidity felt almost languorous as it filtered through the scraggly trees, and he napped, almost able to forget she was there.

"I don' hate you," she said softly, jolting him out of his doze.

"That's big of you," he said disparagingly. "It makes me feel so much better."

"I sorry I use up alla water," she said in a small voice. He finally looked at her, disgusted. She kept her eyes averted from his.

"Sadonya," he said bitterly, "I don' care nodamn your fuckin' sorries. You've been nothing but a pain in my ass, damned near killed us both. I can't say I'm too thrilled to be with you right now. Why couldn't you forget about me, for God's sake, *leave me alone*? Why couldn't you have stayed with the Brethren?"

She stared out across the water, her face stoic. She

blinked and a single tear trickled down her cheek, startling him. "Don' like them," she said sullenly. "They alla buncha meek'n milds, can't speak shit, 'cept alltime don' do this, can' do that. They don' like me, neither. I damnsure never be happy there."

"No kidding." He couldn't help his sardonic tone.

"Y'really hate me?" she asked, refusing still to look at him.

He sighed. Yes, he had to confess, he hated this thirteen-year-old child. Not a pleasant thing to admit to himself, but he simply couldn't make himself like her.

"Not enough to kill you, if that's any comfort," he said finally. He glanced at the sun overhead, glaring through the tops of the trees, and got to his feet heavily. "Come on, Sadonya," he said, resigned. "We got a long way to go, and this river isn't going to be convenient that much longer."

It was roughly fifty miles to Harrisburg, but the sandy riverbank didn't hamper walking, and the swift, running water was clear, cooling the nearby air to an almost tolerable degree. Small patches of scraggly trees grew along the banks, bending their fragile shade over the river. Berk kept the girl walking long after sundown, the trickle of moonlight rippling on the water enough to guide them.

The river had changed course over the centuries, and when they stopped around midnight to rest, they slept beneath an overpass that had once traversed the river now cutting a channel fifty feet from the old bridge.

Berk roused Sadonya a few hours later, the night sky still bright with pinpoint stars, although he had to resist the temptation to sneak away, leaving the sleeping girl behind. Even without his map, he was fairly confident he remembered the way well enough. York lay about ten miles to his left, Lancaster little more than ten to his right. The Harrisburg Domes were more than twenty-five miles up the river, but Berk knew the next bridge over the Susquehanna would be the old Route 76, five miles from the untouchable refuge. They would eat and rest there before crossing the river west.

The desert was behind them. But they would still have a straight fifty-mile race across hot, tinder-dry hills heading up into the low mountains of the Alley Oops. Berk intended to make it in one day, with or without Sadonya. Once with the Hebers, he would be quite willing to stay put until the next supply plane came in to rescue him.

It was a good plan. Not a thing wrong with it.

Except that ten miles or so before Berk expected to find the old auto route and the bridge across the rapid water, he caught sight of dark smoke leisurely roiling up into the early morning sky. A lot of it. On this side of the river. A chorus of quavering warbles vibrated indistinctly in the air, like the humming of insects on the summer breeze. Shit.

Rangers.

The river had widened out, dotted with islands along its course. On one, a pair of distant conical towers gleamed in the pearl-gray dawn. Closer, a smaller island anchored itself in the river's center, like a lifeboat. "We have to cross here," he said to Sadonya, and stepped a foot into the current.

"What?" she demanded. "What you sayin', cross here?"

He turned around, exasperated, then relented when he saw the terror in her eyes. Not fear of the Rangers, if she even understood the threat; she was panicked by the swiftly flowing river.

He pointed to the wall of smoke in the distance, behind the ancient cooling towers. "Those are Rangers, Sadonya. We're cut off from the bridge I wanted to cross. If we're going to get to the other side, we'll have to go here."

"No," she said flatly.

For a moment, he considered grabbing the anxious girl and pulling her across with him. "Fine," he said, tying the hem of his robe around his waist. He pointed back down the river, south. "You just go on back that way, fast as you can, and you should be okay with the Brethren. They'll take care of you. Goodbye and good luck, Sadonya."

He hitched his rolled pack higher onto his shoulders and waded into the water, heading for the north end of the island. The river was shallow, but not shallow enough for him to walk across. The stones under his bare feet were slippery, and he lost his balance when the water reached his chest.

Splashing facedown, he bobbed back up, gasping, and

began to swim for the diminutive island. The water ran fast enough to make swimming difficult and dangerous, and when he scraped his knees on the rough sand, he barely avoided being carried past the southern tip.

He crawled up onto the little beach, coughing, and shaking the water from his hair. Dumping his waterlogged pack onto the ground, he rolled to sit in the sand, letting the water stream away. He blinked, focusing on the girl squatting on the opposite shore.

"Come on, Sadonya!" he said, not even knowing why he was encouraging her to follow him. "It's not that hard!" He got to his feet, and walked to the other tip of the islet. "You can do it, let the water carry you!"

As she stepped apprehensively into the water, he wondered if he was really trying to kill the girl. She couldn't swim. Even in this shallow water, she'd easily drown. And, sure enough, within a half dozen steps, she lost her footing, screamed, and went under.

He leapt back into the water without thinking, thrashing his way to where she was being battered on the rocks, the river tumbling her over and down. She snagged herself against an old tree root thrust upside down out of the water, clutching its slick roots with her head thrown back, eyes closed, wailing.

He grabbed her by the arm and hauled her spitting and coughing, fighting both him and the water in crazed fear. He dragged her up onto the tiny islet beach, where they both lay on their bellies, choking. Amazingly, she hadn't lost her grip on her own small pack, her white-knuckled hand clamped tightly around the leather straps.

She vomited water, weeping hysterically. Berk glanced back at the smoke rising from behind the crest of the hillside, the crackle of flames almost audible. He drew her by her shoulders, dripping wet, and cradled her gently, rocking back and forth murmuring, "Okay, okay, it's okay . . ."

She didn't cry long. She pulled away from him and looked at the river around them in dismay. "It all around us," she said accusingly. "We fuckin' alltime stuck now!"

"No," he said firmly. "We're going to do it again." He

pulled her wet pack onto his back as well as his own and pointed to the opposite shore, the west shore. "I'll help you if you want me to, Sadonya. Or I can beat you senseless and drag you across or just leave you here to fend for yourself. You choose, and choose *now*. There's no more time."

"You right. I hate you, damnsure," she said. She stared up at the wall of smoke as if seeing it for the first time. Scowling, she stood. "Less go."

It was further across, and she lost her nerve halfway, but somehow they managed to make it. Berk didn't wait to dry off, but hauled her to her feet and up the shore at a near run.

A road cut through the remains of a small town, burned into oblivion ages past, leading away from the river, and Berk headed down it blindly, west. He clamped his hand around Sadonya's wrist, tugging her along quickly. His lungs were burning, and the girl panted, wheezing. She fell, crying in pain as he dragged her several more feet along the dry, hard ground before he finally halted.

He stood gasping, trying to catch his own breath as he waited for her. After some hesitation, she got to her feet shakily. Taking her own pack back from him, she hoisted it onto one shoulder and plodded behind him.

Things look very different at ground level than they do in the air, he realized. Distances when measured footstep by footstep seemed agonizingly longer, exhaustingly further than when he had sat suspended five hundred feet above, safe and secure from his advantageous perch.

His memory of the map did not include their exact location now. How far this small road ran, where and what it intersected, he had no idea. He was drawn north towards where he knew the old 76 must be, and driven west by the wall of perilous Ranger smoke.

He was too tired and worried to be relieved when the town road joined an old auto route he knew drove straight south from Harrisburg, the ancient map number he couldn't remember. It didn't matter; he knew it would merge with 76, and he finally let them both rest out the afternoon heat, hiding in the shade of a tumbledown shopping mall.

Sadonya looked at him without speaking for a long time,

then leaned hesitantly against his shoulder. Berk sighed. Ignoring the heat, he put his arm around her and hugged her gently to his chest.

He thought she might cry, but within minutes, she'd simply curled up and fallen asleep.

THIRTY

ALTHOUGH THE MOUNTAINS WERE NOT ALL THAT steep, his legs were tiring. As they climbed the twisting hills following the old road, the food and water were nearly gone, (not her fault, Sadonya paused from her renewed litany of complaints long enough to point out), and his energy and patience were at an end. Dragging her along, he stumbled resolutely up and across the mountain range.

Sadonya grumbled bitterly, resentful and becoming more and more unreasonable and difficult with every step. Berk considered, not for the first time, knocking her brains out with a rock and leaving her behind. It was only a fantasy, he convinced himself. He couldn't do it, not even to her. The animosity between them simmered.

Amazingly enough, they made the Twin Tunnels shortly after sunup the next day, without any problems other than the fact that he was stuck with her, and they were out of water, out of food and out of strength. They hadn't run into any Rangers, thank God.

When the armed Heber boy standing guard spotted the filthy robed pair, Berk was terrified for a moment that he would kill them both. Standing in the sunlight where the boy would have no trouble shooting him, Berk held his empty hands up over his head. Dirty and dressed in rags, he'd lost weight since the Hebers had last seen him. Belatedly, he wished now he had cut off the beard concealing his face.

"It's Berk Nielsen, the City pilot!" he shouted. "Remember me? I've got a girl with me, no one else!"

Another of the Heber boys on watch rose up out of the rock, both guns trained on Berk and Sadonya. The boys crouched, rifles braced against their shoulders, squinting speculatively through the gunsights.

"Put up your hands, Sadonya," Berk said quietly. Grudgingly, she held her hands casually at shoulder height. "Higher," he hissed. She glared venomously at him with narrowed eyes and hiked her hands up a fraction of an inch.

He stood exposed in the light, nervously. The boys exchanged a look. After a tense minute, they lowered their rifles, but kept them aimed in the pair's direction. One of them scrambled down off his perch and vanished. Sadonya dropped her hands.

"Keep them up!" Berk warned her sharply.

"It hot standin' out here inna sun," she complained.

"Just shut the hell up, and do what I tell you."

He was beginning to feel slightly dizzy in the heat himself when the boy returned. To his relief, Old man Heber was with him.

"Berk Nielsen?" the old man shouted down.

"It's me!" Berk yelled weak-kneed with relief. "Just me and a girl, no one else. We need help!"

The old man considered for a disconcerting length of time. "Go round to the back, the Trade store," he said at last. He and the boys scrambled back down out of sight.

"Come on," Berk said, and grabbed Sadonya's wrist. Jogging up the rocky incline, he worked his way to the eastern tunnel. The gate through the razor wire had been left open leading across a dusty no-man's land to the tiny access door into the storage tunnel. The steel door cracked open as they reached it and, as Berk pushed it wider, he heard the sound of multiple rifle bolts pulled back.

They were yanked roughly into the dim interior, and shoved to the floor facedown. A booted foot stamped down hard on Berk's back, knocking his breath out. The metal door clanked shut, locked behind them.

"'Scuse the inconvenience, Mr. Nielsen," a girl's polite voice said apologetically as the cold muzzle of a gun pressed against the back of his skull. He recognized Elissa's voice. "Please put your hands atop your head, if y'don't mind."

They quickly and efficiently frisked him before they let him sit up, then minutely inspected the two packs. Old man Heber stood watching, smoking his pipe serenely.

"No weapons," Berk said. "Except the knife."

Elissa looked up from where she had scattered his few possessions, spreading them out on the floor. "Nothin'," she announced.

Old man Heber nodded, and smiled at Berk. "Nice to see you again, Mr. Nielsen. Sorry for the welcome." He extended his hand to Berk and helped him to his feet.

"I don't even have my pistol any more," Berk said.

Sadonya shook off the hand of the girl who helped her up, scowling angrily. One of the boys handed her her repacked bag, and she jerked it from him. He shrugged.

"We're more concerned about explosives. We've had Rangers bring in dud grenades to trade, so we never take chances. We don't intend to go down like the Tusk Tunnel did. You're not travelin' solo"—the old man eyed Sadonya —"and she looks a little bit like a Ranger."

Sadonya shot him a furious look, and Heber raised his palms placatingly. "From a distance," he added quickly.

The Hebers took them in, fed them, and found places for the two to sleep, thankfully apart. Berk's tiny Spartan room seemed luxurious now, the narrow bed the most comfortable thing he'd ever slept in.

The old man allowed them several days to recuperate before he approached Berk to ask his intentions.

Berk stood in the shade of the tunnel balcony, a cup of steaming herb tea in his hand as he watched the little stream trickle through the garden between the tunnels.

"Glad you're feelin' better, Nielsen," Heber said. He stuffed a wad of homegrown into his pipe, tamping it down firmly with his thumb. The old man's concentration in his task worried Berk.

"I'd like to thank you all again for taking us in, Heber," Berk said uneasily. "We wouldn't have made it otherwise."

"Uh-huh," Heber said noncommittally. He lit the pipe and squinted through the smoke. "How you planning on getting back to the Pit?"

"Wait for the next supply plane out here, and have the pilot take us back," Berk said confidently, firmly.

"Uh-huh," the old man said again. "That's gonna be quite a while. The last pilot out here was you. It ain't likely there'll be another plane out before the end of that hot season, anyway."

"I'll wait."

The old man sucked on the pipe, his eyes searching across the arid mountains. Finally he said, "I ain't running anything for free, Nielsen." He coughed apologetically. "Don't mean to sound hardhearted, you understand. But we're a trading post, not an aid station for the lost and lonely."

"I'll pay."

The old man smiled ironically. "City issue?"

Berk chuckled. "Maybe we just hash out a trade," he said.

"You don't seem to be packing much with you, Cityman. And I'm not fond of takin' IOUs."

Berk shrugged amiably. "Well, we did discuss a service you proposed last time I visited your fine establishment."

Heber raised his eyebrows in surprise. "We got the very strong impression from your lady friend that your services weren't available at the moment. Seems she feels she got some kinda proprietary rights." The old man eyed Berk skeptically. "And she's a rather unpleasant person, I have to tell you."

Berk grimaced. "I'm aware of it, Mr. Heber," he said dryly. "But she's got no claim on me whatsoever, whatever crap she tells you."

"That's something I prefer you work out yourself, son," the old man said laconically. "Please let me explain a few things about Tunnel Families to you, Mr. Nielsen. I know that to you sophisticated City types our little family might seem to be a quaint collection of primitive bumpkins, a convenient harem of nymphomaniac pussy hot for any randy pilot on the route." His voice was bland.

Berk blinked in astonishment. "I'm sorry, Mr. Heber," he said quickly, "if that's the impression I gave you."

"Not at all," Heber said, matter-of-fact. "I do admit you seemed like a better-behaved man than a few others we've had rutting around here like cats in heat. Mr. Wysaigh, while we all liked him fine and sorry seeing him gone, he sometimes could get a little carried away with enjoyin' himself." Heber shrugged. "Cityman," he stated baldly, as if that were explanation enough.

The old man smiled, sucking air into his pipe, sweet gray smoke drifting between them. Berk opened his mouth to speak, but Heber held up one hand gently apologetically.

"I don't deny it's true we can always use new blood, *need* it, that's a fact of life," he said. "Emotions are also a fact of life, and we got a healthy respect for 'em, son. This place is just too damn small not to be payin' attention to feelings." He puffed on the pipe for a moment, savoring the smoke in his lungs before he exhaled. "None of our girls is forced into anything they don't want. If a couple in the Family decide they want to be exclusive, keep things private 'tween themselves for a while, that's respected, too. The girl says she's got some kinda arrangement with you, and jealousy is not something the Family can afford in these close quarters. You understand?"

Unhappily, Berk was afraid he did. "I understand."

"You should have yourself a good heart-to-heart chat with that little friend of yours, if you don't mind a bit of friendly advice. Work things out, and do it fast," Heber suggested, iron in his mild voice. "She's stirrin' up some real bad feeling. We don't need it here."

"I'll take care of it."

"Glad to hear it. After that, then we'll talk about how you gonna pay for room and board, okay?" Heber knocked the ashes from his pipe and left Berk standing alone, his tea cold, his mood soured.

THIRTY-ONE

August 7, 2242

B ERK NEVER GOT THE CHANCE TO TALK IT OUT with Sadonya. He had waited, trying to figure out a way to force her into some semblance of civilized manners. He waited too long.

Heber found him in the morning out in the garden, helping to dig irrigation ditches in an attempt to repay his hosts, but the old man's usual congenial, if impersonal, attitude had vanished. Heber was mad.

"I do believe it's time you and your girl moved along, son," he said without preamble, barely controlling his red-faced anger.

Stunned, Berk gaped at him. "I don't understand," he stammered.

"Seems your little friend had some kind of nasty disagreement with one of my girls," Heber explained, his slow voice dead calm. "I don't know what about. She won't say what, and Elissa's too sick to talk. Don't really care, either."

Dread prickled up Berk's cheeks.

"Your little friend's got quite an interesting ability. Regular Lucretia Borgia, ain't she? She put a little surprise in the kids' afternoon meal. I got five very sick, very scared children right at the moment. She leaves. Now."

A horrible comprehension dawned on Berk. "Oh, no," he groaned, shaken. He didn't know what to say. He leaned against the shovel, eyes squeezed closed, shaking his head numbly. "Your children"—he forced the words out—"are they going to be all right?"

Heber stared at him narrowly. "Yeah," he said slowly, "if you can believe your friend. Said she wasn't trying to 'frag them alltime dead,' just get even with one girl. Nielsen, I'm chuckin' that bitch outta my home. You stay if you want to, doesn't seem to me you owe her much of a damned thing."

Berk took a deep breath, sorely tempted. He tried one last time. "If you throw her out, she'll die. She can't survive Outside on her own."

Heber shook her head. "Not my problem," he said stonily. "My concern is my Family, first and last. Always. Far as I'm concerned, that scrawny vicious child isn't much more than a Ranger, and I shoot Rangers when they threaten me and mine. You feel some kind of responsibility for her, that's *your* problem. You stay or go as you want."

Berk knew better than to plead. His mind finally kicked back into gear. "I'm stupid, Mr. Heber," he admitted. "But I'm not suicidal. It's a goddamned long way back to the City."

Heber smiled thinly. "You stayin', then."

"No," Berk said quietly. "She goes, I'll have to go with her." The old man's eyes widened in surprise. "But I'll need supplies if I've got any chance at all of living long enough to get back. Food. Water. Medicine. A rifle and enough ammunition."

Heber snorted derisively. "You got zero to bargain with, Cityman. I'm just supposed to give this all to you out of the goodness of my heart?"

"Yes," Berk said tightly. "I can't believe you're as mean a bastard as you're trying to make me think."

Heber's face hardened. "I'm a businessman, son, and your City don't carry all that much weight around here," he said. "I can give you food and water, maybe a little medicine, no skin off my nose. But the rifles we can't afford to give away."

"Then consider it an 'investment,'" Berk said. "I'll pay you twice the value of anything you give me, once I get back to the City. I'll send whatever we agree on out with the next supply plane, but if I don't have enough supplies and protection, I won't make it back to pay you off. It's to your advantage."

Heber stared at him; then a smile cracked through the hostility. His eyes crinkled in amusement. "'Course, if you don't get back, I'll lose my 'investment,'" he pointed out.

"That's the risk," Berk pressed. "Keep it in mind, I've made it back this far already without a gun."

Heber looked at him calculatingly before putting out his hand. "*One* rifle," he said. "Only one. A box of bullets, and enough medicine, food and water for two people, four days. Get you as far as the Alley Tunnel. Then you'll have to make your own deal with old Juhamit."

Berk hesitated, looking straight into the old man's eyes unblinkingly. "And in return?"

"Four rifles. New. And a new solar generator."

Berk smiled thinly. "You're a greedy old bastard," he said.

"Yup. If you make it."

"Deal."

They shook hands.

The old man took him into his weapons room, unlocked a gun cage and selected a rifle. He handed it to Berk, and the two walked out to the landing strip where *First Violin* had set down not so long ago.

Berk checked the rifle over carefully, loaded it and squeezed off a round into the distance over the razor-wire fence. It kicked hard against his shoulder, but seemed in order. It sighted a little high, but not too bad. Pulling back the bolt, he ejected the empty cartridge, then slung the rifle over his shoulder.

Sadonya sat cross-legged in the dust outside the storage tunnel door, her hands tied firmly behind her back. She squinted up at Berk as he and Heber walked through the doorway, and Berk stopped to glare at her. Reaching down, he jerked her to her feet.

"You just got us kicked out of here, Sadonya," he said angrily. "Thank you very much."

"They take my things," she said, unfazed. "Want 'em back."

Berk turned to look at Heber, and the boy standing impassively next to him, Sadonya's ratskin bag in one hand. "We don't want this shit," the boy said, holding it out like something tainted.

Berk took it from his hands. It weighed very little. He picked up his own rolled bag, which Heber had packed with food and medicine. Filled water cans thunked inside, and Berk had topped the brass canteen from Amminadab before fastening the bag around the waist of his now clean robe.

"Gimme my things," she demanded.

He looked down at Sadonya, and abruptly spun her around. "Good idea," he said enthusiastically. "And while you're at it, you can carry a bit more, now can't you?" He didn't release her hands, but hung the two packs onto the girl's back, strapping them to her securely.

Sadonya began cursing, struggling until he wrested her around to face him again. Bunching her robe in his fist, he pulled her up until she stood on her toes, pushing his face close to hers.

"Listen, Sadonya," he said very quietly. "I didn't have to come with you. You could have died out there all by yourself while I stayed here nice and cool and safe without you. *You* have fucked up." She blinked, his breath in her wide eyes. "Now, you will do what I tell you, keep your mouth shut, or I'll damnsure quicktime beat the living shit out of you. Do you understand?"

She scowled without answering, her eyes burning spitefully. He took that as a "yes," and shoved her stumbling away.

He shook Heber's hand a last time. "I'm sorry about your children," he said.

Heber didn't comment. "Good luck, Cityman," was all he said before he closed the gate on the razor-wire fence. He and his sons retreated to the safety of the tunnel, locking the steel door firmly behind them.

Berk and the girl crossed the tiny creek that ran between the two tunnels farther down, working their way back onto the old auto route. An hour later, he stopped to rest out of the sun in the rubble of the old Tusk Tunnel. Waves of heat shimmered against the horizon.

"My arms n' hands sore, Berk," Sadonya whined. "Why y'don' cut me loose?"

"Shut up, Sadonya," he said wearily.

Her eyes narrowed. "You like makin' me hurt, huh," she accused him. "You jess like Mouse, think hurtin' fun. I no-time did same to you."

"No," he said. "You just tied me down, poisoned my food, starved me whenever you felt like it, and broke my ribs. Remember?" But much as he didn't want to admit it to himself, he did want to hurt her. He hid his brief flush of guilt by yanking her around and slicing through the ropes with his knife. She shrugged the packs off her back.

Rubbing her wrists, she scowled, surly and unappreciative.

"Why the hell did you put your damned 'cooking' in the Hebers' food?" he asked, reluctantly curious. "Heber said you got into some kind of fight with one of his girls."

"What you care, you fuck," she spat. "Not sayin' nodamn thing to you."

Annoyed, he sighed and shrugged. "Don't make me do something you'll regret," he warned her, and closed his eyes to try and nap.

He leaned against the packs, more to safeguard them from her than as any cushion, and cradled the rifle in his arms. When he roused himself from his lethargy a few hours later, she had curled up among the rocks, sleeping soundly with her back to him.

Getting to his feet groggily, he rubbed his eyes and hoisted his pack to his back, rifle slung across his chest. He kicked her ungently awake. When she scrambled to her hands and knees, startled and cross, he dropped her bag on the ground in front of her. "Let's go, Sleeping Beauty," he said scornfully.

He trudged up the side of the mountain, with Sadonya following some distance behind him. When he reached the crest, he could see the hazy purpled tops of the Alley Oops rising in layers before him, the evening sun turning the sky behind the low peaks ruby-red, lovely and ominous.

This is crazy, he thought. For a moment, he regretted leaving the Hebers, considered turning back, leaving the girl to fend for herself.

And plodded on.

When he stumbled across the remains of a fire, gray ashes scattered on the hilltop, he felt a brief surge of alarm before he suddenly recognized it. He had sat before this same campfire months ago, could see hardened tiny craters in the ash where he had shaken the water out of his lost kettle, thin logs burned black, broken when he had stamped out the fire. To one side, the dry grass was still crushed, the ground scraped where *First Violin* had sat. His jaw hardened, ached.

Then he also noticed the marks of bare footprints in the ash. Small, misshapen. And fresh.

Sadonya hiked up the hill and stopped behind him when she saw him looking around. He quickly scanned the area, staring hard into the surrounding hills, eyeing the shadows in the whip-thin brush that crusted the slopes between the dead stumps of the ancient forest. Nothing moved in the fierce, glaring heat. All the same, he didn't want to stay long.

He clicked off the safety, checked to make sure the rifle had a round in the chamber, and held it tightly as he marched down the road, his nerves on edge, tense and jumpy. Pushing Sadonya ahead of him, he kept his eyes on the hills and gaps around them, seeing nothing. She, he was at least thankful for, had enough sense to keep quiet.

When night fell, with not enough moonlight to see by, they slouched in the inadequate shelter of a tumbled pile of boulders, their backs against the rocks. He slept fretfully, waking at every sound, until the sky began to pale.

They marched on, Berk prodding Sadonya to the limit, every muscle taut in apprehension. She couldn't understand his alarm, and after a few miles of the grueling pace, she began whining in protest. Threats shut her up only briefly before she started muttering again. He pushed her, grumbling and complaining, as hard as he could, towards the Alley Tunnel and safety.

For all his vigilance, it was Sadonya who spotted the boy first. They were within a few miles of the Alley Tunnel, when she pointed to a figure perched on the top of a large boulder.

"Looka him," she said, intrigued, unafraid.

Berk snapped his head around to stare at the boy. His misshapen body wrapped in odd-colored rags, the young Ranger stared down at them, a rifle balanced across his knees. As Berk brought up his own gun, the boy grinned, wriggled and vanished down the other side of the rocks.

Berk kept his rifle ready, eyes scanning the area as he walked, hunched over, up the old road. He was sure a shot would come at any moment. They crept slowly along the road, watching for the Ranger. Berk smelled smoke in the air.

When they were within shouting distance of the Alley Tunnel, Berk discovered it was locked tight, no one going in or out.

"Juhamit!" Berk cupped his hands around his mouth. "It's Berk Nielsen, the City pilot! For God's sake, let us in!"

No one responded to his frantic, repeated calls for help. He yelled until he was hoarse, shouting at the barred, razor-wired walls in frustration.

If the Family in the tunnel could even hear them, they knew Rangers were close by. If they weren't open for trade, it meant the Rangers were on a bloody rampage. Juhamit's Family weren't about to open their fortifications for anyone. Period.

"There he is again," Sadonya said, and pointed.

Berk dropped to one knee, trying to control his shaking hands as he sighted through the rifle scope at the same young Ranger. Squatting in the rocks above, the boy held his rifle beside him like a walking stick, thick stumps of fingers wrapped around the barrel. Berk saw the boy's matted hair hanging down over black irisless eyes, unreadable through the scope. The boy grinned, long, pointed teeth clacking open and shut under his pig snout. He disappeared from the crosshairs just as Berk squeezed the trigger.

The rifle discharge echoed through the barren hillside, the bullet striking in a puff of dust where the Ranger had been a second before.

A second later, a triumphant warble trilled, hysterical animal laughter mocking Berk.

Sadonya peered at him quizzically. "Why you tryin' to frag him?" she asked. "What he done to you?"

"He's a fucking Ranger, Sadonya," Berk snapped, furious at her ignorance.

"So?"

He stared at her blankly, breathing hard. "They've got to let us in," he muttered, ignoring her. He stood and screamed at the unseen inhabitants of the tunnel, until his voice and the dying twilight both gave out.

They camped for the night, backs against the sharp barbed wire surrounding the tunnel, sleeplessly watching the shadows. Berk's eyes stung with exhaustion and fear.

With the first light, he gave up and pulled the girl to her feet. He started walking as fast as he could down the road again, hoping that it was possible simply to outrace the boy to the unknown borders of the Rangers' territory. The boy had not returned in the morning, and Berk prayed they wouldn't see him again.

Although the steepest parts of the mountain range were, for the most part, behind them, they stumbled haggardly to a halt, exhausted, Berk's frantic energy expended. Both his and Sadonya's skin were beginning to peel again, exposed too long to the harsh sun's radiation. He squeezed out the last of the medication, smearing it over their bare skin like some mystical potion he'd lost belief in.

They still had plenty of food, appetites diminished from sickness and dread, but the ruthless sun had leeched away their water. Berk forced himself to stop, to get out of the sun and wait out the hottest part of the day.

Towards late afternoon, he sighted the young Ranger again. A pebble dropped clinking from the rocks above them, then a second and a third before Berk could spin around, bringing the rifle to his shoulder. The boy was silhouetted in the harsh light for a brief moment, then vanished again. Berk heard the weird, warbling noises he remembered as a boy echoing off the rocks above him. His guts contracted.

His energy spurred, he jerked Sadonya to her feet, griping and irritable, and hastened on the road west.

"Why you gettin' so pissed off?" Sadonya grouched. "He not hurtin' you."

"Shut up and move!" He prodded her roughly, shoving her in front of him.

The boy kept popping up, around this corner, up on that bend, relentlessly tossing pebbles at them and grinning, but otherwise leaving them unmolested. In the distance, a trace of smoke hung in the air. Berk wondered if Sadonya could be right, if the boy was simply playing with them, not intending any harm.

He really didn't want to think about it too much, however.

At this pace, he knew they were within a day of the City. He kept them both going until it was too dark to see the road and, worn out, he huddled against the hollow of a large rock, trying desperately to stay awake, keeping guard. He kept his rifle propped up on his knees and reluctantly allowed Sadonya to jostle close to him, pressed against his shoulder as she snored lightly.

He tried not to sleep, his eyes jerking open at every creak in the breeze, every subtle sound in the distance. He stared into the blackness, the stars filling the hollow of the rock with the only light.

Nothing moving in the shadows except the feeble wind scudding clouds high overhead, thin veils across the starlight. The black of the night slowly turned chalky gray, the light so dim it seemed as if it were a badly developed grainy photograph. It was enough, however, to see the Ranger boy squatting not more than five feet away from them, grinning liplessly at Berk.

The boy's rifle was pointed directly at his chest.

THIRTY-TWO

THE RANGER BOY SHUFFLED FORWARD, BLANK ONYX eyes unblinking, and snatched the rifle out of Berk's numb hands. Sadonya stirred, mumbling to herself as she woke. She blinked at the boy in confusion. Her nose wrinkled as she smelled his rancid body odor, an eye-watering stink.

The boy's lipless mouth clicked open and closed, oversized canines sharp and stained brown. He chuckled like a tortured bird, a throaty rasp that could have been either laughter or crude speech. The odd shreds of rags covering his filth-streaked, twisted limbs blended with his matted hair.

He motioned them down towards the road with the rifle, herding them in front of him. They turned north for hours, the boy loping effortlessly mile after mile, prodding them up a barely discernible deer trail, staggering towards the growing clouds of smoke roiling into the air.

Towards late afternoon, Berk faltered to a stop at the crest of the hill, staring down into the wide hollow between two ridges. A frenzied cluster of Rangers churned the dust up to mingle with the sheets of black smoke rising from a roaring fire. Half the Rangers appeared to be dancing in ecstasy between orange flames licking wildly through the brush. The other half lay scattered on the ground, hacked into bloody pieces. Wriggling bound prisoners were trampled under the stomping feet of dancing Rangers.

The boy clubbed Berk in the small of the back with the rifle butt, propelling him down the slope towards the demented camp. Spotting the newcomers, a clot of warbling, howling dancers swirled up to engulf them as they approached. Rough hands snatched at Berk, tearing at his pack, ripping his robe. He was drowning in a sea of grasping hands, pulled down helplessly into the whirl of bodies. He lost sight of Sadonya in the mêlée, and after a brief, futile skirmish, he found himself bound and tossed ignominiously into a group of abject prisoners.

Most of his fellow captives were Rangers, sitting in stoic silence, jet-black eyes staring unseeingly, piglike nostrils snuffling from the dust. Berk glimpsed a few demoralized Aggies huddled together. He inched his way on his belly toward them.

"Dushprek?" he asked. They turned to look at him vacantly. He tried again. "Ferstanda mish?"

One Aggie, a grizzle-bearded man with a deep gash in the side of his head, oozing blood plastering his hair to his face, leaned towards Berk. As Berk bent closer to hear him, the Aggie suddenly spat in his face.

"*Domen tyran*," the man cursed. "*Tuin deef.*"

Berk winked the spit from his eye, pulling away from the hostile Aggies. He couldn't blame them. Unlike the Brethren, these people had obviously had plenty of experience with the domes. To them Berk was as bad as the Rangers, a marauding enemy plundering their land. A *garden thief*.

His eyes and nose stung from the thick smoke hanging in the still air as their guards prodded them tightly together in a close circle. A huge bonfire had been dragged together out of the smoking brush, and the Rangers hauled the corpses and mutilated pieces of bodies towards it, tossing them into the flames. The stench of burning flesh nauseated him.

But he didn't vomit until he saw the Rangers pulling the

charred carcasses back *out* of the fire and devouring them. He heaved until nothing but greenish spittle dribbled from his mouth, and sat upright again, his teary eyes and the heat waves blurring the dancing figures.

One of the forms approached the captives, distorted in the shimmering heat. It waddled clumsily towards Berk, shaded by an open umbrella over its head. He squinted, staring up into the shadowed face of a serious, snub-nosed girl, heavily pregnant.

"You really a City pilot?" she said indifferently.

Stunned, he gaped at her. "Yes," he said quickly, finding his voice. "Berk Nielsen. Who are you?"

The girl didn't smile. "Adria Heber," she said.

Behind her, three lean Ranger men ran up to the group of hostages. Selecting a captive at random, they jerked one of the bound Rangers to his feet, a man who looked identical to themselves, and goaded him stumbling towards a rioting group of dancers.

Berk watched in horror as they fell on the captive and tore him to pieces, shrieking in glee. A few didn't bother cooking their meat before stuffing the bloody chunks into their mouths, fresh blood running down their chins and chests.

"My God!" he breathed, and looked up into the unemotional face of the pregnant girl. "What is going on here?"

She shrugged, unconcerned. "We had a war. We won. They lost. Now we're celebrating."

"*We?*"

Another Ranger shuffled up beside her, the biggest Ranger Berk had ever seen. Had ever imagined. He slouched over the girl, nearly three feet taller than she, peering down at Berk with solid black eyes, huffing. Berk was startled when the girl snuffled back, an incomprehensible wheeze of animal sounds.

"This is Bear, my . . . husband," Adria said. "He's the leader of this band. Come with us."

She turned without looking back, not bothering to see if he followed or not. The huge Ranger shambled behind her, sniffing around her face like a curious dog.

His arms still bound behind him, Berk wrenched himself

awkwardly to his feet and trotted after the girl and her enormous mate. They picked their way through the throngs of celebrating Rangers towards a campfire set near a tumble of boulders. A group of excited Rangers danced in a lumbering jig, wearing necklaces of slime and dirt-covered human entrails. Several others sat torturing feebly squirming captives, carving their bodies with grotesque designs. Berk shuddered, his guts shriveling, as one popped an eye out of a mutilated prisoner staked alive into the ground. The Ranger's companions laughed, scrambling after the eye as it bounced away, its nerve thread whipping over and over, collecting dirt.

Adria appeared not to notice, swaying as she walked with one hand resting on her swollen belly, followed by the squat shouldered Ranger. On the edge of the camp, out of the way of the revelers, a half-dozen tents had been thrown up carelessly, disease-pocked hides over a skeleton of twisted tree branches providing the only shade. A neglected fire burned in the center of a ring of loosely arranged rocks.

Sadonya sat with her back to the flames, her eyes on the Ranger boy who had captured them. He was crouched on splayed feet several feet away with other young Rangers, all of them watching their leader, Bear, with unblinking stolid expectation as he settled himself on the ground. Adria leaned on his shoulder and, grunting, levered her heavy body down beside him. Bear shoved his face into her neck, whining, a throaty, beseeching whimper, startling Berk. Adria pushed him away, scowling, and shifted the umbrella to her other side to block both him and the sun.

"Please sit down, Mr. Nielsen," she said calmly.

With his arms still bound behind his back, Berk awkwardly lowered himself to sit cross-legged on the ground. Bear leaned towards him, sniffing in his face, sharp canines protruding as his upper lip curled back. The big Ranger growled, a low rumble of ominous sound deep in his chest. Berk felt the blood drain from his face.

With an effort, he forced himself to turn away, and stared at Sadonya. "You okay?" he asked.

She looked bewildered, nodding dazedly.

Her pack had been upended, pouches of her "cooking" strewn around, some sprinkled out onto the ground, smeared over with footsteps. His own cloth pack had been ripped open, water cans emptied and tossed aside. A half-eaten sausage lay in the dust. In a sudden rush of horror, Berk watched as a curious Ranger picked up the small sample can of oil, sniffing at it curiously.

"No, please," he whispered to himself, like a lost prayer. The Ranger pried off the lid, glancing down stupidly as it fell to the ground, then stuck his nose into the can, snorting. "No . . ."

Adria Heber glanced at him, as another Ranger shoved Berk facedown on the ground. Annoyed, she leaned over and slapped Berk's assailant away. Bear jumped the aggressive Ranger, biting and growling as they skirmished briefly in the dust.

Berk didn't notice; his horrified eyes were riveted to the curious Ranger. Dipping his finger into the can. He tasted the black oil with a grimace.

"No," Berk breathed, and watched, sick, as two more Rangers plodded over to inspect the can. They dumped the slick substance over their hands, dribbling it onto the ground. "Oh, no." In a few seconds, it was gone. He felt too numb to cry.

Triumphant, Bear lumbered back to Adria and nuzzled her neck insistently. He was rewarded by her inattentive pat. Adria watched the frolicking Rangers with hooded eyes, a faraway, bored expression on her face.

A high-pitched shriek jolted Berk's attention away from the dark stain of oil seeping into the dusty ground. A dozen captive Rangers with their hands tied to stakes driven into the ground circled vainly away from the shambling creatures tormenting them. A carousing Ranger jerked the legs from under one captive and fell onto its back. Grunting, he began humping himself rapidly between its legs and Berk realized these captives were female. Another reveler yanked his companion off the prisoner, and the two scuffled squabbling in the dirt. The female captives bawled, swinging around the stakes in a futile effort to avoid their captors' unwanted lust.

The Ranger boy Berk recognized lurched closer to the group by the fire, his stumpy hand on his crotch as he whined pathetically, groveling before the leader and his mate, pointing to Sadonya.

"They gonna rav for who get me, too," Sadonya said bleakly.

Bear cuffed the boy, sending him sprawling, and the youngster sulked back towards the wailing cluster of captive Ranger women.

"Don't think so," Adria said to Sadonya, her voice cheerless. "I think Bear prefers keeping you for himself."

The leader sat hunched by the pregnant girl, listening but giving no sign he understood their conversation. His black eyes glittered, and only his lack of crazed rollicking seemed to set him apart from the rest of the savages.

"My granddad's traded with this Ranger band a few times," Adria was saying dispassionately. She stretched her legs out in front of her, her hand on her back as she eased her weight. "They're not as bad as most."

Berk had difficulty conjecturing what could possibly be worse.

"Bear is stupid, but not quite as stupid as most," Adria went on. The Ranger leader twisted his head to stare at her when he heard his name, and she reached up and idly stroked his shoulder as if he were a large, shabby dog. He nuzzled her neck again, losing interest as she pushed him away. He studied the grime between his misshapen toes, scratching himself.

"We've been fighting Crooked Arm and his band almost half a year. It didn't take much military genius to defeat them," Adria said. "Even I could do it." She smiled thinly.

"What are they going to do with us?" Berk croaked.

"They don't kill women," Adria said, " 'specially dome and tunnel women. They think we got some kind of magic powers, and they can get magic babies by us." She put her hand on her stomach. "They're somewhat right. If having half a brain is magic to them, my baby should seem like some wizard."

Her gesture brought Bear's attention back to her, and, surprisingly, he placed a stubby, filthy hand tenderly on her belly, making soft wheezing sounds. He lowered his head, sniffing at her lap. The girl pushed him away impatiently.

Berk licked dry lips. "But, what about men?"

Adria stared at him coldly. "They think you've got magic, too. And they want it. They think they can get it by eating you. Like they did Mr. Wysaigh."

Berk forgot about the oil.

THIRTY-THREE

T HE CELEBRATION WENT ON FOR THE NEXT FEW days without much discernible flagging of energy. Rangers, it appeared, didn't care whether they were exposed to the sun's radiation, dancing in the harsh open light until they dropped senseless and were dragged away by their companions. Berk suspected some of them ended up joining the victims toasted in the fires, winning side or not.

Bear and the dominant members of the tribe were saving him for themselves, not about to waste the Cityman's magic flesh on their lesser followers. They had separated him from the rest of the prisoners and he lay half delirious in the shade of a hide-covered tent, his arms bound behind him, ankles strapped to prevent him from walking. A coarse rope around his neck tied to a stake in the ground gave him enough slack to sit, but not enough to stand.

Adria brought him water, most of which he vomited. She cradled his head against her huge belly and forced him to drink until he could hold it down.

"Can't you do something?" he pleaded with her. "Untie me, let me go? Please?"

"I'm Bear's woman. That's all. I can do pretty much what I want, s'long's I don't try leaving, or interfere with Bear's diet. I'm real sorry, but if I helped you escape, Bear'd kill me without thinking twice about it." She patted her belly. "I've got a baby now to worry about."

"A *Ranger* baby," Berk said angrily.

"Half-Ranger. Half-mine," she said. "I'm not trading my life, or my baby's life for yours. I'm the leader's woman, and I do have a little leverage with Bear. I don't mean to seem hardhearted, and I really am doing my best to keep you alive, Mr. Nielsen, but I'm sorry, sooner or later"—she shook her head—"you're lunch." She picked up the brass canteen and left.

Bear himself brought water and food later. The hulking Ranger stopped to peer inquisitively into the tent, then brusquely tossed the brass canteen and a thin, burnt portion of meat on the ground. The dim-witted Ranger hadn't intended torturing Berk; psychological torment was too sophisticated a concept for him to grasp, Berk was sure. It simply hadn't occurred to Bear that the canteen was useless with Berk's hands still shackled behind his back.

The meat he didn't even want to look at.

Outside, night had fallen, firelight wavering through the ragged opening in the crude tent. The shrieks of dying Rangers blended with howls of their mad tortures.

Berk stood hunched over as far as the rope around his throat would allow and pulled desperately, straining to pull the stake from the ground until his neck was rubbed raw and bleeding. He was leaning, choking himself against it when he noticed Sadonya squatting in the tent opening, a shadow against the firelight.

"You walkin' onna razor edge again, outatown man," she said, her voice colorless.

"Jesus, Sadonya, help me!" He stumbled to his knees.

She inched her way into the tent, and crouched on the ground, arms resting on her knees. "Why?"

His rage boiled up. "Then get the fuck out!" he yelled, unafraid that he could be heard above the ghastly din outside. "Take your gloating somewhere else!" Unable to stop himself, he started to weep. He sat down heavily.

"Maybe we make nother deal, huh?" she said quietly.

"No. No more deals. No more of this shit, Sadonya." He was tired. He took a deep breath to ease his throat. "Either help me or go away and leave me alone."

She sat in the dark, saying nothing. He could see her profile in the filtered light.

"Do you think," he said finally, "you could manage to give me some water out of the canteen without having to make me bargain for it?"

Without a word, she retrieved the canteen and pulled the stopper, holding the container to his mouth. He drank greedily, gulping the warm, metallic water down as quickly as he could, draining the canteen within seconds. He sat back on the ground, the last of the water dripping through his beard.

Through the tent flap, he watched a group of Rangers tie a captive Aggie between the trunks of two thin trees, and slowly begin disemboweling him, running his intestines out through a tiny hole where his navel had been. The Aggie shrieked in agony, his screams breaking.

"What kind of deal?" Berk said softly, eyes riveted on the tortured man.

The girl shuffled in front of him, blocking his view of the Aggie. She pointed to his crotch. "Make it hard," she said.

"What?" he said uncomprehendingly.

"Make it hard," she insisted. "I mark you. You and me, we fuck. Now."

He gagged. "You're *crazy*," he said.

"This the deal, outatown man. Real simple. I mark you mine. Then we 'scape." She pushed her face closer to his, her furious eyes glinting red in the light. "No more this 'Sadonya, you a stupid shit.'" She punched him hard in the chest, knocking him on his side. "No more 'Sadonya, you a little bitch,' no more 'Sadonya, you crazy, you shut up, do this, I beat you up you don' do I say.'" She kicked him rhythmically to emphasize her points, her toughened foot slamming painfully into his head, his back, his legs, his ribs, bruisingly hard. She stopped, breathing rapidly, then reached down to jerk open what was left of his shabby robe. "Make it hard."

He stared at her, unable to speak. Outside, the Aggie

began screaming again. Berk glanced through the tent flap, and saw that he'd been decorated, painted with red stripes, understanding a second later when the Rangers ripped another ribbon of skin from the man's writhing body, flaying him slowly. Berk swallowed hard.

"What about your booby trap?" he said desperately. Sadonya stared at him, unblinking. "The little nasties you've got tucked up inside you—what about them?"

She snorted. "That jess t'keep Mouse offa me. Don't get nasties ever. Make it hard *now*, outatown man. Or I leave, you die." Her eyes were pitiless in the darkness. "*Do it*," she hissed softly.

He squeezed his eyes closed and tried to make it hard.

He pushed away the anguished shrieks and howls of rampaging savages. He tried to remember how beautiful December had been, how much he once loved her, focusing all his concentration on the first time he'd ever seen her naked.

He forced his memory to recall how the light had been, how it had blurred across that tiny room overlooking the park, clean, warm highlights glistening from her hair. She had smiled so serenely as she unpinned it, letting it spill over her arms and breasts in cascade of gold.

He had sat on the bed, the crisp smell of starched linen and fresh flowers in the room. Reaching for her blouse, he gently pulled the buttons apart, one by one, slipping his hand in on the swell of warm white flesh, astonished how hard her nipple had been under his hand as the Aggie suddenly cried out in terror and pain.

It wasn't working.

He grit his teeth, trying to resurrect the feel of December's hips pressing against him, the warm smooth skin slick with sweat, the salt on his lips as she kissed him deeply, running her tongue along the edge of his teeth, moaning in his mouth. Her long, slender legs entwined with his as Sadonya said, "Can't wait too long f'you, outatown man."

His eyes snapped open. "It's a little difficult for me to get it up for rape, Sadonya, especially my own."

Like it had been difficult for December to be in a receptive mood when *he* had raped *her* the night before he left.

The unbidden memory surged back. He jerked away the bedclothes in his drunken rage, so righteously convinced she had been sleeping with Markley. He knew the exact angle of her arm as she held up her hand to block the light in her eyes while he dropped his pants. He could still recall her cutting expression of disgust just before he ripped her nightgown away from her breasts.

He remembered how they had fought, striking at each other, kicking and biting, punching each other as they struggled. How they had fallen onto the floor, December infuriated as he forced her legs apart with his knee.

"What did *you* have to do for your prize flying assignment? Say pretty please, bend over his desk and let Cormack plug you in the ass?" she spat at him in his memory. A split-second image of himself tethered by his wrists to a stake while Cormack buggered him on the dusty ground, gnarled bloodstained feet stamping around them in the firelight, swept him with fury.

He felt the soft curve of December's throat as he brutally jammed his forearm under her chin, felt the sting in his hand as he slapped her across the face in trembling wrath.

"You're nothing but a selfish, juvenile, washed-up failure," she said, and he realized, amazed, he *was* hard, his cock achingly stiff.

He lurched against Sadonya, knocking her down as he fell across her body. She grunted, squirming around on the ground beneath him. It felt ridiculous for a moment, trying to make love trussed up like a chicken.

No, not *make love*, he reminded himself, *fucking*. That's all this was, and a rape at that, his *own* rape, which made him angrier. The anger made his cock harder, and it was fitting, he decided, if he was going to be raped—what the hell, might as well be dressed for the part.

Sadonya scooted away from him, the leash around his neck drawing him up short. "Come on, girl," he said coaxingly, feeling himself grinning up at her from the ground like a fiend, rope digging into his skin. "If you're gonna mark me, you'll have to do it where I can reach you."

She regarded him cautiously, then slithered her body awkwardly under his.

"You want me to fuck you, spread your legs apart," he snarled, trying to push between them with his knees, bound at the ankles.

Sadonya's eyes glittered in the firelight as she stared at him, sullen and malevolent. He saw December's hate-filled eyes glaring. It was awkward maneuvering himself across her thin body, his cock throbbing. He thrust blindly, searching. He found the softness between her bones and pushed hard, insistent.

"Ow!" the girl cried out, struggling. "You hurtin' me!"

She clubbed him painfully across the side of his head, knocking him off of her, scrambling out from beneath him. Gasping face down in the dust, his erection scraping against the grit, he saw her feet standing by his head. She pushed him over onto his back with one foot against his shoulder.

"You're not making this easy," he said, winded, looking up at her.

She said nothing. Hitching the tatters of her robe up around her naked hips, she lowered herself to her knees over him, grasping his rigid cock in one hand. He raised his head to look down the curve of his chest, his spine arched over arms pinioned behind his back. "Little more to the right, that's it, no, too far, now to the left," he said mockingly as she groped for the correct position.

"Shut up," she growled.

He felt her flesh resist for a moment; then his cock burst through, slipping inside her blood-warm body.

She yelped, a quick inhalation of pain and surprise, then balanced herself with her hands pressing down on his naked chest.

He lay his head back against the ground, and forced himself up into her, her sharp bones sawing against his pelvis. The girl's eyebrows drew together in concentration as she raised herself, sliding clumsily up and down his erect cock. His arms ached, his body trembling with pain and anger and a strange sexual craving for release. *Oh, yes*, he thought in wonder, *yes*. He closed his eyes.

"You didn't care that I crashed Outside, did you?" he said to his memory wife. His hips moved with an energy of their own, moving without him. Sadonya inhaled through her clenched teeth as he buried himself inside her in another long, furious thrust. "You wanted me to die, so you could fuck Markley."

"I can fuck anyone I want to now," December whispered back. "I can fuck a *lot* of men, not just Markley." Taunting him, hating him.

God, yes.

His thrusts became harder, brutal, and he grinned to himself as he lay under the girl, his hands bound as helplessly as December's wrists when he pinned them by her head, his fingers clenched in her hair. His back flexed, his breath coming quick, hot and dry in his mouth.

But this time, it wasn't December lying unwillingly beneath him as he shuddered against her body. For a moment, with his eyes closed, he saw again her strange smile, the tiny feral grin as she locked her legs around his waist, the odd triumph behind the cynical amusement.

Did he understand it now?

The weird heat began pulsating up through his spine, fire streaking through his arms, his fists clenching under his back as it seethed across his aching shoulders, condensing in his pounding heart. He opened his eyes and stared at the girl hovering above him, her face obscured in a cave of matted hair.

Do you understand . . . ?

Maybe he did. Maybe now . . .

He pressed the soles of his feet against the ground, lifted his hips to slam himself into her. She flinched and whimpered softly. *Yes*—his eyes stung as he stared up at her, his teeth grating together in hate and pain and despair—*maybe he did*, and thrust savagely again.

She wobbled, gasping. Her hands slid down his chest, clutching at his throat as she struggled to keep her balance. Hard fingers dug into his neck, choking him.

Perfect, he thought, as the heat focused into sharp fire sweeping through his nerves, stabbing down into his groin.

He heard himself moan, his breath ragged, and let his desperate anger and nightmare fear blend inextricably in a wave of intense pleasure, agony and tortured desire washing through him, draining him completely.

His head pounded, his exhausted muscles shivering uncontrollably as the girl slid off him. He curled onto his side, away from her, suddenly disgusted and sick.

"Huh," she said behind him. "That not much." Her voice wavered over her bravado.

"So sue me," he muttered.

She stood, walked around to face him. "I notime ever gone back onna deal, Berk," she said quietly. "I know you hate me. Don' care. Now I mark you, y'mine, tha's all. You jess be ready to trot quicktime morrow."

Outside, the Aggie's bubbling wail ended abruptly.

Berk nodded, mutely.

THIRTY-FOUR

August 13, 2242

WHEN HE WOKE, HE COULDN'T BELIEVE IT HAD been possible for him to sleep. What woke him was also unbelievable; the camp was eerily silent. He rolled onto his stomach, lifting himself up on his chest to peer out into the morning light, no more than a slice of pink between the gray sky and the low hills.

The Aggie still hung between the two trees, dead, his head missing from the bloody corpse, but at his amputated feet, curled up on the ground, five Rangers slept peacefully. They looked strangely like small children worn out by too much play, arms draped affectionately around each other as they snored blissfully.

Quickly, Berk hunched himself up onto his knees, crawling as far as the tether would allow towards the tent flap. In every direction he could see, Rangers had fallen asleep, slumping mid-revel onto the ground. The fires had burned down, wisps of dying smoke trailing thinly into the morning air.

Two figures walked through the haze and smoke towards him, stepping casually over dead and sleeping bodies. Sadonya and Adria. He sat back on his haunches and waited.

Sadonya held his knife in one hand and his rolled cloth

bag in the other. A rifle was slung over Adria's shoulder, bouncing against the side of her distended belly as she walked carefully, laboriously. She was too young, he thought, to be that pregnant and that grim.

They stooped into the tent and Sadonya held the knife up to his throat. Her hands and the knife were bloodstained. She locked her gaze with his for a moment, then cut the tether, leaving the collar around his neck, long leash trailing. Adria watched impassively as Sadonya sawed through the thongs around his ankles. He lumbered to his feet, and turned around, his back to Sadonya. But instead of cutting his hands free, she hung the pack around his shoulders.

He looked down at her as she tucked the knife blade under the leather strap around her waist. Adria handed her the rifle.

"I hope you're enjoying getting even with me, Sadonya," he said quietly. She said nothing as she jerked him out of the tent by the leash, then jabbed him forward with the barrel of the rifle.

"I thought you couldn't allow me to escape," he said, turning his attention to Adria as they picked their way carefully around the fallen sleepers.

"Mr. Nielsen," Adria said politely, as if she didn't notice his difficulty, "contrary to what you seem to believe, I don't particularly like living with Bear and these people. I want very much to go home to my family. If I'm careful and smart, keep my position with Bear, someday, maybe soon, I might get the chance."

She glanced at Sadonya with what seemed to be fear and hostility. Understandable. "Bear thinks I've got some kinda magic. I'm just smarter than him, that's all. I know how to keep rifles in working order, and I recognize explosives when I see them. But I can't make poisons or . . . banes"— she said the unfamiliar word as if it were a curse—"and I'm not willin' to become a free-for-all woman. Or dinner."

"Ah." It made sense. She needed to get rid of Sadonya as quickly as possible, fearing a rival. Sadonya had "magical powers" that the Heber girl couldn't match, and that made her a very potent threat to Adria's fragile security. "Are they all dying?" Berk asked. "If they're dead, you could escape with us."

"No," Adria said, disappointed and unhappy. "She said she didn't have enough to kill everyone."

I'll bet, Berk thought, glancing at Sadonya's cold face. *She just didn't want you along for the ride, Adria. Sorry about that. She doesn't want a competitor any more than you do.* He stepped over a prostrate Ranger, saliva running from the side of the man's mouth as he grinned, eyes rolling sightlessly in his head, and his hand groping through the rags between his legs. Berk recognized that particular funbane, all right.

"You could still come with us," he said. "We could try."

Adria snorted. "A pregnant woman? This baby's about to drop outta me any minute, and you ain't gonna have a lot of time as it is to waste it playing midwife. Besides, you're going to need me here."

"Why?"

She grinned, a mean smile. "When Bear wakes up, he's going to be real pissed off he's lost such big strong magic. He'll want you back twice as bad, and you got a long, long way to outrun him. You're gonna need somebody to convince Bear your magic is so strong he's better off not fucking around with it. Let you go."

Berk felt cold even in the simmering hot temperature. "You think you can?"

She shrugged. "Don't know. Bear has an annoying tendency to act first and think later, when he bothers thinkin' at all."

They reached the outskirts of the camp, the borders gaily decorated with severed heads, hands, feet and other body parts too badly mangled to identify impaled on top of crude spears thrust into the ground.

"Go straight north from here," Adria said. "You'll cross a dry river first, then run into an old road heading almost due west. I suggest you go as fast as you can." She hesitated, then put one hand on Berk's arm. "You get a message back to my granddad, okay? If you make it, tell him I'm all right. Tell him that if I can, I'm going to get Bear to come trade again when it gets cooler, when the tribe gets tired of 'celebrating.' Tell him—" her voice broke suddenly, and he saw tears glinting in her eyes, "—tell him I love everybody and I want to come home."

He looked at her for a moment, then impulsively leaned over and kissed her lightly on the forehead. "Thank you," he whispered quickly.

She wiped the tears away with the back of her grimy hands, spun away abruptly without another word, walking back through the smoke and sleeping Rangers, her back very straight.

Sadonya poked him with the rifle and they trotted quickly away, up the ridge of the hill.

"How'd you slip it to them, Sadonya? Put it in the water?" Berk asked, panting cheerfully.

"Blood," Sadonya said without looking at him. "They damnsure drink a lotta blood."

"Right, should've guessed." His breath ran out and he concentrated on keeping his quick pace. Tied behind him for four days, his arms ached, his fingers swollen so badly he couldn't bend the joints. The weight of the pack sent ripples of agony through his shoulders, streaking down his back. They crab-walked down the side of a hill, loose shale rocks skipping out from under their feet.

He lost his balance, teetering. The long piece of rope hanging from his neck tangled around his knees. Jerking instinctively, he fell, toppling over the rocks, crashing through the thorny brush as he slid down the hillside. He skidded to a stop, the skin on his chest scraped raw, loose gravel tinking down to patter against his face.

He lay limp, his cheek pressed against the hot ground, as Sadonya picked her way carefully down the hillside towards him. She jabbed him in the shoulder with the rifle.

"Get up."

"No," he said, not moving. He turned his head to stare up at her harsh face above the black void of the rifle barrel. "Come on, Sadonya. Enough's enough. You've made your point. Untie me."

The hot breeze lifted the hair out of her surly eyes. "Don' trust you," she said.

With very good reason, Berk thought. "You trust Bear more?" he demanded fiercely. "You more interested in revenge than you are in surviving?" She hesitated. "For God's sake, Sadonya, if you want me to beg, I'll beg! *Please*." His voice was hoarse, angry, not a hint of pleading in it. "We're not going to make it like this!"

Reluctantly, she took the knife out of the makeshift belt to cut through the noose, then the leather around his wrists. She backed away as his arms yanked free. He bit back a whimper as pain twitched through his injured muscles. Fingers numb, he tried to massage the circulation back into his arms.

"I keepin' the rifle," she said suspicious, and tucked the knife back into her belt.

He chuckled ruefully, holding up his hands. They looked like fat purple sausages. "I couldn't even hold it, girl."

She stared at him enigmatically. "Less go."

He staggered to his feet, adjusting the pack on his shoulders with clumsy fingers. "You're the boss," he said with false exuberance.

I do believe I'm going to kill her, he thought as they stumped across the burning hills. Somehow, that made him happy. It lightened his step as he walked, plotting how he could whirl suddenly, maybe jerk the rifle out of her surprised hands and frag her ass. Or maybe—he grinned cheerfully—he'd just throttle her, choke her slowly to death while he watched her face turn as purple as his hands. He laughed outright, smiling affectionately at her puzzled face as he imagined her bloodshot eyes bugging out, her tongue blackening as it protruded from her mouth, his fingers crushing her larynx. She smiled back at him hesitantly, perplexed, and he had a sudden wave of fondness for her, thinking *Oh, yes, I'm definitely gonna kill you, bitch*. He had to fight the whim to hug her in lunatic elation. He knew he was losing his mind.

Less than ten miles later, they reached what had once been a man-made aqueduct distributing water from the

Alley River into the long, thirsty fields rolling across the worn hills. Its foundations lost, the man-made controls bending its will vanished, the water had seeped away, back into the streams and gullies, leaving nothing behind to nurture the tough weeds and scraggly brush clinging tenaciously to the sides of the aqueduct.

Fallen chain-link fences so corroded they were no more than wisps of rusted lace stained the ground, stalks of weeds half-burying them. Berk slid down over the side of the dry canal and, despite his abused hands, easily scaled the opposite wall, the girl following behind. He sat at the edge, watching her climb.

Now, he thought, *I could do it now.* She looped the rifle onto her back to free her hands, fingernails digging into the cracks in the stone wall. He grinned so hard his teeth hurt as she dragged herself up to the edge. She froze, staring up at him narrowly, as if she could read the intent in his face. *Now*, warily, she scrambled on hands and knees onto the embankment, and *now* twisted the rifle around, muzzle pointed vaguely at his chest.

He nodded, still grinning maniacally, and got to his feet.

The road was as Adria had promised, a few miles more to the north. He recognized it almost instantly, his sense of direction kicking in so abruptly it made him dizzy. The old Penn road. Forty or fifty miles west, and they'd come in at the back door of the Pit.

He set off down the old road, almost loping in the fierce heat. Giddy and reeling, his vision doubled and he finally staggered to a halt, just before he threw up convulsively. Thin acid drool was all there was.

Sadonya plodded up behind him, and nodded towards the side of a hill, the broken concrete and steel girders of an amputated overpass half blocking the road, providing a tiny oasis of shade in the searing heat.

"We gotta rest a little, Rangers or no Rangers," she said.

"Yes, ma'am, boss, ma'am," he said, and giggled inanely. "Whatever you say, Your Highness." It was all beginning to seem hilariously funny. He tried an exaggerated mock bow, tripping over his own feet as his head spun. She shoved him with her free hand towards the shade, eyes unamused.

Taking the pack from him, she watched him carefully, rifle strapped to her shoulder. She ground a mixture of herbs into a small bowl, spitting into it to make a paste. When she'd finished, she put it down just outside his reach and backed away, balancing the rifle across her lap.

"You eat that. Make you better."

"Thank you, no, if you don't mind," he said.

She shrugged. "Die, then."

He thought about that for a while, then finally reached for the bowl. It tasted as nasty as it looked, but he spooned it with his fingers into his mouth and gagged it down.

"Mmm-mmm," he said, smacking his lips. "Delicious. Yummy-yum."

She took back the little bowl, packing it away in the cloth sack, and sat with the rifle resting across the tops of her knees, staring at him as he leaned back against the rubble of the bridge. His head cleared slightly, and he looked down at his body, seeing the strange white patches of flesh in between peeling red skin and scabbed scratches.

He knew what they were. He could feel how his hair was beginning to fall out in blanched clumps, his smaller injuries refusing to heal. He was going to die the way the old man had, murdered slowly by the sun. It would be the same, the sickness riddled so deeply into the body it couldn't be dug out or hacked away. He wondered for a moment if he could do what his father finally had done, gone down together with the only thing that had ultimately mattered in the old man's life.

Would I, Dad?

The old man didn't answer.

Berk didn't want to think about it too hard, either.

The heat stupefied him, or maybe it was Sadonya's bane, and he slept, if it could honestly have been called sleep, until the sun slanted a burnt red haze across the west. Berk blinked awake and stared at thunderclouds forming low on the horizon, hovering far off behind the hills. The faint rumble of thunder teased his ears.

He bolted up, sitting erect, still light-headed and flushed with fever. Sadonya dozed, head bent over the rifle held lax in her arms.

"Time to go!" he said brightly. The girl jerked in surprise, the muzzle of the rifle leaping up at him. "Oh, sorry," he said in phony chagrin. "May we go now, with your permission, pretty please?"

She scowled in abrupt anger, her hands tightening on the gun as she instantly brought it up to her shoulder. He cringed as she fired. The bullet smashed into the hulk of the old overpass, a bare foot from his head, the explosion ringing in his ears. Powdered concrete dusted over him. He lowered his arms from over his head, face blanched, staring wide-eyed at her.

"Don't," she said, her words very clear and clipped, "make me do something you'll regret."

It took him a moment before he got his breath back. "Right," he agreed soberly, holding up appeasing hands. "Okay."

She tossed him the canteen, and he sipped from it carefully, eyeing her as he drank. The water was already half gone. The pack followed the canteen, hitting the dust in front of him. Shrugging it around his shoulders, he got to his feet and trudged down the road. The spot between his shoulder blades felt itchingly vulnerable, and he glanced nervously behind him. She walked with her eyes lowered, the rifle drooping on its strap, just another piece of baggage.

She was muttering to herself.

They marched another five miles as the sky darkened into night, the remote thunderclouds sparking dim flashes of lightning pulsing through the edges of clouds in the distance. Stars in the west shivered and winked out as unseen clouds covered them.

"Stop," Sadonya called. He came to a standstill, head lowered, and waited. She plodded up next to him. "How far *is* this place?" she whined. "We walk and walk and walk, seem like we walk alltime neverend."

His sense of humor had gone, no wisecracks left. He hadn't even bothered daydreaming about killing her for hours, no joy left in it. Sighing, he squinted into the dark down the road. "I can't tell exactly, but it's about forty miles."

"How far that?" she demanded sourly.

"If we walk all night, we'll get there before we have to stop and get out of the morning sun."

A faint animal call lifted on the night breeze. It might have been only a bird, trilling in the dark. Their heads swiveled towards the sound, straining. "Maybe we walk jess a bit more," Sadonya said slowly.

"Good idea," Berk said. He wasn't being sarcastic.

They were both bone tired, toiling with bodies pushed far beyond reserves. When Berk ran out of energy, fear kept him going. When the fear ran out, he kept walking, oblivious, hypnotized by the rhythm of his own footsteps.

At one point, he was sure he'd fallen asleep on his feet. All he had to do was lean a little forward, let the inertia of his own weight jerk his leg forward reflexively, as if all on its own, drop his numbed foot on the ground and keep on leaning forward, jerk, plod, jerk, plod, on and on. He felt a hand on his arm, startling him back into awareness.

He'd walked completely off the road. The rifle now slung across her back, Sadonya caught up with him, guiding him back to where he could barely make out the tracks of the Penn road in the faint moonlight.

They leaned against each other for support, listless. *Too bad*, he thought. *This would be a perfect time to kill her*. Jerk, plod.

He ran into the next hill as if it were a brick wall, and crumpled to the ground, staring up the incline in a stupor. The leaden gray dawn already lightened the east, the horizon behind them a bumpy silhouette of black mountains. Sadonya dropped beside him, face slack and dull. She glanced up, then closed her eyes as she leaned against him.

When he woke, they were cuddled together in the open, the sky a virulent pink. She mumbled slightly but didn't wake as he gently lifted the rifle from her shoulder, slipping the band out from under her limp arm. She murmured, eyes still shut, and nestled deeper into his lap, dirty hands tucked under her chcck. Hc patted her placidly, stroking her face as he stared off across the barren hills.

She opened gummy eyes finally, and he helped her to her feet. Looking once at the rifle in his hands, she made no protest, nor did she look perplexed when he lifted up the pack to his own shoulder. They walked up the hill, and looked over the crest at another. When they got to the top of that one, another took its place.

"Goddamn it," she said, and stopped halfway up another incline. "You fuckin' lie to me again, huh." She pointed with a skeletally thin arm at the hills rolling endlessly around them. "You lie alltime, lie, lie, *lie*! Nothin' *here*, is there? You lying shit."

Trembling in fury, she turned around and started marching down the way they'd come.

"Where the hell are you going?" he yelled.

Whipping around, she screamed at him, "Home! *My* place!" She bent over in the effort to scream, shoulders hunched.

"You'll never make it," he yelled back, "you skinny stupid ass! You'll be eaten by Rangers!"

"No, I won't! I gonna be King Shit, kick that little bitch Adria out, take her place! She *nothin'*! She like that Elissa bitch, she *nothin'*!"

"Fine!" he howled, not even hearing her any more, and heaved the pack to sail through the air, and thump into her chest. "Take this then, you'll need it."

She staggered back under the blow, catching the pack in her arms. Her face crazed, she flung it back at him. "Don' want it! Don' want *nothin'* from you, you nothin' but a lyin' shit! Don' need no favors from *you*!" The pack fell short of his feet.

"Suit yourself! I don't care!"

He whirled around, stomping up the hill in pure rage. The crest bobbed in front of him, exposing more and more of the valley behind it. His face prickled, and the anger vanished. When he stumbled to a halt, he stood looking down at golden bright domes glittering in the embrace of the blue river.

He turned, and looked at the girl's thin back retreating from him, the pack dragged along on the ground beside her.

He tried. He really tried. He bit his lips, shivering with the effort. His eyes watered, a hot tear splashing its way down his filthy cheek, clinging to his beard. He knew he'd regret it for the rest of his life.

"Sadonya," he called out finally. "Wait . . ."

THIRTY-FIVE

August 15, 2242

T HEY WALKED INTO THE CITY SHORTLY BEFORE THE
morning work shift. He had passed the bleak University ruins without even seeing them, following Center Road like a beacon, straight for the only port on the east side of the domes. He could see only the domes. *Home*, his ears rushing with the sound.

The sleepy kid who responded to his call at the security gate blinked in astonishment, not quite understanding. A Ranger girl and a pathetic Aggie, Berk was sure that's what the scared kid saw. But an Aggie wouldn't have spoke like Berk did, wouldn't have known what he did. Reluctantly convinced, the boy, barely old enough to be a guard, opened the gate.

The kid gaped as Berk handed him the rifle, ragged, filthy girl muttering behind him. "Don't bother waking up your boss, son," Berk said distractedly, "I'll do it myself when I get home."

It was still dark, condensation dripping from the overhead domes in a fine, drizzling mist, a few stragglers from the night shift wandering home on the shiny black wet sidewalk. They stared at the shabby pair curiously, and Berk scanned each face eagerly for recognition. It wasn't that large a City,

and while Berk knew a lot of people, most of the night crews
were strangers to him.

But everyone's face looked familiar, even if he didn't
know any of the people passing him. They obviously found
him familiar, too, but couldn't quite place him, didn't want
to, either. The way he looked, he knew they weren't curious
enough to approach him. How could they have known he'd
just walked three hundred miles, through desert and
Rangers. He was only another poor soul, another emaciated
down and out drunk in filthy rags. Another man lost in his
frustrations, too far gone. Soon, when it became too uncomfortable for the public to watch, the compassionate City
would come and cart him away to a nice safe rehab hospital,
out of sight. Out of his mind.

No messiness.

That wouldn't be civilized, would it?

He wanted to giggle, close to hysteria, but he kept it
locked away tightly, trudging up Sixth Street, the cool fa-
miliarity around him almost surreal. Yearning pulled him
along the streets, an ache he didn't even understand.

He stared up at the Stanwix Street apartment building,
lurching with an eerie sense of time shifting under his feet.
Automatically his eyes counted up the floors and over to the
second window from the end. It could have been yesterday
he'd wandered home, drunk, fat, silly, staring up to catch the
yellow trickle of light squeezed out of the old brick and
stone building.

Not months ago.

Not a lifetime of fear and pain and hunger ago.

The light was on. He stumbled into the building, tears beginning to well dangerously behind his eyelids, blurring his
vision. Sadonya trailed behind him, following him up the endless flights of stairs, still dragging the idiotic pack with what
was left of her nameless powders and herbs. He paid no attention to her at all, not caring that she was there, not hearing
her cursing, softly foul.

He wasn't even sure why he was homing in here. He was
desperately afraid, needing *something* he couldn't name to
anchor him, convince him it was true, he was home. Why

December? Why not Cormack, the son of a bitch. Why not a hospital, which he knew he could surely use? Why not, for God's sake, his *mother*?

All that had held him together, all he had grabbed hold of and dreamed of was up there, before him. His old life, the promise that things could be real again.

"December," he said, his voice coming out in a raspy, strangled whisper. He said it aloud again, studying the sound in confusion, as if he'd never heard it before.

It didn't matter. He had to get up there, had to see her. It drove him, his legs now sticks of brittle pain, jabbing up through his crotch as wooden feet pounded down on each step, only thick deadness ever quite making it through to his brain. He had to open that door, get in there, before . . . before . . .

Before what, he had no idea. Desperation pulled him up the stairs, yanking him on as if he were some grotesque mannequin, grinning and jerking him forward without thought, running on pure exhaustion.

The numbers wavered on the door, so far away it was as if they belonged to someone else. The top of the 6 was still chipped off, making the apartment number "71o," and he felt such warm tenderness and bleary joy to see it, like an old friend greeting him.

Welcome home. Yes, it said, you're home at last.

Somewhere in his mind's eye, he could see himself and loathed his loss of control. Open that door and your whole life will mutate before your very eyes. It's going to hit you square in the face, and you know it, but there isn't anything else you can do. His fist pounded on the door, and his ragged, raw throat bellowed:

"December! DECEMBER!"

The door across the hall opened, and he turned his head reflexively, flinching, annoyed at the intrusion. Mrs. Kerowitz glared at him, a split second of resentment, immediately followed by wide-eyed recognition. Her hands flew to her face and she screamed.

Somehow, it seemed like such a pleasant sound.

The door opened as he was still pounding splinter-pained

fists against it, nearly losing his balance. He gasped, silent, staring.

December.

She stood in the doorway, one hand still on the doorknob, looking at him with a strange, puzzled expression. As if he had just gone down a few hours ago for a beer so why was he standing there banging on the door and screaming like a madman?

She was as beautiful as he had remembered her, memory not adding a thing. He wanted suddenly to touch the skin, still pale and smooth, honey-blond hair like strands of pure gold, just to see if it would disintegrate, and he'd wake up back in the Filly, strapped down, hallucinating in ratshit-filled isolation. He felt the weight of months of filth and blood suddenly sitting on his body, blackening his pores, cracking and caking in the lines on his hands. He felt the white disease, etched in his peeling skin, the clumps of balding hair on his skull, his patchy beard.

His hand faltered and fell before he'd lifted it two inches. He couldn't bring himself to touch her.

"December," he said, whispering her name with so much incredible, sudden love, so much tenderness. His throat hurt and, surprised, he felt the first tear sliding down his face. He blinked, feeling another begin its long trek down dirt-encrusted cheeks.

She made no move at all, not to hug him, not to scream in shock or delight, not even to slam the door in his face. The mildly perplexed look simply sat there, and when Markley's anxious face appeared behind her, it all made sense.

He had held on so tightly, knowing the hurt-filled fantasy he'd accused her of had been a lie. A lie he fostered and made real by forcing it on her. He'd killed what was left of the trust and love between them then, months past, and he'd known what he'd done to her, to himself on some level.

He really had known, but somehow the pain was not nearly as bad as he thought it might have been. The bland look on her face and the guilty scurrying of the man hovering behind her, pulling on a bathrobe, *his* bathrobe, over his pudgy frame, worried that December's prodigal husband, unexpectedly returned from the dead, would rise up and strike him in righteous anger made Berk smile through the tears. He wanted suddenly to reassure the poor man, *it's really okay*.

Her eyes said, Well, now what should I do with you? With no more concern than if he had been a stray cat. Just another problem inconveniently landing on her doorstep for her to handle. But that was just how December was. How she had always been.

And that was all right, too. Everything seemed wonderful and sweet, even the faint shine of sweat on Markley's forehead. Even the way the man darted nervously around in the background, like a rat caught in a maze, unsure of which direction to bolt to safety. Berk started to laugh, feeling such overwhelming affection for her, for them both.

He'd lied. Just like Sadonya said he'd done, yes, he had. And it was the lies he told himself, he knew it now, that had kept him alive, kept driving him. Bringing him home.

And see? Here he was.

I'm home, honey! See? Here I am! Home at last, December! It *was* funny. He laughed harder, tears flowing down his face, and he barely realized it when he fell to his knees, only the sharp shards of pain racing up his thighs, cutting his feet. He wept like a baby, unashamed, laughing hysterically while December and Markley stared at him and Sadonya muttered behind him.

Home at last.

Jiggity jig.

THIRTY-SIX

September 13, 2242

S OMEONE, MAYBE IT HAD BEEN THE STUNNED KID AT the security gate, or probably Mrs. Kerowitz, had had enough sense to call the police. When the ambulance came, the attendants had compassionately scraped him off the floor.

"Hey, not yet," Berk was saying, still giggling as tears ran down his face. "I really should check in first with my boss, you know."

"Sure," one of the attendants had said kindly, just before she stabbed him in the ass with a needle.

He spent the next three days in a delirium, bits and pieces of wakeful minutes cluttered together like a child's montage of picture clippings, nothing connected, messy around the edges. He would wake at the rustle of cloth and open his eyes as cool fingers checked his pulse, or slid a thermometer into his rectum.

"You're beautiful," he'd whisper hoarsely, awed by each and every one of the clean, lovely people, men or women, who touched him gently, smiled cheerfully and patted him as if he were a child.

It felt so wonderful to let himself be taken care of, and so odd to know it was okay to sleep, trusting someone else to watch over him. To lie in a clean bed and let someone else wash his inert body with warm, good-smelling water was such an incredible luxury, while he watched in a wondrous stupor the drips falling out of a bottle down the tube into his emaciated arm. An invisible, soft fuzzy layer a foot thick surrounded him. He floated on it, let himself be buoyed up and carried along by the wonderful whipped cream clouds.

On the third day, his fever finally broke and he stopped feeling quite so good.

"We've decreased your medication, Mr. Nielsen," the nurse explained. "We've had you on intravenous feeding, but we'd like you to try a little solid food, if you can manage."

He tried. After a while, he stopped throwing it all back up, and it began tasting good, too.

His skin sloughed off in patches, bandages peeling away strips whenever they were removed. Murmuring, sympathetic hands brought agony at every touch of the naked, raw tissue underneath. Ulcerations healed slowly.

They finally slid the catheter out of his penis and a sweet, freckle-faced girl let him lean against her as he took weak steps to the toilet. She stood with her back turned to give him the illusion of privacy as he sat on the cold porcelain. He held himself up by holding on tightly to the intravenous pole, and stared at her back, amazed at how her round curves filled out the neat black and white uniform.

"Thank you," he said to her gratefully as she tucked him back into the narrow hospital bed. And been astounded when she'd blushed prettily, shyly bubbling her, oh it's nothing, as if he'd been the most handsome boy she'd ever been infatuated with in medical school.

That was the first indication he had that he'd become a Hero.

After another week, they began apologetically cutting away little parts of his body. Nothing important, they assured him. See? The tops of your ears can be reshaped, they'll just be a bit smaller, and we'll fill in what we take off your nose, nobody'll be able to tell the difference. Just a few scars here and there on your shoulders, a little off your back.

Once your hair grows in, it'll cover that thin line on your forehead quite nicely. Anything deeper, well, we think the gallons of medication we've poured into you should help.

We think.

They'd begin allowing visitors once he'd got his strength up, they told him, which he suspected really meant once he stopped looking like a half-dead corpse about to croak any second and scare somebody. When they came, he was surprised to see how many friends he had. Teddy showed up, and Kilian, and the other fliers he'd never done more than hang around with for a beer. They came solo or in raucous groups, all relentlessly cheerful and encouraging.

He made Kilian promise to send Heber his generator, and his rifles, along with a letter about Adria it took him the better part of a day to finish. Because of the bandages on his hands, he told himself.

His mother came, making him uncomfortable at first as she sat by his bed quietly, sometimes holding his hand so tightly it hurt. She chattered away, trying to fill him in on all that had happened, the gossip around the neighborhood, who was new at the symphony. Then she would fall silent, staring at him as if she couldn't quite believe he was really there. Sometimes, he'd catch the look in her eye, the way she'd looked at the old man during the last two months of his life, knowing he was leaving and never coming back.

And of course, Cormack came. He even brought flowers.

"You're quite the hero around the City, Berkeley," he said as he wandered around the room, looking for something to put them in. He finally settled for the water pitcher, stuffing the flowers casually into its too-small mouth.

"So I've heard," Berk said dryly. "I also heard you got yourself another term."

Cormack seated himself in the bedside chair, leg up over his knee immaculately shaved and smiling, a contented man. "Sure did," he said. "Didn't need your help with PR after all."

Berk stared at him for a moment, then chuckled to himself. "You still hate my guts, don't you?"

"Yes, 'fraid I do," Cormack said amiably, leaning back in

the chair.

Berk hitched himself higher on the pillows to regard the Councilman speculatively. "Why is that?" he asked curiously. There was no animosity in his voice. "I've always wondered."

"Because, son, you're not a team player," Cormack said. "You're first and last interest is yourself. You and the old man both had this real proud individualistic streak. Thought of yourselves as last of the great pioneers. You couldn't fly fixed-wing like the rest of us, not you, gotta be different. Gotta fly around in those airborne lawnmowers to prove how good you are."

"I can fly fixed-wing, Leonard. I just prefer helicopters," Berk said quietly.

"That's another problem, son. No flexibility. Team players are versatile. They're willing to adapt to anything thrown their way. That's how you work together as a team."

Cormack looked down at his fingernails, inspecting them. He fished a nail file from his pocket and concentrated on his hands as he spoke. "You never seemed to understand that the domes exist because people pull together, work together, work for the good of the community. We've done more than simply survive, we've saved human civilization, preserved our knowledge and our heritage by putting the needs of the community first and the individual last."

It sounded like a rehash of a campaign speech. "Led by a few good individuals like yourself," Berk commented wryly.

Cormack continued his grooming. "Mock me all you want to, son. You think I'm some kind of ambitious son of a bitch, and to a certain extent, you're right. I'm ambitious, because I can see the domed Cities are the only true hope of reclaiming the entire planet again, and I want to see that happen. And I'm a son of a bitch, because sometimes . . . a *lot* of times, I have to put the interests of the community first and step on the toes of reckless individuals." He looked up. "Like you."

Berk suddenly knew what Cormack was really saying. "The oil *is* there, Cormack. I had the sample. Goddamn it, I *deserve* something for that at least," he said hotly.

Cormack smiled, putting the nail file back in his pocket. "You're absolutely right, Berkeley. We had a deal, and even if you didn't fulfill your end of it, I can afford to be magnanimous once in a while. Especially for a 'hero.' You've got your priority postings. Guaranteed." He cocked his head slightly to one side. "Um . . . just what are you going to be flying, if you don't mind my asking?"

"You bastard," Berk said softly.

Cormack chuckled and shrugged. "Let me know when you get yourself another lawnmower built, and I'll post you top of the list."

"Get out." Berk rolled over, turning his back on the Councilman.

"We can still talk, Berkeley, any time. There're other options, you know . . ." When Berk didn't answer, Cormack left.

After that, December's news didn't even bother him much. She came, sat by his bed with her back straight, chatting casually about carefully neutral subjects. Her eyes seemed distant, flitting around the room, here, there, looking anywhere but at him.

"They're letting me go tomorrow," Berk said.

She was quiet for a moment. "Yes," she said finally, "I know."

He hesitated. "I hate having to ask you this, December, but do I still have a place to come home to?"

She looked at him then, her blue eyes as clear and cold as a winter's sky. "Of course you do," she said.

He reached over and took her hand cautiously. "Sember, I'm very sorry for a lot of things," he said, watching her impassive face. "I've screwed up our marriage and I know it. I learned a lot while I was out there. I finally understand things better, honest. I've had time to think and I"—he wanted to say *love*, but it refused to come out—"care a great deal about you. Things are different. I want the chance to make it up to you. We could even have that baby you've always wanted—I'd like that now too, I really would. Please, do you think we could try again, one more time?"

She covered his hand with hers, and looked at him for a long time. Slowly, she shook her head. No.

It took a while for it to sink in, and he lay back against the pillows, his hand slipping away from hers. It was as if a great weight had come crashing down on him, and for a moment he thought he'd die. But the feeling slipped away within seconds, leaving behind an odd sense of sad relief.

"I'm sorry," she said. "At least I owe you an explanation."

"No, you don't," he said, and he meant it.

"You're still legally my husband, and you have the right to live in the apartment as much as I do," she went on, not hearing him. "Until the divorce. If you want the apartment, I'll find another place through the Energy Department; you can keep it."

He smiled, and looked at her. Would they be friends afterwards? No, not friends; he knew better. They might meet at parties and be polite to each other, maybe have a drink and reminisce, but the feelings had been too deep and the hurt too painful to pretend they could remain friends.

"Do you love Markley?" he asked, a tinge of pain all he felt.

She regarded him quizzically for a moment. "I don't know," she finally admitted. "I want to live with him."

Why?, he didn't ask.

"He loves me," she answered, anyway. "He adores me, he'll do anything for me. I'm the center of his life, and I like it that way. I don't want a puppet, or a weak man, and he's neither. But I need someone who loves me with that kind of intensity. Even if I can't love him back the same way."

"Poor Markley," he said. And grinned shakily at her.

She smiled back. "Maybe. But he's not stupid. He knows. He understands me, and you just never did. He's willing to take me on my terms, and you weren't. I couldn't be happy with you, Berk. I thought you were exciting and daring, all the things I thought I wanted in a husband. But they're not."

"I was a juvenile, washed-up failure—isn't that what you said?"

For a moment, she looked uncomfortable, the most emotion he'd seen from her in years. "I said that because I wanted to get back at you, hurt you like you were hurting me," she said. Tears glittered at the edges of her eyes. "But you're not a failure any more, are you? Now you're a celebrity, a hero. A real success." There was no sarcasm in her voice.

"Don't you want a hero? Isn't that what you always wanted me to be?" he said, feeling a detached self-pity. "Someone you could be proud of?"

"No," she said simply. "All I've ever wanted, ever needed, was a husband I could live with."

When he left the hospital the next morning, he went to his mother's.

THIRTY-SEVEN

H E WAS LUCKY TO FIND AN APARTMENT ON MAD-
dock after only two weeks, a tiny bachelor studio that
had recently become vacant following the death of its eighty-
seven-year-old tenant. Berk filed his single resident's applica-
tion, and wasn't surprised at how quickly it traveled through
the City Basic Support channels. A Hero couldn't sleep on a
grate, now, could he? Her grandson, another flier, sold Berk
the few bits of furniture the family had no interest in for a
token sum.

The place wasn't bad, and it was cheap enough so that he'd
have a little left over out of his Basic allotment at the end of
the month. The view over the air shaft from its single window
(not counting the tiny frosted-glass vent in the bathroom) was
not much to look at. Berk didn't care, he wasn't interested in
scenery.

He carted up to the studio what few boxes of machine fragments and spare parts December hadn't either sold or given
away after he'd disappeared, dumping them on the floor in a
jumble. His workbench and tools were long gone and it took
only a day to empty out the little workroom in December's
apartment. How strange, and how naturally, the old place had

become *December's apartment*, as if he'd never lived there at all.

It became painfully obvious he didn't have a prayer of building another helicopter out of the odd bits and pieces he had left. He would need to have parts specially made, blades custom-fabricated, the framework welded from scratch, the engine machine-tooled. That took money he didn't have, and there was no money coming in.

What little money he did have, he was spending at Strawberry's, drinking. Everybody had wanted to buy the Hero a drink, at first, but as time went on, his Hero shine began to tarnish, the novelty evaporating. Celebrities had very short lives.

He told his stories over and over, each time adding a bit of polish here, changing a small detail there, to make the tale a little better. Then the alcohol started making the stories fade even to him, the reality worn away by retelling them too many times.

Somehow, a few of the tales got lost in between.

He spoke only rarely about Sadonya, and never about what had happened between them in the Ranger camp. She was gradually transformed into the image of the fair maiden, a valiant companion he had defended, struggling against the odds by his stalwart side. He never saw her, didn't even know where she was, and didn't care. She was gone, out of his life forever, thank God and good riddance. The Brethren he only mumbled about in the vaguest terms, reluctant to say anything at all about them.

And of course, he bragged endlessly about his new helicopter, the one he was building. It would be better than *First Violin* had ever been, he was just working out the last of the plans now. His self-confidence leaked away with the whisky into whining insistence, until not even his friends could muster enough assurance that they believed him.

And he drank. A lot. Every day he would shower and shave, whistling in false bravado, walk briskly over to the downtown pilots' hall, loitering there to watch them come and go, read the assignment boards, gossip over this development or that project. Standing always slightly outside, the painful feeling of not quite being a real flier anymore. Then he'd stroll down to Teddy's place to hang out with his old buddies and slowly drink himself into a stupor.

He was terrified and couldn't admit it, even to himself. He felt like a bird with clipped wings beating itself senseless against the glass walls of an aviary.

He was staring moodily into a scotch when he felt a hand clap him on the back. Surprised, he watched Cormack slip onto the stool next to him.

"Buy you a beer to go with that chaser, Nielsen?" he said affably. Berk glanced around, noting the sudden space that had been created around them, no one even looking in their direction. The Councilman was out of place here, respectfully ignored. Berk looked back down into his drink.

"What do you want, Cormack?" he said dully.

Cormack didn't seem to hear the question. He signaled Teddy, and the bartender put down two beers. Berk didn't touch his, eyeing it as if it held poison.

"Y'ever hear the one about all the parts of the body arguin' about which one was the most important part?" Cormack said conversationally. He picked up his beer, smiling at Berk as if they were the best of friends sharing a good joke. His eyes were humorless, impersonal.

Berk glanced at him warily "No "

"Well, see, first the brain sez, 'I'm the most important part, because if it weren't for me, the body wouldn't be able to move, or think, or feed itself, and we'd all die.' "

Cormack took a long pull on his beer, as Berk watched him silently, eyes narrowed.

"Then the heart sez, 'no, I'm the most important part. If I didn't pump all the blood to the body, including you, brain, then you'd die from oxygen starvation.'

"Then the lungs say, 'you're both wrong, I'm the most important, because if it weren't for me, there wouldn't be any oxygen for you to pump to the brain, and we'd all die.' "

Cormack paused, turning on his stool to lean his elbow on the bar. He grinned at Berk.

"Then this little voice sez, 'I'm the most important,' and when the rest of them look down, it's the asshole. All the other parts start laughing. 'The asshole! That's ridiculous, the asshole isn't the most important part of the body.' So the asshole gets real mad, see, and he just stops working. Clams up tight. It takes about four days, everything's backed up, the body is feeling pretty shitty." Cormack chuckled at his own pun. "So the rest of the parts finally get together and decide, 'Okay, okay, we give up. You win. The asshole *is* the most important part of the body.' "

Berk stared at him goggle-eyed. "I don't think I get your point," he said cautiously.

"The point is, Berkeley"—Berk's eyes shut for a moment, a momentary scrape against his eardrums— "the point is, this City's a lot like the body. We need every part of it working, every person doing what they're good at to the best of their ability. Even assholes like you."

Cormack waited for a response, smiling. But Berk's mind seemed to have stopped working, baffled into incomprehensibility. He didn't know what to say, so said nothing. Finally Cormack nodded.

"I told you we could still talk, so let's put it down on the table, Nielsen. This 'hero' shtick's wearing a little thin, isn't it? You're a pilot. But you don't have a machine any more. That's a waste of talent."

"You offering me a plane, Cormack?" Berk asked, bewildered.

The Councilman grinned, showing his square white teeth. "You could say that."

And Berk knew.

Come work in the stables, boy.

This wasn't an offer. It was a contest of wills. A declaration of war. Cormack waited, his eyes glittering like a snake's. Berk stood. He was trembling with anger. "As the asshole said to the brain, Cormack, eat shit and die."

He could feel eyes on his back as he stalked out of Strawberry's, hatred seething poison through his blood.

THIRTY-EIGHT

November 18, 2242

CORMACK WAS A HEARTLESS BASTARD, BUT NOT foolish. He had taken everything that mattered away from Berk, not to crush him, just to prove that he could. But he knew enough never to take everything away from a man; you give him nothing to lose. So he dangled his bait.

The offer ate at Berk like an ulcer, a hunger filling his entire body. He needed to fly. He was starving, a drive within him deeper than the need for food, more intense than sex. It hung in the air at night, whispered like a succubus in his ear as he tossed sleeplessly.

What am I supposed to do now, Dad?

The old man was silent.

He walked out in the fields, stood watching planes come and go, the hurt like an iron band wound too tight around his chest. He never made it as far as the hangar before he would turn around and go back, unable to face the machines. He would never be just another hired lackey, had too much pride to be sucked into Cormack's trap. He'd find another way, build another copter, out of sheet metal and rubber bands if he had to.

He stopped boasting about the illusionary helicopter he was building in his studio apartment. It had begun to sound stupid even to him. Now, instead of bragging over his beer, he simply drank.

His Hero half-life finally extinguished itself. While other fliers didn't exactly shun him, they tended to leave him to brood by himself, unwilling to get in the way of the dark depression Berk was spiraling down into. Even Teddy no longer bothered with his impression of bartender-cum-psychiatrist.

Berk either sat immobile in his tiny apartment, gazing at the collection of spare parts scattered on the floor until he couldn't stand it, or at Strawberry's, drinking until he couldn't stand.

Today was pretty much the same as the day before.

And the day before that.

He'd finished his fifth double whisky and blearily waved at Teddy for another, leaning his elbows on the bar to keep himself upright. The pot-bellied bartender stood behind the counter, wiping a glass, over and over.

"Gimme 'nother, Teddy, ol' boy." Berk grinned sloppily.

"Come on, Berk," Teddy said. "I think you've had enough. Why don't you go on home now?"

Berk blinked, trying to focus his spinning vision on the bartender's face. "Whaddya talkin' 'bout?" he said, in confused belligerence. "I wanna 'nother *drink*."

"Go home, Berk," Teddy said softly.

Berk squinted at him, and saw pity in the man's eyes. Pity. Looking straight at him. Pity for him.

He jerked upright and turned on the stool to glare around the room. He was drunk, but not so drunk he couldn't see the way the pilots quickly glanced away, eyeing him sideways, shifting in their seats uncomfortably.

They all feel sorry for me, Berk thought slowly.

He spotted Kilian several tables away talking quietly to two City pilots, part of Cormack's stable. They all wore Cormack's shiny new leather City Transportation jackets, the gold thread in the City emblems untarnished. A wave of intense hatred for that jacket washed over Berk. He scowled at Kilian as the pilot glanced up at him, troubled eyes darting right, left, down, searching for something else to look at.

Kilian. Old pal, old chum. Cormack's chief stable pilot. Sold out your *Laser Chaser* a few years back to the City, couldn't afford the upkeep any more. Now you fly your own plane on the City's budget, don't you, ol' Kilian, buddy? Sold yourself out to Cormack, didn't you, lick his boots to keep your shine, you whore.

And before Berk realized it, he was on his feet, reeling towards the pilot, a vague anger welling up in his chest. The room spiraled around his head, and he staggered up to Kilian's table, glaring down at him drunkenly.

Irritable and tense, Kilian snapped, "What do *you* want, Berk?"

Berserker Berk. Berk the Jerk was more like it, he knew. He put his hand on the table to steady himself.

"Certify me on fixed-wing, Kilian," he blurted out.

That wasn't what he'd meant to say at all.

The two other pilots glanced at him in uneasy surprise. He ignored them. It was taking all his effort to keep his head up, keep looking straight into Kilian's perplexed eyes.

"Why?"

"I'm going to die if I don't fly," Berk said, the words ripped up from his soul. "I'll do whatever it takes, Kilian. I'll join the stable. I'll get down on both knees and kiss Cormack's ring if he wants me to. I'll fly whatever he gives me, go on any assignment he says. I'll be a good boy from now on, team member all the way, I promise . . ."

He stuttered, not understanding the horror on Kilian's face.

"Just please"—he had to whisper to get the words past the huge lump in his throat—"*please* . . . get me back in the air!"

THIRTY-NINE

December 29, 2242

I IT WASN'T SO DIFFICULT. IT HAD BEEN YEARS
since he'd been in *The Kid*, but he hadn't forgotten. The
reflexes were a little different, the way it felt was a bit
strange, but Kilian was competent. He walked Berk through
his qualifying run, troubleshot the bureaucracy and got him
signed up as a City pilot. Another stableboy.

Then Berk simply waited. He checked the boards every
morning and made no complaint when his name didn't come
up week after week. When it finally appeared, he stared at it
for a moment as if it belonged to someone else. Then he
shrugged on his brand new City Transportation jacket and
walked out to the City co-operative hangar.

They assigned him the worst planes, sky slugs, cobbled
together flying turds, dangerously neglected pieces of tin
foil and balsa wood. He flew them out, dropped mail runs,
did short-range reconnaissance, flew in supplies to the strike
plate crews and flew them back. When he didn't fly, he rebuilt engines, repaired broken struts and repatched old fuse-
lages.

And when he wasn't doing that, he was standing with his
hands in his pockets, staring at *Cloud Tripper*.

With a wingspan over ninety feet long, the glider plane

had a special hangar all to herself. Her sleek hull blended back into the wings and on their curving length fragile black panels of sun-collectors had been embedded flush with the skin. Twin verticle fins flowed into the horizontal stabilizers at her tail as if it had all been molded from a single cast. Hinged props folded against her nose like whiskers on a sleeping cat. Dark bubble-glass swept down the length of the narrow two-seater cabin, hiding the interior with mystery smoke.

Berk didn't need to see the interior; it looked all too singularly familiar.

"Beautiful, huh?" Kilian said behind him.

Berk didn't answer as the pilot walked up beside him to admire the slender gliderplane.

"She's delicate, almost everything's composite, but she's tough. She'll hold two hundred pounds over the passenger weight but she's got just enough power and fuel for takeoff." He gestured towards the graceful wings. "Once she's got enough lift, the solar cells kick in and she can cruise at a hundred twenty knots on power. There's about a thousand little Artie coils under the skin. She uses just about every photon she can soak up, and as an extra-feature benefit, the conduction wiring creates its own magnetic field as a hard radiation shield. She's got a ceiling so high you can see the stars, and range"—he laughed—"shit, half-plane, half-glider mostly wet dream. Get the right thermal updrafts, s'long as the sun shines, who knows how far she can go!"

Berk turned to look at him. "Whose is it?" he asked quietly.

"Cormack's." Kilian hesitated, then amended, "The City's." He paused again, and grinned. "Same thing."

Berk swallowed suddenly, a bitter taste at the back of his throat. "Not private, then?" he asked, managing to keep his voice casual.

"Hell, no," Kilian snorted. "Cormack doesn't believe in private ownership. But it's his design. He sketched the plans out for the engineering boys, they put the prototype together under his direction, funded through the Council as an experimental model. Unveiled it a month'r so after you . . . left."

Kilian cleared his throat, glancing at Berk sideways. "Cormack even gave you credit at the opening speech, said you'd come up with some vague ideas a couple years ago that got him thinking, stimulated his imagination," Kilian was explaining. He seemed earnest, anxious to find good even in the Devil. "He's like that, Berk. Likes to give credit to a good team instead of hogging the glory for himself."

Berk stood silently, the cold, dry breeze icy against his now smooth-shaven face.

"Supposed to be for long-range reconnaissance, see what's still around farther south, up north," Kilian steered the conversation, such as it was, back onto safer ground.

Berk studied the plane again. "Who flies it?"

"I do. Cormack. Lynda Youngston. Roz Kwang." Kilian glanced at him. "Senior co-op pilots only, Berk. Sorry. Maybe . . . someday," he said lamely. "They'll be making more, real quick if it works. It's part of Cormack's plan to motivate pilots into joining the co-op. You know, design better planes than you can build for yourself."

Berk nodded. It would work, too. He knew it would.

He turned his back on the glider plane and walked away.

At first the pilots had welcomed him back, and he even got a little more mileage out of the waning Hero bit, getting laid once in a while by some easily impressed starry-eyed girl. They were sweet, and the sex gave him some release, but it seemed detached, something happening far away. He chummed with his buddies and laughed at jokes, but even his new group of co-workers sensed something odd about him. Outside the necessities of social contact, he rarely spoke or even smiled anymore. Mostly he was left alone, and he didn't discourage that. All he wanted was to fly. Nothing more.

At least that's what he kept telling himself.

Once, walking back from a flight along the protected corridor into the City, he stopped as a small group of co-opted Aggies crossed the road, heading west. They held their tools as if they didn't quite have the intelligence to understand what the equipment was for, listless and stone-faced. The foreman, a kid not much more than eighteen years old, lagged behind them, bored and sullen, rifle on her shoulder. Protection against Rangers.

Sure.

One of the Aggies looked up at Berk. It was no one he knew. He hadn't expected to see any Brethren. It was just another anonymous Aggie. He didn't attempt to speak to him. The Aggie's dark eyes were lifeless. He shuffled on, the wind blowing his frayed dun-colored robes under his second-hand City Agricultural Department jacket. Berk watched them until they disappeared over a rise, then walked home.

Cormack, unseen but certainly felt in the daily dispatch sheets posted, slowly gave him a bit more rein. Berk took the assignments, expressed the appropriate amount of enthusiasm and gratitude.

And flew.

He was up in *The Pig*, a fat sluggish single engine that grumbled constantly, leaked an obscene amount of synthetic oil and flew about as aerodynamically as a brick. He didn't particularly like flying *The Pig*, but he didn't loathe the old plane as much as the rest of the co-pilots did. It flew.

He had dropped altitude slightly, coming into the Cherry Valley temporary domes, another group of strike plates being planted into the ground. At a little more than a thousand feet, he spotted the irregular patch of brown some distance to his left. It was just a bit off, the slightest hint of not quite belonging.

He banked *The Pig*, the ailerons' cables chittering just enough to set his teeth on edge, and took a second look. An Aggie garden. A big one, with hidden traces of disguised irrigation pipes leading from the Pymatuning reservoir, siphoning off water into the camouflaged fields.

Berk pulled the plane around and flew a straight, strafing-type run directly overhead to be sure. He was sure. He could almost pick out the little boulders dotted around the ground that were really human beings, almost see which tiny clumps of dry brush would sprout legs and bleat once he'd gone. Marking the location on his map carefully, he tried not to think much as he flew on.

He dropped off the supplies, passing up the offer of lunch,

and kicked *The Pig*'s reluctant ass back into the air, heading
for the Pit. Once he landed, he hunted down Kilian and du-
tifully filled out his report. The ink wasn't even dry before
three spotter planes were on their way. Before the end of the
shift, it was confirmed.

"Damn!" Kilian was grinning split-faced cheerful. "Biggest
Aggie field I think I've seen!" He clapped Berk on the back
ebulliently. "Fertilized, tilled, irrigated, they must have been
there for *decades*, and we never saw a thing! You just got
yourself a fat bonus, Berk. Ought to buy you a couple nice
airplane parts of your very own."

Berk smiled. The Right Smile. The Company Man.
"Thanks," he said. It felt like somebody else speaking.

He was surrounded by company-owned tools, probing
once again for *The Pig*'s elusive oil leak, when Kilian told
him Cormack wanted to see him down at the Council Hall,
right now.

Berk nodded, packed up. He washed the oil off his hands,
combed his hair back and took a pedalcab across the Alley
bridge to save time. When he got to the hall, he announced
himself to the secretary and stood patiently by the man's
desk. Cormack kept him waiting just long enough to remind
him how busy he really was, then opened the door to his
office.

"Come on in, Berkeley," he said jovially.

Berk sat on the edge of the rigid-backed chair.

"A little coffee?" Cormack offered.

"No, thank you." Berk wondered idly for a moment if his
refusal was the prudently correct choice. Cormack didn't
seem to care.

The Councilman poured a single mug of the bitter grain
coffee. "Guess I should congratulate you, son," he said. He
leaned back, triumphant, smug. "I really didn't expect you'd
ever be able to adjust. But you've turned out to be a genuine
asset to the City, after all. A real team member." It was a declaration of victory.

"Thank you," Berk said calmly.

He sat with his spine so erect the muscles in his back
tightened into a dull ache. Hands folded in his lap, he dis-

tantly watched the Councilman talk. Cormack seemed like something from an old video, flickering with age and overuse.

"You've proven yourself today, son. That find deserves a little reward." He eyed Berk calculatingly. "How's the plane? Wouldn't you be happier with something else?"

Berk weighed his reply carefully. He didn't want gifts from Cormack. "No," he said finally, "*The Pig*'s fine."

"Good, good." The Councilman didn't seem happy with the answer. "Maybe sometime we should take a look into the feasibility of a helicopter for the co-op, might be some eventual use for the City." Berk's gaze stayed on Cormack's face, his hands steady. Cormack smiled tightly. "Something musta happened to you out there, shaken some sense into you, got you to grow up a little. The old man would have been proud of you, I'm sure of it. Good work, son."

Berk didn't trust himself to respond, so he nodded and forced the semblance of a friendly, modest smile onto his lips. He stood when he realized the meeting was over, shook Cormack's hand congenially, and left for Strawberry's.

Teddy's place was half filled with pilots, and a few of the neighborhood regulars, when he walked in. He smiled self-deprecatingly as a couple of the fliers congratulated him, slapped him on the back or shook his hand.

"Just a beer," he said quietly to Teddy. He heard a creak overhead and glanced up. Some of the frothy yellow liquid spilled onto the glass topped counter as the barman set the beer down in front of Berk. Berk didn't notice.

He was staring up at the little metal helicopter Teddy had restored, hanging from the ceiling. He could read the small, shaky letters even from here. *First Violin*. Tiny rotor blades squeaked around the hub, the slight air currents in the tavern causing the model to sway gently. Teddy followed his gaze and smiled, leaning his elbows on the bar.

"Never took it down, Berk," he said with quiet pride. "The whole time you were Outside it stayed up."

Berk stared at the little helicopter, his mouth open, slack. He had forgotten it was there. His chest suddenly hurt so badly, he thought he was going to be sick.

Teddy bent closer to look at him quizzically. "You okay?" he asked, concerned.

The question wrenched Berk's attention back. He looked at the bartender and took a deep breath. "Yeah," he said. "I'm fine." He reached into his pocket, dragged out enough change for the beer and left the tavern, his drink untouched.

He walked back to his Maddock street studio, and sat on the worn sofa until the room turned too dark to see. He tried to conjure up Amminadab's face, force the cheerful little man's stained dark smile into his mind's eye. Berk couldn't recall what he looked like. It blurred away, as if he were peering through running water at the shadows of flitting fish.

What was I supposed to do, Dad?

Outside, traffic moved, people walked in the street, laughed and talked, a dog barked somewhere, chasing children in the lamplit park.

The little room on Maddock was silent.

Finally he got up, flicked on the bathroom light, bare bulb swinging overhead, knelt by the stained toilet and heaved. He threw up again and again, until his stomach had completely emptied and his abdominal muscles ached with the strain. Shivering and sweating, lightheaded, he flushed the toilet, listening to the water as it gurgled into the recycling system.

Turning on the tap, he waited for the hot water to come on, then splashed his face with water, rubbing hard with his hands until his skin hurt and he gasped for breath. The water ran in rivulets off the spiked wet ends of his hair, dribbling into the sink as the tap bubbled, chuckling to itself as it ran.

When he looked up into the mirror, it startled him. He saw the Aggie's desolate eyes. A stranger's face with haunted eyes stared back at him.

FORTY

W HEN HE WAS TOLD THEY WERE GOING TO CALL it the Nielsen Reclamation Field, he didn't object. He didn't give a damn what it was called. Cormack boosted his rating and he got the chance to pick between flight assignments, once in a while even flying one of the more enjoyable planes. He flew, he worked, he tinkered on *The Pig*.

He had no more bouts of nausea, although he spent more and more time sitting alone in the dark in his apartment, trying not to think too much, trying to keep his mind from running around in panicked circles. Sleeping became difficult. He hated the dreams.

The divorce summons arrived. He turned up on time at the Court Hall, murmured his assent, and shook hands cordially with December. He was grateful Markley had the courtesy not to show up. Then he went back to the grungy little studio on Maddock.

The spare parts that littered his floor had been kicked out of the way to make little paths through them, one to the kitchenette, one to the toilet, one to the front door. Neglected, their oily surfaces eventually gathered a thin gray coating of dust. He slept on the couch, the blanket wedged between the cushions, his crumpled pillow jammed against the armrest.

When someone knocked on his door, he started awake, blinking fatigue-swollen eyes open in the dark. He had finally managed to drift off to dreamless sleep, and sat up groggily as someone rapped on the door again, impatient, irritating. Glancing at the clock, he groaned. Too late to go back to sleep, too early to get up. Whoever it was, it had better be important.

"All right, all right, wait a minute," he croaked, and yanked his pants up over his legs, struggling to fasten them as he padded barefoot through the machine parts path to the door. When he opened it, he jumped back in horror, as if someone had dumped a box full of venomous snakes on his doorstep.

"Hello," Sadonya said.

"Jesus," he breathed, suddenly wide-awake and jittery.

"Mind if I come in?" she said, smiling crookedly.

"*Yes*, go away!" He groaned as she walked in, looked around and sat on the couch. "What do you want?" he said tiredly.

"Thank you, I fine too," she said, sarcastic and mean.

She shrugged off her thin schoolgirl's jacket, flinging it carelessly over the back of the couch. Her face had been scrubbed clean, and she was dressed in a fresh-pressed City Education uniform. Her long, matted hair had been cut off, short black curls fitting like a cap around her head. She had fleshed out, the skeletally thin body acquiring almost feminine curves. Manicured hands, nails trimmed and clean, held onto the straps of an oversized bookbag with the City emblem on its flap. She could barely lift whatever she had in it. Two gold earrings glinted from holes pierced in her lobes. A tiny gold chain was looped demurely around her dark neck. She looked almost like a normal schoolgirl.

Except for the eyes. They were as hard and as dark as flint, an old woman's eyes in a child's face.

"Okay," he said cautiously. "How did you know where I live?"

She grinned, professionally cleaned white teeth startlingly

bright. "I go that first place timeback ago, an' that slit look like she be Ferryman's sister, she say you here now, but she say y'don' like visits." She shrugged. "So, I lee you alone. Till now."

He had no desire to go anywhere near her, but the couch was the only place to sit. He leaned against the kitchen counter. "The *slit's* name is December, Sadonya," he said. "She's my wife." He hesitated. "Was my wife."

"She say that," Sadonya agreed.

"Why are you here now?" he asked, wearied. Pain began around his forehead, and he rubbed his palm above his eyes.

"I hate this place, Berk."

He chortled harshly. "It's the maid's day off," he said.

She sneered, pulling the corner of her lip up. "You still-time making fun on me, think I'm real stupid." She dragged the huge bookbag next to her feet. "I talk 'bout this *City*. I hate your *City*."

"Really," he commented. There didn't seem to be anything else to say.

"I'm leavin'," she said.

He looked at her obtusely. "Bon voyage," he said finally.

"You come'n w'me."

He laughed outright. "Fuck you, Sadonya," he said, wiping his eyes. She was studying him seriously, and he couldn't help it. He exploded into laughter again, his sides beginning to ache. She waited until it had subsided.

"Back my place, you alltime talk 'bout this big ag-ri-cul-chrull dome, member?" She pronounced her words very carefully. "Well, I there long time now. City people, they think I special 'cause I a cook, make me alla time work f'them. It 'Sadonya, taste this plant, Sadonya, smell that seed, what you see in y'head, huh?' They make me taste all kinda things, make me draw pictures. Then they get all 'cited 'cause I say, this no good, it die quicktime inna sun, this one kay, 'cause it taste right." Her face screwed up in outrage. "They stick *dirt* in my mouth, say, what this, what that, drive me crazy w'their fuckin' shit."

He didn't say anything, his lips curling up in a bemused smile in spite of himself. Her eyes hardened, glimmering spitefully. "But they say no cookin', not f'me, not f'nobody. No funbanes. Not even smoke. Nothin'."

He *tsked*. "What a shame," he said casually. Laughter threatened again, and his shoulders shook silently.

She sneered, matching his smile with a sarcastic grin, as if she knew something more than he did and was only waiting for an opening to spring it on him. That idea dampened his mirth. He eyed her suspiciously.

"Don' like my place I live, neither," she said quietly. "First they make me live with nother buncha slits, they alltime chat-chat like fuckin' birds, no quiet notime. I say I don' like it, they send me stayin' inna place with old people, alla time don't do this, can't do that, treat me like I two-year-old baby buck."

"What can I say, Sadonya," he responded. "Nobody ever gets everything they want." Wasn't it the truth.

"You lie to me," she said, ignoring his comment. Her eyes narrowed. "You say everybody happy, do enything they want, nobody do ravs, love each other alltime, go la-la-la down th'streets."

He'd half believed the fairy tales he'd spun out to her, and for a moment he felt insulted. The domes were a hundred times better than the deadly squalor of the ruins. She had no right to criticize the City. *His* City.

"Come off it, girl," he snapped, annoyed. "What about you, you telling me you never lied, huh? You're some kind of sweet little angel, never tell a fib in your whole life? What about your phony little nasties? Tell me that wasn't a lie."

She shook her head, as if she pitied him. For some reason, it made him hate her more than he already did. "Sure, that a lie. But not f'you. That a kinda lie to Mouse I tell keep me alive."

"What the hell do you think I was telling you, then," he said more calmly. "It's everything I said it was, Sadonya. So it's just not paradise." He clenched his fists, unable to stop himself. "At least it's civilized."

She snorted. "Only difference I see tween me and *civilized* is least I *know* when I lyin'."

That hurt, and he didn't know why. He didn't answer.

"You happy here?" she demanded softly.

He didn't answer that, either. "Go home, Sadonya."

She grinned triumphantly, an animal snarl. "You wanna know what I got here, maybe?" she said, suddenly conspiratorial, kicking at the large pack. It thumped solidly under her shoe. It alarmed him, a warning buzzer sounding in the back of his head.

"No, don't think I do," he said.

"Seeds. Lots of 'em." Her grin widened. "I member you sayin' 'bout that mister, what his name, he go la-la-la, kay, all cross went everywhere, dropping seeds and putting plants inna ground, so he make everyplace like it here, everything green."

"Seeds," he said, and stared at the pack as if it held a bomb.

"Special gentick en-gen-eared seeds, made special for Outside," she said, patting the bookbag affectionately. "I leavin', go west, I gonna be like this seed mister, go plant seeds everywhere." She laughed demoniacally. "Got all kinda seeds, all kinda spee-shee."

"You are out of your goddamned mind!" he yelled, then dropped his voice. "You've stolen supplies from the Agricultural Division, and you're going to get both of us in trouble!"

"No, I not," she said reasonably, surprised. "How I get in trouble if I gone?"

"Take them back where you got them, and *go home*!" It was a cry of total desperation.

"Can't." Her eyes glinted maliciously.

He knew that look. It chilled him, his skin prickling on the back of his neck.

"Why not?" he asked with more calm than he felt.

She shrugged laconically. "They send me stayin' inna place with them old people, they got fatass baby bucks, say everybody gotta be nice. Fatass baby bucks'r not nice, don' see why I gotta."

"Oh, no." He leaned heavily against the counter, his head hanging down as he listened, numb.

"I say alla time, don't touch my things. This buck slit, she don' respect that. She get in my face, say I jess a nobody, I nothin' but some kinda special Aggie, *I* the one gotta be nice, 'cause otherwise, *civilized* people send me Outside, make me work inna field till the sun fry me dead." She snorted contemptuously. "I catch her in my things, stealin' my smoke . . ." She paused. "So I frag her."

He listened to the sounds outside the window. A pedalcab *screak-screaked* by in the street below, and a cat yowled. Pipes buried in the walls of the old apartment gurgled with the sound of running water, sluggish night life stirring around him. All he could think of was if he called the police, somehow it would discredit him, too. Somehow, it would jeopardize the delicate balance he'd worked so hard to maintain. He felt the floor shifting under his feet, defenseless.

"Y'know, outatown man, I don' think these *civilized* people gonna listen t'me," she continued, no remorse in her voice. "They don' want my splains. So, I leavin'."

"You're crazy," he said, his throat tight with anger. "You've just killed somebody. *Another* somebody. For stealing your things. Then you turn around and steal seeds. You goddamned murdering bitch, you *deserve* to die." He glared at her, his eyes burning. "So go ahead, Sadonya, you just trot on Outside toting a sackful of stolen seeds." He gestured towards the window for emphasis. "That desert we walked across? That's a little, tiny, baby desert. It's *nothing*. You won't make it ten miles before you bake to death."

"I know that," she said. "That why I need you steal a plane."

He was shocked speechless, his mouth hanging open.

"I got it planned right, Berk. Lotta time to think here. What you think I doin' all this time, huh? You been tellin' lies 'bout me, y'think I don' hear em? Y'think I jess be sweet and quiet, not go askin' my ownsum questions? Y'think I damnsure *stupid*." He could see the glimmer of rage behind her eyes, the dead look just before she broke his ribs . . . before she pushed Third out the window . . .

"I know all 'bout planes now, outatown man. We steal a plane, and fly straighttime over this big fuckin' desert.

Maybe we drop some seeds we go by, then we onna nother side, and plant seeds there, too. Maybe it nice there, maybe they no Rangers live that far out."

Too paralyzed to think for a moment, he blinked at her stupidly, then picked her jacket off the couch and thrust it at her. "You'd better leave before I call the police." He tried to keep his voice from shaking. "Get out of here. Don't come back, ever."

She stood up, angry, yanking the jacket out of his hand. "Fine, don' go. You *civilized* people all the same. Buncha lying shits. Who need you anyway? You want stay here, y'like have buncha union bosses say can't do this, can't do nother, you sleep here, you eat this, wear that, you work there, don't say this, don't think that. Y'like being their toadyboy, you stay. I never toady *nobody*, not Mouse, not you, not that ratnose slit, not this fuckin' City. I goin'."

The hurt that he'd felt in his chest in Strawberry's looking up at Teddy's little model came back. "So go," he said quietly, teeth clenched. "Go on and die out there all by yourself, you stupid bitch." The pain grew.

She glared at him, and heaved the pack to her shoulder. "I know you hate me, I hate you. I don' need you. I do fine myself, if you *member*. Who save who w'the Rangers, huh?" The fair maiden of his barroom tales hurled the truth back in his face like dirt. He flinched, and couldn't meet her eyes. "*Me*, that who save y'dumb ass. I do just fine, fuck you, you lyin' shit."

She stomped towards the door, the pack thumping against her back.

He swallowed. "Wait," he said. When she turned and stared at him, he spread his hands, helpless. "You really will die alone trying to walk out in the desert, Sadonya . . . Maybe, maybe I can talk to the authorities, work something out . . ." It was lame, weak. He knew as well as she did what they would do to her.

"What you care, Berk?" she said, her voice strangely gentle. "You jess tell me I deserve to die anyway. Know what? *I* don't care, neither. I rather die bein' my own person than stay here."

"Don't do this to me," he begged.

She stared at him gravely. "Not doin' nothin' to you, out-atown man," she said. He suddenly heard the same pity in her voice that had been in Teddy's. "You come w' me, or not. But you choose."

She waited, watching him with lizard-cool eyes.

"This is insane . . ."

Something snapped inside him.

It was the last lie dying under its own weight. He had traded in everything to fly. He'd had to give up his right to self-respect, accept his humiliation, press himself into a mold he despised, believing it was worth it. He'd convinced himself that Cormack was right, the greater good demanded he swallowed his pride, conform, obey. He'd needed the freedom of wings in the air to feel alive again.

But the funny thing was, he didn't feel alive.

He saw the rest of his life in the City. Flying *The Pig* forever, or until the treacherous pile of junk killed him. Getting laid by telling pathetic lies about his past heroic deeds. Drinking with his buddies as he schemed how to get enough parts to build his own helicopter again, knowing full well Cormack would obstruct every effort. Or take it away from him.

He saw the face of that nameless Aggie woman holding her child tightly against her crying out voicelessly, terrified by the machine hovering above them, whipping the dust around their thin bodies. Saw the face of Amminadab, the little man turning his head to chuckle kindly over his shoulder at the strange pale Cityman stumbling blind and ignorant through the desert wastelands. Saw the bleak eyes of the co-opted Aggie, the face of the stranger he'd become in the mirror, and hated himself for giving in, giving up.

Despised himself for not dying.

He saw the end of his life, getting old, having more pieces of sunblasted flesh cut out of him until he couldn't take the pain anymore, couldn't stand to see the distress in the eyes of his friends. Couldn't fly.

And if they got caught . . . he'd spend the rest of his miserable life grounded, probably imprisoned for aiding and abetting a murderer. His wife had divorced him. He'd never be able to build another *First Violin*. His life in the domes didn't seem to have any real existence anymore.

He was trembling uncontrollably.

City say they own you, the old man whispered.

Berk almost cried.

Where have you been, Dad? Where the hell have you been?

The old man grinned, gap-toothed, *Maybe so, own everything else*. His sunburned face was radiant as he crossed his thin brown arms. *But Outside*—Berk could see the fine sun bleached hairs blowing in the hot breeze—*outside the City, you own the rest of the world*.

I'm an orphan, Dad. I'm an orphan of my own City.

Like Sadonya.

"I'm not yours," he said slowly. She squinted, puzzled. "You ever touch me again, you ever try to 'mark' me, I really will kill you. Do you understand?"

Slowly, she grinned. "Don' worry, outatown man. Y'still ugly, and I never like you either. Jess fly the fuckin' plane."

"We'll need more than just seeds, girl," Berk said.

He felt as if he'd stepped through a door in the dark and fallen through a hole in the floor, the breath knocked out of him. But once his decision was made, it swept him along, powerless and unwilling to stop. He had her take off the schoolgirl uniform, and gave her a pair of his own pants and a shirt, rolling up the cuffs. He found an extra pair of protective glasses and taped the broken earpiece together for her.

He turned the old canvas bag he used for laundry upside down and shook out a month's worth of dirty underwear, oil-stained pants, sour armpit-scented wrinkled shirts. Emptying the refrigerator and the cabinets, he stuffed the bag with food and filled every watertight jar he could find with water. It was heavy, but manageable.

He had two rifles, the one his father had left him after the old man had taken his last flight, and the other the one that he'd brought with him from the Ranger camp. He'd reclaimed it as a souvenir and the Security Department hadn't argued with a Hero. They'd been stored in the closet, behind a hodgepodge of discarded clothes. He handed one unloaded rifle to Sadonya, shoved the boxes of ammunition in his bag, a few loose bullets in his jacket pocket, and loaded his father's rifle before slinging it over one shoulder.

"Let's go."

He closed the door of the little studio, but didn't bother locking it. Sadonya's bookbag held nearly twenty-five pounds of neatly marked experimental seed packets crammed together. She had two more twenty-five-pound bags stashed under the stairwell on the bottom floor. She had stolen some child's play wagon, little daisies painted on its sides, and it bumped along behind her, carrying seventy-five pounds of pilfered seed. Daddy and little girl, just out for the day, having some fun; he smiled benignly at the perplexed looks they got in the street.

No one stopped them.

He thought he might have felt regret, or maybe a sense of loss as they made their way down Duquesne Street to the bridge. As he walked, Berk's heart was buoyant, the air suddenly cool and clean against his skin. They walked across the bridge, the pedalcar traffic clicking by on one side as he glanced at the sparkling water of the Alley River below. He tried to think, *This is the last time I'll ever see this river*, striving to induce a feeling of finality, and failed.

He was committing suicide.

He didn't care. He laughed just for the joy of it.

They walked out of the Commons dome, towards the low humps of the City co-op hangars slouched in the bleak winter light. The sky had lightened, the sun not quite up, pastel pink and amber light painting the undersides of cumulus clouds beginning to form against the pale indigo sky. Still too early in the morning for assignments to be posted, only the supervisors and chief pilots were out. The hangars were deserted.

Kilian strode out of the field office next to the main hangar, hands in his pockets against the cold. He grinned when he saw Berk walking towards him.

"Hey, there, Berk," he said in a friendly tone. He looked

puzzled at the guns and the girl. "You're up bright and early. What's going on?"

Berk lowered his sack to the ground and brought the muzzle of the rifle up to bear on the pilot. The bolt pulled back with a satisfactory thunk, sliding a shell into the chamber. "I'm stealing a plane, Kilian," he said calmly. Sadonya dropped the handle of the kiddy wagon to bring her rifle around to point at the pilot.

Kilian's eyes went wide and he slowly pulled his hands from his pockets. "Whoa-ho," he said, staring at the guns in disbelief. Another man wearing glasses and a crisp Transportation Department jacket opened the door of the office, stepping out. Some accountant flunky of Cormack's, by the look of him, Berk guessed.

"Kilian?" he said, "What's going on here? Who's this?" He looked bewildered, his eyes darting back and forth between Berk and the girl. He stared at the rifles as if they were completely unfamiliar objects to him.

Berk grinned. "Don't you recognize me? I'm Johnny Appleseed," he said. "This is my faithful but somewhat psychotic companion, Janey Cherryblossom. Say hello, Janey."

She squinted up at him suspiciously. "You making fun on me again?" she demanded angrily.

"Don't worry, it's not catching," he said, still grinning.

"I don't understand," the man in the jacket protested.

"He's stealing a plane, Mr. Vickry," Kilian said, his hands held up away from his sides, astonished gaze locked on Berk.

Vickry stared through thick glasses at Berk, then at Kilian in incredulity. "Stealing a plane? To go where?" He turned to Berk. "Why would anybody *steal* a plane?"

"Because I'm crazy," Berk assured him reasonably. It didn't seem to comfort the bespectacled man. "Open up the hangar, Kilian."

"Any particular plane you got in mind, Berk?" Kilian asked. His eyes crinkled in a ghost of a smile, as if he were somehow enjoying this. Maybe he was. There was obviously only one plane. Berk jerked his head towards the hangar.

His hands held out from his sides, Kilian turned and walked to the doors. He pushed his weight against them, grunting as they slid back on well-greased tracks.

She lay close to the ground, ninety feet of delicate white wings, black speckles of solar cells along their backs. Smoke-dark glass glittered like the enigmatic eyes of a moth. "Pull her out, old buddy," Berk said quietly.

Kilian hauled *Cloud Tripper* straight out of the hangar, the sleek glider plane light on her tiny wheels. Slender wings shuddered. The sun broke over the horizon. Desolate winter light hit the plane in a sudden explosion of gleaming white brilliance that hurt Berk's eyes. The plane spoke to him.

I know you . . .

"You can't take that!" Vickry objected. "That's Cormack's prototype!"

"I thought it was City property," Berk said mildly. "I'm a City pilot, what's the problem?"

The man sputtered as Kilian eyed Berk, now with a definite smile. "Just where the hell do you think you're going to go in her, Berk if you don't mind my asking?" he said.

"Up and away," Berk said. "Get the right air currents up high enough, stay in the light long enough, who knows?" Kilian nodded slowly, as if he got the joke. Berk glanced at Sadonya. "Open the door and get this crap stashed quicktime," he said.

She fumbled with the unfamiliar latch, but got it open. Muttering, one hand juggling her rifle, she struggled with the packs. Kilian turned his head to watch her; then, his hands still up, he looked back at Berk. "Should I give the girl a hand there?"

"Why not? That'd be very civilized," Berk said. He took Sadonya's unloaded gun, slipped it over his shoulder while he kept his rifle trained on Vickry.

His head felt light, giddy with affection for the plane, for Kilian—hell, even Sadonya. He laughed outright as Vickry continued sputtering, grumbling indignantly as Kilian stowed the three packs and Berk's rattling supply bag into the slender hold behind the passenger's seat, then helped

Sadonya into the plane. He buckled her in and closed the door carefully.

"How can you help him steal Cormack's plane?" Vickry griped. He glared peevishly at Berk, bloodshot eyes made small behind his glasses.

"He's got a gun, I don't," Kilian pointed out. He turned to grin goodnaturedly at Berk. "I'd wish you luck, Berk," he said, "but Vickry here would probably report me."

Berk nodded, and backed away towards *Cloud Tripper*, rifle still trained on the two men. "Thanks, Kilian," he said. He popped the door of the plane open, sliding his body into the narrow space, his rifle aimed at the two men until he pulled the door down, locking it securely, the guns wedged into the space beside him. He smiled tightly as Vickry took a few steps towards the plane before Kilian grabbed him by his fine jacket, restraining the red-faced man. Their mouths moved in silent argument as Berk ran his hands over the control panel, wishing he could have done a preflight check. Then he laughed to himself.

If anything went wrong, what difference would it make now?

It felt *right*, everything exactly where it should have been, as Berk knew it would be. He flicked on the instruments, one by one, the lights coming alive under his fingers. His heart pulsing in his throat, he turned on the engine, giving it throttle.

The prop twisted falteringly, *hup-pup*, caught and blurred into a low hum vibrating through the long, slender craft. Slowly she crept forward, bounced over the rocks and dried clumps of grass as Berk taxied to the dirt strip. He turned the plane's nose down the runway, glancing towards Kilian and Vickry. Kilian was grinning broadly and shaking his head, standing with his hands back in his pockets while Cormack's toadyboy pranced around him in frustration and backwashed dust. There'd be no chase.

Then he rolled past, and gave the plane more throttle. She shivered, trembling like a lover in anticipation, the dirt runway a blur behind her spinning props. She sped forward, feeling good under his hands, and when she nosed up in the air, Berk realized he'd grinned so hard his cheeks hurt. He glanced behind him. Sadonya was gripping the sides of the seat, white-knuckled and wide-eyed. She watched the world whip past, gasping as it fell away underneath her.

He banked the plane around to circle the domes, just once, huge jewels gleaming in the snug safety of the river's arms. He wasn't saying goodbye as much as simply appreciating how beautiful they were. He turned and headed west, the sun at his back, the early morning warmth misting steam from the cold ground beneath them. Circling under the flat expanse of cloud, he searched for a thermal updraft that would carry them higher, float them upwards on the heat of the killing sun. A gentle bump lifted the wing, and he tucked into the thermal, cutting the engines to save whatever fuel might be left to eke out another takeoff, if he needed it. They had the whole day to fly in, but Berk knew it wouldn't be enough.

He soared between a low layer of wispy clouds, thunderheads dotting the horizon in the distance. For a few moments, he saw a pilot's halo on the clouds below him, a double rainbow ring, one bright, one faint, shimmering around the silhouette of *Cloud Tripper* at its core. The light outside the circle seemed brighter than on the inside. He watched it flicker across the cloud, and vanish as he broke into brilliant sunlight. Early morning light flooded the clouds with gold, burnished crimson, radiant streaks of sunbeams cutting through the hollows between clouds, a surreal, breathtaking vista only flight could show.

Flying on a wing and a prayer—wasn't that the way it went? He had the wing, but he knew they hadn't a prayer, and he didn't care. It was insane. It was doomed, and it didn't matter in the least whether the sleek little plane could fly a thousand miles over the Great Desert, and up across the jagged peaks of the Rockies. One day, two days, it made no difference.

When the fuel ran out and the sun set, they'd come down. And they'd stay down. Then they both would die.

His life in the domes receded behind them. The future, for what little it was worth, or for however long it lasted, was here, Outside.

He owned the rest of the world.